by Tessa Dawn

A Blood Curse Novel
Book Twelve
In the Blood Curse Series

Published by Ghost Pines Publishing, LLC
Volume XII of the Blood Curse Series by Tessa Dawn
First Edition Trade Paperback Published March 9, 2021 10 9 8 7 6 5 4 3 2 1
First Edition eBook Published March 9, 2021 10 9 8 7 6 5 4 3 2 1

Ghost Pines Publishing, LLC

For Angel L Gende

*In fond friendship, loving memory,
and because I promised Braden's book would be yours!*

Forever in my heart.

ACKNOWLEDGMENTS

Credits and Acknowledgments

Ghost Pines Publishing, LLC, *Publishing*
  Damonza, *Cover Art*
  Lidia Bircea, *Romanian Translations*
  Reba Hilbert, *Editing*

Passing Mentions

The Cheshire cat: A fictional cat made popular by Lewis Carroll in Alice in Wonderland's various adventures, circa 1865.

Dr. Jekyll & Mr. Hyde: The main character in the 1886 novella, *Strange Case of Dr Jekyll and Mr Hyde,* by Robert Louis Stevenson.

Excalibur: The legendary sword of King Arthur which may originate in the work *Culhwch and Olwen from the Mabinogion,* a collection of Welsh legends, circa 1100 CE.

For every time, there is a season: The Holy Bible: Ecclesiastes 3.

Nothing comes from nothing: An ancient Greek philosophical dictum first argued by Parmenides.

Punct: Also referred to as a *point* or a *prick*, a quarter of an hour in Medieval Europe.

Rock of Ages: A hymn written by the Reverend Augustus Toplady in 1763.

THE BLOOD CURSE

In 800 BC, Prince Jadon and Prince Jaegar Demir were banished from their Romanian homeland after being cursed by a ghostly apparition: the reincarnated Blood of their numerous female victims. The princes belonged to an ancient society that sacrificed its females to the point of extinction, and the punishment was severe.

They were forced to roam the earth in darkness as creatures of the night. They were condemned to feed on the blood of the innocent and stripped of their ability to produce female offspring. They were damned to father twin sons by human hosts who would die wretchedly upon giving birth; and the firstborn of the first set would forever be required as a sacrifice of atonement for the sins of their forefathers.

Staggered by the enormity of the Curse, Prince Jadon, whose own hands had never shed blood, begged his accuser for leniency and received four small mercies—four exceptions to the Curse that would apply to his house and his descendants, alone.

Ѱ Though still creatures of the night, they would be allowed to walk in the sun.

Ѱ Though still required to live on blood, they would not be forced to take the lives of the innocent.

Ѱ While still incapable of producing female offspring, they would be given one opportunity and thirty days to obtain a mate —a human *destiny* chosen by the gods—following a sign that appeared in the heavens.

Ѱ While they were still required to sacrifice a firstborn son, their twins would be born as one child of darkness and one child of light, allowing them to sacrifice the former while keeping the latter to carry on their race.

And so...forever banished from their homeland in the Transylvanian mountains of Eastern Europe, the descendants of Jaegar and the descendants of Jadon became the Vampyr of legend: roaming the earth, ruling the elements, living on the blood of others...forever bound by an ancient curse. They were brothers of the same species, separated only by degrees of light and shadow.

PROLOGUE

Braden Bratianu paced restlessly, back and forth, in front of the floor-to-ceiling windows in Kristina's lavish penthouse apartment on the top floor of the Dark Moon Casino, feeling more like a restless tiger than a seventeen-year-old vampire male. He swept his hand through his shoulder-length, chestnut brown hair and shook his head in disbelief.

He couldn't believe it was actually happening.

The Millenia Harvest Moon would rise tomorrow, and only the gods knew what the omen would bring.

And as for what Kristina Riley-Silivasi had just offered to give him...

Shit...

Just shit...

Braden knew she didn't mean it.

They had been back and forth, covering the same territory, again and again: What would happen tomorrow when the celestial gods poured their power down upon the earth, when the dormant blood of a prince roused inside Braden's young body: quickened, stirred...awakened?

1

Would Braden still know Kristina?

Would Kristina still know him?

Would Napolean continue to enforce his decree—insist upon seeing the unusual couple mated, two vampires who were both exempt from the Blood Curse? Or would the soul, the spirit—the *what the actual fuck?*—of Prince Jadon be so strong that it ultimately took over? And if so, would Braden actually have a Blood Moon one day, a blood *destiny*, a female chosen by the gods, whom he had to claim, cherish, and mate?

What would happen to Kristina then?

Could Braden still potentially sire female offspring after tomorrow night, or would the Curse placed upon all the sons of King Sakarias—Prince Jadon's progeny and Prince Jaegar's alike —usurp the rare, singular circumstance of Braden's siring?

Braden was *made*, not born, to vampirism.

And thus, he was immune to the punishment—and the required sacrifice—demanded of all biological sons...and their sons...*and their sons*, for all perpetuity, of the original celestial progeny.

If Kristina and Braden made love tonight—if the young, fledgling vampire commanded a pregnancy—then he would have two, not one, offspring to bring to the house of Jadon, possibly rare, precious, coveted female children, and they would belong to him.

To him...

To Braden and Kristina.

Not to Prince Jadon and not to some yet unknown *destiny*, not to some horrible dreamtime mistake made in a fit of madness and desperation by a sleeping High Mage.

"Shiiiit," Braden murmured beneath his breath, glancing over his shoulder to study Kristina's features for the umpteenth time. His head was beginning to spin, and her expression was just as confounded: Her beautiful, normally bright blue eyes were dark with shadows, thick with fear, nearly glazed over with uncertainty...and desperation. Why else would she have offered to do something so personal, so intimate, so permanent? Something she had never been willing to do before?

To couple with Braden before their mating.

To give herself to a seventeen-year-old boy...

Because isn't that how she really saw him?

Always had...

Likely always would.

Despite the fact that Braden had finally stopped growing at six feet, two inches tall; despite the fact that he was now 200 pounds of hard, sinewy muscle, all strength and cords packed around rock-hard abs—strong as an ox and fast as a cougar; imbued with powers, insights, visions, and wisdom well beyond his years—Kristina Riley-Silivasi had always seen him as a kid, someone she might have to wait a decade to be with.

"Say something, Bray," Kristina nearly whimpered, twirling a curly lock of red hair around her finger, nervously, even as she sank back into the cream-colored cushions on the large, plush sectional, beneath several soft, glowing, recessed lights, and crossed her ankles in front of her, interlocking the spikes of her stiletto heels.

Damn, Braden thought. She looked so damn beautiful. So damn vulnerable. And what could he say?

He wanted her.

He always had.

And yeah, screw being a seventeen-year-old neophyte in the house of Jadon; he had no doubts whatsoever that he could give her pleasure, make her call out his name, make love to her like a grown-ass male with passion, skill, and dominance.

The instincts were in his blood.

The vampiric passion had always been there, stirring, waiting...rising.

He may have been made by a sire, as opposed to born of the

Curse, but he was still a fully matured male vampire. "You don't mean it, Red," he finally murmured.

She crossed her arms over her chest and shivered, probably hoping Braden didn't notice the latter. "Bray, *I do*. I mean, tomorrow is no longer promised, and we've always been really close, you and me. We've always been great—"

"*Friends*," he interjected.

She shook her head sadly. "I was going to say: 'We've always been great together.' More than friends, Braden." She took a deep breath for courage, or at least that was the way Braden read it. "The way you look at me...that time you kissed me, that time you stole my breath...we've always been more than friends."

Braden angled his broad shoulders to face her squarely. "And what if I change so much tomorrow that I no longer remember you, Kristina? What if I really do end up promised to another, and meanwhile, you have two of my kids?"

Kristina blanched at his bluntness, then quickly recovered. "Would that be so terrible?"

Braden shrugged. "For me? No. For you, yeah. *Shit yeah*, Kristina; that's not who you are. You could never share me or anyone else. The situation would drive you crazy."

Kristina studied her bright-pink manicured nails. "I guess I would learn to live with it," she muttered beneath her breath.

Braden stared at the crease in her eyebrows, the deep lines of worry etched into her frown—did she even know she was frowning? She was sitting on her couch, wearing a nearly see-through white silk blouse over a killer hip-hugging pink-and-white skirt—smooth, bare legs and painted toenails slipped into a designer pair of stiletto heels—trying to appear calm, ready, and certain, even as her soft, sculpted lips were curved into a frown.

One thing Braden knew for certain: The female truly loved him.

She had to.

Because what she was offering was *everything*.

Her whole heart, her body, the rest of her life.

And for a moment, just a fleeting second, Braden wished he were selfish enough to take her up on it.

He strolled across the living room floor to where she sat on the sofa, braced one heavy knee on the cushion beside her hip, and leaned into her, grasping her high, angular cheeks in his palms, his thumbs anchored beneath her jaw. And then he bent down to kiss her, and he let years of pent-up frustration... restrained desire...flow into the kiss.

She gasped and reached for his shoulders, but he just as quickly pulled away.

He still had to meet with Nachari, the rest of the Silivasi brothers—the sentinels and Julien, the king and Fabian, even the High Mage—at Napolean's manse.

Time was running out.

Without looking back, he headed to the elegant sliding doors that led to Kristina's wrap-around balcony, brushed them open with two stiff fingers and a backward flick of his wrist, then strolled across the decking, leaped over the banister, and shifted into a glorious eagle the moment his body hit the cool night air.

Because yeah, he had gotten better at that shit too...

Even though, with the exception of Nachari, who could shift into a panther—and now, Fabian Antonescu, the great High Mage who could probably do all kinds of miraculous crap—most vampires were restricted to only bats or mist.

As he tilted his outstretched wings in the direction of the Vampyr king's compound, Braden did his best not to think of the complicated, confused, beautiful redhead still seated on her couch.

* * *

Achilles Zahora, the Dark One otherwise known as The Executioner, was feeling restless, twitchy, amped up, and loaded for bear...

But he had no idea why.

Salvatore Nistor had been right about one thing: Achilles had always been a bloodthirsty savage, a giant of a vampire, and a killing machine...a force to be reckoned with.

He reveled in the slaughter.

He luxuriated in the taste and feel of fresh blood on his tongue, the thick, sticky fluid snaking down his fangs; and he could never get enough carnage, destruction, or bloodshed.

Maybe it was just as simple as that...

Achilles hadn't fed in a while; he hadn't left a string of brutalized human bodies in his wake for at least two or three moons; and he hadn't executed a rebel or a sinner in the house of Jaegar for just as many months. Still, tomorrow night marked the coming of the Millenia Harvest Moon, and the house of Jaegar would be busy, indeed: busy *feeding* on human hosts so younger siblings could feed their fathers...their brothers...in the ancient familial rite; busy satiating carnal appetites of every bent and perverse imagining; busy impregnating beautiful young women who would give birth to two dark sons, forty-eight hours later, and die a wretched death as the younglings, the evil offspring, clawed their way out of their sensual, fertile bodies.

Achilles wanted no part in the latter, to become a father...just yet.

True, in the house of Jaegar, it was every male's ultimate duty to procreate, and Achilles' offspring would be a coveted prize to his dark brethren. Yet and still, he wasn't ready. It was as simple as that.

Two years back, when that brutish son of Jadon, Marquis Silivasi, had discovered one of the last remaining females of a proud and ancient race—Ciopori Demir—and managed to claim her as his own, seduce her, even as he was caught up in a wicked deceitful love triangle, believing Kristina Riley to be his true *destiny*, chosen by the gods, Salvatore had managed to abduct the careless princess and bring her back to the Colony: The promise of heated nights, thrusting inside that royal womb; the mystery and allure of a female who might not die—who *might* still have access to celestial magic and *might* be able to circumvent the Curse, and thus give birth to female offspring?—had been too strong for Salvatore to pass up. Salvatore had needed to know more. So much remained a puzzle. And he had pulled the trigger, taken the princess, a bit too soon.

He had been reckless, selfish, premature.

And as a result, the sons of Jadon had invaded the Dark Ones' Colony, entering the underground settlement from a tunnel in the back of the sacrificial cave under the cover of night to rescue the missing princess, and they had slaughtered—annihilated—*fifty* sons of Jaegar, malevolent infant offspring who had just begun their eternal reigns of terror. In reply, Oskar Vadovsky, the new chair of the Dark Council, had ordered every male over the age of five hundred to go out and reproduce, to replace the lost, slain souls, until at least 250 new demon spawn slept in new cribs.

Achilles Zahora was over a thousand years old, but the Colony Guard and the illustrious council were exceptions to the edict, as were many other males whose seed was not ultimately needed, as 250 women were impregnated rather...quickly.

As far as Achilles was concerned, it was just as well.

He had always craved something better...different...worthy of his rank and file.

Perhaps a female human, corrupt to her core, who would relinquish her immortal soul for the promise of everlasting life on earth—immortality—a woman drenched in iniquity: a dark, soulless vessel who could bear Achilles offspring, again and again.

Or perhaps a blue-eyed redhead who was already Vampyr...

A cherished daughter to the Silivasi clan; a loyal servant of Napolean Mondragon; a hot, ditzy, prime piece of ass who strutted around in stiletto heels and whose soul would taste like honey, whose innocence...goodness...ultimate light would supersede and overshadow the familiar taste and taint of an already immoral soul.

Yeah...

Achilles would rather claim a female from the light than convert a soul already lost to darkness.

He was perverse that way.

The thought of defiling her innocence...again and again... forcing her to bear children for the house of Jaegar, taking her away from those arrogant, worthless, motherfucking halfwits from the house of Jadon was just too damn tempting...

First, he would take her away from Nachari Silivasi, a bastard who had once almost bested Achilles in battle outside Saber Alexiares' cave when Diablo had shown up to kill the *"dragon"*: Achilles had stabbed the Master Wizard with a ten-inch-dagger. Nachari had shifted into that detestable black panther, and the cat had nearly eviscerated Achilles' throat.

And second, he would take her away from Braden Bratianu, who had eluded Ian Lacusta's nefarious plot to kill the youngster at River Rock Creek: Ian had managed to grasp Braden's heart, and he had almost extracted it from the kid's adolescent body, but not unlike Nachari, Braden had shifted just in time, leaving Ian with a fistful of eagle feathers instead.

And last, but not least, Achilles would take the female from Napolean-freakin'-Mondragon's collection of faithful servants, from the monarch who had single-handedly slaughtered eighty-seven dark soldiers during that first Colony raid...

Using only his eyes and his power...

So yeah—*shit yeah*—it would be worth having a ditzy bitch

for a consort, just to irritate, insult, and outwit the house of Jackasses...

And that's why Achilles had no intentions of siring offspring tomorrow night.

While he would join his dark brothers in celebrating all the bloody sacrifices Prince Jaegar, their forefather, once performed in Romania—while he would take his fair share of innocent lives in the most brutal and imaginative ways possible, slaking his itch and assuaging his restless, brutal nature—he would opt out of the procreation...

For now.

He would wait to claim a richer prize...

Kristina Riley Silivasi.

CHAPTER ONE

T hey were waiting for him in the Ceremonial Hall of Justice.

All of them: Marquis, Nathaniel, Kagen, Nachari, and even Keitaro; all four sentinels, including the notorious fifth-wheel tracker, Julien Lacusta; and of course, Napolean himself and the closest thing the king had ever had to an equal, the infamous High Mage, Fabien Antonescu.

Way too formal.

The whole ominous setting.

Braden would have just as well preferred the outdoor terrace, a bunch of Master Warriors, sentinels, wizards, a Master Healer, and the supreme Master Justice huddled around the veranda's fireplace; hell, roasting a few marshmallows over the pit just to keep it simple...to keep it real...somewhat normal. It wasn't like they actually had to eat them—the low-key ambiance would have at least been inviting, maybe even relaxing. As it stood, Braden was keenly aware that his stepdad, his mother, and his little brother, Conrad, were waiting as well at the Dark Moon Lodge. They had been in the valley since early August, and yeah, didn't that just underscore the ultra-serious nature of the whole situation—the Bratianu family back together, at least in theory and definitely in urgency. In truth, the reunion had gone well. Everything was the way it should be: Braden had never been closer to his mother, Lily, and he and Conrad were making some great brotherly inroads.

He blinked away the distraction.

He had to maintain his focus on the immediate cluster of hardcore vampires at hand, the imminent crisis before him—well, *conference*, not crisis—but why parse words. He had to keep his full attention on the upcoming meeting.

As he approached the two heavy, wooden arched doors at the end of the long, circular, underground tunnel, the cobblestone floor feeling uneven beneath his boots, he paused just for a second before reaching to grasp the thick iron handle on the left. That door on the right—the one that led to the Chamber of Sacrifice and Atonement, the one that abutted another door bearing crossbones and an eerie warning inscribed in the Old Language, *Behold the portal to the corridor of the dead*, the one that ultimately ushered one into the Death Chamber—caused a chill of pure ice to prickle along Braden's spine. It had never really bothered him before, knowing it was there, knowing all that creepy shit was there. But he was riding a razor's edge tonight.

He grasped the handle on the left more firmly and yanked it open with sheer determination and iron will, stepping confidently into the safe and benign Hall of Justice, and the breath he didn't know he was holding left his body.

Holy.

Shit.

For all intents and purposes, Braden may as well have been the biblical Moses, placing the tip of his staff into the Red Sea, the way the vampires on the other side of the door suddenly rose, stepped back, and parted. Like equal halves of the same body of water, rolling in two fluid waves, they ascended from their various perches in the middle pews of the hall and stood in some reflexive formation, falling to the left and the right: Ramsey, Saxson, Santos, and Saber lined up against the nearest anterior wall, with Fabien at the head of the line, closest to the stage; and Keitaro, Marquis, Nathaniel, Kagen and, oddly, Julien lined up opposite, on the farthest posterior wall, closest to the king. Was it Braden's imagination or was Saber's characteristic smirk just a little bit less sarcastic?

Braden didn't meet the dragon's eyes as he passed the sentinel by.

And shit, his imagination continued to work overtime as he caught a glimpse of both Julien on the right, and then Ramsey on the left, catching each male in turn in the crosshairs of his peripheral vision. The tracker's typical caustic nod was definitely a bit subdued, and Ramsey Olaru, that hard-ass rebel, actually removed the toothpick from the corner of his mouth, twirled it beneath his fingers, and folded it into the palm of his hand, concealing the small wooden stick as if it were somehow disrespectful to suck on it in Braden's presence.

What the actual hell...

Braden drew back his shoulders and raised his chin, determined to appear both relaxed and proud—just a few more strides until he reached the king and Fabien—he could do this.

Just breathe...

Just breathe.

"Welcome, son." Napolean stepped forward, his proud noble features appearing serene, and his calming, authoritative voice helped to settle Braden's nerves. Well, at least a little.

Braden nodded because he couldn't speak, and that's when Nachari stepped forward, smiled, and placed a warm, loving hand on Braden's shoulder. "Good to see you, *fiule*."

He called him *son* in Romanian.

Shit.

Just shit.

A hot, moist tear pooled in the corner of Braden's eye, and he tried to blink it away.

Nachari inhaled slowly, angled his head to the side, and bent a little lower to study Braden's eyes, deep forest green seeking glassy burnt sienna, and then the Master Wizard let all pretense go as he drew the six-foot-two, broad-shouldered, two-hundred-pound fledgling into a full-bodied embrace and locked his powerful arms around Braden's stiff, resolute shoulders.

Keitaro placed a firm, steady hand on Braden's back, even as Julien sauntered to the front of the room, cut to the top of the line, and sort of palmed Braden's head, mussing his hair in a gesture of affection.

Damnit...

The last thing Braden wanted to do was cry.

He was not the same young neophyte he had been when he first came to the vale. At a minimum, he was showing signs of not only burgeoning maturity and power but promising wizardry and the traits of a warrior—blubbering like an idiot or a child would not help...or change...a thing.

The king expected more of him.

Hell, he expected more of himself.

He drew back from Nachari's welcoming embrace and sighed, this time, stiffening his back.

"It's all good," Nachari reassured him, no doubt reading Braden's emotions effortlessly.

"Yeah. *Yeah*," Braden muttered. "Thanks. I just...I think...the shit's just getting real, isn't it?" He shook his head in wary exasperation. What had happened to that focused, stalwart male vampire, the one who had just turned his back and walked away from Kristina, when all he had wanted to do was take her in his arms and explore her...soul?

"Very real indeed," the king chimed in, ushering an open palm toward an open pew a few rows forward at the front of the hall. "Sit." His statuesque mouth curved up in a smile. "Stay a while."

Braden didn't have to be asked twice.

He ambled quickly to the front row, and his knees nearly buckled beneath him as he sank down onto the wooden bench, stretched out both legs in front of him, and crossed his boots at the ankles. Nachari followed suit on his right, Keitaro took a seat to his left, and all the other warriors, sentinels, and the healer crowded into the pews behind him. The king scanned the hall until he eyed a pair of extra upholstered, high-backed, armless chairs—he pointed in their general direction and crooked his fingers forward. The chairs floated softly through the air, sliding into place *just so*, both across from and facing Braden, about three to four feet apart. The king took his seat silently, across from Braden and to the vampire's right, while Fabian Antonescu just sort of appeared like a desert mirage in the seat adjacent to Napolean's.

Braden blinked a few times and inadvertently shook his head.

It was always a little disconcerting when the High Mage did that, just sort of moved or appeared out of the ether. True, vampires could travel faster than the speed of light. They could fly, flash in and out, transport anywhere they liked. And their motions were often so fluid, so seamless, so animalistic in nature, one didn't always see them approach. But this was something different. Fabian had a way of willing things into being—it was more like he had a fleeting thought, released a desire or intention into the universe, and then manifested it instantly.

I'd like to sit in that chair...

Done.

The ancient wizard cleared his throat. "Just for the record— and so that we may concentrate fully on the most pressing matters at hand—we already discussed tomorrow's festivities, the formal and informal rites and celebrations taking place for all in the house of Jadon, the prayers and worship, the ceremonies and events, the traditions which accompany this new millennium..." His voice trailed off, and he waved a dismissive hand through the air, his burnt-copper, almond-shaped eyes narrowing with purpose. "The princesses will lead the people in the Homage Ceremony; the Master Wizards will see to the valley's sacred Rites of Magick, Renaissance & Renewal; and the Vampyr at large, all the families and individuals in the vale, those not directly present in this hall tonight, will complete the sacred Rite of Peace, Prosperity & Protection on their own, as usual." He waved his hand again, this time in a wide arc to indicate all those present in the Ceremonial Hall of Justice. "We, however, are primarily at your disposal, available at all times should the need arise." He allowed a moment of silence to punctuate the gravity of his words. "Now then, the moon will rise at 8:59 p.m. tomorrow."

Braden blanched—talk about getting straight to the point—and then he struggled to suppress a shiver: *Blessed Monoceros*, Braden's ruling lord, despite the gravity and great historical significance of the moon at hand, the High Mage, the sentinels, Julien, the Silivasis, and even the king were all at Braden's disposal? They had divested of their prominent roles and divided their conventional duties in order to attend to...whatever Braden might need.

Damn.

If Braden thought the shit was real before, it just got critical.

Hell, *severe.*

The High Mage closed his eyes as if listening to the elements around him; maybe listening wasn't the right word... "This night's moon will fully set by 10:49 tomorrow morning...at two hundred ninety-three degrees." He paused for the space of several heartbeats. "Then the next night's moon—tomorrow's blood-tinted moon, the Millenia Harvest Moon—will rise at 8:59 p.m., sixty-five degrees, Meridian Passing at 3:34 a.m., and moonset, the next morn at 11:46."

Braden drew back in his seat and gave Napolean a quizzical glance.

The king smiled warmly. "Any changes that might occur as a result of your imbibing Prince Jadon's royal blood could begin as early as 10:49 tomorrow morning, but they will be at their peak, reach their zenith as it were, by nine o'clock tomorrow night—"

"Eight fifty-nine p.m., " Fabian interjected.

The king regarded him with an impatient glance. "Yes, 8:59 to be exact." He refocused his attention on Braden. "If nothing happens, or if the moon loses its power, we should start to see the waning around 3:30 a.m."—he eyed the High Mage crosswise —"3:34 a.m. to be exact. And the full cycle of the moon's rotation will be complete by 11:46 the next morning. In other words, today is the fifteenth, tomorrow is the sixteenth, and if all is... unchanged by 11:46 on the seventeenth, then I think—we think— that nothing is going to happen."

At this, Braden's countenance lit up. "You think that's actually possible?"

"No," Fabian said brusquely. "But it gives us a timeline to follow."

Julien, who had become a sort of mentor if not a faithful friend to Braden over the past seven months, ever since the tracker had pulled Braden aside to dig deeper into the young vampire's past by way of the history with his parents, leaned forward in the pew behind him and placed a hand on Braden's upper arm. "We think you're good to go tonight. You can stay at the brownstone, the king's manse, wherever you like, but we don't want you to be alone come 10:49 a.m. tomorrow." He glanced down the row toward the four seated sentinels. "Ramsey, Saxson,

Santos, and Saber are going to be close at hand, at least within earshot if you get my drift, and as the day progresses, as we approach 8:59 p.m., the king, Fabian, Nachari, and myself are probably gonna be riding your six like an old drunken one-night stand—that poor, misled girl you can never get rid of."

"Like white on rice," Ramsey amended.

Julien sat back, just a little, and held up both hands, even as Braden twisted on the pew, straining his neck to see him. "Pardon the crude mixed metaphors," Julien pressed on, "but point being: You're not gonna be alone."

At this, Santos Olaru chimed in, his typically crystal blue eyes shadowed with intensity. "Just a precaution, Braden. Napolean needs to be right in the mix for obvious reasons—I think the same holds true for Fabian, who will also have the Master Wizards, Jankiel and Niko, at his beck and call. And as for Nachari, we know the two of you share an especially close bond, and well, after riding out more than four horrible months in the Abyss himself, Nachari has his own set of special skills. Intuition. The panther. We're just trying to cover all bases."

Braden swallowed a lump in his throat and fidgeted with his fingers, rubbed the back of his neck, then shifted his weight in the pew. "So, you guys will all be there, pretty much through the night? At least until 11:30 the next morning?" Acutely aware of Fabian, he paused to search his memory—he wanted to be precise. "At least until 11:46 the next morning?"

"Yep," Ramsey Olaru said, brusque and to the point. "And if everything's still copasetic at 3:30 a.m., we might even let you get some sleep." He chuckled, deep and low, from the back of his throat, trying to interject some much-needed humor in the moment, and a few of the warriors joined in. But all in all, the sound rang hollow—the humor was forced, and everyone knew it.

Braden swiveled back around in his seat.

He appreciated everything everyone was doing, and he

knew instinctively that the warriors, the sentinels...his Vampyr family and friends had likely discussed things—and in such great detail—that they had never dared to share with him. They probably had a plan B, plan C, and plan D through X. Hell, they had shared a lot of it with Braden over the past two months, but right now, this night, on the eve of the Millenia Harvest Moon, he just wanted it straight. All of it. Simplified, of course, but straight as an arrow. "Fabian," he said, reaching for courage, "what do you really expect? I mean, all of it. Best-case scenario to worst."

The High Mage rubbed his chin between his thumb and fore-finger, his almond-shaped eyes narrowing within rims of black, and the heart-shaped birthmark on his right shoulder seemed to glow in contrast to his copper skin. "You already know the answers to those questions, young Braden. Best-case scenario: Nothing occurs. The celestial gods do as they always have—they pour their power upon the earth and aid in our rites and celebra-tions. The dark lords of the underworld drench the earth with their malevolent powers as well, and the house of Jaegar performs its own depraved observance—but nothing out of the ordinary. And Prince Jadon's blood, the life-giving elixir of our revered patriarch himself, awakens in your veins, but your soul does not succumb to its ancient powers. It is not overtaken...over-whelmed...by the same. Your essence stays put. Perhaps you become wise beyond your years. Perhaps you share a rare, enlightening fusion, absorbing the Ancient One's wisdom, history, talents...but nothing material happens." He shifted in his seat, betraying his true discomfort. "Worst-case scenario: The sheer power of such an ancient soul, of such a mystic and super-natural occurrence, is far too much for your mortal body, vampiric as it may be, and your soul departs this world. You return to the Valley of Spirit & Light...forever."

"You mean, I die?" Braden blurted, needing the clarification.

"That's not going to happen," Nachari whispered, sounding more than a little miffed with Fabian.

Fabian shrugged. "I didn't say it would. Best case. Worst case. You already know each scenario. But you have asked me about probabilities...likelihoods...and I could pontificate over a dozen potential outcomes. The truth is, I believe it will be something in the middle, between those two extremes. Will something powerful, something extraordinary, happen? Yes, it will. Will your soul be lost or supplanted by Prince Jadon's? I do not know. I expect, perhaps, some amalgamation of the two, however that will look. Will it make you physically ill, change your anatomy...your chemistry? Unknown. Will you be the same male you are today, come the seventeenth day of September? No, you won't. But you must know, you must keep in mind, who the spirit of Prince Jadon is... who he was...a male of honor, not unlike yourself, a warrior of great power and skill. A leader who spared his people, his followers, for generations in perpetuity, from the worst of the Curse— the one who brought us the *four mercies*. A brother who loved his sisters so much he sent them ahead to a foreign land and asked me to guide and protect them. A prince who ruled with nobility and honor and who, in his wisdom and foresight, gave us a vial of his blood...on purpose. I am an alchemist, Braden. To you and your generation, this means my feet are most firmly planted in what you might call science, even as the sphere of that word is very broad, but in this matter, I am also what one might deem religious...a high priest...and I would cautiously advise you to have some faith. The celestial deities are neither unaware nor powerless, and Prince Jadon is not malevolent. Perhaps you should sleep this night as Ramsey suggests, but perhaps you should also pray."

Braden crossed his arms over his chest, pondering the High Mage's words.

He sat back in the pew and withdrew quietly inward, even as

Nachari Silivasi leaned closer. "Do you want to stay at the brownstone tonight?" Nachari asked.

"The lake house is there if you want it," Santos added. "Water is one of the primary sacred elements, and it does wonders for the spirit...for prayer."

"Ciopori and I would welcome you at the farmhouse," Marquis Silivasi said. "She is an original female."

"As is Vanya," Saber chimed in. "If you think the lodge, spending the night with your parents and your brother, is the right call, I'm sure the princess would be happy to take a room nearby. I'd ask you to stay at the Gothic Victorian, but Lucien is likely to be up all night—and ain't gonna lie, I suck as a host."

Keitaro spoke next. "It's just me and Zayda at the homestead."

"The manse might make the most sense," Napolean offered, matter-of-factly, his brow knitting downward in concern and compassion.

Braden held up his hand to halt any further offers. "I want to be at home." He eyed Nachari with a knowing, brotherly glance. "I want to be with Nachari and Deanna. The brownstone is still where I live." His mind shifted rapidly, wandering to Kristina and her warm, elegant penthouse: *I'd like to be with Kristina*, he thought, but he shoved the musing aside. And then he turned his attention back to the two most powerful beings in front of him: Napolean Mondragon, king of the Vampyr, the leader who had almost single-handedly formed and saved the house of Jadon, and Fabian Antonescu, the godfather whom the only remaining original females called *nanaşule*, the most powerful magician who had ever lived. "Napolean," he said softly. "Fabian..." He eyed each ancient male in turn. "Will you pray, too? For me? For my family? For the whole house of Jadon? If the gods are still listening, if Prince Jadon is still...somewhere out there, able to hear, tell him he can use me however he wishes, but I still have a lot of life to live, people who love me, talents to explore, heck, maybe even gifts to one day give. Ask them to watch over our valley. Ask them to somehow, when it's all said and done, make this Millenia Harvest Moon into a blessing, not a curse, and to protect each and every soul in the house of Jadon, the fraternity of friendship, family, and fealty we all revere." He paused, thinking it over...that special request. *Yeah*, he figured, feeling quite certain: "I think, maybe, they'll listen to you."

CHAPTER TWO

Kristina took the upcoming S-curve at about eighty-five miles per hour, leaning into the gas pedal of her pink Corvette with a heavy stiletto-clad foot and an even heavier heart.

She wasn't sure where she was going, and she really didn't care as she attacked the narrow, winding roads of the steep mountain pass like a reckless banshee, heedless of the potential consequences, dead set on venting her turbulent emotions. She only knew that she had to get the hell out of dodge, away from her penthouse apartment, and away from Dark Moon Vale...just for a couple of hours.

She needed to clear her mind and somehow quiet her soul.

She had to try to reclaim just a little bit of her sanity.

As for integrity...

Dignity?

Yeah, well, she didn't have much of those left.

She'd exposed her heart and left her self-respect on the penthouse floor when she'd offered her passion, her body, and her soul to Braden, and the vampire had strolled across the floor, kissed her with unrestrained hunger, then shrugged it off as if it were nothing—as if *she* were nothing—before turning his back and vaulting from the penthouse balcony.

He hadn't even bothered to look back.

But what was new?

This was the story of Kristina's life: a deceased, alcoholic father who had not wanted Kristina or her mother—she had never even met the man who had impregnated *Mommy Dearest*; a hellish run with Dirk, who had abused her emotionally and physically; that horrid experience with Ramsey—*Saber*—where she had been played like a desperate, love-starved fool. And then there was Braden, possibly the best friend she'd ever had—

But Kristina couldn't love.

She couldn't allow herself to *be loved*...

To completely open up.

She could do sister.

She could do friend.

She could even do smart-mouthed redhead, but she couldn't do vulnerable, and she couldn't do...trust. Kristina hid her scars like a master illusionist, but deep down inside, far beneath the surface, the wounds—and the pain—were still bloody and raw.

Still, she had tried...

Earlier that night.

Heaven knew she had exposed her true soul to Braden.

The car's rear tires spun out on a loose patch of gravel, and Kristina tightened her fingers around the wheel, pressing the tips of her fuchsia-pink manicured nails into the palms of her hands as she steered out of the skid and regained control before heading into another bend in the road.

What the hell was going to happen tomorrow when the Millenia Harvest Moon rose?

What the heck did Braden think of her now?

And since when had she cared...*so much*?

A staggered steppe of large, jagged boulders leaned toward the road about a half mile ahead, jutting out from a sudden vertical crevasse, a protrusion in the mountain, dotted with pines, blue furs, and quaking aspens, many of the native trees growing straight out of the rocks. She let up on the gas just a bit to maximize her control, and that's when she saw the shadow.

The ghost in the darkness.

The silhouette of a hulking male, blending almost seamlessly with the rocky shelf, just behind a thick, leaning bristlecone pine.

She blinked several times in quick succession, her vampire-senses coming alive, and then she leaned into the steering wheel, narrowed her gaze through the dew-drenched, foggy window, and scanned the shadow again.

Holy shit!

Both feet hit the brake, and the car skidded sideways.

That wasn't a shadow, and it wasn't a lone human hiker.

Last time Kristina checked, shadows didn't have pale, citrine-colored eyes, black-and-red chin-length hair, or circular bands of black mambas with jeweled red eyes wrapped around their upper right biceps.

And humans were rarely seven feet tall.

She gulped, swallowing what felt like a gallon of air, threw the Corvette into reverse, and glanced frantically in the rearview mirror as she hit the gas and tore off backward.

Shit-shit-shit!

The road was too narrow—she almost drove straight into the side of the boulder.

She screeched forward, then darted back, shifting the gears again and again while spinning the wheel left, then right—whatever was necessary—in a desperate attempt to turn the car around.

Damnit!

She came way too close to the edge of the road—two or three

inches more, and she would have driven straight off the bluff! She craned her neck to look behind her. Where was the shadow now? "Oh fuck," she whispered frantically. "Just get out of here, Kristina." She threw the car into reverse once more, praying no one would come down the pass and sideswipe her before she could get off the road.

Her mind raced frantically, her thoughts spinning faster than her tires...

What had she learned in Nathaniel's self-defense class?

What vampiric skills had she mastered in the two short years since Marquis had turned her Nosferatu?

What...who...there had to be something!

Shit.

That's right.

She wasn't alone.

Kristina Silivasi was never truly alone...

From the moment she had stumbled upon Dark Moon Vale as a lost, homeless runaway, when Kagen Silivasi had rescued her from certain death at the hands of a Dark One, to the day she had begun working at the Dark Moon Casino, under the Vampyr's protection, to that awful night on the front porch of Marquis' farmhouse, when the Ancient Master Warrior had converted her under the supposed protection of Lord Draco—it had been an elaborate deception for sure; Marquis had believed Kristina was his *destiny*—but still, from that night to all the days, weeks, and months thereafter, Kristina had been welcome in the house of Jadon. Hell, Nachari and Deanna were like her brother and sister...

No, Kristina was not alone.

An inexplicable calm settled over her, and she finally managed to shimmy the car out of the middle of the road, pop it back into first gear, and point her front wheels forward, facing home.

And that's when she saw him.

Again.

Planted in the middle of the road.

Only this time, he was in front of her, looming like a massive, ancient oak tree staking its claim on the banks of a river.

"Achilles Zahora." She whispered the name, and it left a disgusting taste on her tongue.

Even though she had never technically met the infamous Dark One, she was absolutely sure who he was—his description was undeniable, and his reputation, his terrifying persona, preceded him. The Executioner, as the vampire was also called, belonged to the Dark Ones' formal Colony Guard, and nearly eight months earlier, he had ordered Ian Lacusta—Julien's long-lost dark twin, who had escaped being sacrificed to the Curse at birth and returned to Dark Moon Vale—to seek vengeance for the house of Jaegar by murdering Braden at River Rock Creek. Julien had almost died during the fiery confrontation, and Braden had only survived because of his quick thinking and agile shape-shifting—he had escaped in the body of an eagle. As if that were not enough, Braden had faced Achilles once more, along with the Chair of the Dark Ones' Council, Oskar Vadovsky, when the two dark vampires had tried to extract Braden's heart in the basement of the Fortress. If not for Nachari and Nathaniel's intervention, Kristina would have lost Bray forever...

The thought curdled her gut, and her teeth began to chatter.

She hit the brakes again—softer this time, more in control—and a single telepathic word flowed from her mind like a prayer, swirling through running water: *Papa.*

She steeled her resolve and sharpened her focus...

Keitaro.

She didn't know how she did it, but her mind went blank of all fear, all chatter, as she projected three crystal-clear, vital images to her HOJ father: her Corvette speeding along the mountain pass, the jutting rocks and the ghost in the shadows, her car, turned around, and the ominous male planted like an oak in front of it.

Achilles Zahora.

She sent the name along the same fluid bandwidth, praying— no, believing—that the eldest Silivasi would hear it.

And just like that, her car was surrounded.

Keitaro Silivasi stood in front of the hood, his thick black hair shining in the moonlight, so dark the purple hues reflected like flowing prisms, dazzling in the dim yellow headlights. Marquis materialized next to Kristina's driver's-side window, his expression carved in granite, with a crude ancient cestus on his fisted right hand, and Nathaniel appeared to the right of the car, his dark eyes brimming with lethal purpose, his mouth curved into a slow, easy smile, wielding two razor-sharp stilettos with hand-crafted grips and polished silver blades—the Ancient Master Warrior was ready to strike, and by the look on his face, his inner child had come to play.

Kagen leaned against the back of the car—Kristina could see his profile in the rearview mirror—and the good-natured vampire looked more like Mr. Hyde than Dr. Jekyll, his jaw locked in a firm, contemptuous line, his tall, muscular shoulders taut with tension and twitching every couple of seconds. And *celestial gods, bless him*; Nachari Silivasi emerged, not as a green-eyed Master Wizard but as a full-fledged black panther, slowly slinking back and forth along the Corvette's front bumper.

Kristina's eyes glossed over with tears.

They were here.

All of them.

Just like that.

But where was Braden?

Her gut clenched, and she slapped a mental Band-Aid over the persistent, painful wound beneath her latest scar: *"Don't go there, Kristina,*" she whispered to herself. "*It's the eve of the Millenia Harvest Moon—you know he can't get away, not even if he wants to.*" It was enough—more than enough—that Napolean had allowed three Ancient Master Warriors, an Ancient Master Healer, and a gifted Master Wizard to leave the critical meeting.

She blinked several times, swiping tears from beneath her lower lids.

It didn't matter anyhow.

There was nothing to be done...

Keitaro was scanning the road and the nearby woods; Marquis was thumbing a pile of gravel, then scenting it beneath his nostrils; Kagen's dark brown eyes, which typically shimmered with reflections of silver, were emitting two infrared rays of light as he skimmed the mountaintops, the tree line, and the forest, searching for the faintest sign of life or movement. And Nachari —the panther—was pacing systematically, back and forth, in tight, even rows, examining every inch of the adjacent pass, every tire track, every footprint, every heat wave.

Achilles was nowhere to be found.

The bastard had vanished the moment Kristina had opened the telepathic call.

* * *

"Fucking-A!" Achilles bristled, his heavy black boots kicking up gravel in the dimly lit parking lot outside the Dark Moon Casino. He narrowed his citrine peepers on a tall, blonde beanpole who had just gotten off her shift—the human barista must have been anorexic; it was a wonder she could walk to her car—and then he scanned the parking lot a second time, just to make sure there were no vamps in the nearby vicinity, no watchmen or security guards of the blood-sucking persuasion.

"*Fuck!*" he vented his frustration, once again.

Having stalked the sexy redhead from a relatively safe distance, off and on since an hour past sunset, he had hardly believed his good fortune when she'd climbed into her car around 10:30 p.m., and it would've been so much easier to catch Kristina and speak to her directly—kindly and gallantly, of course—alone on the mountain pass. But she had obviously called the cocksucking calvary, and he had no intentions of starting a war on the eve of the Millenia Harvest Moon, nor of taking on five viperous vampires by himself.

As it stood, and for reasons he couldn't really place a finger on, he wanted the challenge, he needed the chase, he craved the internal satisfaction of catching her, deceiving her, manipulating Kristina's free will—getting her to come to him freely—not just grabbing and snatching.

Maybe he was old.

Maybe he was tired.

Hell, maybe he was just...bored.

At any rate, it was time for *plan B* and the Dark Moon Casino...

Finding a less conspicuous cohort.

His attention went back to the waiflike barista and ensuring the absence of vampire guards, sentries patrolling the lucrative establishment on behalf of the house of Jadon. He knew he had been careful to remain invisible, but still, vampires could easily sense their own kind.

And speaking of the local house of Jackasses—what the hell was up with them anyway?

For weeks now, if not months, the males had been acting like a skittish colony of ants: gathering in clandestine clusters, marching in and out of the king's heavily fortified compound, and circling around that ancient high...*priestess*—well, High Mage, as the bastards were now calling Fabian—the prehistoric wizard, arisen from the dead. Point being: They were acting like a clique of teenage girls, gossiping around a junior high lunch table, and they all had their panties wadded up in a bunch.

But why?

The skinny barista picked up her pace, reached into her slender handbag to retrieve a key fob, and rounded the hood of her 2010, maybe 2011, Toyota Camry.

Bingo.

Time to move.

As Achilles gathered his invisible molecules and prepared to transport, then materialize inside the human's way too tiny car, he shrugged his ethereal shoulders. Who the hell cared what was going on with the house of Jadon—the surge in activity had given him a chance to approach Kristina Silivasi on that barren mountain road, and by the looks of the locked-and-loaded entourage that had showed up in an instant, the second Kristina had transmitted a mental SOS, the Bloodstreet Boys were not *that* busy—not *that* distracted—they still had time to circle the wagons at the drop of a hat, and that meant whatever they had been chattering about all these months could not be that important.

It also meant Achilles had to be more careful.

He couldn't let down his guard.

Millenia Harvest Moon coming or no, he couldn't just step up to Kristina and start a casual chat. And if he was being honest —if he was being fair—he had to admit that whatever was plaguing the house of Jadon, whatever was in the air, the house of Jaegar was drinking at the same cantina, sucking down the same potent spirits and swallowing their fair share as well: Salvatore Nistor had all but merged with that insidious cube of his, and as a consequence, he had visited Achilles' lair every other night since early July; Oscar Vadovsky had held at least a dozen council meetings over the same period of time; and well, yeah, Achilles was both twitchy and antsy as hell. Something funky was definitely in the air.

"Boo!" He barked the word just as Blondie reached beyond her steering wheel and pressed her key fob into the pre-fitted slot. The female squeaked more than she screamed, but the sound was loud, shrill, and annoying as hell. "Shh," Achilles whispered, leaning forward from the back seat of the car. *Shit*, the chick was hyperventilating. He encircled her diminutive chest with a tight, bulging arm and placed his huge, heavy hand around her convulsing throat, massaging both sides of her windpipe. "What's your name, little girl?" His voice sounded like it had been ground through broken glass.

"M-M-Mindy," she stuttered, starting to sob.

"Mindy," he repeated, this time lacing the word in a velvet compulsion. "Breathe, little darling. That's it, just take in some air and chill. The Grim Reaper's not gonna visit you tonight." She took several deep breaths, but her entire body trembled. Achilles sent an electrical pulse down her larynx, through her lungs, and into her heart, slowing the beats himself. "How does that feel?" He rotated his thumb beneath her chin, then slowly massaged her lymph nodes. "Better?"

She nodded tentatively.

"Good," he crooned, "good."

She turned her head to the side to try to steal a glance at him, but he flicked her cheeks with the backs of two fingers. "Look," he said, his boorish voice thick with compulsion. "I need you to do me a favor." He reached into the pocket of his long, leather duster, retrieved a plain eight-by-ten envelope, and dropped it in her lap. "First thing tomorrow morning, you're going to come back to the casino, head up to the top, penthouse floor, and knock on Kristina Riley Silivasi's front door. When she opens it, you're gonna hand her that envelope and simply tell her, 'I have an urgent message from Braden Bratianu—he said to keep it a secret.' If she doesn't answer the door, you come back, again and again, every hour on the hour. Got it?"

Mindy nodded zealously, like a programmed bobblehead doll, then glanced down at the envelope. "But what do I say if she asks—"

"Shh," Achilles repeated. "Not another word to me *or* Kristina. *I have an urgent message from Braden Bratianu, and he said to keep it a secret.* That's it. That's all. You walk away. And the moment you get back in the elevator, you're going to forget me. You're going to forget this night and our private conversation. You're going to forget the letter and handing it to Kristina. The last memory you will have is getting in your car and driving home without incident. Got it?" He sat there for a minute or two, giving his words a chance to linger and the compulsion a chance to take hold, while allowing his mind to wander to other topics, including the upcoming rare, significant observance: tomorrow night's festivities...

Achilles had only been two years old at the last Millenia Harvest Moon, but the tales chronicled in the historic almanacs, those told by Oskar and the Colony's sorcerer, were legendary in their descriptions, detailing how the house of Jaegar celebrated the unholy night: Youngest brothers fed their fathers and siblings until all were satiated and replete. Piles of dead bodies were left in the Vampyr's wake as they engaged in countless orgies and profane rites. Terrified women were ravished and brutalized, giving birth to dozens of newborn Dark Ones forty-eight hours later—no, not giving birth! The babes clawed their way out of broken carcasses, amidst plaintive screams, unbearable agony, and the fetid stench of death. And when it was all said and done, the house of Jaegar was revived...replenished...

Refreshed.

For just a moment, Achilles wondered if Mindy's shrill scream would add elocution to the disharmonic chorus, and his manhood stirred.

He lowered his hand from her throat to her blouse.

He grasped her breast and flicked a nipple...

Wondering...thinking...considering.

But nah, not enough there physically to make it worthwhile, and not enough there mentally to hold his interest. Nothing about Mindy beckoned: *Come back.*

He withdrew his hand and leaned back against the stiff, uncomfortable leather; his enormous seven-foot frame packed into the Camry's back seat like a folded sardine. "Fuck," he growled. He needed to get out of there. "Do you understand the directive, Mindy?"

The female tried to answer, but once again, she only squeaked.

At least this time it wasn't so shrill.

"Good," Achilles barked. Enough was enough. She would deliver the letter to Kristina—she had no other choice—but just in case she started to get cold feet, sweat like a pig, or the redhead asked too many questions, he leaned forward, the best he could, and snarled in her ear: "Oh, and Mindy? If you fuck this up, if Kristina doesn't accept the letter, or if you say one word outside the script I gave you, I'll be back to snap your little chicken neck."

Luckily for Achilles, he climbed out of the car and vanished before the smell of Mindy's urine, pooling atop the front leather seat, could grow any more pungent.

CHAPTER THREE

THE DARK ONES' COLONY ~ 3 A.M.

Salvatore Nistor sat up in bed, swung both feet over the side of his overstuffed mattress, and pinched the bridge of his nose. "What in tarnation?" The limestone floor was cold beneath his feet, it felt like the ancient walls of the subterraneous lair were closing in on him, and the heavy antique chandelier looming above his head almost seemed to be mocking him. He flashed an evil sideways glance at his cube and shook his head in exasperation: Achilles Zahora, stuffed like one of the feathers inside Salvatore's downy mattress in the back seat of an emaciated human woman's Toyota, and he wasn't even *feeding* or abusing the female—well, not really. The scene went dark, much like the lair all around him, but that was just fine with Salvatore—at this point, he didn't even want to know.

As far as the ancient vampire was concerned, every day brought something stranger, more confusing than the last, and he couldn't make heads nor tails out of any of it.

He lowered his heavy, weary lids, catching a peripheral glimpse of the random papers—notecards, sticky notes, and wadded-up scribblings—scattered about his nightstand, and his brow furrowed. He didn't have to read them to remember what they said.

Nonsense.

Gibberish.

Arbitrary, meaningless omens portending something vitally important—but what?

King Silvano's grandfather, 988 BC.

Maiden voyage, North America, 799 BC.

Hawk, circled twice; raven, underlined with an explanation point; Achilles Zahora, blood, blood, blood...

Yada, yada, yada.

The accompanying portents—or the cube's visual revelations, as it were—were just as clear in the sorcerer's mind as the notes and all the scrawlings: Achilles Zahora, "The Executioner," bathing in an ancient tub of blood, imbibing the substance through his mouth, ears, and nostrils, swirling it around on his tongue; Achilles Zahora, "The Executioner," rising from a shallow grave like a mythical phoenix ascending from ash...

Yeah, Salvatore had seen and heard it all before: He had drunk the Kool-Aid, bought the T-shirt, and now, he just wanted the visions—and the nonsense—to end.

Oh, but there was more...

Over the last several weeks, Salvatore had also seen the damnedest string of words, mystical quotes floating through the air like the trail of an invisible skywriter, gliding through his lair:

Light cleaves to light, and darkness cleaves to darkness.

Drink this blood and welcome life.

Drink this blood and welcome death.

What. The. Hell. Did. That. Mean?

"Fine," he said out loud, as if the cavern had ears and the ancient stalactites could hear him. "I get it. The Millenia Harvest Moon only occurs every one thousand years. Tomorrow is no ordinary day. It's momentous, extraordinary, unequaled in scope and weight!" A snarl escaped his taut lips, cool air grazing his fangs, and he took a deep breath to quell his rising temper. "I get it," he repeated, "I wasn't born when the ancestors celebrated the first chiliad moon in antiquity, before the sons of Jaegar were claimed by the Curse, nor was I born during the second Millenia Harvest—I did not get to participate in all its delicacies, all its wicked delights—but alas, I was there in 1011 A.D., and I will never forget that night...that moon...that overwhelming surge of power." He folded his hands in his lap and bowed his head in reverence. "So, what the fuck is up with this cube, and how long do you intend to toy with me?" He sighed. So much for restraining his temper.

From across the room, Salvatore's nephew whimpered, and the sorcerer rose from his bed. His musings must have roused the young vampire, which was a pity in its own right as the two-year-old usually slept like the dead. Salvatore chuckled, and the sound ricocheted throughout the lair: *Slept like the dead.* What a clever vampiric witticism, though make no mistake, the Vampyr were not the undead—they were not the cold-blooded, inorganic, walking corpses that filled so many human novels and nightmares. Nay, the Dark Ones were very much alive.

He crossed the floor in a handful of fluid strides, avoiding a particularly sharp stalagmite jutting up from the floor, and reached into the crib where the toddler was now standing. "Ah yes, sweet Derrian." He picked him up. "Did your uncle Salvatore wake you? Apologies." He slid his fingers into the child's thick, wavy black-and-red hair, the same texture as his father's, and gazed lovingly, all the while smiling, into the two bottomless deep-green orbs staring back at him. The reflection was uncanny, if not a bit unsettling, how the boy's eyes were the spitting image of his mother's: Dalia Montano-Silivasi, the human *destiny* of Shelby Silivasi who never had a chance to be fully claimed and converted. Valentine had seen to that when he had abducted her, ravished her body, and forced her to bear his offspring—well, bear was not quite the appropriate term. It was more like a volcanic eruption that eviscerated the human female's skeleton, and the impulsive act, the insult to the house of Jadon, had cost Valentine Nistor his life.

Salvatore's fangs elongated at the memory...

Marquis Silivasi and his little brother, Nachari, had exacted such a horrific Blood Vengeance on Valentine, but no matter— Salvatore tucked the memory away, stuffed it deep into the recesses of his subconscious, much like a kitten being held under water.

Somehow...

Someway...

Eventually, Marquis and that incessant, arrogant Master Wizard would get what the pair had coming to them.

He pressed Darrien's head to his shoulder and gently rubbed his back—the toddler settled in nicely, emitting a barely audible purr. "It's a pity you may not remember your father. He was such a magnificent male." He leaned his head against the child's. "But your future is very bright, indeed, little one. Tomorrow is the dawning of a brand-new day, and despite all the confusion emanating from my cube"—he glanced over his shoulder, eyed the nightstand briefly, then turned his attention back to Darrien —"the Millenia Harvest Moon will bring amazingly good tidings for you. If nothing else, you will have dozens and dozens of new playmates: vampires to grow up with, hunt with, kill with, brothers who will always have your back, and who may one day seek Blood Vengeance, retaliation, on your behalf."

Darrien heaved a sigh, nestled into his uncle's shoulder, and drifted off to sleep.

"Yes," Salvatore whispered, placing him gently back in the crib. "While the sons of Jadon must await their chosen *destinies* in order to mate and repopulate their house, the sons of Jaegar can reproduce at will. One day soon, there will be a reckoning, and not even Napolean Mondragon with all his celestial powers, nor that High Mage, Fabian, will be able to save them. The Dark Ones will reign supreme."

He crossed the room, climbed back in bed, and rolled onto his side, tuning out the cube and the omens. *"Bring on the harvest moon."*

CHAPTER FOUR

SUNRISE ~ MORNING OF THE MILLENIA HARVEST
MOON

A ray of soft golden sunlight streamed through the bedroom window as Braden rolled over in bed, wiped his eyes with his forearm, and slowly stretched his arms. His head turned toward the open window, he yawned, and then he gasped.

Holy shit!

He sat straight up.

It was September 16th, dawn of the Millenia Harvest Moon!

What the hell time was it?

He closed his eyes and steadied his breath, feeling for the moon's magnetic pull on the earth, the rotation of the planet, the vibrations in the solar system...

6:41 a.m.

He threw back the covers, rose to his feet, and chuckled softly as his eyes caught the brass, sunflower-shaped wall clock hanging on the painted drywall: *Yep, 6:41 a.m.*

He slowly looked down at his chest, his legs, then his feet.

He patted his pecs, feeling the hard rise of the muscles and the lines between ridges.

He counted his fingers and his toes: Ten each—that was good.

He ran through a quick, albeit human, cognitive test, asking himself several basic questions: *What year is this? Who's the human president? Count backward from one hundred, by fours...*

One hundred.

Ninety-six.

Ninety-two.

Eighty-eight...

His brain appeared to be functioning just fine.

He made a beeline to the en suite bathroom, padded across the travertine tiles, and pressed his nose against the heavy antique mirror hanging above the pedestal sink.

Too close.

Way too close!

He backed up and stared at his reflection.

Burnt sienna eyes with golden pupils. Chestnut-brown, shoulder-length hair with an occasional blond highlight. Six-foot-two, at least two hundred pounds—he flexed his right bicep and then the same triceps. *Damn*, he was really getting strong. He shook his head, dismissing the thought, then drew back his lips and stared at his teeth: thirty-two pearly white choppers, two particularly sharp canines on top, and equally powerful incisors. He ran his tongue around the latter, emitting a couple drops of venom from the glands situated beneath them, just to prove he could.

Yep, he was definitely still a vampire.

"Braden?" He called his own name in the mirror.

Nothing felt different, and nothing happened.

He swiped his lower lip with his tongue, then bit down on the same out of anxiety. "Prince Jadon?" He spoke the words in a whisper, his heart skipped a beat, his hackles rose, and his breaths became quick and shallow.

Still, nothing happened.

He breathed a heavy sigh of relief.

"Braden?" Nachari's familiar melodic voice echoed from the threshold where the Master Wizard stood, clad only in a pair of black silk pajama-shorts, the ones Deanna had given him for Christmas, and that familiar amulet his twin Shelby had bequeathed him from the other side of eternal existence. "You okay?" Nachari asked. His deep, forest-green eyes looked tired. "How long have you been up?"

"Not long," Braden shot back, turning around to face him and leaning back against the sink. "Did I wake you?"

At this, Nachari chuckled. "Not hardly."

Braden smiled sheepishly. *Shit*, if anything Nachari had probably been up all night, coming into Braden's room to check on him every hour on the hour, just like a newborn babe, and it was Braden who had slept through it all. "Cool," Braden replied —he didn't know what else to say.

Nachari pointed at the heavy antique mirror, and Braden sighed.

Double shit.

So, Nachari had probably seen and heard everything. "Just, you know," Braden mumbled, "checking things out, first thing in the morning."

Nachari nodded with empathy and raised his eyebrows. "And what did you find?"

"I'm still me." Braden swept his hand through his hair. "Is Deanna up, too?"

"Oh yeah," Nachari said. "She's been up for a while. Sebastian did his thing again."

Nachari and Deanna's son, Sebastian Lucas, was seventeen months old already, and being that vampire children developed much, *much* faster than human children, Sebastian had gone from crawling to walking, from walking to running, and from running to trying out his wings, months ago. Although he still slept in a large, padded bed—a crib that transformed into both a daybed and a toddler bed, fairly easily—Nachari and Deanna kept the sides up at night, primarily for Sebastian's safety. Just the same, whenever the boy got hungry or restless, whenever he wanted his mother or father, he would simply stretch his wings, float over the spindles to get out of his crib, then fly to Nachari and Deanna's master bedroom, where he would hover directly above the sleeping couple. According to Nachari, he loved his son dearly, but the behavior was creepy as hell, waking up to a hovering vampire staring down into one's eyes, with peepers the exact same color...

Braden couldn't help but chuckle.

There was something oddly reassuring about Sebastian waking up his parents—however creepy the manner—on the morning of the Millenia Harvest Moon. It was almost as if the universe was sending a calming message: Business as usual—nothing to see here, folks.

If only that were true...

"So, what's on your agenda?" Nachari asked.

Braden's eyebrows hitched up and his jaw dropped open. *Was he kidding?*

Nachari shook his head. "I meant this morning. One hour, one minute at a time. Lots of ceremonies and festivities today—you're welcome to all of them, any of them, just as long as you stay tight with your entourage."

Braden nodded. "Yeah, I get the protocol." He pushed off the sink, folded his arms beneath his pecs, and quickly changed gears, shifting back to Nachari's question. "Fabian said that last night's moon will fully set by 10:49 a.m., and tonight's moon will begin rising at 8:59 p.m., 'to be exact.' So, my thought is, hop in the shower, swing by the Dark Moon Lodge to visit with my parents and Conrad, then maybe meet up with the sentinels, Napolean, and Fabian by 10:45. You know, just to be safe."

Nachari nodded in agreement. "Makes sense to me. Were you thinking the King's manse?"

"No," Braden answered abruptly. "Not the manse." He shook his head, emphatically. "The queen will be there, at least in and out, and Tiffany will be wherever Brooke is, with Roman in tow, and that's to say nothing about all the decorating and preparations going on in the courtyard, whatever Ciopori and Vanya are whipping up for tonight's Homage Ceremony. Nachari, I don't..." He paused to collect his thoughts and choose his words more carefully. "I don't want anyone who doesn't have to be around me —*that* close around me—to be anywhere near me when the harvest moon rises. Does that make sense?"

Nachari nodded slowly. "So then..."

"What about the lake?" Braden offered. "I mean, not the huge one outside the Dark Moon Lodge, or the southeast basin near the hot springs, but Santos' private reservoir, part of his hidden cove? The way I figure, the sentinels have to be with me anyway, right?"

"True."

"Do you think Napolean and Fabian will mind?"

Nachari shook his head. "I think Napolean and Fabian will be mostly in and out. While they've divided their duties and placed others in charge of the various ceremonies, events, and sacred rites, I'm sure they're still gonna want to stop in, participate here and there. But definitely by 8:59, they'll make their way to the lake house if that's the place you desire."

Braden closed his eyes. "Oh, shit." He opened them and frowned. "What about Natalia and Zeri—they'll still be there, won't they?"

Nachari averted his eyes for a second, focusing inward as if puzzling it out. "No," he finally answered. "I'll give Keitaro a call. I'm sure he won't mind if Natalia and Zeri join him and Zayda at the Homage Ceremony this night, then remain at the homestead until morning—Zayda and Natalia are very good friends. But do you mind if I ask..." His voice trailed off as Braden waited. "If I ask about Kristina? Don't you want to see her, hang out with her today, maybe at least—"

Braden waved his hand through the air, cutting Nachari off in midsentence. "I already handled that last night."

"*Handled that?*" Nachari drew back, his expression instantly wary. "What does that mean?"

Braden swallowed a lump in his throat and avoided direct eye contact. "It's not what it sounds like." He sighed. "I just meant..." He paused to catch his breath—*what did he mean?* "I already went to see her last night, before I showed up at the compound. We said everything we needed to say."

Nachari's forehead creased with concern, and his expression dimmed. "You said everything you needed to say?" He repeated Braden again. "Son?"

Braden shook his head. "I, um, I can't, Nachari. Can we just leave that alone?"

Nachari became the epitome of stillness. His brow smoothed out, but the wariness still showed in his eyes. "The two of you are promised, Braden. Maybe not right now, but sometime in the future, Kristina will be your—"

"Leave it alone," Braden repeated, his voice sounding deeper than he remembered.

Nachari took a measured step back and linked his hands behind his back, appraising Braden thoughtfully. "A lot on your plate, isn't it?"

"Yeah," Braden said.

"I get it. I do, but just keep in mind, son, that fear is a horrible counselor. You've got this, Braden. *We've* got this, Braden. Everything is going to be okay."

Braden met the wizard's thoughtful, penetrating eyes and held his gaze for a pregnant moment.

Nachari didn't know that.

No one could possibly know that.

The blood of an ancient, powerful prince was flowing through Braden's veins, and when the clock struck nine—okay, well, 8:59 to be exact—how had Fabian put it? The celestial gods would drench the earth with power and open a channel between the celestial sphere and this planet, allowing their offspring access to pure, undiluted energy from all six directions. As would the dark lords...

And while, technically, Braden was not the offspring of the original celestial ancestors—he had been made Vampyr, sired, not born—that blood in his veins was still churning: *Drink this blood and welcome life.* Fabian had placed Prince Jadon's blood in Braden for safekeeping, and he had commanded it—*no, conjured it*—actually bonded the blood itself to this night's Millenia Harvest Moon. According to the High Mage, who had done the deed, the blood would ripen, fully awaken, and activate.

Sure, it was originally supposed to be a catalyst, an insurance policy to protect the princesses, make sure they were found wherever Fabian had placed them to rest in an enchanted sleep, but now?

Who the hell knew...

Not Fabian.

Not Napolean.

And despite the goodness in his heart, not Nachari Silivasi, though Braden wished his mentor were right.

"Son, are you okay?" Nachari asked.

Braden nodded, unconvincingly.

"You sure?"

He shrugged his shoulders and tilted his head in a brief *come-what-may* gesture.

"What about Kristina?" Nachari held up one hand in a sign of both peace and apology. "Not gonna pry. I'll leave it alone. Just tell me one thing: With regard to the two of you, is Kristina okay?"

Well, wasn't that just the million-dollar question, the one Braden refused to dwell on. He couldn't. He just...couldn't. But Nachari was way too insightful to bullshit. He had to give the Master Wizard...something. "Truth?"

"Always," Nachari said.

"No. I doubt she's okay." There. He had said it. He moved the topic along, just as swiftly, uncrossing his arms but stiffening his shoulders. "But she will be. I'm sure of it."

Nachari didn't press any further. He gestured toward the large, walk-in shower, encased in slabs of marble, frameless glass walls, and fitted with a sleek copper Roman soaking tub at the back of the enclosure, and did his damnedest to lighten the mood and change the subject. "Well, you'd better hop to it. I'll go get dressed, myself. Just one more question?"

Braden started to frown, but he caught it and checked it, on purpose.

"The Dark Moon Lodge: Whose Mustang are we taking? Your King Cobra or my vintage Calypso?"

Braden smiled, immediately perking up. "I say both. Maybe we engage in a little harvest moon competition of our own?" His smile ripened into a mischievous, taunting smirk. "Unless, of course, you're afraid to race me."

Nachari's ensuing laughter filled the lofty brownstone to the rafters. "*Afraid to race you...*"

"You're repeating me again."

That grin...that regal, stunning, arrogant grin...the one that made females swoon and males roll their eyes; Nachari was the same proud, powerful male he had been that night Braden had accompanied him to meet Jocelyn Levi, Nathaniel's newfound *destiny*, in the Ancient Master Warrior's downstairs living room. So maybe...

Just maybe...

Nothing had changed.

At least, for this moment, all was right with the world.

* * *

Kristina stood in the narrow, softly lit hallway just outside her penthouse front door, her bare feet nestled on dark, large-planked floors, one hand on her hip, the other clutching a plain white envelope, as she watched a skinny, batshit-crazy human practically run down the hall and dart into an elevator, having just handed Kristina the envelope.

"I have an urgent message from Bray-den-brat-ee-ahn-ooo." She'd pronounced Braden's name so slowly and carefully, emphasizing every single syllable as if her life depended upon her diction, that Kristina had been rendered speechless. "He said to keep it a secret." And then just like that, the slight, skinny woman had turned tail and run. If Kristina hadn't known better, she would have sworn the crazy lady thought Kristina had a hidden gat and, any moment now, she was going to pull it out and shoot her.

Kristina had almost stopped her.

She had almost run after her.

But the poor, loony female had been perspiring like she'd just finished a two-hour cardio workout, and her knobby knees had been trembling so violently, she had run in wobbly, unbalanced zigzags.

Who the hell knocks on a stranger's door at seven in the morning, anyway?

Just fifteen minutes after sunrise?

And where the hell did Braden find this crazy female?

Why?

He could've just called Kristina...

Curiosity getting the best of her, she glanced one last time down the hall toward the elevator, then padded back inside. The moment she locked her front door behind her, she leaned back against the eight-foot, solid mahogany-and-glass panel and tore open the envelope.

The letter was at least a page long, and the handwriting—

This wasn't Braden's!

The loops were too lavish, as in not from this century, the strokes were too bold, and the ink, well, it didn't resemble a Bic pen or Sharpie—it looked more like deep black oil, as if someone had actually used a quill and liquid toner.

Her stomach tightened.

Something wasn't right.

Braden would have never taken the time to do something this lavish—he would have just hit Kristina up with a text.

She started reading...

Princess Red,

Kind of has a nice ring to it, doesn't it? Or at least it could if you would give me a chance...

I'm not one for wasting time or words, so I'll cut right to the chase—I want you. I always have.

Seems to me your life in the house of Jadon is only half what it was meant to be: living all by yourself in that lonely penthouse apartment, waiting for the day when you might—or might not— mate Braden Bratianu, assuming he doesn't find another, or the gods don't give him a chosen destiny. Stranger shit has happened in the vale!

By now you know I'm not just a human, and you also know I do my research. Fuck yeah, when I really want something...someone...I go all out. And that's how I know how the house of Jadon has really treated you: how Marquis killed your lover, Dirk (guy was an asshole, no doubt, but still, not Marquis' call to make); how Marquis claimed you when he didn't really want you, all the while messing around with Ciopori behind your back; how he agreed to take care of you like a favorite puppy, pay all your bills and "house you" close to home (the car was a nice touch, but damn, you're meant to be a princess, are you not?). It's also how I know that Saber played you, that "Ramsey" played you, and that Braden is playing you now. You're like that one single vampire female that no one really wants, but everyone likes to toy with. Sure, you're a member of the family but always on the perimeter, kind of like the redheaded stepchild...with braces. LOL No pun intended.

Don't hate, Kristina. Truth is truth. Except for the "truth" you've been taught about the house of Jaegar.

No torture, no death, no trading your soul for immortality.

No submission, no degradation, no constant rejection—

AT LEAST NOT FOR YOU. Never for you!

You're different, Kristina. You're already a vampire. You, my love, would be treated like a queen. The one and only queen in the entire house of Jaegar. You would live in wealth and splendor; you could come and go as you please; sex, pregnancy, and bringing a child into this world would not be a death sentence, not for you and me. Our children would be demigods. Hell, they might even be born female. And don't get it twisted, I would never share you— when was the last time a man loved you so well it made your toes curl as you screamed his name? When was the last time your body caught fire and burned with so much pleasure you forgot your own name? When was the last time you felt wanted, safe, and completely worshipped? Probably never.

Think it over, Princess Red—what have you got to lose?

What do you stand to gain...

Other than power, pleasure, privilege, passion, and position.

You weren't created to be with a boy—you were perfected to be with the best. I see it. I know it. I want it.

I want you, Kristina. Forever by my side.

Yes, in the house of Jaegar, among your own kind. So don't knock it until you try it. Just let your mind wander a bit, consider the possibilities...my hands on your breasts...my lips on your...

Every day.

Every night.

Come to me, Kristina. No compulsion, no tricks, no fear of abduction—come to me of your own free will and let me love you as you were meant to be loved. Think about it. I'll be in touch.

Forever, your not-so-secret admirer,

AZ

P.S. I didn't mean to frighten you last night—I only wanted to catch you alone so the two of us could talk.

Kristina dropped the letter like the paper was on fire. She leaped away from the door—*and the letter*—prancing on her tiptoes, as if it might grow teeth and bite her. And then she ran to the other side of the room. She gagged, almost retching in her mouth, as she stared at the unfolded paper on the foyer floor and shivered.

AZ.

Achilles Zahora.

Oh gods, oh gods, oh gods...

What the actual hell?

Why?

How?

Since when?

Achilles wanted Kristina!?

No way.

No. Way.

This wasn't happening.

She drew several deep breaths in through her nose, out through her mouth, her petite chest rising with every breath as she tried to calm her nerves. She should call Deanna, or maybe Vanya? Perhaps Ciopori—she was both family *and* a powerful princess!

No, she should call Keitaro or Marquis—

Fuck that—maybe she should just go straight to the king!

And Braden...

*Holy shit...*Braden!

Braden would be apoplectic; *enraged* wasn't even the word.

And he had so much on his plate right now, the Millenia Harvest Moon...

Shit—that was today, wasn't it? The omen was already here...

Dear gods, she didn't know what to do.

Three hard, crisp knocks sounded against the penthouse front door, and Kristina nearly leaped out of her skin. Her adrenaline surged, the hair stood up on her arms, and her heart began to race in earnest. Eyes frightened and wide, she froze in place, her feet planted to the floor like two concrete blocks cemented to the plush ivory throw rug. She scanned the room, glancing left then right, before eyeing the floor-to-ceiling wall of glass sliders that provided a panoramic view of the vale.

The patio!

She couldn't shape-shift or fly like Braden, but she was Vampyr—she could jump.

She could call out to Keitaro again...and jump!

"Room service." A human male called out from the other side of the door, and Kristina knew he was human because she recognized the concierge's voice: Adam Dorsey. He had been at the casino longer than Kristina, and although she had never pried or asked, she assumed he worked directly for Marquis, one of the house of Jadon's loyal human servants from a generational family who knew about their kind.

Still, she couldn't be sure.

Achilles had gotten to the skinny blonde woman, the one who had delivered the letter. No wonder she was so strange—scared shitless. What kind of compulsion had he seared into her head? And he could possibly get to Adam too.

She gulped, her Adam's apple rolling up and down. "I didn't order anything, Adam," she croaked from across the room.

Nothing.

No response.

He probably hadn't heard her.

She tiptoed quietly across the floor to the door, all the while glancing back and forth at the patio sliders—she might not have time to open them, but it didn't matter. She was a vampire. She could heal. If she had to run and dive through the glass, so be it. If Adam touched the door, if the handle moved, even an inch, if she heard a crack, a pop, anything that felt suspicious...

Run!

She held her breath for a protracted moment, then gathered every ounce of courage she could muster. "Adam." She projected her voice through the thick mahogany panel. "I didn't order anything from room service."

"Good morning, K!" he called in a perfectly normal, cheery voice. "I know that. I have some flowers for you." He sounded so pleased, so excited.

The horizontal glass panels in Kristina's front door were stacked one above the other, between alternate panels of solid wood, and heavily frosted for privacy. No one could see in or out. And since Kristina didn't have her smartphone in hand—nor was she seated in front of her monitor—she could not make use of the hallway security camera. She rose to the tips of her toes and glanced through the old-fashioned peephole. *Yep*, Adam Dorsey, all five feet, nine inches of the prim and proper concierge, his meticulous dark brown hair combed into place, standing in the hall with his chin up, back arched, and spine ruler-straight, holding a gargantuan, heavy, exorbitant glass vase filled with twelve long-stem red roses, the petals the deepest red Kristina had ever seen, the thorns shaved away, and all surrounded by baby's breath and resplendent pale green foliage.

Against her better judgment, Kristina stepped back and opened the door. It wasn't that she had lost her wariness or that she trusted Adam, fully—it was just that she needed a minute to think. She needed Adam to go away. She needed a chance to collect her wits, and it was only a vase full of flowers. Besides, what if the arrangement was from Braden?

"Thank you," she said kindly, forcing the warble of fear out of her voice.

"You're welcome," Adam said brightly. He leaned in conspiratorially, and she almost turned tail and ran. "Who do you think they're from?" He winked as if he knew anything whatsoever about Kristina's private life.

"Don't know," she said, shrugging her shoulders as she reached for the vase to take it from Adam.

"It's heavy as hell," he warned her.

Kristina smiled wanly. "That's okay." She placed both hands beneath the heavy vase, and sure as heck, she had to use her vampiric strength to heft it. "I've got it." She backed into her apartment and nodded at the door, signaling for Adam to close it. "Thanks again," she called.

His eyebrows furrowed. She was usually more friendly, but being a good concierge, he nodded professionally, reached for the handle, and shut the door, disappearing behind the frosted panels. Thankfully, he never expected a tip—all the casino's employees were paid handsomely, and Marquis had made it crystal clear that Kristina was casino royalty. Whatever she wanted, she got. No hesitation, no expectation, and no gratuities.

She lumbered across the floor and set the arrangement down on the glass and bronzed-metal coffee table, stepping back to take a closer look at it. Her breath caught in her throat, and she stepped forward to trace the vase with the tip of her forefinger. The heavy crystal amphora vessel was crafted to look as if it had been transported from another period in time, with its flaring lip, cylindrical handles, and curved body, just above the base, but that wasn't what commanded Kristina's attention: The entire vessel shimmered, reflecting light like a prism. And why wouldn't it? The crystal glass was inset with black diamonds, along with onyx, agate, jasper, and bright red rubies...garnets and coral...red and black...*red and black.*

The house of Jaegar.

This gift was not from Braden.

She tentatively reached for the neatly folded card tucked behind a bundle of baby's breath, and she winced when her vampiric senses confirmed what her eyes were also telling her: The deep red, velvety petals had somehow been brushed with— or dipped in—blood, which was why they possessed such a rich, supernatural color. Instinctively, Kristina's stomach clenched, and pangs of hunger stirred. She couldn't help it, she couldn't control it, she couldn't stop it if she tried. And for the first time since she had finally, fully embraced becoming a vampire, she wished she were something else, anything...else.

She lifted the card gingerly, careful to avoid touching any of the flora, and brought it closer to her eyes: *"All five senses should be awakened, nurtured, imbibed,"* it read. *"Touch, taste, smell, sight, and especially hunger. Sound is overrated unless it's the sound of your laughter, your sighs—you, speaking the simple word, 'Yes.' Think it over, Kristina. AZ"*

Kristina tossed the card on the coffee table, backed away, and choked back a sob.

Absently, without even thinking, she rounded the glass-and-bronzed corner of the tabletop, darted to the fireplace mantel, and opened the lid of an antique velvet-lined box. Attached to the lid, against the velvet liner, was another note, a glossy five-by-seven card, but she didn't pick it up and read it—she didn't have to—she knew exactly what it said: *Thank you for always having my back,* the words embossed on the front, and *passion, death and foreboding are not quite as frightening with you here to help me breathe,* the words engraved in the interior.

It was the note Braden had given her when he had been suffering from headaches...having recurring visions...channeling the mystery and the omens surrounding Saxson Olaru's Blood Moon. And the card had come with a special gift: a sleek platinum band attached to a thin platinum chain, peppered with flawless, brilliant onyx and rubies, gemstones that were also black and red. Only, there was nothing dark or tainted about them—Braden had made the bracelet with his own two hands at the Dark Moon Mineral Plant, with the help of a few Ancient Master Warriors.

He had made it...*for Kristina.*

At the age of *fifteen*...

A friendship bracelet.

Without true awareness or deliberate intent, Kristina reached into the box, retrieved the bracelet, and slipped it around her slender left wrist. Then she thumbed it absently...reverently, while wandering back to the sofa.

She crawled onto the oversized cushions, leaned back against the overstuffed pillows, and drew her knees to her chin. Then she wrapped her arms around two trembling shins, burrowed her head in her knees, and wept.

Oh, dear gods...

This wasn't happening...

None of it...

Any of it!

The Millenia Harvest Moon had barely begun, and the entire world was already topsy-turvy.

And as for Achilles Zahora...

Oh gods...

Just, no.

CHAPTER FIVE

10:00 A.M.

"You feel that?" Niko Durciak asked Jankiel Luzanski, as he arched his back to stretch and glanced furtively at the clear blue sky from the back patio behind the secluded manor house.

Jankiel nodded. "Yeah, the coming moon's gravitational pull is already electric."

"What time is it anyway?"

"Nineteen minutes 'til moonset."

"Then the harvest moon takes over," Niko said.

"Takes over and rises at 8:59."

"Yep."

The two Master Wizards stood in companionable silence, surveying the elaborate gardens, exquisite fountains, and the portion of the lap pool that wound around the back of their property, as they collected their thoughts and took a moment to enjoy the cool, crisp morning air on the eastern-most edge of Dark Moon Vale.

"You ready for the ceremonies?" Jankiel finally asked.

"Yeah, you?"

"As ready as I'm going to be," Jankiel said.

As far as Niko understood it, in the broader context of the earth's history, the Vampyr were still a relatively new species, emerging in 800 BC, and the first Millenia Harvest Moon had been an elaborate veneration of the Autumn Equinox, already celebrated by the original half-human, half-celestial ancestors: Where the half-human ancestors had primarily focused upon their crops, the harvests winding down, and the fact that the fields would soon be empty—bountiful yields had been plucked and stored for the coming winter, and autumn was a time to stop, take a few moments and honor the changing seasons, give thanks for the quarter's blessings and abundance—the ensuing Vampyr had adapted the early festivals to focus far more on celestial rites, rituals, and ceremonies.

Where the ancient half-celestial kings and queens focused on the balance between light and shadow, a time when the hours counted in a day would soon equal night, the house of Jadon now focused upon the gifts and powers born from the original Curse and the ensuing *four mercies*: the benevolence bestowed upon the Vampyr as a result of Prince Jadon's pleading, the understanding that the universe demands balance in all things, and the realization that both cold and warmth inevitably lie ahead, as life unfolds in metaphorical seasons. And in light of this, it was Napolean's privilege and place to lead the Homage Ceremony— to pay respect to the six directions and the natural elements, to guide the Vampyr in rites of balance and reflection, and to humble himself in acts of thanksgiving and worship: expressing gratitude for community, family, and friendship.

Strength, loyalty, and honor...

Only this year, Ciopori Demir Silivasi and Vanya Demir Alexiares would lead the hallowed ceremony.

Where the ancient half-celestial mages and high priests once focused on mystery and divinity, the enchantment that caused a seed to unfurrow in the ground and yield such bountiful harvests, it was the wizards, the mages—and it should have been the High Mage, Fabian—who would now lead the Rites of Magick: a public display of the power in the heavens by arousing solar winds, conjuring the illusion of exploding geysers, and manifesting winter snows, all carefully controlled in a mystic funnel, through the use of focused intent and harnessed emotion.

This year, it would be Niko taking on that role.

And where the ancient half-celestial, half-human inhabitants would equally be led by a practitioner of magick in the ceremony of Renaissance & Renewal—*the circle of drumming*—Jankiel would lead the vampires this equinox in the communal ritual of weaving light, focusing inward to sharpen one's senses, and aligning each heartbeat in one harmonious symphony of rhythms: hearts, not drums; blood, not drumsticks; inhaling and exhaling in place of tapping.

And of course, all the people—all the Vampyr in the house of Jadon—would singularly and collectively take place in the Rite of Peace, Prosperity, & Protection by creating an ethereal, harmonious perimeter around their homes or properties, using elemental and cosmic forces in place of corn stalks, apples, grapevines, or acorns. At least for this rite, each individual or family was on their own.

Niko shook his head: *Crazy.*

It all seemed so crazy to him, to be going forward as if nothing were different, other than the names and titles of those leading the ceremonies, when in truth, the entire world as they knew it— life in the house of Jadon—was hanging in the balance.

Just then, Jankiel took two steps forward and squinted, and Niko followed his gaze. "What are you looking at, my friend?" Niko asked.

"Not looking," Jankiel said, "thinking...*feeling.*"

"*Feeling* toward the southwest?" Niko inquired, his voice tinged with skepticism.

Jankiel smiled. "Yeah, guess so. More like toward the Dark Moon Casino. It's like there's some sort of dense solar shadow shrouding the area, faint but enormous at the very same time."

Niko sidled up beside his housemate and stared more intently in the same direction, tuning in all six senses more acutely, one sense at a time. "Yeah, I think I get what you're saying. Like the whole galaxy, the entire Milky Way is involved— which is why it feels enormous—yet the influence is so negligible that it also feels faint: like a single drop of a foreign liquid added to the ocean. On one hand, the ocean is an enormous body of water, so you feel the energy of the shift as one vast whole, but on the other hand, a single drop of liquid is so infinitesimal, it doesn't even make a ripple."

Jankiel planted his hands on his hips and furrowed his brows in confusion. "So in this case, the shadow represents—"

"The entire galaxy," Niko cut in.

"Right. All the celestial gods and goddesses. And the drop of water represents?"

"An errant energy," Niko supplied.

"Exactly," Jankiel said. "But I don't get it. What's big enough to represent the entire galaxy, all the celestial gods and goddesses, yet small enough—singular enough—to almost remain commonplace...undetected? What...*who* is big enough to invoke them all?"

Niko shrugged. "Well, the most obvious answer is the harvest moon. On one hand, the moon rises and sets every day, quite common, but on the other hand, this particular Harvest Moon is once in a millennium. However, if you're speaking of living souls, individual beings, or vampires, then I'd have to say Napolean or the High Mage."

Jankiel nodded slowly. "That's what I was thinking too, but

close your eyes: Do you feel the goddess Andromeda or Corona Borealis any stronger than the rest?"

Niko closed his eyes. *Hmm*; Jankiel was right. The presence, the weight, the feel of the gods throughout the galaxy was even, all of them as a cohesive unit, at least within the shadow they were sensing—the *shadow* they were sensing. "Shadow, not light," he whispered to Jankiel, reopening his eyes.

"Bingo," Jankiel replied. "*Shadow.*"

"Not all the celestial gods and goddesses but all the dark lords."

"Yep," Jankiel said, "at least that's what I'm thinking."

Niko worked the puzzle in his mind, trying to fit the odd pieces together. "Okay, well, then doesn't the same thing apply? It's tied to the oncoming harvest moon, because Dark Ones don't have individual dark lords or ruling constellations—they might pray and tender offerings to different idols, depending upon what they want or the individual spell they're casting—but I don't think a soul, even one as particularly dark and evil as Salvatore Nistor or Oskar Vadovsky, by example, could conjure or evoke that strong of an influence on the entire galaxy."

"I agree, my brother," Jankiel offered, even though the two were not related by blood. "The only vampires known who could create a rift in the entire solar system—evoke every single god and goddess, or dark lord, male or female—are Prince Jadon and Prince Jaegar themselves, and last I checked, they weren't gambling at the Dark Moon Casino."

At this, Niko chuckled, which at least released some tension. "Shit. I have no idea..." He ran his hand through his dark ebony hair, and the loose, layered waves fell back into place. "So, what then?"

Jankiel shrugged. "I dunno. I-don't-know." He emphasized each word, individually.

Niko sighed, flashing back to everything he knew about the

Millenia Harvest Moon and this imminent holiday, in particular. Obviously, things were very different. Fabian Antonescu, the legendary High Mage from the original time of the Curse, was with them, and he had revealed to Napolean, Braden, and Nachari, during an exorcism spell designed to extract inner demons and reveal inner secrets by blending the High Mage's mind with Napolean's, the fact that he had indeed kept an unconscious secret: Two years back, while sleeping beneath an aged stone well, his spirit had flown in the body of a hawk and then a raven, each time carrying a sacred vial of blood. The first, the elixir of Prince Jadon's very essence, had been placed into the sleeping body of Braden Bratianu. The second, the extract of Prince Jaegar's very soul, had been placed in the body of Achilles Zahora...

Subsequently, and over the past two months, Napolean had selectively shared the information with those whom he felt might be directly affected or add insight into the tenuous situation, such as immediate family members and mates of key players, the Council of Wizards and the valley's sentinels, the original princesses with their celestial magic, and any other crucial individuals who might prove instrumental in untangling the mystery...deciphering the unknown implications.

The blood...

What would happen when the blood of the Ancients quickened?

Jankiel turned his head sharply to the left as if hearing Niko's thoughts. "Light cleaves to light, and darkness cleaves to darkness."

"Braden and Achilles?" Niko asked.

"Maybe," Jankiel said.

They both looked toward the southwest again—the shadow was still there, and it was still just as faint. Niko threw both hands up in frustration. "Achilles would be northwest of here, not southwest, somewhere 'round about the Red Canyons, the Valley of Shadows, on the other side of the vale. He sure as hell wouldn't be hanging out at the Dark Moon Casino."

Jankiel rubbed his chin with his thumb. "Yeah, you're right, and I feel like we're chasing rabbits down random holes. So there's a very faint shadow over the Dark Moon Casino, one that implies the deities in reverse, a gathering of all the dark lords at once, but it's so negligible, so infinitesimal as not to even account for a singular body, an identifiable soul. I think we just have to chalk this one up to Millenia Harvest Moon jitters. Are we sensing something real? Yeah, you bet we are. But is it anything we can discern, follow up with, using magick—is it anything worth sending out an SOS? No, I don't think so. Let's just remain aware."

Niko considered Jankiel's words carefully—*very carefully*—before chiming in with an additional suggestion. "Agreed," he said evenly, "only, let's also err on the side of caution with this one. An SOS? No. Not that serious...at least not yet. No need to put out an urgent telepathic call, disrupt anyone's train of thought, or intrude on their inner sanctum. But a heads-up? Yeah...*definitely*. Better safe than sorry."

Napolean had already ceded the Homage Ceremony to Ciopori and Vanya—the king had more than enough on his plate. Fabian, the High Mage and Niko's personal idol, had relinquished the Rites of Magick to Niko and the *circle of drumming* to Jankiel—the ancient wizard was clearly laser-focused on Braden and the moonrise as well. And as for the remainder of the house of Jadon, most of the Vampyr were none the wiser. The king had not shared what had happened regarding Fabian and the ancient vials of blood with anyone outside the tight, need-to-know circle, the vampires Niko had already pondered. Napolean was waiting to see what happened first, waiting to make sure it was necessary.

So yeah, to Niko's way of thinking, that left Nachari Silivasi.

He reached into his back pocket, retrieved his cell phone, and dialed the green-eyed wizard's number.

* * *

Braden and his little brother, Conrad, now twelve years old and on the verge of adolescence, leaned back against the side of Braden's sleek, pristine Mustang as they crossed their arms, tapped their toes in unison, and stared out beyond the parking lot, toward the lodge's deep blue lake.

Nachari had won the race to the lodge but only by a hair, and he had spent the past half hour talking on the phone. From what Braden could gather, the Master Wizard had spoken to Niko Durciak first, then appeared to try another number several times without getting an answer, at which point he had hastily called his mate, Deanna.

Whatever that was all about...

Now, as Nachari sat on the hood of his own vintage Calypso Coral Mustang, about twenty feet away, still speaking on the phone with his *destiny*, Braden struggled to find the right words to connect with his younger sibling. Braden had asked both Dario, his stepdad and Conrad's father, as well as their mother, Lily, to remain inside the lodge while he and Conrad stepped outside—yet his mind was drawing a blank, and his mouth was curiously dry.

He had wanted a moment alone with his little brother, and now, the internal clock in his head was *tick-tick-ticking...*

Ten o'clock.

Ten fifteen.

Drawing nigh on ten thirty...

It was almost time to blaze a trail, yet silence still hovered between the two brothers like vapor over a kettle of stew.

"So..." They both spoke the word in unison.

"You go first," Braden offered.

Conrad sighed, and he ran the tips of his fingers through his short, spiked, dirty blond hair. "I'm glad you came by." He twiddled his fingers. "It's really good that you and Mom are getting so close again. She talks about you all the time, ya know? How much she loves you, how badly she misses you, whether texting you ten times an hour, every hour, might be a little too much? *Hey, Conrad,* she always says. *What do you think Braden's doing?*" He chuckled softly. "She even gets out that old embroidered prayer pillow, the one Great-Grandma gave her, kneels at the side of her bed, and asks the gods for your protection—every single night." He groaned conspiratorially. "And I know Dad worries about you too, sometimes." He bit his bottom lip. "Not like that. I mean...not in general. He knows you're grown and have a lot of warriors around you...mentors, stuff like that. He's just been worried about this Millenia Harvest Moon." He winced, lowered his gaze, and stared at the ground, immediately feeling sorry for mentioning the great big millennia-elephant in the room. The family had already hashed the subject into the ground, and they had all done their level best to avoid the worst of the *what ifs...* They had all gone out of their way to impersonate Pollyanna, assuring Braden, half a dozen times, that everything was going to be A-okay, and when that hadn't quite worked, they had finally wrapped their arms around him, as a family unit, and offered a prayer to both Lord Pegasus, Dario's ruling celestial god, and Lord Monoceros, the deity who had chosen Braden.

"You know what I mean, though, don't you?" Conrad said, interrupting Braden's train of thought.

Braden nodded amiably. He reached over and mussed Conrad's hair. "I do know what you mean, Conny. And you know what I'm grateful for right now?"

Conrad's gunmetal-gray eyes lit up.

"I'm grateful for you, my favorite little brother, the fact that, even though we might not know exactly what to say in this moment, there's no more...misunderstanding or personal distance between us. Grateful that we're finally getting a chance to know each other better. Blood brothers, you know? Not just HOJ vamps."

Conrad's answering smile rivaled the sun for its warmth and brightness. "I'm your *only* little brother, but...you mean that?" He stood up straighter and angled his body toward Braden.

"Of course I do."

Conrad bit his bottom lip again. "You know, I may only be twelve, but I get that things were different, the way I always traveled around with Mom and Dad, got so much of their time and attention. I know you probably thought I was a little spoiled or...I dunno...different." He frowned. "Self-important." He shook his head. "It's just, I know your real dad was an asshole, and Dario sired you—I guess I always thought you didn't like me much, so I kind of put up a wall."

Braden stepped away from the car, turned to face Conrad directly, and planted two large hands on the kid's eager shoulders. "Conrad..." He drew in a deep, measured breath. "Brotherhood is *everything* in the house of Jadon. Blood is life, and life is blood. I never blamed you for either of our circumstances. To tell you the truth, I was so busy growing up, just trying to find my way, figuring out who I was and where I belonged in the whole scheme of things, not just our family, that I didn't really have time...didn't notice or stop to think what everything looked like from your point of view. But you were always my little brother, Conny, and I always loved you."

Conrad's soft, resplendent eyes teared up. "Not so little anymore though, right?" He raised his chin and puffed out his chest, trying to show off his burgeoning muscles, and Braden chuckled out loud.

Yep, they were definitely cut from the same genetic cloth.

He shook his head in the affirmative. "Definitely not so little anymore, and soon, if you like, I'll swing by and pick you up so we can work out together at the academy's gym or maybe at Ramsey's cliff house—he has a state-of-the-art weight room and swimming pool—see how your training is coming along." He pointed at the driver's side window of the Mustang. "I'll even let you drive my car—just don't tell Mom or Dario."

Conrad laughed and rolled his eyes. "They can be so drastic and overprotective sometimes. Seriously, though, I'm a vampire, right? I can already fly, dematerialize, and feed on my own—you would think I could handle a car." He bent over to look inside the window. "I mean, what's the worst that's gonna happen? Not like I can't regenerate."

"Hey," Braden said sternly. "Not worried about you, but you'd better not wreck my shit, or we're gonna have words. Feel me?"

Conrad spun back around and laughed again. "Deal," he said, and then his expression grew all at once solemn. "Braden?"

"What's up?"

"I'm gonna say a prayer of my own for you tonight."

Braden tilted his head to the side and summarily dismissed the comment—he just wasn't willing to go there...again. Things were going exceedingly well, and he didn't want to dampen the mood with concerns about things no one could predict...or change. "Thank you, Conny." His words were crisp, purposefully abrupt, and then he reached in his pocket, pulled out his car keys, and whistled to catch Nachari's attention. "Ten thirty-five!" he called, tapping his naked wrist in demonstration. "We need to head out, Nachari." He turned back to Conrad and smiled. "You say that prayer, and text me if you feel like it. I'll hit you back as soon as I can, and everything's gonna be fine." He was lying through his teeth, but oh well—

Maybe it would turn out to be true.

At this, Conrad reached out and grasped Braden's arm. "You're making that shit up, but it's all good—I get it. Just... Braden?" He waited until the two made eye contact. "Here's what I know: My big brother has the stealth of a warrior, the skills of a wizard, and the heartbeat of the house of Jadon in his veins. He can shape-shift, unlock mysteries from the Blood Canon, and fight with the best of them. And he hasn't even chosen a formal discipline or trained at the Romanian University yet. I think, maybe, one day, you might end up being one of the greatest vampires that ever lived, and maybe tonight is just part of that." He drew back his hand, bowed his head, and averted his eyes in a formal vampiric show of deference and obedience, a younger brother paying respect to his older sibling. "Be well, my brother."

A formal tiding.

A warrior's parting.

Braden blinked several times to clear the mist from his eyes. "Be well, Conrad." He spoke the words softly, and although he wanted to pull the kid into his arms, he knew the greatest love and respect he could show Conny was to honor the age-old custom, male-to-male, brother-to-brother, strong, courageous warrior...to warrior.

He opened the door to his Mustang instead and regarded the approaching Master Wizard: "Nachari, let's go."

CHAPTER SIX

The air was crisp, thanks to an occasional cool cross-breeze, even though the sun was shining high in a pale blue sky. Princess Ciopori and her sister, Vanya, surveyed the open, outdoor courtyard along the left side of Napolean's compound, checking the decorations for the night's Homage Ceremony. The sisters had overseen the construction of twelve elegant white pavilions with pergola-style roofs for clear, uninhibited viewing of the moon and sky, along with several slatted wooden walkways arching between them, and among the taller trees, along the exposed, unobscured branches, they had hung numerous glass-and-iron lanterns, each encasing a single autumn-colored candle, all suspended by a length of braided rope.

The folded chairs were decorated with leafy lianas cascading across the top rails and hanging down along the back posts to the legs, and everywhere the eye could turn there were wooden barrels, hay bales, and ornate trellises, either wrapped in pale yellow roses and sage-green vines, or festooned with harvest fruits, pine cones, and mixed bushels of stems, plantings in the full array of harvest colors.

Ciopori brushed her long, raven hair behind an elegant shoulder, ran her finger along a decorative loop inside a tall, arcing trellis, then sat down on the bench below it, watching her sister studiously as Vanya first tied a knot, and then a bow, in a loop of twine around the final bushel.

"That's lovely," Ciopori said.

Vanya smiled, and her pale rose eyes shined like moonlight, illuminating the scattered blonde highlights in her flaxen-gold hair. "Why, thank you, sister." She placed the bushel atop a barrel, *just so*, and stood up straight to survey her handiwork. "All in all, I think the courtyard looks like a royal garden. In fact, it reminds me of the happier times, growing up in the palace."

Ciopori nodded her head, then sighed. She had been thinking along the same lines as Vanya, remembering life in Romania, before the Curse, before the worst of the female genocide, before the growing anarchy and deadly divisions had escalated in their father's kingdom...before Jaegar's henchmen and Jadon's loyalists had become as two opposing nations in one fractured monarchy.

Vanya met her sister's eyes. "You're thinking of them too? Our brothers."

Ciopori nodded. "How could I not?" She shook her head in consternation. "With all that is going on, the return of Nanaşule, and the knowledge of what he did with those vials..." Her voice trailed off, and she shivered.

"Yes," Vanya said frankly, taking a seat beside her sister and smoothing the pleated hemline of her skirt, "if I'm being perfectly honest, it keeps me up at night...the revelation. My mind wanders incessantly in so many different directions." She fidgeted with her fingers, rotating her thumbs before placing both hands palm down in her lap. "While I feel so very sorry for Braden, I can't

help but admit there's a part of me that wonders...perhaps wishes...even hopes—"

"To catch a glimpse of Jadon?" Ciopori interrupted.

"Yes." Vanya nodded. She leaned back against the wooden bench, shifted her weight from side to side, and crossed her arms in front of her. "But then..."

"Jaegar," Ciopori supplied, acutely aware of her sister's nervousness. Heck, she felt it too.

Vanya rolled her eyes in embellished emphasis as opposed to annoyance. "I was terrified of him toward the end, Ciopori. I truly was. There was just...his soul...something missing, something twisted. Something rotten to the core. I don't know that I have ever encountered a more perverted being."

"You mean a more perverted vampire," Ciopori said.

Vanya shrugged. "Perhaps. We never got to see that side of him, our brother after the change, after the Curse. Toward the end, we were so consumed with running, hiding...eventually relocating. I dare say the thought of Jaegar with all these added powers... I honestly can't conceive of it."

"Nor I," Ciopori agreed. Despite her own much calmer demeanor, she shivered before redirecting the conversation to the present. "Do you feel anything different?" she asked. "The gravitational pull of this coming moon? Any portent or premonition of what is soon to come?"

Vanya furrowed her brows. "Mm. That's hard to say. I do know that my celestial magick is awake...astir...like static electricity coursing through my veins. More alive, more present, more kinetic than usual, and earlier this morning, I felt a darkness like a dense, turbulent cloud hovering above the eastern end of the vale, but I don't even know if I can trust my instincts: What is insight? What is divination? What is just fear or anxiety?" She shook her head in a visible attempt to shake the thoughts loose from her head. "We should change the subject."

Ciopori held up one finger. "Wait—not yet." Her shoulders tensed. "You said the eastern end of the vale?"

"Mm hmm," Vanya said. "Why? Does that mean something to you?"

"Not quite sure," Ciopori replied. "I got a call from Deanna, about thirty minutes ago—she wanted to know if I had spoken with Kristina this morning. Apparently, Nachari tried to reach her, but she isn't answering her phone. And while Nachari did not want to disturb her telepathically, he thinks she might be upset, perhaps taking some personal time to deal with the whole precarious situation. He was concerned enough to ask Deanna to call each of the Silivasi sisters, his brother's mates, to ask us to keep an eye out, to keep checking up on Kristina. Much like you, Niko Durciak and Jankiel Luzanski also got a really strange vibe earlier, a sense of darkness or foreboding, centered around the Dark Moon Casino, and Niko alerted Nachari. Just a heads-up but still...the casino is on the eastern end of the vale."

Vanya worried her bottom lip while considering Ciopori's words thoughtfully. "Hmm, that is interesting, very...interesting. Do you think you should try to reach Kristina right now?"

Ciopori frowned. "Not really. I mean, I would, but Deanna said that she, Arielle, and Jocelyn would keep trying Kristina's number, and neither Niko, nor Jankiel, sensed anything... definitive. Like Nachari, they do not want to intrude if Kristina is just...retreating inward. But they are going to keep an eye out."

Seemingly satisfied with the answer, Vanya slowly nodded. "Very well then." She took a deep breath and exhaled slowly to release some tension. "Speaking of being *upset*...the whole precarious situation...I've been meaning to ask: How is Marquis?" She injected a clearly forced note of cheer into her voice. "I know my brother-in-law is very close to Braden—the young vampire has a special place in Marquis' heart, even if the Ancient Master

Warrior doesn't always show it." She chuckled softly, and Ciopori smiled.

"I dare say Marquis is anxious as well. Loaded for bear. Determined to face this Millenia Harvest Moon the way he faces everything else: directly, head-on, and with an iron fist." She sighed, demonstrating both her understanding of her fearsome mate, and her concern for the warrior's welfare. "And Saber? How does he feel about all that is happening? Has he said much about it recently?"

Vanya narrowed her gaze on a loose, pale strand of thread lying crosswise against a seam in her skirt. She picked it out between her nails, studied it absently, then flicked it into the dirt. "Well, being a sentinel, of course his first concern is the safety of the king and the continued well-being of the house of Jadon. He's not one to let his imagination get the best of him, and I would assume, being raised in the house of Jaegar, he isn't as...threatened...by the potential of dark cosmic forces, some universal evil being loosed on the land this nightfall. I would say, it's fifty-fifty —his concern that something odious might happen versus his belief that all will be well. Nonetheless, he will be very relieved— as will I—when this Millenia Harvest Moon business is behind us."

"Amen." Ciopori stressed the word, once again eyeing all the festive decorations. "Even as we prepare and plan for what should be a night filled with sacred, rejuvenating ceremonies, it's hard to feel celebratory or as reverent as we ought... In truth, I just want it over with, as well."

Just then, the sound of tires skidding to a halt on the other side of the outdoor terrace, the veranda that edged the courtyard, interrupted their conversation. Seconds later, a single car door slammed shut, and the crisp *clip-clop* of hurried footfalls—the underside of a toe, quickly followed by a balancing heel— ascended along the steps to the patio.

Both Ciopori and Vanya leaned forward, eager to catch a glimpse of the approaching visitor.

Ah, it's Kristina! Ciopori noted inwardly. *Speak of the devil...*

Relieved to see her sister-in-law in the flesh, she cleared her mind of all recent conversation and turned her full attention on the always well-dressed, five-foot-six female. "Greetings, sister," she called, gracefully waving her fingers.

"Hey, sis," Kristina called back. She crossed the terrace and stopped short, four or five feet in front of Vanya. "Hey, V—what's up? How are you?" She didn't wait for an answer. Rather, she planted two delicate hands on her narrow but curvy hips and glanced around the courtyard. "This looks great!" she exclaimed, but the enthusiasm in her voice was largely manufactured.

"Thank you," Vanya said.

"Rest assured, we didn't do all this work ourselves," Ciopori added, "but yes, we believe it came out quite nicely." She waved her hand through the air. "But enough of all that, dear sister. Do you realize half the family has been trying to get in touch with you?" Kristina scrunched up her forehead, pretending to be confused, and Ciopori immediately called her out on it. "You have not been answering your phone, Kristina." She paused to let the accusation settle in. "Nachari... Deanna...Jocelyn and Arielle. Everyone has been worried about you."

"Oh, that," Kristina said sheepishly. "Yeah. I'm sorry. I had my phone turned off. Haven't really been in the mood for talking, but I texted Joss before I left to come see you, so everyone knows I'm fine."

Ciopori reached below the bench to retrieve her small leather handbag, took out her cell phone, and brought up the message screen. She scanned the list until she came to the most recent group message from Jocelyn: *Heard from Kristina. She says she's just fine!* (Smiley emoji and a heart.) Ciopori tucked the device back into her handbag and nodded with satisfaction at Vanya.

Only, Vanya wasn't having any of it.

She was staring at Kristina like the devil was standing behind her, as if taking her measure from the inside out. "You're fine?" she queried. "I can see that. And I would almost buy it, based on your hair, your makeup, and your clothing, except your aura reeks of dark, turbulent energy. It's hanging all over you like a muddy cloud."

Ciopori held out her hand to soften Vanya's approach. Sometimes the princess could be a bit...too direct. "What brings you here to the compound?" she asked Kristina, casting a sideways, chastising glance at Vanya. She raised her brows and turned her attention back to Kristina.

Kristina's eyes shot from Ciopori to Vanya, then back to Ciopori, like a nervous child's, before drifting downward and settling on a pine cone. "Nothing major, I just...just wanted to run something by you."

Vanya softly harrumphed.

"By me?" Ciopori asked. "Or by Vanya?" There was a hint of both confusion and urgency evident in her voice, and she told herself to pull it back...proceed with caution. Otherwise, Kristina was not likely to confide in either one of them. And it wasn't that the two of them weren't family, or that the three of them weren't quite good friends—they were. In fact, considering Kristina and Ciopori's odd, convoluted history—the whole debacle with Marquis' Blood Moon, when both females had been mated to the Ancient Master Warrior, each in turn—their relationship was surprisingly natural and amiable. They both loved their brothers dearly, practically worshipped their father, Keitaro, and they were both firmly entrenched in the Silivasi family. But—and it was a glaring *but*—Kristina rarely drove out to the farmhouse or sought Ciopori for counsel or companionship. She wasn't sure if she had ever been to Saber and Vanya's Gothic Victorian, and outside of informal family gatherings, or formal HOJ functions,

Kristina was more likely to hang out with Deanna or even Arielle.

"Both of you," Kristina clarified, and then she bit her bottom lip and tapped her toe nervously against the ground, still staring at the same tired pine cone. "But—" She held up one finger. "You both have to swear that you won't say a word to anyone, at least not until tomorrow."

"A word about what?" Vanya asked, pointedly.

"What are we talking about, Kristina?" Ciopori leaned forward.

"That's just it," Kristina said. "I need to show you something, but I have to know that it stays between the three of us."

Now this made Ciopori nervous.

What the heck?

"You're not making any sense, little sister," Ciopori said. "Does this have something to do with Marquis or Saber?" She shared a second stolen glance with Vanya. "Maybe Braden?"

"Everyone," Kristina answered. "And no one. It has more to do with me and my crazy, chaotic life."

Silence hovered in the courtyard for a protracted moment, and then Vanya finally stood up and held out her hands. "Okay, so what do you have to show us?"

"I have your word?" Kristina repeated.

"Yes," Vanya insisted, sounding a little impatient.

"And yours?" Kristina stared at Ciopori.

The princess shrugged her shoulders and gestured anxiously with her hands. "If I say *no*, then what?"

Kristina planted her hands on her hips.

"Well?" Ciopori prompted.

Kristina just stood there, waiting.

"Is anyone in danger?"

Kristina blinked several times, her long, dark auburn lashes fluttering like the wings of a butterfly.

"*Kristina!*" Ciopori chided. "What is this concerning!" She stood up next to Vanya and took an exasperated step forward.

Kristina took a generous step back.

Ciopori angled her head. "Is someone we love in danger?" Her voice was both calm and even.

This time, it was Kristina who shrugged. "I don't know—do you love me?" Her voice warbled as she spoke that last word.

Ciopori frowned. "You do realize..." She paused to choose her wording carefully. "At this point, we could take the information from your mind if we chose to?"

Kristina's eyes narrowed with contempt, and her hot, redheaded temper flashed in her pupils, but she banked it just as swiftly. She stood her ground and shook her head. "You're not going to do that. It would be rude and unacceptable. And I came here because I needed...I came here to get your advice." She continued to defy the gently implied threat with silence.

"Fine," Ciopori relented. "You have my word, and for the record: Yes, we love you."

Kristina released a long, slow breath, shook out her hands, then massaged her temples. *Lords, she had really been nervous.* She reached into an elegant raspberry wine-colored purse hanging over her right shoulder by a skinny leather strap, and retrieved a horribly crumpled piece of paper. She handed it over to Ciopori, and Vanya immediately grasped the upper corner, while Ciopori smoothed the parchment.

Both sisters leaned in and began to read in unison, mouthing the words beneath their collective, nervous breath: "*Princess Red, kind of has a nice ring to it, doesn't it? Or at least it could if you would give me a chance...*"

The moment they finished reading the letter, Ciopori drew back, eyes wide as saucers, and recoiled. "AZ!" she exclaimed. "A.Z.? As in, Achilles—"

"Zahora," Kristina supplied. She reached into her purse

again. "And there's this as well. A card. It came along with a flower arrangement, that and a zillion-dollar vase."

Vanya snatched it before Ciopori could open her hand, and she began to read out loud: "*All five senses should be awakened, nurtured, imbibed. Touch, taste, smell, sight, and especially hunger. Sound is overrated unless it's the sound of your laughter, your sighs—you, speaking the simple word, "Yes."* Think it over, Kristina. AZ" Vanya's hand shot to her mouth. "Gross!"

Ciopori's jaw dropped open. "Whaa...*what*...what the hell!? Is this somehow related to the other night, when Marquis and his brothers met you on the mountain pass?"

"You said you'd seen Achilles Zahora," Vanya chimed in.

"But he was gone when the warriors arrived," Ciopori added.

"Geez Louise!" Kristina yelped, gawking at both princesses, her eyes bouncing back and forth between them. "Does the entire house of Jadon know?" She leveled an irritated glare at Ciopori. "You're mated to Marquis, so...yeah, I get that one. *But Vanya?*" She turned her gaze on the startled, ashen princess.

Vanya shook her head. "Sisters," she said by way of explanation. "Besides, I'm mated to a sentinel—surely you had to know they would be informed."

Kristina shook her head. "Fine. Whatever. The point is: Tonight is the Millenia Harvest Moon, and Braden would be—"

"Apoplectic!" Ciopori cried.

Kristina frowned. She started to nod her head, and then she stopped, pulled it back, and shrugged instead. "Maybe not," she whispered. "He doesn't care quite as much as I...as we...once thought."

Vanya hung her head, shook it from side to side, then raised it slowly like it was too heavy to lift. "Oh, good goddess, Kristina. If that boy *cared* any more about you, he would have his heart placed on a silver platter, your name carved into all four chambers, and then he'd drop to his knees and present it to you happily, even as he drew his last breath." She sighed in an exaggerated manner, hoping she had made her point. "And yes, he would be beyond apoplectic. But Keitaro, Marquis, Nathaniel, and Kagen, and especially *Nachari*—they would just be pissed, knowing you didn't share this information. You must let them know immediately."

Kristina shook her head emphatically. "No. And I swear to you, Vanya...Ciopori." She narrowed her gaze in warning. "You promised—both of you. You swore. My brothers, the wizards, and the sentinels, they all need to be laser-focused on Braden and the harvest moon rising. They don't need to divide their attention or place any focus on me. Not tonight."

"I think you're being reckless," Vanya said, pointedly.

"I hate to say it, but I agree," Ciopori added.

At this, Kristina's eyes began to tear up and when she next spoke, her voice intermittently warbled: "Reckless," she repeated. "You think I haven't thought this over? Well, how's this for reckless: I have, and I think I would probably rather die than see something happen to Braden because of my crazy drama. And it's not like I'm not being careful. I'm here, after all, not alone in my penthouse. It can keep for one more day."

Ciopori drew back, astonished. "My gods," she whispered. "You love him."

Kristina eyes dried up, and she huffed in exasperation. "That's not the point."

Vanya sighed again, less dramatically this time. "Of course it's the point. Otherwise, you would be handing the letter and the card to the Silivasi clan or even the king, instead of to myself and Ciopori. Otherwise, you would be tucked away in Napolean's manse, surrounded by a half-dozen warriors...being guarded."

"And that's just it," Kristina said softly. "I can't. I just...can't. Braden is already linked to the entire house of Jadon by some psychic connection...he shares a heartbeat with the king...and that's all before this crazy moon rises! Lock me up, surround me with guards, and tell me he's not going to feel that? He's not going to worry, want to be wherever I am? Bullshit."

Ciopori studied Kristina thoughtfully. "I thought you just said he didn't care." It was more of a statement than a question.

Kristina shook her head, and her eyes were so incredibly sad. "He doesn't have to love me to want to protect me—he's a vampire male, a male of honor. We couldn't keep him from it." She held up her hand, signaling that she was weary of arguing. "Regardless," she said, "this isn't about my...connection...to Braden, whatever is or isn't going on between us. It's about that seven-foot monster." She thumbed the edge of the letter, then the card, before holding them up in the air. "As Ciopori so fittingly put it: What the actual hell!"

Vanya shook her head slowly. "No telling." She raised her chin, and her keen eyes brightened as she visibly shifted from arguing to trying to solve the problem. "Kristina"—she spoke evenly—"Saber knows Achilles, personally. Heck, he's known him for centuries, and the gods know, Saber can keep a secret. Can we at least ask the *dragon* what he thinks Achilles is up to... what he believes Achilles is thinking...trying to get away with... going to do next?"

"No."

"Can we at least tell Nachari?" Ciopori persisted. "He's a wizard; he may have some insight."

"*No.*"

"Very well," Ciopori said, capitulating. After all, they had given Kristina their word, and she was right about the house of Jadon's resources, to say nothing about the wickedness...and wild-ness...taking place in the house of Jaegar this night. There was no telling what the Dark Ones might do—every sentinel, warrior, and wizard, as well as the king, might be needed before the night was over and the Harvest Moon set.

"I'll be fine for another twenty-five hours," Kristina reassured both princesses. "And honestly, that's why I came here. I was hoping..." She glanced around the courtyard, and her voice trailed off.

"What were you hoping?" Ciopori asked.

"I was hoping I could just hang out with the two of you for the rest of the day...for the rest of the night...like somewhere in the background, where I won't get in the way. I was planning to attend the Homage Ceremony anyway, and there's gonna be a whole lot of warriors at the ceremony, right? Not to mention, unless I haven't been paying attention since I was tossed into this testosterone-loaded family, your mates are gonna check in on you, all night long, regardless of Braden, because that's what possessive, protective, abnormally controlling vampires do." She forced a tentative smile. "Aaand," she drew the word out, pressing on, "Brooke, the little princes, and Tiffany are going to be here tonight in the manse. In other words, the king is gonna have this compound locked down like Fort Knox—I think I'll be safer here than anywhere else in the vale. Besides, it's just too lonely at the casino right now."

The casino....

Every word Kristina had spoken had made perfect sense to Ciopori, but the word that jumped out and struck her like a two-by-four to the forehead was...casino.

Niko and Jankiel's psychic trepidation, centered around the Dark Moon Casino...

Vanya's description of a dense, turbulent cloud hovering over the eastern end of the vale...

They must have all been picking up on something from Kristina...and Achilles...the letters, or maybe the floral delivery.

The thought made Ciopori shiver.

Just then, a rust-brown squirrel with an unusually bushy tail scurried down the trunk of a nearby ponderosa, careful to avoid a hanging lantern, and darted across the courtyard to the closest bale of hay, where it scampered up the straw, snatched an acorn, and turned around to face the women, as if checking to see if they were watching. All three females stared in amusement—and silence—perhaps grateful for the momentary distraction, and the squirrel craned its neck, stood a little taller, and clutched the acorn to its breast.

Ciopori giggled.

"Achilles?" Vanya crooned, leaning forward in the critter's direction.

The squirrel puffed out its cheeks and squeaked.

"You know you can't be out in sunlight," Vanya chided, staring at the animal more closely.

This time, Kristina laughed, even as the squirrel chortled angrily.

"Hmm," Vanya intoned. "Does make one wonder."

"I don't believe the Colony Guard can actually shape-shift," Ciopori observed.

"*Well!*" Kristina demanded, throwing both hands up in the air to distract the women from the squirrel. "Can I hang out with you guys or not? Just 'til tomorrow...or whenever this whole moon-thing is over?"

"*Yes,*" Ciopori said with emphasis, "and when the ceremony is over, if you would like, you can come back to the farmhouse for the remainder of the night."

Kristina grimaced, ostensibly remembering her time as a pseudo-captive in Marquis' lair.

"Or she can stay with me and Lucien at the Victorian, near the hot springs," Vanya offered. "No telling what time Saber will be home, but I would certainly welcome the company."

"Very well," Ciopori said, "then it's all settled." She extended her hand to Vanya, who accepted it gracefully and took an immediate step to the left, even as Ciopori took two measured steps to the right. Then both females drew closer to Kristina, until they ultimately linked both hands around her waist and pinned her inside an oblong circle, in the center of their arms.

"Kneel," Ciopori said, without preamble.

Kristina cocked an eyebrow and drew back her chin as if suddenly feeling claustrophobic. "Excuse me?"

"A spell," Vanya explained.

"For protection," Ciopori clarified.

"We may not be able to tell our mates, the sentinels, or the king...quite yet," Vanya continued, "but we can place a protective ward around your body...your anima. The spell will hold until tomorrow at dawn, and should you feel fear, or an overwhelming sense of dread, the spell will trigger a psychic alarm of sorts. The signal will be broadcast instantly to your brothers and the sentinels. They will know your location. They will be promptly aware of the letter, the card, and the flowers..."

"Non-negotiable," Ciopori added. "They will be able to see through your eyes, hear through your ears, and feel through your senses, and they will also be able to track you...to find you, unerringly."

Kristina's fair skin flushed a pale shade of pink. "Shit," she whispered. "You can do all that?"

"We insist," Ciopori said.

"'Tis our price for the secrecy you ask of us." Vanya smirked, then winked.

Kristina's heart-shaped lips curved up in a smile, and her bright blue eyes shone with warmth.

At last, Ciopori thought, *she gets it. Of course she is loved and always protected.*

"Thank you," Kristina said humbly. Then she slowly lowered her body to the ground and placed one knee, covered in a sheer stocking, in the dirt, albeit gingerly. "I hope someone did this for Braden too," she murmured absently.

At this, Ciopori released Vanya's hand and stroked Kristina's hair maternally, allowing her fingers to play along a lock of loosely curled red tresses before it fell away and linked, once more, with Vanya's. "The most powerful beings in the house of Jadon will have their eyes on Braden this night, and even the celestial gods will be watching. But if it will calm your spirits and bolster your faith, we will say a prayer for Braden, also. We will ask Monoceros, his ruling lord, to look after him; we will beseech our own lineage, the goddess Cygnus, to defend him; and we will ask the Millenia Harvest Moon to shine down favor upon him."

Kristina opened her mouth to reply, but her utterance was too hushed to discern.

Nonetheless, Ciopori got it—

And so did Vanya...

Whatever was happening between Kristina and Braden, whatever the Millenia Harvest Moon would bring to the latter, their fates were inextricably intertwined. For all intents and purposes, Braden Bratianu and Kristina Riley Silivasi were already mated, as friends...as sojourning souls, and whatever befell one would befall the other.

CHAPTER SEVEN

THE VALLEY OF SPIRIT & LIGHT

Deep inside the midnight void—a cross-shaped cluster of northern stars within the remains of the Veil Nebula—Cygnus, the Swan, spread her golden wings and peered into the turquoise-blue ocean of living water beneath her. As her waist-length, snow-white hair fell across one shoulder, the glistening pure silver highlights reflected off the tranquil sea, and her bright silver eyes narrowed ever so slightly.

Lord Monoceros, sensing her unease, placed a strong but gentle hand on her shoulder. "Your ancestors pray," he said softly. "The females of your lineage beseech your favor."

"All the valley prays," Lord Pegasus added, having ventured from his home amidst the Globular Cluster to visit the god and goddess at the pristine shore, several short clusters beyond Cygnus' palace.

"Well," Cygnus mused, "they are rightfully concerned about Braden." She smiled then, regarding Monoceros' hand with a sweep of silken lashes. "Your chosen son is now a wise and powerful, full-grown male, even if he does not fully realize it."

"Indeed," Monoceros said, "and I have made the forest ready."

She nodded before shifting her gaze back to Pegasus, who now kneeled on the sand beside her. "And the protection you provided, Lord Pegasus, when Dario converted the child has served him well these past twelve years."

"Yet?" Pegasus queried, crossing his powerful arms in front of him.

"Mm." Cygnus sighed. "Yet here we are, the winged horse, the unicorn, and the swan, celestial deities who rule the heavens, helpless to do naught but await the fate...and the free will...of our beloved children—knowing that the forest has been made ready, realizing the dark lords will bolster and entice their own—yet hoping we have taught and led our scions well." She swept her hand in the turquoise-blue water, and all three divine beings gazed at the ensuing ripples, watching as the water cascaded, rose in subtle waves, and finally settled into a brilliant, still, translucent pool, reflective like a mirror. "Ah," she breathed as she leaned forward to peer into it, "alas, it begins, history revisited."

"Aye." Monoceros squeezed her shoulder, and then the mirror began to shimmer, to coalesce, as faint, distant images became more and more vivid: a desolate mountaintop rising over 8,000 feet high in the Transylvanian Alps, festooned by two massive, jagged boulders; thick, swirling, low-lying clouds descending in an unholy blizzard; a swelling storm chilling the air with unforgiving winds and bitter vortices of ice—the land, the gloomy moonlight, the pungent scent of rotting corpses and burning juniper, all living manifestations of rage, fear, and strife.

Cygnus shivered as she waited. "Two thousand, eight hundred and seven years past," she mumbled absently, grasping Monoceros' hand and gently squeezing it before dipping her forefinger back in the water.

"Aye," he said again.

Pegasus seemed to be holding his breath, and Cygnus wondered if he was aware of the silence, the deafening quiet, left in the absence of his usual breathy exhalations. For truly, the stillness between the three deities was unsettling.

And then the liquid mirror filled with faint, swirling images from the past, began to churn more urgently, and at last, came to life in full, vivid, living color...

"So, it has finally come to this." Prince Jadon's baleful words echoed from antiquity as he placed the toe, then the heel, of a high, stiff black boot on the top of a ragged, dark gray rock and shifted his weight to mount the boulder. He squinted into the blistering snow, ignoring the rising howl of the wind as he set his deep, dark brown eyes—no longer placid but determined and fixed dead ahead—on his twin brother, Jaegar. "Did you think I wouldn't show?"

"Gah," Jaegar grunted in a guttural clip, his own cold, stark onyx glare boring into Jadon's. "I knew you would come—the stakes were much too high to play possum."

Prince Jadon swept his right hand down to the top of his scabbard, even as his cold, bare thumb brushed along the hilt of his blade, moonlight reflecting off the burnished iron, and cold, moist air blistering his unclad chest. His nostrils constricted as he breathed in and out, steeling his resolve, and his mouth turned down in a frown. His eyes swept the valley below them. "The storm," he observed, "you do realize we are the cause of it, don't you?"

Beneath a heavy cloak of finely honed wool, Prince Jaegar shrugged his broad, muscular shoulders in indifference, snorting as he displayed his apathy. "Amazing, isn't it?" he said. "Still coming to terms with all the side effects of being a...vampire?" He licked his bottom lip, lapping frost with his tongue. "*Vampire.*

That's what they're calling it—the change, the Curse, this new way of life." He cackled, a sinister sound. "Vampyr, Nosferatu, creatures of the night—I rather prefer it to celestial progeny. It's more masculine, don't you think? More bloodthirsty. More powerful."

Jadon shook his head in disgust. "After all this time..." His voice trailed off, and his heart grew heavy—there would be no reasoning with his twin, no changing Prince Jaegar's ingrained contempt. "Our civilization is in tatters; our loyal servants, cursed; our women, slaughtered, gone like the long days of summer, warmth giving way to cold. And yet you maintain your stubborn arrogance, continue your reckless defiance. You stand on this mountain and gloat, eager to reign over a graveyard."

Cygnus couldn't help but admire Prince Jadon's self-control —with every breath in the prince's weary body, he wanted to blurt out a curse of his own, reveal an arrogant secret he had kept for so long...for too long: *Foolish as ever, my ignorant brother, despite this night's outcome, let it be known forever—may it reside in what's left of your soul—that our sisters still live. Yes, Jaegar; Ciopori and Vanya still live.*

But he dared not...

He did not.

On that hallowed eve, October 31st, in the season of the Autumn Equinox, 795 BC, Fabian Antonescu and his two female wards, Ciopori and Vanya Demir, were alive and well on the other side of the world, in a new land upon a rich, abundant continent. Yea, it had been five years and five months since the monstrous Curse, since the males of King Sakarias' monarchy were splintered, immutably divided, and changed into a species as base and instinctive as animals. Yet and still, two original females lived because Prince Jadon Demir had stolen them out of the castle six years hence, sent them deep into the Carpathian

Mountains, where they might flee—and survive—with a band of rebel warriors and mercenaries, and seen to their lives...to their care...along with the wizard Fabian, until passage upon the seaworthy vessel had been procured.

Moreover, he had given the powerful wizard a vial of his blood.

He had instructed him to keep it safe but to only use it in the direst of circumstances. Should Prince Jadon never arrive in the strange new world, should another soul need to protect the princesses, then Prince Jadon's blood—and thus, Prince Jadon's awareness—could be used to preserve this most critical mission. The elixir itself would act as a beacon.

And now, if the prince could only prevail in this battle—one last tempest—their great civilization might yet live...

Brother against brother.

Prince against prince.

Vampire against vampire for the whole of the race.

One soul marred by evil, one soul redeemed through mercy, two souls engaged in a final mortal contest so that legions of souls might live...so that armies of cursed males, many of whom still crawled on the ground and writhed in the frozen mud, stricken with dreadful bouts of bloodlust, would be spared eternal conflict, war without end. As Prince Jaegar had once said on the eve of that most fateful of days: *Lasa pe cei puternici sa mosteneasca pamantul.*

Let the mighty inherit the earth.

"If I fall," Prince Jadon said solemnly, "you must swear to keep your word. You will rule, uncontested, over the survivors of our kind—my soldiers, my loyalists, my Vampyr—but should any soul in my fellowship refuse to yield to your rule, refuse to bow before a new master or offer his eternal fealty, you must give me your word: That soul shall receive a swift and honorable death."

Prince Jaegar rolled his eyes in annoyance. "Of course I will." The corner of his cold, bloodred lips turned up in a smirk. "And if I fall," he countered, shrugging facetiously, "which is never going to happen, you may co-opt, lead, or slaughter my minions however you see fit." He chuckled, seemingly impressed by his own barbarous cruelty. "No need to display hypocrisy at the end." He held out both arms as if embracing the sky, the storm, and the upcoming battle, then drew in a deep, heady breath. "Do you smell that, brother? Immortality! The gods gave us favor after all." He thumped his chest with vigor. "We don't die like we used to, so I hope you'll at least aim for the heart." He swiped the side of his forefinger along his neck. "Remember to remove the head." He held his palms upward and glanced at his wrists. "Can you honestly believe how much it takes to kill a wayward brother? I am still getting accustomed to all the changes: drain the blood, incinerate the body, or just toss the royal fuck up into the sun." He spoke like they were bantering over a routine supper—he laughed like he was endlessly clever, and this further stirred Prince Jadon's ire.

"All but the last one, dear brother," Prince Jadon snarled. "You see, my loyalists and I do just fine in the sun. 'Tis why I was willing to meet *you*...at night."

Prince Jaegar's eyes turned cold...vacant...void of any lingering wit, and his lips curled back in a snarl. "Enough! Did we come here to exchange barbs, or did we come here to die? Did we come here to gossip as little girls, or to settle this matter as men? For all our followers, all our loyalists, for all the servants and battles yet to come—for the fate of a cursed and terrible species—brother against brother, winner take all. May the mighty inherit the earth." With that, he dropped down, settled into an offensive squat, and began to step sideways, circling Prince Jadon like the earth rotating around the sun, each stealthy, silent sidestep crossing forward, then back, above one ankle...behind the next.

Dark, empty onyx eyes deepened with rage, even as Jaegar's heavy woolen cloak, cinched beneath his neck by a circular, ornamented clasp, heart side, below his left shoulder, flapped in the wind, and the muscles in his bare, exposed chest rose and fell with steady, measured breaths and flat, uniform heartbeats.

Prince Jadon followed suit.

He stepped lithely to the left, maintaining an equal distance from Prince Jaegar, and a savage snarl escaped his lips as his dark brown gaze narrowed in intensity...and focus.

The brothers circled like dire wolves from the Late Pleistocene era, ferocious relics, more beast than man, their eyes locked, their jaws set, their muscles bunching and contracting in a primordial, bestial rhythm. And then Prince Jaegar gnashed his teeth, released his fangs, and stopped short beside a jutting rock formation. He stood up straight and widened his stance; his feet fell a shoulder's width apart; and faster than Prince Jadon could track with his vision, he reached behind a crag in the boulder, retrieved a sturdy wooden bow and three bronze-tipped arrows, and released all three with a hiss, the missiles flying straight and true, toward Prince Jadon's heart.

Prince Jadon sharpened his senses.

He closed his eyes, stretched out his arms, and reached for the soul of the elements, becoming one with the wind, the snow, and the air, as his body fractured... dematerialized...and the arrows sailed right through him, soaring over the edge of the cliff. He felt his pupils burning, undoubtedly glowing red, as he regathered his form—his muscle, bone, and sinew—and dropped into a squat.

Jaegar was several heartbeats ahead of him, talons protracted, left leg bent at the knee and right leg extended backward, resting on the toes. He snarled like a hellish creature and sprang forward, hurtling through the air like a ball from a catapult, in a brazen effort to sever Prince Jadon's jugular.

Prince Jadon fell into a low, extended backbend, arched his chest forward, aligned his neck with his arms, and planted both palms, upside down, on the ground. Prince Jaegar flew right over him, landed on his feet, and swiftly spun around, even as Prince Jadon sprang upright, leaped several yards forward, and twisted to face his brother once again. The princes effectively traded places, and Prince Jaegar lunged a second time.

This time, Prince Jadon threw back his head, thrust both hands outward, and caught Prince Jaegar by the chest. He shoved his brother upward, rotated backward, and flipped both of them over in a converse somersault, landing on top of Jaegar's chest. He heard a vertebrae crack and went in for the kill, releasing his lethal canines and striking Jaegar's throat.

Two hard, iron fists slammed into Jadon's chest. Jaegar pressed Jadon's torso upward with the backs of his fingers, the bones of his knuckles, and then drew back his knees, planted the soles of his feet squarely against Prince Jadon's midriff, and shoved him upward—propelled him back—into the air and over the edge of the cliff.

Prince Jadon flew through a dense, black, low-lying cloud. Grappling to halt his trajectory and reorient in the air, he bowed his back, flipped his body upright, and released two pitch-black wings. He could hardly see two inches in front of his face as he floated upward, felt for the floor of the rocky crevasse, and slowly descended once again, placing his feet on solid ground. A ghostly hand shot out of the mist, a claw nicked Prince Jadon's jugular, and then five curled fingers wrapped around his throat.

Prince Jadon reached across his chest, grasped wildly at his tethered waistband, and withdrew a sharp, crescent-shaped dagger just as Prince Jaegar struck at his heart. The evil prince's talons pierced Prince Jadon's breastbone, and Prince Jadon clasped his brother's forearms by the wrists. "Not like this! Not tonight," he snarled.

Prince Jaegar withdrew his claws, snatched the hilt of the dagger from Jadon's hand, fisted it like a battle flag, and sank it deep into Prince Jadon's neck.

Prince Jadon flailed wildly for a moment, and then he grasped Prince Jaegar's forearm and snapped it with a sharp turn of the wrist, breaking the vulnerable radius beneath the decorative armband.

Fire shot out of the clouds, blazed all around them, and hail began to tumble with the snow. Prince Jaegar inhaled deeply, taking the fire into his lungs, and then he spewed the combustion outward, streaming hot flaming breath, like a fire-breathing dragon, into Prince Jadon's eyes.

Prince Jadon recoiled in shock, jerked back, and swiped the flames from his eyelids—the pain in his chest was unrelenting, and he did not have a moment to spare. He swept Jaegar's legs out from underneath him, fell forward on top of him, and the feral vampires rolled around on the ground until, at last, Prince Jadon achieved a dominant position. He sank his fangs deep into Jaegar's femoral artery, latched on like a savage wolf, and as the blood of Jaegar's twisted soul flowed down the back of Prince Jadon's throat—rancid, fermented, and hard to swallow—he struggled not to gag.

Still, he refused to let go.

He snarled, gulped, and guzzled like the vampire he was, desperate to drain Prince Jaegar's essence...to siphon as much of the wicked male's life force as his fangs could draw out.

Pinned, depleted, and desperate, Prince Jaegar slammed his fist into Jadon's skull. He fisted Jadon's hair and wrenched his mouth away from the gushing artery. He struck at Jadon's eyes with two piercing talons, blinding the prince in the night. And then he scrambled to his knees, shuffled backward, and withdrew his sword from its scabbard...with a broken arm and a spurting artery...shoring it up with his uninjured hand.

Prince Jadon froze as he listened...

Like the cry of a ghoul from a shallow grave, the steel rang out in the oppressive, ominous darkness, and the remainder of Prince Jadon's senses heightened.

His breaths grew shallow, and the hairs stood up on his arms.

A slash across the stomach—Prince Jadon cried out in pain.

A lunge, a stab, a twist of iron—Prince Jaegar's steel pierced Jadon's heart.

Prince Jadon grunted, sucked in air, and spit out a glob of blood.

No!

No...

It couldn't end like this.

There was far too much riding on this battle.

His fingers splayed, his left hand trembling, Prince Jadon pressed his palm against his chest and breathed...focused...*felt* for each shift in energy.

Static.

Electricity.

Lightning flickered inside the clouds.

Spurting.

Gushing...

Blood spewed from Prince Jaegar's thigh.

Falling, swirling—ice settled like the morning dew all around them.

The lingering...persistent...pungent scent of rotting corpses and burning juniper.

Yea, but Fabian had the women!

Jadon's sisters.

Fabian had the vial of blood.

The vampire males would follow the High Mage to the new

land, the new world, and the progeny of celestial gods and men—Prince Jadon's descendants, Prince Jadon's legacy—would not perish from the earth.

So it was settled...

Listing from both blood loss and blindness, Prince Jadon swayed in the darkness, felt for the pommel of his sword, slid his hand down to the grip, and drew it from its sheath. He *heard* Prince Jaegar's blade slicing through the air—drawing closer, nearer, about to fall on his throat—and he conjured the supernatural speed of a million celestial deities, borrowed Prince Jaegar's momentum, seized the surrounding kinetic energy, and multiplied each advantage ten-thousand-fold.

His back arched, his spine stiffened, and he choked on a gurgle of blood, gasping for air.

The band on his forearm seemed to tighten, and his bicep flexed as he drew back his steel, raised it over his head, and slashed downward with all his might, urging the energy of the blade forward, through flesh, blood, and bone, even as his own throat was sliced.

Silence.

A haunting, unrelenting quiet.

The snow stopped falling.

The lightning ceased.

The cold, barren ground gave way beneath him...and then...

There was only darkness.

Kneeling at the side of the sea on the celestial shore, still within the remains of the Veil Nebula, Cygnus drew back from her anxious perch and stared soberly into the translucent, liquid mirror. She watched breathlessly as the ancient mountain began to tremble, split open, and eventually swallow the princes before closing...collapsing...and settling, still, along with the turbulent storm. And then she breathed a heavy sigh of both weariness and relief. "The awakening has been long in coming."

"Indeed," Monoceros said, closing his heavenly, moondust eyes. "So many seasons have come and gone, bitter winters, joy-filled summers...so much planted in each celestial spring. Yet now comes the time of harvest..."

Pegasus held his tongue.

CHAPTER EIGHT

8:30 P.M.

Braden stared out at the placid, almost silver-blue water, marveling at the way the lake grew still in the evenings, its steady waves and choppy swells receding into a shimmering liquid platform, as he ran his fingers absently through the smooth, fine sand beside the edge of his blanket.

Santos' private, hidden cove was equally quiet.

Tranquil...

Cottonwood trees stood as still as statues, surrounded by random sprinklings of reeds and bramble, the latter gathered around like eager children waiting to hear an evening story, and as the pale red moon shone higher...brighter...more portentous in the sky, replacing the 7 p.m. sunset, Braden stifled a shiver.

Nothing had happened at 10:49 a.m.

Nor at noon, or at two, or even early evening.

For all intents and purposes, the day had been anticlimactic, pleasant, and wholly uneventful.

Marquis, Nathaniel, Kagen, and Nachari had joined Braden, the sentinels, and the tracker at the private oasis around 4:00 p.m., and they had sat on the beach passing time like family, sharing company, laughter, and nostalgic memories: Nathaniel had told the story of Jocelyn and the lycans, how Braden had saved his *destiny* during a terrible winter blizzard when he had crouched behind a heavy door at the back of an old, dilapidated shed and pounced on Tristan Hart—a hulking, fearsome were-wolf—actually going for the lycan's jugular. Marquis had chimed in, more than once, recanting his own chilling tale of Draco's Blood Moon, the confusion surrounding Kristina and Ciopori, and how Braden had divined the mystery from the Blood Canon, the ancient book of black magic, interpreting the spell that had been cast by Salvatore Nistor—how Braden had been the one to realize the dark vampire had switched the women. Kagen, a masterful storyteller in his own right, had practically waxed poetic about his journey through Mhier, a land beyond a portal where he had found Arielle, and how Braden had virtually saved all of them by coming to the grove every day—in fact, every hour on the hour for twelve hours a day at first, and then eventually at noon and midnight—to open the portal and await their return.

Saxson had given Braden credit for his future with Kiera, emphasizing the fact that Braden had once again unraveled an omen: a two-toned rose that was crimson and black, the black petals swallowing the red. The female who had been at Saxson's side from the rising of his Cetus Blood Moon had not been his *destiny*, Kiera Sparrow, but her dangerous, conniving twin, Kyla.

And then Julien had chimed in, on behalf of himself and the wizard Fabian, thanking Braden for luring Julien's dark twin, Ian, to River Rock Creek and acting as a decoy, while Julien hid beneath the ground, ready and eager for the violent confrontation. He had thanked him for possessing the courage to help set the trap in the first place and for ultimately creating the conditions which had at last freed the tracker from a lifetime of haunting inner demons. He had thanked Braden, as well, for saving Gwendolyn Marie Hamilton, the High Mage's strong-willed *destiny*. Braden had been the one to find the captive female in The Fortress, to rescue her from the ductwork, and to immediately recognize something in her soul and bring her back to the house of Jadon. Braden had been the reason Gwen's path had ultimately intersected with Fabian's.

Ramsey, in his own blunt, brutish style, all the while speaking around a mint-flavored toothpick, had lightened the mood just a little with his tale of how Braden had confronted the Master Warrior in defense of Kristina Riley Silivasi's honor. The fledgling had only been fifteen years old, three months shy of his sixteenth birthday, yet he had beat his chest like a primal ape, hurled a stone at Ramsey's back, and lunged for Ramsey's throat —fangs released, claws extended—determined to provoke the six-foot-five, 240-pound pit bull. Yet in the end, his courage and his honor had likely saved Nachari's *destiny*, Deanna, from a wicked plot devised by Salvatore Nistor and Oskar Vadovsky, and carried out by Saber Alexiares, pretending to be Ramsey Olaru— well, at least before Saber had known he was actually a son of Jadon.

Kristina Riley Silivasi...

Her name had carried to Braden's ear and lingered in the air like the distinct dewy scent of the hidden lake's deep waters. He had placed his hand over his back hip pocket and absently felt for his cell phone—*Dear Gods*, how he had wanted to text her...

Call her...

Reach out to her.

Just check up on her and tell her...he was sorry.

Nothing about the night before—he did not want to bring up their time together, how he had kissed her, how badly he had wanted her, how...or why...he had turned and walked away.

He had only wanted—

Only wanted....

Gods, he was just so...sorry.

So confused.

And in that moment, it had finally hit him—he might never get another chance to tell her, another opportunity to explain his behavior.

Luckily, Nachari had abruptly rescued him from his self-pitying musings by recalling several intimate tales of his own: He'd shared how Braden had likely saved King Napolean Mondragon himself during the monarch's horrific Blood Possession by once again channeling mysterious, cryptic information. The way Nachari had told the story, something had happened on that day, on the side of the road, two or three miles east of Tall Pines, where the Snake Creek River forked just outside the county line. A gateway of some sort had opened, a bridge between Braden and the collective house of Jadon, the genetic memories, the living history...the shared celestial origins. And while his body had been racked with pain—he had nearly thrown up his guts—he had also managed to utter several critical facts that had given the warriors the power to rescue Napolean: the sickness wasn't Braden's—it was Napolean's. The king had been possessed by a worm. And the worm had a name: the dark lord Ademordna. He was going to violate Napolean's *destiny*, and he was going to kill the king.

As if instinctively knowing that the tale was too dark and depressing, in spite of its happy ending, Nachari had seamlessly switched to reciting happier memories: how Braden had once accidentally erased the memories of a twelve-year-old girl named Katie Bell but also, how he had shown endless patience, kindness, and compassion with Deanna when she had first arrived in the valley, by regaling her with facts, stories, and information about Nachari while he was away...unconscious...trapped in the underworld.

And then Nachari had ended with the best tale of all: the first time he had introduced Braden to his family. Braden had cringed through the entire description of a fifteen-year-old fledgling, dressed in black trousers and a silk white shirt, trailing a cape behind him, his face painted ghastly white in order to look like Count Dracula, while he'd dragged a half-formed wing behind him, having failed miserably in an audacious attempt to shape-shift "for the Ancient Master Warriors."

Even Braden had to chuckle when Nachari mentioned the "bat cave," a clever form of *time-out* devised by Marquis Silivasi. Yet through it all—perhaps out of empathy, perhaps out of propriety—no one had spoken a word about the prevailing, underlying thread.

No one had pointed out the obvious.

No one had mentioned the *why, what,* or *how* beneath all these divine, almost karmic occurrences.

That kid with the painted face and the broken wing, the one who had accidentally erased the memory of a child, had played the hero in all these stories—that five-year-old human, not even a descendent of the original progeny, who had been sired, not born, into vampirism, had rescued warriors, interpreted omens, dreamed the future, saved many *destinies,* and somehow just magically shaped the entire house of Jadon.

Hell no, it wasn't a coincidence.

Braden peered once again at the moon, studying the shadows, divots, and murky surfaces.

Shit.

Just shit.

It had been smooth sailing so far, but there was no denying what was irrefutable: The spirit of an ancient prince had been with Braden, even as the prince's blood was now running through his veins, for a really long time. Truly, there was no other explanation.

Braden knew himself.

He knew his thoughts, his blunders, and all his hidden insecurities.

He knew all that care, divine intervention—hell, insight and wisdom—the courage, strength, and decisions of a hero that had popped up here and there since day one had to have come from an outside source...a greater power.

It had to have come from...Prince Jadon.

"How are you doing, son?" Napolean Mondragon shimmered into view, appearing on the beach like a Viking from the past, his dark onyx eyes contrasted with the moonlight, the silver irises gleaming like the stars, his waist-length hair blending with the black of his shirt, his slightly faded jeans, and his heavy tactical boots. He stepped forward from the apex of the loosely knit circle of warriors and squatted to meet Braden's eyes. "Still no change?"

Braden smiled wanly. "So far, so good. Are the ceremonies kicking off?" The king and the High Mage had promised to arrive at the lake by 8:45 at the latest—before the full rising of the moon —and based upon the position of the stars, their proximity to the celestial poles, it was nearing 8:40, and the king had probably completed his rounds.

"So far, so good," Napolean echoed, dipping slightly lower to study Braden's features.

"What?" Braden asked. *Thump-thump, thump-thump.* His heartbeat slowed down.

"Your pupils," the king said cautiously, "they're glowing like lanterns, and the golden pupils, they're enveloped in glowing light, like the rings of...Saturn."

Braden furrowed his brows.

Thump-thump. Thump. Thump. Thump.

His heartbeat evened out, slowed down, six to eight breaths per minute, and then a whirring drone, a faint white noise growing louder...coming closer...ringing in his ears.

The king was asking him...something...but he couldn't make out Napolean's words.

Braden instinctively glanced up at the sky, once again searching the heavens for answers: The moon was growing darker, more crimson, more oblique...more ominous. And for lack of a better description, the sky was filled with colors—white, silver, eddies of gold...black, red, faint hints of green—swirling in soft neon waves like the Aurora Borealis. "Do you see that?" Braden asked.

"See what?" Napolean said.

Or maybe that was Nachari...

Maybe it was both.

A current of air, like a chill winter's wind, swept through Braden's lungs, and he tilted his head to the side, listening...feeling... The constant drone was not white noise—it was the sound of his blood circulating through his veins.

His senses heightened, and the hair on the back of his neck stood up.

Cold, ragged, dark gray rocks closed in all around him.

Blistering snow.

Howling wind.

Dense, low-lying clouds hovering, settling...constricting.

"*Say something, Bray,*" Kristina nearly whimpered as she twirled a lock of curly red hair around her finger and sank back into the cream-colored sofa.

Then lightning, danger, the overwhelming stench of rotting corpses and burning juniper.

Kristina crossed her ankles in front of her, interlocking the spikes of her familiar stiletto heels, while Braden swayed in the darkness, listing from blood loss and blindness. He felt for the pommel of his sword, slid his hand downward to the familiar grip, and drew the heavy iron from its sheath.

Another blade!

Slicing downward...

Drawing closer, nearer, about to fall against his throat...

Kristina!

Kristina...

So damn beautiful. So damn vulnerable. Her voice so alluring as she spoke: *"The way you look at me...that time you kissed me, that time you stole my breath...we've always been more than friends."*

Braden's back arched, his spine stiffened, and he choked on a gurgle of blood, gasping for air. The band on his forearm seemed to tighten, and his bicep flexed as he drew back his sword, raised it over his head, and brought it downward with the full strength of his will, slashing through flesh, blood, and bone...his *brother's* flesh, blood, and bone!

His eyes began to water. He blinked several times, then jolted, his chest caving inward. He was now strolling across the living room floor, eyes transfixed on Kristina. He braced one knee on the cushion beside her, leaned in, cupped her cheeks, and bent down to kiss her.

Passion.

Frustration.

Two years of pent-up desire...

She gasped and grasped at his shoulders before he pulled away—pulled away and stole away—without looking back. She had returned the kiss with equal ardor and clung to his shoulders as if he were her lifeline, while he, on the other hand, had fled to the balcony, leaped over the banister, and sailed on the wings of an eagle, his only cleaving embrace the cool night air.

The cool night air...

The cold, bitter, frigid Transylvanian air...

A sharp, piercing pain along the side of his neck and then silence—all-pervasive, unrelenting, and hallow—paired with finite darkness.

The snow stopped falling.

The lightning ceased.

And Braden tossed back his head and roared.

* * *

Achilles Zahora catapulted off the cold stone slab in the snake pit, also known as the Chamber of Cobras, feeling both hyped up and rejuvenated from the numerous fresh snakebites, exciting his nerves, scoring his flesh, and the ensuing, erotic venom now flowing through his veins. Not only had the session heightened his senses for the night's festivities, but it had also given the brutal vampire one hell of a powerful orgasm, which had been his goal from the moment he'd entered the chamber.

After all, it was the night of the Millenia Harvest Moon...

And now, despite the impending carnage to come, however he chose to celebrate the auspicious holiday, he would at least be able to restrain his carnal urges and forego any frenzied, craven acts that might lead to reproduction...accidentally inseminating some poor, wretched bitch and siring an heir forty-eight-hours later—an heir he really didn't want.

Nah, not for him.

Not like that.

And not this night.

He had his sights set on a much grander prize...

Kristina Silivasi and the blue-eyed offspring she might one day provide him.

He jogged down the back circular hallway on the main level of the underground Colony, turned sharp left when he reached the narrow vestibule that led to the inner council chambers, and picked up the pace down another diagonal passage, on his way to a particular family cluster of lairs: the Dragavei family unit; only, minus a father, a grandparent, or any siblings.

So...minus the "family" part.

Achilles chuckled.

Zeus Dragavei had the entire cluster of lairs to himself.

At four hundred years old, the savage beast of a male was as wild as a hungry wolf. With a gnarly, pointed beard and multiple piercings in his eyebrows, ears, and upper lip, he looked as crazed as he behaved, and he was also joining the formal Colony Guard on this most auspicious of nights, finally taking the place of Blaise Liska, who had been killed by Saber Alexiares nearly seventeen months past in a battle outside the dragon's isolated cave in the Red Canyons. Right about now, Silas, Nuri, and Falcon would be finishing up Z's tat: a circular band, wrapped around Z's upper right bicep, of a black mamba with jeweled red eyes. The least Achilles could do was welcome the inglorious bastard into the fold and make it crystal fucking clear that he, The Executioner, was the de facto leader of the pack.

No questions asked.

No delusional aspirations.

No bullshit or ballsy plots to one day challenge Achilles' authority.

At 1002 years old, Achilles was not about to cede his prestige or his commanding influence to a savage but wily whelping pup, who for all intents and purposes was still wet behind the ears.

The Executioner slowed his roll as he approached the tail of the cluster—the storage rooms, wood and metal shops, nurseries, and human slave quarters at the end of every family unit—and that's when the vertigo hit him.

One moment, he was staggering back; the next, his chest felt like it might cave in; still, a few seconds later, his feet left the floor, his body rotated upward and back, and he cartwheeled onto the cold, prehistoric floor, the vertebrae in his lower back snapping like flimsy, brittle twigs, even as an unholy pain pierced his jugular—it felt like someone was ripping his throat out.

Achilles shook his head wildly and grunted.

What the actual fuck...

He caught his breath, grasped his throat, then released his jagged incisors, excreting a handful of venom into the palm of his hand, before arching forward to press it against his lower spine.

The vertebrae knit back into place.

His torso shot upward, and he was catapulted, retrograde, onto his feet, almost as if someone had yanked him off the floor by a pully or a crane. "Son of a bitch!" he shouted, spitting a lump of phlegm onto the cold stone beneath him—another sharp, piercing stab along the side of his neck. "*Fute-m-aş!*" he cursed in Romanian; it felt like an icepick dissecting his flesh.

And then an even stranger phenomenon: The natural, jagged, prehistoric limestone, dotted with calcite formations all above him, gave way to dense, low-lying clouds, and fire shot out of the vapor and gas—hail pinged like haphazard pinballs, ricocheting off the colony walls.

Then snow...

Bitter cold.

The overwhelming scent of rotted corpses and burning juniper filled the underground cavern hall.

Achilles hit the floor with a thud, his legs swept out beneath him.

He jackknifed off the ground, brought his knee to his chest, and clutched his femoral artery. "Salvatore!" he bellowed angrily, calling for the Colony's sorcerer. This shit was getting way out of hand, and it had *supernatural, underworld,* lethal *black magic* written all over it.

The sensation of blood—spurting, gushing, spewing from his thigh.

The mirage of ice and snow—falling, swirling, then settling like morning mist on wild mountain grass.

What manner of witchcraft was this?

The six-foot-tall Dark One materialized in the hall before him, Salvatore's stark widow's peak mapping a line to the crown of his long, black-and-red hair, his dark sapphire eyes gleaming with surprise, then purpose, his thin, arched brows curved into a frown.

"Counselor!" Achilles barked. "Now might be as good a time as any to step the fuck up and do something!" He lumbered to his knees and raised a heavy, blood-soaked hand toward the powerful ancient vampire. And then he jolted, his body seized, and his jaw dropped open, as the flesh, bone, and sinew on the side of his neck shredded like a flimsy piece of paper.

"Achilles?" Salvatore queried, his dark sapphire eyes wide with horror.

The Executioner listed to the side.

Was he dead?

Alive?

Or trapped in a nightmare?

"Achilles!"

He stared at the bloody floor, feeling oddly...disembodied.

"Vampire!" Salvatore roared, both angry and confused. The Executioner was covered in blood, and his eyes were thoroughly vacant. "What is wrong with you? Get up!"

Achilles' nostrils flared, he took a long, slow, deep breath, and the corners of his mouth curved upward in a smile. He raised his head—ever so slowly—then his massive, barrel chest inflated with a fresh breath of life—of power—and he levitated to his feet.

He turned his head to the left, then the right.

He surveyed the dimly lit hallway.

And then he licked his bottom lip like a Cheshire cat.

Salvatore took several cautious steps backward, which only

inflamed Achilles' predatory instincts—The Executioner took three tyrannical steps forward, snatched the sorcerer by the throat, and raised him high off the ground, before tossing him fifteen feet through the air into a sharp, protruding stalactite. The preglacial outgrowth, formed from epochs of calcifying salts, pierced Salvatore's back, and he winced in pain...and rage. "Are you insane?" he growled, staring down at his dangling feet.

"Two seconds," Achilles snarled, and his deep, chilling voice snaked along the walls of the stony hall, reverberating like icy thunder.

Salvatore's eyes bulged in their sockets, and he clenched his jaw in pain. He stared at Achilles like he was beholding a ghost and began to shiver from head to toe. "Two seconds to do what?" he queried warily, his voice no longer defiant.

"To come down from that archaic cross and kneel before your prince!"

CHAPTER NINE

Braden!

Kristina sat forward in her chair and gasped. She grasped her left wrist with a strained right hand and anxiously thumbed the gemstones in her bracelet. Despite the weather remaining fairly warm—the day's high was seventy-five degrees at noon, sixty-six degrees around 6 p.m., and somewhere around fifty-five, now, at 9:00 p.m.—a cold chill gathered at the base of her spine and slowly traveled upward toward her neck.

Something felt off.

Something was wrong.

Something terrifying, bigger than life, and supernatural was happening.

She glanced around the outdoor audience, eyeing several of the familiar guests as they convened in their various pavilions: Deanna Silivasi shifted nervously in her elegantly decorated folded chair, Sebastian in her lap, playing busily with a tiny toy figurine; yet she didn't appear unduly alarmed. Gwendolyn Antonescu sat beside Deanna, her son Falcon asleep in a portable child carrier, nestled snugly by her feet; again, the pretty blonde *destiny* seemed relaxed. Across the arched wooden walkway, in an adjacent pavilion, the queen, Brooke Mondragon, shared the space with a loyal human governess, Brooke's bestie, Tiffany Olaru, and their collective gaggle of kids: Phoenix Lane, Paris, Parker, and Santiago "Roman," Ramsey's high-strung, rambunctious son—nothing appeared amiss.

One by one, Kristina glanced inside each pavilion, evaluating the facial expressions and body language of all the guests, until she finally settled on the farthest rotunda, the structure encasing Aric Zander, Kristos and Colette Nastase, Natalia Olaru and baby Zeri, Keitaro Silivasi and his companion, Zayda, as well as Dario, Lily, and Conrad Bratianu. If anyone else could feel the stark unease, it would be Braden's blood-kin, his immediate family. She strained her eyes to see more clearly, even though she could have simply zoomed in with her vampiric vision. Dario looked restless but not overly distraught, Lily was wringing her hands in her lap, and Conrad—his brow was moist with sweat, and he kept glancing anxiously around the courtyard.

Bingo, Kristina thought.

He feels it too.

She shifted her attention to the front of the gathering, the decorative stage, festooned with hay bales, sage-green vines, and harvest fruits in every autumn color, and she may as well have been staring into her own reflection: Ciopori Demir was doing her best to lead the majestic, sacred ceremony, to pretend she was fully present in the moment, but the raven-haired princess looked rattled. Her eyes darted left, then right, scanning the courtyard every couple of minutes. She would occasionally pause, right in the middle of a sentence, her eyebrows would furrow, and then she would continue. And Princess Vanya, her sister? Her lips were gently parted, and they would move from time to time as if she were whispering beneath her breath—yet she wasn't uttering a sound. Her pale rose eyes were transfixed beyond the audience, sometimes above the tree line, cast upward toward the sky, and she appeared to be scanning...something...*nothing*...searching the forest for clues...or boogeymen.

Yeah, the sisters were rattled, all right.

They were picking up the same energy as Kristina, and *concern* was written all over their faces.

Just the same, Kristina had to hand it to the royal females—Ciopori kept right on speaking in a lyrical, almost mesmerizing lilt, and Vanya's hands kept moving, gesturing eloquently, as the two women continued to deliver a reverent soliloquy, paying homage to the six directions, weaving in and out of celestial history, and teaching about the elements—earth's mysteries—as they went along. Their royal upbringing still served them faithfully. Their parents had taught them well.

As if her first pang of worry had not been enough, another errant thought flashed through Kristina's mind, even more unwelcome and disturbing—

Achilles!

Shit, where had that come from?

Kristina shook her head, clenched and unclenched her fists, then shook out her fingers to discharge some energy. She forced herself to sit back in her chair, smoothed out her skirt, and slowly turned her head, once again, to peek inside Keitaro's pavilion. There was no doubt in her mind, the watchful patriarch would stay in touch with his family, and that meant his sons would be reaching out, all night, telepathically. That meant Keitaro would have secondhand access to both the king and Fabian. It meant, if anyone would receive up-to-date news about Braden—and consequently, about Achilles Zahora—it would be Keitaro Silivasi. She tried as subtly as possible to catch his attention, turn his head, and force some eye contact.

He didn't respond.

She leaned forward, then rocked back, hoping the motion

would trigger his predatory vampire instincts and cause him to follow the movement.

Still nothing...

Father. She sent out the word on what she hoped was a private, telepathic bandwidth and watched as he settled deeper in his chair, raised his left arm, and placed it protectively, if not possessively, along the back of Zayda's seat. *Hmm,* Kristina thought absently, wondering if the two of them were growing... closer. Still, *his hand didn't actually touch her shoulder...*

Her mind was wandering.

Then—*oh, shit*—the entire pavilion, including Keitaro, turned and looked right at her.

Well, hell...

Apparently, she had sent the telepathic word as well as her entire train of thought about Keitaro and Zayda to the whole damn pavilion.

Oh, well...

Keitaro smiled warmly, and Kristina felt her face flush. "Sorry." She mouthed the word and shrugged.

He raised his dark, sculpted eyebrows and chuckled softly beneath his breath. And then he sat up straighter. *No word yet from my sons.* Unlike her own, his telepathic voice was clear, concise, and laser-focused, appearing in only one person's mind.

Kristina nodded her head.

Are you sure you wouldn't rather join us? Keitaro asked. He had invited her to sit with the guests in the farthest pavilion earlier, but Kristina had politely declined: She had so much on her mind. She was carrying an explosive secret. And the last thing she needed was the close-up-and-personal scrutiny of an Ancient Master Warrior, who could probably read her like a book with one warm, cozy, intimate glance. The last thing she wanted was to say or do anything that might get back to Braden before the harvest moon had passed. Yes, she desired the protection of the paternal vampire, but she still felt solitude was best.

She opened her mouth to answer, then closed it.

Keitaro was on the other side of the courtyard, and knowing herself, she would blurt something out, and it would be way too flippant and loud. She tried to focus her telepathic vocal cords but figured, what the hell was the point? She wasn't very consistent with the whole telepathy thing—Keitaro would understand her silence.

Very well, he said, instantly proving her point. *I promise, I will let you know the moment the boys send any word.*

Now this made her smile.

The boys...

Kristina could think of a lot of ways to describe Marquis, Nathaniel, Kagen, and Nachari, but *the boys* wasn't one of them. She closed her eyes, folded her hands in her lap, and concentrated on taking slow, deep breaths, placing her full attention on the rise and fall of her chest. This kind of worry didn't become her. Besides, it was pointless—it wouldn't change anything. Kristina had lived through far worse uncertainty and much, *much* darker nights. Hadn't she?

"Kristina! *Kristina?* Come out of that closet." Kiki Riley's hoarse, gravelly voice, compliments of two packs a day for just as many decades.

Mommy Dearest was calling, but Kristina wasn't answering.

"I swear to you, girl; you come out or else!" Kiki pounded her fist against the wall. "You disobedient little redheaded bitch—come out of there, Kristina! Right now!"

How old had Kristina been...that time?

Seven?

Maybe eight?

And who was the boyfriend, the unhinged, brutal, one-sided lover, the latest drug partner, this night? Was it Tom, or was it

Joe? No...*no*...it was the guy who stacked boxes in the back of the corner liquor store, the one with three missing teeth, a grimy goatee, and filthy, tattered blue jeans with a broken zipper—Chuck, short for Charlie—the one who also didn't wear any underwear and loved to flash his toothless smile whenever his junk was hanging out.

Kristina cringed in her seat as the memory came flooding back: Kiki, stumbling around the fetid motel room, searching for a used, misplaced syringe. Chuck, cursing like a sailor, threatening to do things to Kiki no child should ever hear—that is, if Kiki had used up all the heroin before he got there—and Kristina, cowering in the three-by-three-foot-deep closet, dirty knees pressed to her chest, bony arms encircling her shins, dainty hands pressed over her ears, shivering.

She had fetched Old Lady McGuire's groceries for five weeks and, one day, scrubbed her toilets and mopped her floors, with a mop that was almost too tall and heavy to push, all in exchange for leftover food and whatever loose change Old Lady McGuire was kind enough to give her. And she had managed to save up nine dollars and thirty-eight cents. She had stuffed three pleated skirts, three pairs of undies, and one pair of socks in a brown paper grocery bag, along with her bright-pink mermaid toothbrush, her bubble-gum-flavored toothpaste, and her old, ratty hairbrush—just in case something really terrible happened, and she had no other choice but to run.

Kiki kept telling her that Chuck was her new dad, that he was a misunderstood genius and a brilliant inventor. She'd said that one day they would all move in together, once he got a patent for his hands-free beer-bottle opener, and then Chuck would buy the Rileys a house.

The Rileys...

That would be Kiki and Kristina, as Mother had suffered too many miscarriages to have any more kids, and she never missed an opportunity to remind Kristina that her real dad was a lowlife scum who had left her mother while she was eight months' pregnant, that her real dad drank himself to death on the floor of a roach-infested motel after being robbed by a prostitute and her nineteen-year-old pimp.

Still, even at seven or eight years old, Kristina knew that Chuck wasn't anyone's dad, that he could never afford a real house, and that a hands-free beer-bottle opener didn't make any sense! Who the hell wanted to bother with some moronic contraption when they could just twist off the cap, or use a regular bottle-opener, with one flick of the wrist? And how was that supposed to work, anyway? Hands-free! Stupid. That's what it was. And Kiki was just as dumb for believing him.

Kiki was silent now, compliments of Charlie's fist, and he was rattling the closet doors.

Damnit.

Kristina trembled from head to toe.

He knew she had some money in her grocery bag, but this time, she wouldn't give it up.

She couldn't give it up.

This time, she would use it to get away!

She shook like a dried-out leaf in autumn as she unraveled the neck beneath the hook on a wire hanger, straightened the wire out, and grasped it in her tiny fist, the tip of the wire sticking out between her first and third fingers. She shifted her weight onto her knees and waited.

"Open the door, Kristina! Your mother's asleep, and I need to borrow some money."

Borrow some money! Her cheeks felt hot, and she grit her teeth in anger. "Go away!" she'd cried out, still hoping to avoid a fight, still hoping to avoid getting hit, like Kiki. But she had already made up her mind: Old Lady McGuire had a dark, empty attic just above the tiny back kitchen, and Kristina had already made herself a bed in the loft with a bath towel rolled up as a pillow, and one of the panels from the motel curtains. She had already removed the screen from the ground-floor window and left the pane unlatched, and if she had to leave Kiki and set out on her own, then at least she knew where she could go for the weekend. The rest? Well, fear became the huge invisible monster in the motel closet, haunting the darkness and a little girl's soul—but anger, red-hot and steamy, stamped it out.

She tightened her fist around the wire hanger, kicked open the door with two bare feet—if she ever got out of this chaos and filth, she would only wear shoes fit for a queen, or maybe a model, sparkly, pretty, high-heeled treasures, just like she'd seen in a magazine—and sprang from the closet with a shout.

Chuck's eyes bulged wide, and his hands shot up, which gave Kristina the perfect target.

Stab!

Wrench back.

Stab again, even harder.

Hit the bull's-eye, between the whites of the bulges.

Chuck screamed like a stuck pig, and Kristina bolted around him.

Holy crap!

It had worked.

She snatched her bag, choked back her tears, and barreled out of the motel, running as fast as her tiny naked feet could take her, along an empty concrete city sidewalk.

Kristina opened her eyes, crossed her arms over her chest, and tried to refocus her attention on the beautiful princesses now leading an ancient prayer from the stage. She bit her bottom lip and stiffened her spine. Where had that memory come from? And who the hell cared? She had been on her own since the day she had left that motel room, and she had grown up in the streets, pulled herself out of poverty, taught herself to read and write, even enrolled in some classes to get her GED. Point being, Kristina was no one's babe in the woods, and she was no stranger to dark nights, overwhelming worry, or being cast out into the world alone.

Braden...

Achilles...

The house of Jadon...

Thoughts of the former two were terrifying—the questions, the uncertainty, the invisible monster still in the closet—but the latter was her home. Once again, she glanced over her shoulder at Keitaro, her more-or-less adoptive father, and her eyes swelled up with tears.

Keitaro was her dad now.

He seemed to genuinely love her, and either way, he was far enough removed from her daily life—*safe enough*—to love in return without risking rejection. Without setting herself up for abandonment.

And the Silivasis were her brothers. They had rescued her—literally and figuratively—time and time again. Jocelyn, Ciopori, Arielle, and Deanna were her sisters, and they also had her back. Hell, Kristina lived in a penthouse apartment above a classy, upscale casino, and Marquis provided for her every need. He had even bought her a pink Corvette. Staring down at her feet, she smiled—five-inch-high platform black pumps with a thin, dainty ankle strap—she was wearing one of her favorite raspberry wine-colored skirts, her feet were covered, and her clothes were clean.

She raised her chin and refocused on the stage.

Braden would come through the Millenia Harvest Moon just fine—he had to!

He had to...

And the HOJ warriors, the sentinels, her brothers—maybe even Napolean, the king—they would deal with Achilles Zahora. Everything was going to be all right.

You disobedient little redheaded bitch—come out of there, Kristina...

The voice echoed in her head one last time as she sat back, relaxed her shoulders, and crossed one shapely leg over the other. "Fuck you," she whispered beneath her breath, covering all the old scars with fresh Band-Aids.

CHAPTER TEN

The rumble of the feral roar filled the night sky.

The sharp, piercing pain along the side of Braden's neck ceased abruptly, all sensation gone, and the all-pervasive, unrelenting void collapsed into an ocean of stark but welcoming darkness.

One minute, Braden had been standing on the shore, lurching, reeling, and moving in and out of past then present memories. The next, he had been enveloped in oblivion, and now he was simply roaring...and falling.

Falling...

Falling.

Only, he didn't sink down to his knees in the sand, nor topple over into the still, silver-blue water; it was more like he merged into an endless sea of thick black clouds, and the vapor closed in all around him.

Tight.

Dense.

But also comforting...familiar?

And then he began to spin and spiral, tunneling backward in

a fetal position, curiously traversing a parallel dimension, traveling across eons of time in a narrow tunnel. He could hear snippets of his life pass by him, streaming into his consciousness like short, cascading spools of moving pictures, three-dimensional videos...floating, swirling movies:

Braden, is that your new report card? His mother's voice when he was seven years old, Lily smiling as she removed the folded slip of paper from the front pocket of his superhero backpack.

Boy, put that damn train set away, or I'll toss it in the fire and burn it! His biological father on Christmas morning—Braden was only three years old.

I'm so sorry I couldn't help him...there was just no way. He saved me. Jocelyn's voice. *You should have seen how he went after Tristan.* They were inside the old, dilapidated cabin, secluded in a remote, pristine basin in the Dark Moon Forest, and the Silivasis were about to wage war with the lycans.

Then, *Braden! Braden!* Nachari's frantic voice, closer, like it was anchored to the present. *Son, can you hear me?*

The sound of an oncoming freight train whooshed by him —*through him*—the light of a thousand suns flashed like a burst from a cannon, and the thick, welcoming, dense black cloud all around him exploded with power and vibrant, living energy.

Braden's heart leapt in his chest.

He stood up, straight as an arrow.

And then he simply left his corporeal body behind him, slipped gracefully into his ethereal matter, and stepped out of the void—the clouds, the light, the multidimensional tunnel—into the most brilliant yet tranquil, enchanting forest.

His eyes had never beheld anything like it.

* * *

"Braden! *Braden!*" Nachari Silivasi stared frantically into Braden's ever more vacant burnt sienna eyes, wide pupils swiftly transitioning into two deep, dark brown orbs, the former giving way to the latter as the Master Wizard shook him by the shoulders. "Son, can you hear me? Look at me!"

Their gazes met for a fleeting second: life recognizing life, friend reaching out to friend, and then, as if someone reached into the seat of Braden's soul, snatched it, and yanked it backward, the transient moment passed.

Dark brown orbs grew vivid, haunting...solid as the ascending harvest moon.

Braden cocked one strong, muscular shoulder in a sharp *get-off-me* gesture, breaking Nachari's hold. He took a tentative step backward, blinked three times, and swiped his eyes with the back of his hand. He looked left, then right, before raising his left pointer finger, gently flicking his wrist, and fixing his gaze, once again, on Nachari. Though he didn't speak a word, the message in the commanding wave and autocratic stare was unmistakable: *Step back.*

Instinctively, Nachari averted his eyes and took a cautious step back.

Braden's broad shoulders seemed to rise, inflate, in a proud, almost regal manner, and confidence—nay, *certainty*—the innate projection of self-assurance drew a line around his lower jaw and settled into his stance. "Who are you?" he asked, his voice a steady tenor. He followed up, before Nachari could answer, immediately surveying the shore and the warriors all around him. "Where am I?"

Nachari opened his mouth. Closed it. Cleared his throat. "Excuse me?"

"Warrior, I would know your name and your lineage?" He paused, cocked his head to the side, and amended, "Nay, not warrior...mage."

Nachari heard the words, and in his formal HOJ brain, they made sense, but his heart was still reaching for his acolyte. "Braden?" He answered the question with a query of his own.

The boy—no, the man—shook his head.

And that's when Nachari knew...

He took another step back, dropped to one knee, and bowed his head in reverence. "Prince Jadon?"

"Aye," the austere monarch said. "Your name, wizard?"

Nachari cleared his throat, trying not to stutter. *Holy Perseus, the Victorious Hero*, he was kneeling before a legend—but where was Braden? What had happened? "I am known as Nachari Silivasi. I hail from the ancient line of the god Canes Venatici and his human consort, Ophelia. Chosen by our lord Perseus; the youngest son of the Ancient Master Warrior Keitaro and his once-human *destiny*, Serena; a Master Wizard and member of the esteemed fellowship of the same in the venerable house of Ja—" His breath caught, and he had to reform the words. "In the venerable house of Jadon, the communal society of your ancestry."

The male seemed to mull it over for a moment, as if trying to make sense of the various nuances while straining the English through a Romanian filter, perhaps relying on his soul's timeless Transylvanian awareness while depending upon a relatively young North American brain to sort it all out. He processed very quickly. "Silivasi." He tried the word once more on his tongue. "*Silivasi...*" His eyes narrowed and his brows furrowed ever so slightly. "From the house of Canes Venatici and his human mate, Ophelia." He flicked his wrist yet again, this time in an almost self-deprecating, unpretentious manner. "House of Jadon...*yes*." And then his eyes lit up. "Are you...of relation...to Timaos Silivasi?"

Nachari opened his mouth to answer but only stuttered, and Marquis Silivasi stepped forward.

The Ancient Master Warrior placed his hand on Nachari's shoulder. "Descendants," he barked, his own voice sounding hoarse. "We are the *very* distant descendants of Timaos Silivasi."

Now this gave Prince Jadon pause. "Descendants," he whispered, swiftly deciphering the meaning of the word. His eyes swept the totality of the males now gathered around him, and he slowly nodded his head. "Your name?"

"Marquis Silivasi, eldest son of Keitaro and Serena."

Short and sweet, Nachari noted, still straining to unscramble his brain.

"And you...the two of you?" Braden—*no, the prince*—pointed loosely...generally...at Nathaniel and Kagen.

"Brothers," Nathaniel answered for both. "Twins. I am Nathaniel Jozef Silivasi, and this is my brother Kagen; we are chosen of the goddess Cassiopeia and Lord Auriga, the Charioteer, each in turn."

"Twins," Prince Jadon repeated, and then he briefly closed his eyes. "*Chosen...*" He opened them again. "Ah, but of course; you were all born after the Curse, then? And you are each Vampyr?"

Nathaniel nodded solemnly.

"Yes, Your Grace," Kagen whispered, his tone reflecting his stupefaction.

Prince Jadon gazed upward at the night sky. "Gathered together under the cover of darkness, on this rarest of occasions— the Millenia Harvest Moon." His spine elongated, he stood up straight, and his hand shot swiftly to his hip, as if feeling for a blade or a scabbard that was no longer there. "You!" he bellowed, his voice both chilling and commanding, "to which house do you pledge your loyalty?" He took a swift, stealthy step backward, incredibly light of foot, and rocked subtly from the balls of his feet to his toes. "All of you, each male here: To which sovereign prince do you swear your fealty?"

Nachari's eyes shot quickly across the shoreline, following Prince Jadon's fixed, wary gaze, and he winced the moment he caught sight of the tall, muscular vampire the ancient monarch was focused upon: *Saber Alexiares*. Six feet of hard, taut muscle; wild black-and-red hair falling just below his shoulders; and that characteristic, upper right corner of his mouth turned up, as usual, in that automatic, distinctive smirk.

"Saber Alexiares." The sentinel spoke for himself. "And I have pledged my loyalty to you and your house." He swept his hand through his wild, bicolored locks. "Trust me," he said on the trail of a snarl, "I know how it looks, but I was born to the house of Jadon, son of Rafael Dzuna and his *destiny*, Lorna Madison, chosen by the celestial god Serpens." He flicked the ends of his hair with two flippant fingers. "*This*," he added, "is a really long story."

Prince Jadon studied him carefully, and then his deep brown eyes turned upward and to the left. He was clearly accessing a memory—*Braden's memories*—and Nachari's heart constricted in his chest. "Yes," he murmured softly, "I have a...faint sense of this."

As if of one accord, every warrior on the shoreline descended to one knee and bowed his head in reverence—the gesture in perfect unison—and the communal demonstration spoke louder than words.

Prince Jadon shifted his weight and widened his stance. "Look up," he commanded, and the warriors obeyed. "You." He gestured toward Julien Lacusta, whose moonstone gray eyes were practically glowing with veneration.

"I am Julien Zechariah Lacusta, son of Micah and his *destiny*, Harietta Noel, chosen by the god Hercules, and I too serve your house, both as a tracker and an Ancient Master Warrior."

Prince Jadon nodded with deference before turning his attention to Ramsey. "And you?"

"Ramsey Demetrios Olaru," the sentinel said. He swept his hand to the side, indicating his brothers. "And these are my brothers—my twin, Saxson, and our eldest sibling, Santos. All three of us serve in the house of our lord as warrior-sentinels to our ancient king."

To his credit, Prince Jadon remained silent as Saxson and then Santos introduced themselves to the original monarch, each relaying their titles and their lineage before reaffirming their fealty to him. And then, without preamble or hesitation, he leveled his gaze on Napolean Mondragon, having had no trouble whatsoever singling him out—whether through Braden's memories or Napolean's unmistakable regal bearing and prominent presence, Nachari couldn't say.

"Our ancient king..." Prince Jadon repeated Ramsey's words. "Please, come forward."

Napolean rose with all the grace and dignity of his title, his own broad shoulders drawn majestically back, and he strode forward with both dignity and purpose, wearing his own station like a royal cloak. "Your Grace."

Prince Jadon took the king's full measure. "My Lord." He held both palms up and outward, acknowledging the full...stature of the male before him. "*King*...of the house of Jadon." He paused, his stoic manner giving nothing away. "From whose line do you hail, King Napolean?"

While steady, even proud, Napolean's deference and awe were apparent in the subtle, almost subservient, downward cast of his head. "My Prince, I am Napolean Mondragon, born on the third day of May 810 BC, to my father, Sebastian, and my matron, Katalina Constantin. Our house descended from the goddess Andromeda and her human mate, Demetrius, and I was chosen by the former celestial deity, having survived the Curse. I am an Ancient Master Justice, and yes, the leader...*the founder*... of all those who, alas, survived the brutal pronouncement and torment, all those who eventually—through great hardship and over time—migrated to North America."

Once again, Prince Jadon's discerning eyes flashed upward and to the left but only for an instant—he was accessing Braden's memories more swiftly now, almost instantaneously. "Mondragon." He nearly exhaled the word. "I know this house!" He stared at Napolean in rapt fascination. "And I know...*I knew*...your father, Sebastian. He was one of my loyalists. He was there at the Curse. He was—" His voice cut off abruptly.

"Yes," Napolean said sadly. "He was murdered. Beheaded. By your brother, Prince Jaegar, immediately following the change."

If eyes could reflect both empathy and gratitude, Prince Jadon's pupils glowed with each, and then he tilted his head to the side. "Words are inadequate to express my depth of sympathy —my soul...the monarchy weeps for your loss. And congruently, it is beyond the skill of the tongue to express the immense—nay, staggering—gratitude you are owed for all you have done. For leading our soldiers across the sea, for holding my house together, for founding a society that has survived so long—nay, I cannot do such fealty justice with words, but with all my heart, I thank you, King Napolean." The words lingered as if they were living entities, and then Prince Jadon's eyes lit up with enhanced awareness. "Napolean," he repeated, his voice thick with wonder. "Sebastian's young son." Yet again, he paused. "You are not the same child who was saved by Timaos from the wrath of Ravi Apostu, are you?"

"I am."

Prince Jadon nodded crisply, and then he suddenly switched gears and spun around. "*Oh gods!* My brother! Prince Jaegar! Where is he now? What...when...what year is this? *My sisters!*" His eyes swept the shoreline, and his voice rose with angst. "The princesses, Ciopori and Vanya! They boarded the vessel with the High Mage, Fabian. They voyaged across the great sea."

"Yes, they did. *We* did," Fabian Antonescu said bluntly as he both shimmered into view on the sands of the shore and strolled unapologetically to Prince Jadon's side. "Your Grace...Your Highness...*my beloved friend*. By all that is holy, it is good to hear your voice."

Once again, Nachari shivered inwardly: Fabian couldn't say, *It is good to see you*, because the face he beheld was Braden Bratianu's, even as the voice belonged to another being, another vampire. Nachari closed his eyes and whispered in his mind, into the vast, uncertain silence: *Braden, son...where are you?* He stared longingly at Prince Jadon, studied each and every one of Braden's fine, angular features, hoping for a sign...

Anything.

A wink.

A nod.

A twitch of his fingers...

But nothing subtle nor exceptional happened, nothing that might indicate Braden had heard him.

"Fabian!" Prince Jadon's tone took a familiar, almost human lilt. His hands shot up to his jaw, and his eyes lit up with pleasure. "You're here. You're alive. Then my—"

"Sisters?" Fabian interjected. "Aye, your sisters are alive. The royal princesses yet live."

Prince Jadon closed his eyes—ostensibly, and once again, scanning Braden's memories—only this time, rather feverishly. When at last he opened his lids, his eyes were moist with tears, and he exhaled with deep emotion. "My gods..." He placed both hands on Fabian's shoulders, and Fabian covered the prince's hands with his own. "Then you made it," Prince Jadon said, sounding both relieved and astonished, "all three of you." He gestured with his chin to indicate the shoreline and all the warriors still kneeling before him. "What of the others, the whole of my loyalists? You not only survived the Curse but all the tumult that followed? My males? My loyal subjects? What of the house of—"

"Whoa..." Fabian interrupted. He shook his head slowly. "*No*, my prince. Few of the original soldiers survived. I'm sorry, but much has changed over the long, hard years, the many centuries since we left Romania." He cupped Prince Jadon's face firmly in his hands, and the gesture was uncharacteristically intimate. "It's all there, in your memories, the memory of the vampire whose body you inhabit, and whatever is missing, I will supply. But for now, this moment, this fateful night, there is much we need to attend to...much, I'm afraid, that is terribly urgent."

Prince Jadon drew back and held up one hand, silencing Fabian with one gesture. "Wait," he said, "before you go on. Fill in these blanks right now...three queries."

He must have sent the questions through a private, telepathic bandwidth because the two men stood silently while Fabian nodded. After the space of several heartbeats, perhaps a minute, the High Mage stepped back and spoke aloud, so that all who were present could hear the answers. "We boarded the vessel on February first, 799 BC. We arrived in North America, now Dark Moon Vale, on May first, three months hence. The soldiers, your loyalists—the Vampyr—began arriving in May of 791 BC, but the full migration took many years, spanned several decades in time. And even then, many of the remaining males scattered across the mainland—it took centuries for Napolean to gather them together and create the society we know now. As for your second question, the answer is more painful, the truth more difficult to confess: Fearful that your sisters might never awaken, I panicked while in a...volatile...state of mind. While sleeping...dreaming...I traveled in the breast of a dark brown hawk and fed your blood to the male whose body you now possess. Your Grace, I stole a second vial from the castle apothecary, a vial containing your brother's blood, and while traveling in the body of a midnight-black raven, I fed it to a Dark One in the house of Jaegar. The universe demands balance, and I feared the spell might not work—your sisters might never be awakened—if I had not done both, provided the celestial sphere with balance by paying homage to both the light...and the darkness."

"And my third query?" Prince Jadon asked, showing no hint of judgment or disapproval.

"In answer to your third question: This night, the Millenia Harvest Moon—it has now fully risen, and it will wane at 3:34 a.m. The young one's name is Braden Bratianu, and he now embarks on a journey of his own, a journey that will, one way or the other, prove consequential to the entire fate of the house of Jadon. While I do not know where he is for certain—divination is an imprecise art—I feel...*I sense*...or perhaps I just hope that he is somewhere in the realm of spirit, yet sentient, somewhere far beyond our grasp. And I believe, although I cannot be certain, that he battles forces, engages...spirits...that are neither earthborn, nor made of flesh.

"No, I did not know what to expect—I had no idea what would happen when the full moon rose at 8:59 p.m., when your blood awakened in the vampire's body—but now I am fairly certain at least of this much: The body you inhabit will remain in your care until such time as the Millenia Harvest Moon wanes. After that, it is anyone's guess. Perhaps it depends upon the young one's journey."

Prince Jadon considered Fabian's words thoughtfully, taking a moment to process all the High Mage had said.

He rubbed his chin and bit his lower lip.

He turned his back on Fabian and the nearby vampires and strolled along the bank of the shore.

He turned around and rejoined his comrades.

And then he beckoned the kneeling males to rise with a regal lift of his hand.

Once all were standing, quiet and waiting, he angled his shoulders toward Fabian. "One more question, my wise, forthright friend..."

Fabian raised his brows.

"Who"—Prince Jadon said softly—"is Kristina Silivasi?"

CHAPTER ELEVEN

Achilles could not make sense of what was happening.

One moment, he was heading to see Zeus. The next, he was staggering sideways in the underground passageway, his body flailing, flipping, cartwheeling backward, his vertebrae snapping against the cold limestone floor, his neck throbbing, his jugular on fire...the sense that something or someone was about to tear his throat out.

Then snow...

Icy cold.

He had called out to Salvatore in hopes that the sorcerer could put an end to the...*witchcraft?* The otherworldly assault. But Salvatore had only shouted—"Get up!"—and then things had gone truly haywire...insane...utterly inexplicable.

Achilles' body had no longer been his own.

Like a puppet dangling from the masterful strings of a marionette, he had started to levitate to his feet—

And that's when the Colony had faded out.

Gone black.

That's when a gale-force wind had hit Achilles like a freight train, tunneling in through the back of his head, ping-ponging around his brain, and streaming down his spinal column, before spreading throughout his arms and legs.

Now, Achilles was flailing again...

Flailing, falling, and tunneling backward into a dense, thick void formed from mist.

Clouds?

Smoke?

A hot vat of inky tar?

The whirring drone of that damnable passing freight train!

He was traveling too fast to make sense of it, summersaulting backward, yet again...and again.

And then just like that, he stopped.

The sound subsided.

The spinning ceased.

And Achilles was ejected from the tunnel like a ball from a catapult, swiftly deposited— without fanfare or preamble—into a dark, barren, haunted forest.

Salvatore Nistor spat a wad of phlegm tinged in blood, braced both hands, palms facing backward, against either side of the underground cavern walls, and wrenched his body off the prehistoric spike, falling like a heavy sack of potatoes to the ground.

He swiped his bloody mouth with the back of his hand and stared fixedly at the Dark One before him—he could heal the damnable hole in his back later, assuming Achilles allowed him to live.

Shit, fire, and brimstone...

Not Achilles...

Not.

Achilles.

Salvatore stared intently into the stark onyx orbs leveled directly back at Salvatore, and for a moment, his labored breath left his body: Achilles Zahora, The Executioner, had pale, rich, citrine-colored irises—these were the eyes of *death*.

Dark.

Ageless.

Consumed by rage, if not madness.

Yet sharp, intentional, discerning.

Determined.

And in an instant, a rare moment of magus clarity, everything his cube had been telling him for the last two and a half months came back in a flash...

King Silvano's grandfather, 988 BC.

Maiden voyage, North America, 799 BC.

A hawk. A raven. Achilles Zahora, blood, blood, blood—The Executioner bathing in an ancient tub of blood, imbibing the substance through his mouth, ears, and nostrils, swirling it around on his tongue—Achilles Zahora, The Executioner, rising from a shallow grave like a mythical phoenix ascending from ash...

Light cleaves to light, and darkness cleaves to darkness.

Drink this blood and welcome life.

Drink this blood and welcome death.

Salvatore had no idea when...or how...but the evidence was irrefutable—and glaring—and standing right in front of him. Somehow. Someway. Achilles Zahora had imbibed the blood of a very ancient and deadly creature, an infamous tyrant, patriarch, and prince. Nay, the very genesis of the house of Jaegar, himself.

Salvatore sank to his knees.

And then he fell forward onto his face, prostrating his body before the hulking, murderous vampire. "Your Majesty," he crooned. "Welcome to the house of Jaegar—*your house*, your legacy, the descendants of your venerable line of loyalists, all such surviving Vampyr of darkness, those who owe their eternal allegiance to the greatest soul who has ever lived: our most cherished forefather, Prince Jaegar Demir."

Prince Jaegar strode forward and grunted. "Get off the floor."

Salvatore scrambled to his feet, careful to keep his head bowed, low.

"You are?"

"Salvatore Rafael Nistor, son of Johann Nistor and whatever suffering wench he used to spawn me: an elder in the house of Jaegar, a member of the esteemed Dark Council, and a highly skilled practitioner of dark magick—the Colony's most revered sorcerer."

Prince Jaegar listened attentively, and Salvatore could almost hear the wheels turning in his mind—in the mind of Achilles Zahora—as the ancient prince processed every utterance efficiently...strategically.

Salvatore needed to make his next move, and quickly. "Should you allow me to live, Your Excellence"—he spoke delicately, eloquently, and above all, submissively—"I believe I can be of service. Much time and history has come and gone since you last walked among your followers."

Prince Jaegar rocked back on his heels, ran his hand through Achilles' chin-length, black-and-red banded hair, then crossed his arms in front of his chest. He stared down at the faded black denim constricting his waist and thighs, and tugged at the constricting crotch, pulled at the hem of the odd cotton muscle-shirt. "Can you fix this shit?"

Salvatore startled. He blinked three times. And then he slowly raised his head and nodded. *Holy crap—nearly 2,807 years since he purportedly died, and the first thing the prince of our colony has to say is, can you fix these foreign clothes?* "Of course, Your Majesty," Salvatore assured him, searching his memory for an image—the portraits of the ancient monarchs stored in the Colony's library, recorded in the annals of history. With the tentative wave of a trembling hand and a few cryptic Latin incantations, Salvatore focused all his energy on the too-tight T-shirt and faded jeans, and voilà: a loose-fitting pair of cloth trousers, falling just beyond his knees, plenty of room in the crotch, high, supple boots, and a long-sleeved tunic, with ruffled sleeves and girded wrist cuffs—nothing too snug around his chest.

Silence hovered in the limestone hall while the reincarnated semi-deity checked the feel, fit, and familiarity of his conjured garments.

Salvatore bit his lower lip. "Do you have any—"

"This body," Prince Jaegar interrupted. "Whose is it?"

Salvatore nodded. "Your corporeal flesh belongs to an incredibly powerful soldier, one who defends the Dark Council as well as the entire house of Jaegar as the de facto head of the Colony Guard. He is, in point of detail, known as The Executioner, due to his unusual delight and brutality in carrying out—"

"Fucking-A!" Prince Jaegar snarled. "Do you always speak so much? Because let it be known, right here and now, I would just as soon behead you as listen to you ramble. I do not require such frivolous detail—I've already absorbed your language; I can see a mental blueprint of this underground settlement; and I have a fairly crisp concept of how the government is structured—but his name is just outside of my reach. So, let's try again: I asked you his fucking name."

Salvatore shuffled a few steps back. "Achilles Zahora."

"Finally," Prince Jaegar groused. "Achilles...Zahora." He held his right hand in front of his face, focused intently to rearrange the molecules, and glimpsed into his palm like a flesh-and-blood looking glass. "His appearance. Can you change it?"

Salvatore mulled that over.

This prince was a male of considerable ego—that was swiftly becoming clear. *As well as he should be,* Salvatore thought. "Yes," he said, foregoing the words *Your Majesty* in the interest and demonstration of brevity. "May I expound?" He winced and held his breath.

Prince Jaegar rolled his eyes. "You may but take caution."

"If you would like, I can restore your former appearance, but it will only be an illusion—I believe you will still walk within Achilles' body; you will still have access to his mind and knowledge. But if you feel it might be beneficial, I can do one better—I can provide you with the ability to go in and out of both personas, to sound and appear as yourself, Prince Jaegar, when you wish, or to sound and appear as The Executioner when it suits you." He folded his lips around his teeth to force his mouth to stop moving.

Prince Jaegar thought it over. "The latter."

Taken aback once more by the prince's brevity, Salvatore nodded tersely. He referred again to the likenesses of the ancient monarchs stored in the Colony Library, and commanded every neuron in his brain to fire correctly—*by all the dark lords, he had better get this right*—until a full 3D image of Prince Jaegar's ancient features—his body, his stance, his expression—were crystal clear in his parietal lobe.

This time, as he waved his hand, he also weaved his fingers in several intricate pattens, adjusting the configuration and the mystical spell as the visage of the prince transformed in front of him: thick, wavy, raven-black hair, streaked with red veins as a result of the Curse, stark onyx cutthroat eyes—soulless, merciless, and dead—six feet tall rather than seven, with broad, muscular shoulders and a large, ornate royal crest ring on the prince's right hand.

Salvatore bowed at the neck and waited as, once again, Prince Jaegar gazed into his palm.

Seemingly satisfied, the prince transmuted the glassy surface back into flesh and bone. "Very well," he said curtly. "Now then, is the High Mage, Fabian, yet living?" He raised one hand, looked up and to the left, then answered his own pointed question. "Ah, yes...he is. And the son of Sebastian is now a king—King Napolean Mondragon—hmm." He chuckled sardonically. "The descendants of Timaos Silivasi...Petraeus Olaru's line...and yes, *oh, yes*, my beautiful, no-longer-virgin sisters. Where is this... manse? This compound which houses Napolean and his ilk?"

Salvatore almost recoiled, but he caught the reaction and stifled it. *Um, not the place to go,* he thought. "It's, uh, directly above us, across a ribbon of thick forest and slightly northeast," he said. "About fifteen miles north of a gorge we refer to as the—"

"Red Canyons," Prince Jaegar cut in. "Yes, I see how the valley is situated. This night—it is the Millenia Harvest Moon?"

"Yes," Salvatore said.

"And this has something—*no, this has everything*—to do with why I am standing here before you?"

"That, I do not quite understand. You see—" *Shut up, Salvatore—short and sweet.* He linked his hands behind his back. "I don't know."

"This blood, my blood, the life-force which animates this body; tell me this much, sorcerer: Has such a mystery—such a miracle—also occurred with my brother, Prince Jadon?"

"That, I do not know."

"I see, but—"

"But I do recall a premonition which foretold your resurrection, Your Majesty: *Light cleaves to light, and darkness cleaves to darkness. Drink this blood and welcome life. Drink this blood and welcome death.* I do not know how Achilles came to imbibe your essence, nor do I know who may have imbibed the essence of light. But if the portent was accurate—and we can hardly refute it —then the odds are quite strong that your brother now lives in the body of a vampire from the house of Jadon."

Prince Jaegar nodded thoughtfully.

He furrowed his brows as if deep in thought, and took two casual steps forward.

Then he drew back his arm, balled his fist, and slammed the full force of his knuckles into Salvatore's prostrated jaw.

The bone shattered.

Salvatore's teeth scattered.

And blood pooled from his nose, drenched his lips, and meandered like a river along the curve of his mouth, staining an ivory canine lodged sideways in his cheek.

"If you ever interrupt me again, I will kill you." Despite Prince Jaegar's barely audible whisper, the words rang out like clamoring cymbals. "You may heal that shit with your venom in a moment but first, I have one last question."

"My Phlence?" Salvatore slurred the words, unable to pronounce *prince* properly. He stared at the ground, ignored his double vision, and waited.

"Who the hell is Kristina Silivasi, and why did Achilles want her?"

CHAPTER TWELVE

THE FORESTS...

B raden's breaths were steady and even, and he felt as if a giant weight had been lifted off his shoulders as he strolled further into the resplendent forest toward a massive, perfectly symmetrical, ageless tree imbued with radiance. At first glance, it looked like a mighty oak—the trunk was strong, robust, and wide; the thick, heavy branches curved in multiple directions, some nearly touching the ground, others stretching toward the sky; and the foliage, the leaves, were bright and healthy, not a single sparse section on the limbs, only, some were green, as found on earth, while many others were white or gold. At second glance, he knew it was something more, a species nonexistent on earth.

A literal Tree of Light.

As he rolled his ethereal shoulders and stretched his back, he realized he was no longer wearing his familiar clothes: His waist was covered in a simple, crude tie of cotton voile cloth, which fell to mid-thigh and cascaded as he walked, his feet were wrapped in simple leather sandals, as weightless as the burdens he had just shrugged off, and his arms, chest, and legs were bare. Somehow, it did not seem peculiar or off-putting. Nothing about his surroundings concerned him...at least not yet. He noticed a swaying scrap of parchment hanging from a lower branch in the tree, and immediately strolled toward it, inexorably drawn by its golden light. He clutched the parchment in his hand and plucked it from the limb like a delicate piece of fruit, feeling the fine, silken texture between his thumb and forefinger before bringing it to his eyes.

It was a missive.

A decorative note, written in an elegant, ancient hand: calligraphy for sure—but more—the golden letters were both raised, embossed, yet also part of the paper.

He narrowed his gaze on the words:

My son,

The forest you have entered is a bridge between two worlds, the life you have come to know on earth and the realm of eternal life, the Valley of Spirit & Light. I have brought you here so that you might remember—remember and make a choice—for what lies ahead of you, should you return to the former, will require courage, contain great sorrow, and demand the use of every badge you collect. But again, the choice will be yours. Pay attention. Learn. And remember, my son. Nothing that has ever befallen you is by accident, and I am ever near.

Lord Monoceros

P.S. I chose you on purpose.

A flock of small birds flew overhead, chirping a joyful song, and Braden glanced upward to watch them flutter, glide, and dance in the sky before returning his attention to the missive.

Remember and choose.

Courage, sorrow, badges...

And just like that he remembered everything, each detail in perfect clarity: Kristina offering her heart and her passion, leaving her alone on the couch; waking on the morning of the Millenia Harvest Moon, visiting his family and Conrad;

spending the afternoon and evening with the warriors by the shore, and spinning...falling...traveling. He knew, without a doubt, that Prince Jadon's blood had truly awakened inside him, and that the prince had taken his place on earth—the ancient one had usurped and inhabited Braden's corporeal body...for a reason.

Nothing was random.

And he was here.

In this enchanted forest, standing in front of a tree of light...

Tasked with remembering...collecting...badges?

And ultimately making a choice.

A serene smile curved along the corners of his mouth as he thumbed the parchment again—Lord Monoceros had scribed this missive with his own celestial hand, and he had done it for Braden Bratianu!

For Braden...

Of all vampires.

Holy crap.

An empty leather satchel appeared in Braden's free hand, connected to a long loop of cord, and he instinctively slipped it over his neck and one arm, causing it to fall at his hip, before carefully—and with reverence—folding the missive into a perfectly proportioned square and slipping it into the pouch.

"I'm ready," he said out loud, understanding intuitively that there was much more to come, and time was somehow of the essence.

* * *

Achilles Zahora staggered forward, extending both arms outward to catch his balance.

What the actual hell—where was he?

His breaths were ragged as he sucked in air and spun around

in a wary circle: The ground was cold beneath his bare, exposed feet, his clothing had been replaced by a bearskin loincloth, and smack-dab in the middle of the parched, fruitless woodland stood one lone gigantic tree, blood seeping from the trunk like thick, gooey sap.

Achilles stopped turning.

He drew back his shoulders, raised his chin, and bounded across the cracked, dry ground to get a closer look at it: asymmetric, ancient, and twisted, yet the wide trunk was sturdy and powerful. The copious gnarled branches were covered in ancient foliage, leaves of brittle green, scarlet, and black, and if he listened carefully, he could hear the tree moaning, the sap faintly hissing—it was a literal Tree of Darkness.

And without knowing why—or how—he knew, Achilles instantly understood that he was here to draw sustenance from both the tree and the forest: Somehow, it would make him stronger. Even more defiant...*ready*.

A murder of crows flew overhead, screeching an ear-piercing chorus, and Achilles welcomed the clamor and the discord as he extended his claws, dipped them in the crimson sap, and striped two lines beneath his lower eyelids like war paint. He pressed his bare back against the trunk, slid down to the ground, and extended one leg in front of him, drawing the other knee up as an armrest.

"Whatever the hell this corrupt shit is, I'm here, I'm ready...so *bring it*."

CHAPTER THIRTEEN

DARK MOON VALE

Even as the princesses were occupied at Napolean's compound, leading the Homage Ceremony in the courtyard, and Niko was on the opposite end of the vale, nestled between the thick of the northern forest and the Dark Moon Academy, performing the Rites of Magick, Jankiel Luzanski was in a clearing just west of the hot springs, leading several warriors, *destinies*, and Vampyr families in the Renaissance & Renewal Ceremony, midway through the *circle of drumming*.

He had already woven the necessary ritual bands of light, focused inward, and sharpened his senses, and the rapt audience had already aligned their immortal heartbeats in a single harmonious rhythm: a symphony of pulses, not drumbeats; blood, not drumsticks; inhales and exhales in place of tapping.

Badump-badump.

Thrum-thrum-thrum.

The collective heartbeat of the house of Jadon soared in the clearing.

And that's when Niko interrupted the ceremony: *Wizard*, he

called out on a private, telepathic bandwidth. *Jankiel, are you there?*

Jankiel drew back, losing his focus, and instinctively turned his head toward the north. *Niko, what is it?* It was no small thing to interrupt a sacred ceremony—surely, Niko was midway through a very difficult sequence of rites, himself, evoking solar winds, conjuring magical geysers, and manifesting a contained winter snowstorm—something had to be wrong.

I don't know how else to say this, Niko said, his psychic voice thick with emotion, *but our ancient patriarch lives. Jankiel, Prince Jadon is alive!*

Jankiel staggered backward, and several watchful vampires immediately fixed their eyes upon him: Arielle Silivasi, with little Ryder seated on her lap; Rebecca Lacusta, as she lounged on a blanket beside Jayce Gideon; Rafael and Lorna Dzuna, seated toward the head of the throng; and the Master Warrior Mateo Devera, who had once taught self-defense along with Nathaniel and Jocelyn, the vampire's keen senses instantly alerted.

Stunned by the extraordinary statement, Jankiel's mind went blank—but only for a second—and then it filled with a dozen competing thoughts at once...

How could this be?

Where was Braden—what had happened?

What of the blood in the second vial—the blood Fabian had fed to Achilles?

As a Master Wizard he was intrigued, curious...drawn by the supernatural phenomenon, but as a loyal son in the house of Jadon, he was immediately concerned for his kinsmen, the children, the beloved destined daughters. *Niko, I don't know where to begin,* he murmured. *My mind is so full of questions—what is it you would have me do?*

Yeah, tell me about it, Niko shot back. *Same here, and I still don't have many answers. But this much I know—the prince took possession of Braden's corporeal body in the cove outside Santos' lake house, pretty much the moment the harvest moon rose, and Fabian believes, Prince Jadon agrees, that Prince Jaegar has likely taken over Achilles Zahora.*

Jankiel gasped, and Mateo Devera stood up.

Arielle Nightsong Silivasi set Ryder down beside her.

What are you saying, wizard? Jankiel asked, staring, dumbstruck, out at the crowd.

Napolean does not want to alarm the Vampyr. As of yet, there is no reason to overreact, but needless to say, extreme caution is the name of the game. He wants every male, female, and child in the house of Jadon either safely sequestered inside their homes—wards and alarms fully activated—or gathered in the courtyard at the compound. Niko sighed, then pressed on. *Look, the warriors are spread out all over the vale, and so are the* destinies *and their offspring. As we well know, the Dark Ones are engaged in full-fledged debauchery and wicked blood rites this night, so only the gods know how this moon will turn out. Fabian believes—or maybe he just hopes—the changes will reverse themselves when the harvest moon wanes at 3:34 a.m. If not at 3:34, then at the latest, when the moon fully sets tomorrow morning at 11:46. He believes Braden's soul—his persona—will ultimately return, but of course, he can't make any promises. Same holds true for the house of Jaegar, whatever the hell is going on there. Either way, Napolean wants everyone in one place where they can be protected by the warriors, the sentinels, and if necessary, by him. And blessed Lyra, it goes without saying, Prince Jadon—Prince Jadon!—is with him.*

* * *

Prince Jaegar Demir, in the body of Achilles Zahora, leaned back in Oskar Vadovsky's high-backed leather chair at the head of the esteemed council table and crossed one leg over one knee. He eyed the descendants of his own venerable, ancient line, each one in turn, as the vampires sat obsequiously around the worn limestone tabletop, awaiting the monarch's instructions: Oskar Vadovsky's jaw still hung open; Salvatore, who still flinched at Jaegar's every word and movement, shifted back and forth like a restless child in his seat; Sergei Gervasi, the son of a previous, murdered council member—and kudos to the duplicitous rebels for engineering the coup—kept digging for gold beneath his fingernails; Milano Marandici, with his disturbingly beautiful right profile, brutally scarred left temple, and one missing eye, constantly worried his bottom lip; and Demitri Zeclos, who was apparently missing something else—something far more valuable, situated quite a bit lower—kept tensing his shoulders and wiping his brow.

Ominous torchlight flickered in the darkness, illuminating the craggy, ancient chamber, and silence hung like a phantom in the air as Prince Jaegar carefully considered his options and the Dark Ones' next move.

"Your Majesty..." Oskar breached the silence, his grayish-black eyes cast low. "Do you have any further questions for the council?"

Prince Jaegar studied Oskar's eager, servile expression as well as his submissive body language—though head of the Dark Ones' Council, the vampire dared not show even a hint of offense for being seated in a more lowly position, for giving Prince Jaegar his plush, preeminent chair at the head of the council table. The ancient prince flicked his wrist in a haughty, dismissive gesture. "No," he said bluntly. "I believe I have sufficiently queried the council, and at this juncture, I am quite confident I have the lay of the land." Indeed, Oskar had already shown Prince Jaegar all three levels of the underground structure, the prince was fully acquainted with the Colony Guard, including its newest member, Zeus Dragavei, and the ancient monarch had scanned Achilles Zahora's memories, ad nauseum, making internal note of the most pertinent details.

In addition, Prince Jaegar had spoken at greater length with Salvatore Nistor, and according to that curious object, that strange, enigmatic "cube," it was indeed quite likely that Prince Jadon had reanimated in an immortal vampiric body as well. Yea, Prince Jaegar and the sorcerer were in tacit agreement: Both princes' time in their borrowed bodies was limited at best, the possession was most likely transient, and that meant there was no time to waste. Prince Jaegar had been given a rare opportunity to right what had once gone...so wrong. And at this point, the only thing that mattered to the reanimated prince was making full and efficient use of the auspicious occasion.

While the majority of the house of Jaegar—*his house*—could remain blissfully unaware, free to celebrate the Millenia Harvest Moon, indulging in carnage, debauchery, and bestial pleasures, Prince Jaegar would remain laser-focused on enacting timeless Blood Vengeance on his piteous twin and finishing what he could not accomplish so many centuries past: the ritualistic sacrifice of the most divine, royal progeny of celestial gods and men, his sisters, Ciopori and Vanya.

If possible, he would lure Kristina Silivasi to Achilles' lair, leave her as a gift for the faithful executioner, but such an act of generosity was not his primary focus. He wanted to look, at least once more, into his twin's placid, dark brown eyes. Only this time, he yearned to see pain, anguish, and abject failure reflected back in Prince Jadon's pupils—he wanted to revisit that fateful night in Transylvania when brother had slain brother and prince had murdered prince—and he wanted to change the course of history for all of time immemorial.

He wanted to right what had gone so wrong.

"I shall utilize the Colony Guard as my personal sentry and

militia," he stated, matter-of-factly, "in order to carry out my own private vengeance on those I once held dear. And if"—he shrugged a cocky shoulder—"during this intimate process, I manage—*we manage*—to slay every beating heart of every female *destiny* in the piteous house of Jadon, well, that would be a bonus, to be sure. However, I will not—*I cannot*—allow such petty, infantile fancies to distract me from my aim or thwart my ultimate desire...to circumvent my path. My brother. My sisters. One final sacrifice to the ancient gods. 'Tis all I give five fucks about."

The council sat in silence—clearly, they were still getting accustomed to Jaegar's blunt, yet introspective, personality.

Whatever...

Finally, Oskar Vadovsky rubbed his hands together and leaned forward in his subordinate seat, daring to pierce the silence once more. "It shall be as you wish, Your Majesty, but if I might ask one indulgence, there is something I have long desired to know...to understand." His voice trailed off into the chilly night, and his audacity stirred, then settled, like eddies of snow caught in a sudden gust of wind, all around the council chamber.

Prince Jaegar furrowed his brows and frowned.

Despite the vampire's arrogance, Oskar was indeed a leader... a thinker...one who led the Colony with an iron hand and ruthless authority. He was curious but not to a fault—there seemed to be a method to his madness—and Prince Jaegar had already glimpsed enough of the Dark One's mind to know the question he desired to ask had vexed the vampire for centuries. It would not do to emasculate the authoritarian leader before the very males he would still need to control once the venerable prince was gone.

"What is it, Oskar?" Prince Jaegar asked, summoning the patience to spare five more minutes, placating the council chair.

"Your Highness," Oskar began, speaking in a low, respectful tone, "it has long perplexed me...angered me...nay, *disgusted* and confused me...our inability to walk in the sun, the challenge of propagating our race, bringing sons into the world when we cannot keep a female alive, the challenge of—"

"Get on with it, Oskar."

"Yes. *Yes*, of course. It is written that at the time of the change —at the time of the Curse—the blood of the slain rose up to torment the princes, to curse both you and your twin brother, Jadon, as punishment for sacrificing your females—*our females*— to the point of extinction. It is recorded in the annals that the maiden Jessenia Groza was the last female slain, and her sacrifice —her death—brought the plague upon us. But we now know...you now know...that there were two females yet living, your royal sisters, the daughters of King Sakarias and Queen Jade. I have often wondered why the Blood did not know this, did not *respect* this"—his voice rose in anger—"why the Curse was allowed to go forward."

Once again, Prince Jaegar studied Oskar mindfully, and then he thought, *I really don't have time for this shit.* But he could see why the question would have haunted the councilman over a lifetime, living with the Curse, and it was not that difficult to provide an answer, especially since Prince Jaegar had spent several lifetimes hence, residing in the Valley of Death & Shadows.

"Oskar," Prince Jaegar purred, his voice thick with conviction, "on this earth, where you reside, you only see what is right in front of you. You only hear with your ears, see with your eyes, and feel with your external senses, but there is much more going on in the realm of spirit. Indeed, all that you behold around you is merely thought, manifest as form. It was created—it was done— long before it appeared to your carnal eyes. Quite literally, thoughts are deeds." He sat back and sighed. *How to illustrate this in a more elementary fashion?*

"Imagine this scenario: a marketplace in the village square, where a poor vendor peddles fresh-baked bread from a cart, the first thing every morning. On one particular daybreak, a child born to wealth, privilege, and prone to boredom idly passes by and steals a loaf of bread...for pleasure, but the vendor catches the boy in the act and seizes him by the arm. The boy, in turn, flicks a coin at the vendor's feet, laughs, and strolls along. The child has committed no sin. He has broken no laws. He did not in fact steal the loaf of bread. In truth, he paid a fair coin. Now then, imagine a destitute child who lives in a hovel with his impoverished family. This child also takes a loaf of bread from the merchant's cart, but when the merchant sees him, attempts to seize him, the child wriggles out of his grasp. He runs away with the bread in hand. By law, this child has committed a crime—the second lad is guilty of theft." He paused to let his words sink in, hoping Oskar was following his logic. "Ah, but that is not how it is seen in spirit, you see. In the underworld—yea, in the celestial realms—intention is nine-tenths of the law. The first child set out to sin; he believed wholeheartedly in the crime he was committing; and the theft occurred in spirit long before it occurred in flesh. Whether or not he returned the bread, paid for the loaf, or circumvented the theft is of no matter—he *intended* to steal from the vendor, and he believed it was theft when he did so. His thoughts were his deeds, Oskar. Congruently, the second child was absent of malice. He never intended to steal from the merchant—yea, his hunger drove him to violate the law—but he had no such corrupt intention."

Prince Jaegar sighed; the whole damn tale was making him weary, and he was going way too far out of his way to explain. "Trust me, Dark One," he grunted, "when I and my soldiers slayed Jessenia Groza, we thought she was the last female living; we believed we were sacrificing the final wench to the gods, we absolutely intended to spill her blood in exchange for power and glory, and the Blood judged us accordingly. Our thoughts were our deeds. It is not the same in spirit. It mattered not that Ciopori and Vanya had been sequestered away in the Transylvanian mountains. We believed—*I believed*—that we had sacrificed the very last female, and make no mistake, we relished the iniquity." He sat back and crossed his arms over his chest. "Also," he added, circumspectly, "those bitches were crazy. The Blood. It was twisted. It wanted to curse the men, and Jessenia's sacrifice was all the excuse it needed. The Blood was not inclined to split hairs."

Oskar nodded his head, and the other Dark Ones sucked in air, ostensibly trying to grasp the concept. "So, in this analogy," Oskar said, "my prince, you would be the wealthy child of privilege, and Prince Jadon would be the poor, starving pauper. Do you believe the Blood would have spared Prince Jadon—offered your twin the Four Mercies—even if he had not pleaded his case?"

At this, Prince Jaegar tilted his head to the side, considered the query for a fleeting moment, then tossed back his head and laughed, uproariously. "No," he said with finite conviction. "I don't think you grasp the full picture. My brother, Jadon, was a male, just like myself. And the Blood was well and truly pissed off. Trust me, you had to be there."

Oskar's slate gray-and-black eyes grew darker, and Prince Jaegar knew he finally understood: This was not about some higher theological judgment—right versus wrong, degrees of sin— it was about an age-old struggle between good versus evil...

And evil had corrupted innocence.

With regard to the Blood of the Slain, darkness pierced the light, not the other way around, and Prince Jaegar had been on the side of darkness.

He still was.

They all were.

And that meant, this night—this Millenia Harvest Moon— was a second chance to revisit a primordial battle: to punish

Prince Jadon, the celestial order, and to enact equal vengeance on the Blood itself.

Light was weak.

Goodness was overrated.

And if Prince Jadon was back, in the body of one of his far-removed loyalists, his indirect descendants, then both were likely weak as well.

This time, Prince Jaegar would prevail.

CHAPTER FOURTEEN

THE ENCHANTED FOREST

"Remember and make a choice," Braden whispered, but he had already remembered everything that had happened, at least leading up to arriving in the forest —and nothing transformational had occurred.

At least not yet.

So remember what?

He sat down at the base of the Tree of Light, raked the tips of his fingers through the rich, loose soil, and stared up at the brilliant tricolored foliage. The gold and white leaves began to rustle, making a soft, almost harmonic sound, as if separate voices in a heavenly chorus were singing a pure, organic ballad, and time seemed to stand still...

As he listened...

And tuned in to the enchanted melody.

Closed his eyes.

Aligned his heartbeat.

His thoughts began to drift, as thoughts often do, and he found himself thinking of Kristina: the first time he'd kissed her on Valentine's Day, outside Nachari's brownstone...that time she had appraised him approvingly, from head to toe, when he was wearing his worn leather bomber-jacket and a pair of faded blue jeans—the way she had whispered *"Damn"* beneath her breath—and the proud way she had displayed his gemstone bracelet, showing it off to his mother, Dario, and Conrad...

Her bright blue eyes and her carefree laughter...

The shades of red in her soft, layered curls.

The dozens—no, hundreds—of shoes she collected: azure-blue ankle boots to go with her form-fitting blue and gray pencil skirt, cobalt-blue spikes with thin, dainty ankle straps, to go with her next suede ensemble.

He chuckled softly, relishing the memories.

And then his mind meandered, naturally, to Conrad: *I'm gonna say a prayer of my own for you tonight...my big brother has the stealth of a warrior, the skills of a wizard, and the heartbeat of the house of Jadon in his veins.* How true that statement had become...

A low-hanging branch brushed Braden's right upper arm, and he opened his eyes, turned his head to glance at it. As the ends of the branch curled around his shoulder, like a friend reaching out to reassure a comrade, he absently thought, *how strange*—it should have been unsettling, but it wasn't.

And then the branch disappeared.

The tree was no longer there.

And Braden was standing in a clearing, in a beautiful, plush green meadow on a warm, arid day, in the center of Dark Moon Vale...

"Braden," Nachari Silivasi said softly. "You remember what we discussed, right? For the next thirty days, no matter what, you will return to this meadow, every hour on the hour, *to this exact spot*, and you will reopen this portal. Understood?"

Ah yes, Braden remembered.

Sixteen months past, the Silivasi brothers had slipped

through the portal in order to enter the land of the lycan, the bizarre dimension of Mhier. They had embarked on a terrifying, dangerous journey in the desperate hope of finding and retrieving their father, Keitaro, and Braden, not knowing if or when the brothers would come back, had returned to that spot to reopen the gateway—*every hour on the hour*—dozens and dozens of times, for five straight days.

Following Nachari's instructions to the letter, he had drawn a crude circle on the ground, then placed the bark from a tree in the north and stones from the eastern cliffs in the east. He had emptied a vial of clear water from the Winding Snake River in the south and tossed a chunk of uneven rock from the Red Canyons in the west. With each placement, he had repeated a rhythmic Latin phrase he had heard Nachari speak the first time they had opened the portal, and then he had placed a piece of the lycan's hair in the center of the haphazard circle, careful to bury it just below the surface, exactly as Nachari had shown him.

Though the Silivasis were never there when Braden opened the portal, and everyone in Dark Moon Vale had grown restless, concerned, and even bereft, Braden had not given up. He had opened that damn portal time and again, counted backward from ten to one, then closed it.

Rinse and repeat...

Rinse and repeat.

On some level, he had wanted to prove his worth to the warriors—Marquis and Nachari had trusted him, and all the Silivasis were counting on the acolyte's faithful allegiance to ensure their safe return to the vale. On another, more personal level, it had simply been Braden's...duty.

He was a male in the house of Jadon—displaying honor was not something special.

But more than that—more than any of it—he had loved

Nachari like a brother, and opening that portal, day after day, hour after hour, had been Braden's special way of showing it.

The meadow faded, the memory dimmed, and Braden shook his head, coming back to the Enchanted Forest and the Tree of Light behind him. He exhaled slowly, and the curled end of the branch released his shoulder.

Remember and make a choice...

"I remember," Braden said, "but what is the choice? Is there something I need to do to prove my honor—or my loyalty—once again, to the Silivasis?" His forehead creased as he frowned. "I don't get it."

And just like that, the ground in front of him began to glow with a golden light, and slowly, yet distinctly, two silver oblong discs appeared in front of him, the edges filling in before the centers. Braden bent to one knee and leaned over to study them, even as the branch of the tree, the limb that had just cradled his shoulder, extended in length, like a wiry arm with elongated kindling for fingers.

The forefinger burst into flames, a gold-and-purple blazing stylus, and began to scribe letters on the first of the two discs, until at last, it had written the word *patience*. It moved seamlessly, like flowing water, to the second of the silver plates and inscribed the word *kindness* over the silver.

And that's when Braden got it.

It was suddenly so clear...so obvious.

These discs were his badges, and he had collected each of them, one choice at a time.

Tears filled his eyes, and he blinked to remove them: All those long days, those fear-filled nights, wanting so desperately to prove himself—praying that the Silivasis would return—had not been an exercise in futility, nor had it been about duty or proving his worth as a vampire. Every hour on the hour—day after day— had been orchestrated and necessary for the lessons to be learned.

The strongest swords were forged in fire, and the gods had forged *patience* in Braden's character—they had cemented *kindness* deep in his heart. And these attributes, these hard-earned characteristics, were badges he would carry for the rest of his life, whether on earth or in the spirit world.

He tapped the top of each forged disc, testing the temperature with his forefinger, then scooped them up, one at a time, and held them up to the light of the tree, to get a better look.

Beautiful.

Perfect.

His heart swelled with pride and gratitude, and then he silently slipped the badges into his pouch and cinched it shut with reverence. "I remember," he whispered softly. "I get it now."

And in time—with patience—he would come to understand the elusive...*choice* he would need to make.

CHAPTER FIFTEEN

DARK MOON VALE

K ristina stood toward the outskirts of the courtyard, once again clasping her wrist and Braden's bracelet, only at this point, she absently held both against her heart. She was shrouded in the pale haze of a dangling tree lantern, watching the mesmerizing, eloquent Homage Ceremony, when all at once, the peaceful milieu exploded with frantic activity,

It was already 11 p.m.

The ceremony was only half over, yet males and females, warriors and *destinies*, young and old vampires from the house of Jadon began to appear in the outdoor square, joining the service from every region of the valley: First came Jankiel's audience from the *circle of drumming*, then Niko's attendants from the Rites of Magick, and from what Kristina could tell, or overhear, many families who had otherwise been at home, performing their own Rites of Peace, Prosperity, & Protection, had also material-ized at Napolean's compound.

Many simply shimmered into view.

Still others, especially those with children, came in their cars and SUVs—one by one, two by two, or family by family—all flowing into the lantern-lit yard, gathering in chaotic, chattering circles, and ushering the children—*all of the children*—swiftly into Napolean's manse. Apparently, they were to be watched by the queen's nanny and a handful of *destinies*—Jocelyn, Gwen, Brooke, and Tiffany—as well as two of the warriors, Mateo Devera and Tyce Tanase, the latter being one of Braden's closest friends at the local Academy, a vampire no older than Bray.

Dear gods, what is happening? Kristina wondered.

She strained to hear more of the chatter—more of Napolean's orders...

Something about Prince Jadon!

Something about protection in numbers.

A passing murmur about the Dark Ones—*holy shit!*

Where the hell was Braden?

The Millenia Harvest Moon shone high in the sky, its orange-and red-tinged light illuminating the pavilions as Kristina again scanned the furthest rotunda, narrowing her gaze on Keitaro Silivasi. He was speaking attentively with Aric Zander, Kristos Nastase, Dario Bratianu, and Arielle Nightsong, while Conrad, Lily, Colette, Zayda, and Natalia hung back—little Zeri and Shelbie Ryder were already inside the house.

And *gods have mercy*—Arielle had her bow and quiver!

What the hell was going on?

Kristina knew she should've made a beeline across the courtyard to Keitaro's pavilion—asked her adopted father what had happened to Braden, what was happening in the vale—but she backed further into the shadows instead, her fear warring with regret, her concern warring with her shame...

In truth, she didn't want to know—

Not yet!

If Braden was gone...

If something horrible had happened...

She wasn't ready to deal with the possibility of never seeing Bray again.

She stomped her foot against the ground in frustration, dirtying the toe of her high-heeled pump against a divot filled with pine needles, and fought against an onslaught of tears: How many times had she walked beside Braden through the upper halls of the casino, the top few floors which housed the penthouse apartments? How many times had they hung out casually, outside Nachari's brownstone, on their way into town to go shopping, or while exploring a new path through the forest...a scenic trail around one of the valley's crystal lakes—*just once*, why hadn't she taken his hand?

His hand!

How hard would that have been?

How improper or inappropriate was it, just to hold someone's hand?

How many times had Braden stood inside her walk-in closet, matching her shoes to her skirts like a professional fashion designer. She could have flirted, she could have kissed him—hell, they could have fooled around *just a little* on the closet floor.

They didn't have to go...that far.

She could've waited for Bray to come of age, while still acknowledging the strong, handsome, *loyal* male he was becoming. The best friend she had ever had. She could've wrestled her own inner demons—*told him she didn't know how to love!*—told him she had scars that no one ever saw or knew about.

She could have told him she believed he was destined for greatness...

To become one of the greatest warriors or wizards—maybe both—the house of Jadon had ever known, that he would one day become so powerful, so exceptional...so gorgeous...that she believed she would no longer turn his head. And she could have admitted that when she looked into his burnt sienna eyes, and those golden pupils stared back at her, they were so damn beautiful—*so damn amazing*—that her heart hurt just to look at him. She could have at least tried to explain that the situation, being promised to each other by Napolean, scared her shitless because she knew, deep down inside where there were no Band-Aids, that one day, Braden would see all of her too, and he would know—he would find out—that she was both damaged and unworthy.

Braden was infinitely kind and endlessly patient—she could have told him the *truth*.

He would have understood.

And now, she might never have the chance.

Why the hell was half the house of Jadon gathering at Napolean's manse, in the courtyard? Why did Arielle need her bow and quiver? And why were the Vampyr whispering about Prince Jadon, when Braden was the one who had swallowed the prince's blood? *Oh gods*...her chest ached, and she felt...ashamed.

"Kristina..."

She heard her name and she spun around.

"Kristina Riley Silivasi?"

It was spoken more as a question than a familiar shout-out, and the hairs on her arms stood up. "Who's there?" she called into the darkness, peering behind the base of a large, leaning ponderosa pine. Her head began to tingle, the tightness matching the ache in her chest, almost as if her thoughts were being extracted and replaced with cotton, and her entire body felt suddenly weak...limp...as if it had just been drained of energy. Kristina took a cautious, staggered step back. "Who's there!" she demanded.

A tall male, maybe six feet even, stepped out from behind the tree, his stark onyx eyes as dark as midnight, his mouth curved into a wicked, self-satisfied smirk. "Nice to meet you...*Red*."

Her stomach lurched, and her eyes shot immediately to his hair—*the vampires in the courtyard had been whispering about*

Dark Ones!—but it was oddly shrouded, eclipsed like a mirage in the ponderosa's branches, and Kristina couldn't make out any colors. "Do I know you?" *Keitaro!* the voice inside her head clamored loudly. *Call out to Keitaro...now!*

"Shh," the male whispered. "You don't want to do that. Don't be afraid, just listen to my voice."

The compulsion in his tone was thick as honey, and Kristina shook her head in an effort to break the spell. She was Vampyr now. That shouldn't work on her so easily. She had to keep her wits about her...try to push him out of her mind. "There are a dozen warriors in this courtyard!" she warned him. "And they will all come running if I call."

"But you aren't going to do that," he purred.

Shit.

His voice was so...alluring.

And there was something dark, ancient, and irrefutable in his tone, like he commanded the entire night sky: the canvas, the stars, and the Millenia Harvest Moon. Why couldn't anyone else see him? Hear him? And what did he want with Kristina?

"Come to me. Quickly." He held out his hand.

Kristina drew back and shivered.

She tried to cry out, but her voice was constricted.

No way! she thought, but she couldn't say it—this could not be happening, not right here in Napolean's courtyard...not with half the house of Jadon a stone's throw away.

"Come to me, Kristina. Take my hand, Princess Red."

Princess Red?

Oh, fuck!

Achilles Zahora...

But this male was a foot too short—

Before she could process this new information, figure out what was happening, and reason her way out of it—come up with a plan—she picked up one foot, placed it in front of the other, and reached for the Dark One's hand.

* * *

How perfect was this?

How timely and fortuitous!

Having made his decision to enact timeless vengeance and having directed the Colony Guard on how to best serve him, Prince Jaegar Demir had set out on a reconnaissance mission of sorts: to survey the valley, learn more of his brother, and alas, to find his long-lost sisters.

The latter had been fairly easy as Oskar, Salvatore, and half the house of Jaegar knew exactly what the sons of Jadon were doing for the Millenia Harvest Moon celebration. Among several trite, predictable rites and ceremonies, they were offering homage to the gods, right out in the open, in the courtyard of that ten-year-old boy who had eluded being murdered by Ravi Apostu over two and a half millennia past.

Napolean Mondragon...

Go figure.

Needless to say, Prince Jaegar and his Guard had rendered their bodies invisible, and they had flown, swift as the wind, silent as the night, cloaked in the scent and energy of the native vegetation and wildlife, courtesy of Salvatore's sorcery. The prince had landed just outside the courtyard's perimeter—*go big or go home,* a phrase borrowed from Achilles' vernacular—blending his form and anima behind a thick, pyramidal pine tree. And wouldn't you know it, less than five feet away stood a captivating, pretty redhead in soft, sheer stockings, shoes placed on stilts, a form-fitting kilt—the current word was *skirt*—and an ivory, long-sleeved tunic, a *shirt* made of something akin to wool that hugged her breasts and waist like a bodice. She stood deliberately apart from the fray, surveying the courtyard and eavesdropping on conversations, while hiding like a fox in the brush, masked in lantern light and obscured in shadows.

The obfuscation made no difference.

The moment she tilted her head and craned her neck in order to peer inside a distant structure, she revealed her profile, and Prince Jaegar recognized her...instantly.

"Kristina..." He tried her name on his tongue, and she whirled around like a frightened rabbit. *Oh yes*, he was correct in his identification. "Kristina Riley Silivasi?"

"Who's there?" she had called into the darkness, and Jaegar had immediately assessed the situation like a seasoned foot soldier, like a strategic prince, like an ancient, instinctive vampire. He had delved into her mind, quickly extracted both thoughts and memories. She was distracted by musings and plagued with worry...with regret...over a boy named Braden, a boy who had consumed a vial of blood preserved by Fabian Antonescu and given to the lad without his knowledge.

Oh...

Dark lords.

This impossible rebirth—this enigmatic, extraordinary phenomenon—had been orchestrated by the ancient High Mage, starting as far back as 799 BC: So Jadon had given Fabian a vial of his blood before the mage had sailed to the New World with their sisters...before that fateful night in the Transylvanian mountains? *Well, bully for him!* And the wily wizard had also stolen a second vial, long before the Curse had been enacted, from King Sakarias' castle apothecary. *You seditious little devil...*

Prince Jaegar had never been dull of wit or lacking reason, and he understood, instinctively, all that had happened, who had swallowed the second vial—Achilles Zahora, of course. And in truth, if he were being fair, the ancient mage's actions made sense: The universe always demanded balance, and while Prince

Jaegar did not know the when, where, or why of the whole sordid occurrence, he frankly didn't give a shit.

It was no longer relevant at this juncture.

So who cared?

They were both here now—they had both been reanimated— Prince Jaegar and Prince Jadon were alive and well and free to move about a glorious new world. They were legends, living patriarchs, the leaders of two thriving societies, each created by their surviving successors in a valley called Dark Moon Vale.

Shiiiiit.

This is wild...

They were gods among men—well, gods among vampires.

No sooner had he made the connection between the past and the present than he noticed his sisters' fingerprints—they were clear and unmistakable, prominent in fact, and littered all over Kristina's body in the fashion of a spell-cast ward.

Delightful, he had smirked inwardly.

So the girls were still practicing the original, celestial magick, and they had coated this female in protection, some sort of energetic snare, set to snap the moment she felt dread or fear, set to alert a family of vampires—and sentinels—with knowledge or Kristina's prior dealings with Achilles and, far more important, of her exact position in the valley.

Jaegar had rolled his eyes and sneered.

He had spent millennia in the Valley of Death & Shadows— the silly ward was child's play to him. He had unraveled it in under a minute.

"Who's there?" she'd repeated, taking a cautious step back.

Time to play, he'd thought. "Nice to meet you...*Red.*"

To her credit, her eyes had shot directly to his hair—she was trying to discern his allegiance, *his house*—a Dark One, marked by the Blood at the Curse, or a son of Jadon, spared from the red- and-black banded coloring?

Jaegar had shrouded his hair in darkness.

"Do I know you?" she'd asked, once again being crafty—she'd intended to call out to a warrior named Keitaro. *Not gonna happen...*

He had blocked all transmissions.

"Shh," he'd cajoled, "you don't want to do that." He had laced his tone in overwhelming compulsion. "Don't be afraid, just listen to my voice."

"There are a dozen warriors in this courtyard, and they will all come running if I call."

"But you aren't going to do that," he'd countered. "Come to me. Quickly." He had held out his hand, even as he had constricted her vocal cords. She had drawn back, her skin growing pale, her entire body had quivered, and her eyes had reflected her defeat. "Come to me, Kristina. Take my hand, Princess Red."

And that was the second she had gotten it.

Yeah, little lady—you are summarily screwed.

Only, the poor insecure woman—no, the abused broken child —was just naive enough to think she had been taken by Achilles Zahora.

"Hah!" He grasped her hand, spat on the ground, then encircled her slender, trembling shoulders. "Welcome to *my* house," he whispered as he dragged her backward, further into the shadows. "Zeus!" he barked, glaring into the darkness, knowing the veiled soldier was close by. "Take her back to Achilles' lair, lock her inside, then rejoin my entourage. I still have a family reunion to attend to."

CHAPTER SIXTEEN

THE VALLEY OF DEATH & SHADOWS

I n the deepest bowels of the underworld, the dark lord Soreconom, twin energy to the celestial god Monoceros, watched through the reflection of a boiling cauldron as one of his favorite vampires, Achilles Zahora, sprawled beneath the Tree of Darkness in one of the many bridges between worlds, the Forest of Evil, eager to eat from the dark tree's fruit.

As noxious gases swirled from the cauldron, wafting to Lord Soreconom's nostrils, he considered the facts and this rare opportunity—after all, Achilles was neither alive, nor dead, in this predetermined moment. Rather, he had ceded his body to Prince Jaegar for a time, and Soreconom intended to make good use of the interlude. To be sure, Achilles Zahora was already a masterpiece, born of rage and reared in darkness. He possessed every attribute of a true, minacious soul: cruelty and envy; arrogance and deceit; dishonor, self-absorption, and a vile, quick temper. He didn't just dole out punishment or enact vengeance with a fury—he kept a detailed, long-lasting record of anyone who had ever wronged him, and he positively delighted in retribution and evil.

He would never love.

He would never show true kindness.

His soul was as murky as the sap in that tree.

And he was right about Kristina Silivasi, with one important exception—the Dark Ones were cursed, down to the very last male—they were in fact "damned to father twin sons by human hosts who would die wretchedly upon giving birth, and the firstborn of the first set would forever be required as a sacrifice of atonement for the sins of their forefathers." In other words, Kristina was no longer a *human* host—she could indeed bear children without dying wretchedly upon giving birth. Only, unlike Braden Bratianu, who was born of man, then later sired into vampirism, Achilles was a true, full-blooded vampire, born of a son who was the son of another, on and on...ad nauseum.

He could not circumvent the Curse.

His children would be born as twin *sons* of darkness, and like any other male in the house of Jaegar, he would be required to sacrifice the firstborn of the first set. Indeed, the only difference would be the eternal life of Kristina, bearing son after son...after son.

In perpetuity...

Soreconom absently stroked the gnarled antler protruding from the center of his forehead. It wasn't quite the magnificent horn Lord Monoceros, the Unicorn, could don at will, but it was far more fitting for a deity of the underworld.

He turned his attention back to the cauldron—time to stir things up a bit.

Yes, Achilles would grow angry and rebellious over time, once he realized he could not provide immortal females for the house of Jaegar, females to distribute, use as chattel, and ravage. He could not proliferate the species with the redhead. And he would eventually grow tired of her endless existence and mayhap snap her skinny neck, but before then...until then...she could magnify and multiply the best of the best: Kristina would give Achilles numerous, exceptional offspring.

And that's why Lord Soreconom had chosen to step in.

Well, that, and his utter disgust for the celestial regions and Lord Monoceros.

That, and the fact that two could play this game, two pantheons, that is: If the celestial gods thought they could play chess with Braden, well then, *game on*—Soreconom would gladly move his pawn, Achilles, forward across the board. And luckily for the dark lord, Achilles did not require...a whole lot of nudging. A little shoring up here, a little influence there—ratchet up the cruelty and envy; cement the arrogance and deceit; pour a little gasoline on the fires of dishonor, selfishness, and temper; and stoke the vengeance, fury, and evil—give him more of what he already possessed.

Make him more of what he already is...

Soreconom dipped his hand in the cauldron and swirled it around in circles, groaning as his flesh melted off his bones—it would grow back the moment he withdrew it—and he conjured a female siren with curly red hair, bright blue eyes, and a supple, beckoning body. She looked enough like Kristina to entice The Executioner but not enough to satisfy his yearning...his longing... to command, possess, and multiply his seed.

And so, *envy* would grow.

Followed shortly thereafter by grossly enhanced cruelty.

Hell, Achilles Zahora would take the conjured female beneath the Tree of Darkness in every bestial manner imaginable, until he had finally had his fill. He would savage her body, drink her blood—he might even break her fragile bones—until at last, she perished beneath him. And the desire for the real thing, for Kristina Silivasi—Achilles' envy of Braden and the house of Jadon—would grow, along with the Dark One's savagery.

Yes, Soreconom would strengthen each vice, one at a time,

each iniquity in turn, until this singular dark vampire was even *more* of a masterpiece. And the dark lord was free to do so, at will, to pour his powers upon the earth or the forest of evil, to drench the cosmos, atmosphere, and even the soil with sin. He was free to drench Dark Moon Vale—and this bridge between worlds— due to the rarest of omens, occurring this night...the Millenia Harvest Moon.

CHAPTER SEVENTEEN

DARK MOON VALE

wiser male, a younger male, a male who had not lived —and died—over 2,800 years ago might have exercised more caution.

But Prince Jaegar Demir was not that male.

Clad in his familiar ancient clothing—a cinched pair of trousers, high leather boots, and a long-sleeved tunic with ruffled sleeves and girded wrist cuffs—he once again stepped boldly into the courtyard from behind the pyramidal pine tree. Only this time, he was not stalking a redhead.

He was strolling toward center stage...

Stalking his ancient sisters.

His thick, wavy, raven black-and-red hair cascaded about his shoulders as he prowled forward with all the stealth, grace, and confidence of a jungle cat, a predator...a minacious ancient monarch. And his entourage—Silas Slovinsky, Nuri Bolasek, Falcon Zvara, and Zeus Dragavei, who had already returned from depositing Kristina in Achilles' lair—were close behind him in a loose semicircle, still invisible and still cloaked in the energy and scent of the native flora and fauna.

Jaegar knew the warriors from the house of Jadon would spot him immediately, but honestly, he didn't give a shit. The immediate element of surprise was half the battle, and no one in this courtyard could match his ageless skill, his unconscionable savagery, or his awesome power.

Ciopori was the first to see him, and Vanya, maybe a half second later.

The eldest of Jaegar's two royal sisters swept her waist-length, midnight-black hair behind one shoulder in an absent yet defiant gesture and trained her golden gaze directly upon him. Vanya crossed to the front of the stage without hesitation and began descending the makeshift staircase, newly constructed for the festive occasion, her pale-rose eyes ablaze with fury. "You bastard," she practically snarled.

They were walking right toward him.

Could this get any better?

Ciopori halted about five yards away and extended a braced arm in front of Vanya's chest to stop her. "After all these years, all these centuries..." Her voice trailed off in disgust and disbelief.

"Back from the dead, dear brother?" Vanya goaded.

Prince Jaegar declined his head in a mockery of a male curtsy, an archaic gesture of respect to the monarchy. "You didn't think I would let you get away?" he countered.

Ciopori let out a quiet, drawn-out hiss, the air passing over her lips like venom. "Be it known, you vile creature, that we did get away. We escaped the castle, and we escaped Romania. We escaped you and your depraved, soulless army of failures. For that is what you are, Jaegar, what you have always been: a failure, a nothing, a bygone relic of triviality and irrelevance."

"We have children," Vanya added, her nostrils twitching in anger. "Children and mates, an entire life here in this valley. And we still practice the ancient magick; we are able to share it with our people. You destroyed nothing but yourself, even as you condemned your followers for eternity. How was the Valley of Death & Shadows? Were you irrelevant there as well?"

Prince Jaegar smiled, even as his gums began to throb, and his fangs descended in his mouth. How bold, how arrogant—so the girls had grown up? The haughty, self-righteous wenches! He released his claws, took an angry stride forward, and that's when the warriors appeared in front of him, looming like a stone-and-mortar fortress between Jaegar and his sisters.

According to Achilles' memories, to the left, now blocking Ciopori, stood Marquis Silivasi, his right hand cloaked and fisted in an ancient, well-worn cestus. His brothers, Nathaniel and Kagen, the former wielding a razor-sharp stiletto with a hand-crafted grip, the latter flashing only a calm yet dangerous, cagey smile, swiftly filled in the space between Jaegar and his eldest sister. And hackles raised, front paws forward, an enormous black panther also crouched in front of her, head low, ears back, forest-green eyes trained on Jaegar, alert and ready to pounce.

Ah yes, Nachari Silivasi...

The wizard.

To the right, surrounding Vanya, were all three Olaru brothers, Santos, Ramsey, and Saxson, an iron stake, a three-pronged, barbed trident, and a medieval axe in their hands. And then there was Saber Alexiares, menacing toward the fore, every muscle in his chest and arms twitching from bloodlust...and the desire to strike.

Prince Jaegar glared at Saber with loathing—this male had once been a member of Prince Jaegar's house, the traitor, the infidel, the weak, spineless bastard. He wanted to kill Saber most of all. "So," he carped, eyeing each warrior in turn. "This is what you bring me to contend with?" He glanced over his left shoulder, and then his right, remaining motionless, proud, and defiant as Silas, Nuri, Falcon, and Zeus revealed their presence and flashed into view.

"Prince Jaegar." A deep, sonorous, commanding tone of voice.

The prince's head snapped forward, dead center, as Napolean Mondragon flanked the black panther, took a brazen step forward to stand directly before Jaegar, and glowed from head to toe with a burnished, sizzling orange-and-red light. "Move one inch closer to these women. I dare you—no, I *beg you.*"

Prince Jaegar studied him more closely, taking the king's full measure...

Dark lords, the mighty vampire was channeling the celestial bodies—*nay, the very miasma of the sun*—even in the thick of night, and he was holding his palms forward, all ten fingers splayed, the tips pointed at Jaegar and the Dark Ones. He was ready to cremate the males where they stood, in spite of the fact that he would also scorch—and destroy—his beloved valley. Perhaps his beloved followers.

Interesting.

Brilliant.

This little boy from the indigenous village...

"You!" Jaegar spat the word. "The child who changed the course of history without lifting a single finger, without knowing what he did." Napolean did not flinch or look away, and Prince Jaegar chuckled haughtily. "My High Priest, Ravi Apostu; he had visions about a ten-year-old child, several days before the Curse. At the time, he told no one; yet and still, he was determined to extinguish your life." He fixed his gaze on the brothers and the panther perched in front of Ciopori. "Only your ancestor, Timaos Silivasi, treacherous as he was, convinced me that he'd had a change of heart, that he was loyal to my line and my cause, just long enough to slay the priest, before once again pledging loyalty to my brother, Jadon. It was all for you, Napolean." He glanced upward at the red-tinged moon, then back at the formidable king. "To save the child pauper who would one day be a monarch. You see, what is hidden in life is revealed in death: each act, each thought, each intention. So much orchestration on behalf of one inferior lineage." He shrugged a cocky shoulder in contemptuous dismissal. "I see now that the gods chose well but not well enough, dear king. Not well enough."

He held his own hands outward, palms facing the bowels of the earth, to draw symbolic energy from the dark lords of the underworld and power from the Millenia Harvest Moon. "You are not the only male of great prowess," he said, as thick, dark vapor coalesced around his fingers. "You are not the only remnant from the Old World in this courtyard." The vapor began to harden like cement, and Prince Jaegar raised his arms. "Release your power, dear king, and it will strike a wall of darkness, ricochet off, and incinerate every soul in this courtyard, including your own. You will destroy your beloved valley, every heart in the house of Jadon, as well as every innocent human inhabitant." He reached, once again, into Achilles' memories to find a more apt vernacular. "You don't have to take my word for it: If you're feeling froggy, *leap!*"

Napolean stared at Prince Jaegar's hands, studying the mystical, thickening vapor. "Fabian?" he whispered under his breath, and the ancient High Mage appeared beside him.

"Yes, he speaks the truth," Fabian said bluntly.

Prince Jaegar's breath left his body as he regarded the latest newcomer: burnt copper eyes rimmed in black and shaped like graceful almonds; long, layered, golden bronze hair and perfectly symmetrical features: a powerful physique, fit for a god, chiseled as if animated from a statue.

"*Nanaşule.*" Jaegar breathed the word, recalling his sisters' pet name for the male. "Fabian Antonescu, son of Fortino, child of Koryn Anne, High Mage to my father, King Sakarias."

"Yes, Prince Jaegar, one and the same."

Prince Jaegar blinked three times; then his mouth turned down in a scowl. "I see you served my brother well, but you sure as shit made a mess of things, didn't you? Vials of blood and all that. What the actual fuck were you thinking?"

"There is nothing for you here, Prince Jaegar," Fabian said with authority. "Go back to the Colony, enjoy this night with your progeny, mingle with the Dark Ones until the harvest moon wanes. You will not procure your sisters. You will not sacrifice another female. You will not complete what you failed at, so long ago in antiquity. The house of Jadon will leave you unmolested if you return to your own for the duration of the millennium moon."

"I see," Prince Jaegar mocked. "You will leave me unmolested —*you*, and what army?" He glared at Marquis, whose shoulders tightened. "Him?" He turned his gaze on Saber, who was gutturally snarling. "Or him?" He swept one hand forward, gesturing toward Ramsey and the other...*sentinels*...before placing it back, palms down, in front of him. "Or these ragtag warriors and so-called guardians?" Now he was just being deliberately provocative. "Will you protect Kristina Riley Silivasi?" His top lip turned up in a menacing snicker. "Oh yes, too late—we already have her. She is resting comfortably in a colony lair. You didn't think I would over-look the redhead, did you? Not with her intimate relationship to Braden." He paused to let the boy's name settle in their ears. "Yes, Braden Bratianu; shall we talk about the body my twin has taken over? Jadon *has* inhabited Braden's body, has he not?" The prince was looking for a signal, anything—a twitch, a sideways glance, any type of tell which might confirm the proffered information—but it honestly didn't matter. He had already put the pieces together. Higher reasoning was never one of Prince Jaegar's weaknesses.

"What's happened to Braden?" he heard a female murmur in angst, somewhere off to the right in the background, from the cover of a distant pavilion, and the rapid spike in the female's heart rate, as well as her preternatural hearing, her palpable maternal energy, told Prince Jaegar everything he needed to know.

Hmm.

Such information was golden.

Ripe in the moment...

So, the female was both a *destiny* in the house of Jadon and the vampire—the matron—who brought Braden into the world.

"What have you done with Kristina!" Ciopori demanded, recapturing Prince Jaegar's attention. In her ire and dismay, she elbowed her way forward, edging her body beyond Marquis' huge shoulder, and she was immediately shoved back by his large, unsheathed hand, his eyes flashing crimson with terror, rage, and overwhelming possessiveness.

Huh...

So Marquis was Ciopori's mate...

Good to know.

"I tell you what," Prince Jaegar snarled, "come back with me to the Colony, dear sister, and all this will end right here, right now. I will even leave Vanya alone...for the moment. Correction, I shall leave her *unmolested.*"

"Fuck you!" Vanya retorted, lashing out from behind the protection of Saber's shoulder. *Yes, of course, these two were mated as well.* "Your magick against ours; we're right here and willing. And unlike that night you came for us in the castle, we are no longer young, naïve, or helpless maidens!"

"Tsk-tsk," Jaegar warned her. "You were never that. But now, as then, you should listen to *Nanaşule.* If we all behave neatly, retreat to our separate houses, we might all remain unmolested, Vanya." He linked both hands behind his back and flashed his canines, while emitting an audible snarl. "But as for giving up entirely—neither procuring my sisters, nor sacrificing another female—I'm sorry, but I'm afraid I cannot do that."

His chest rose.

His shoulders fell back.

And he raised his chin in rebellious derision.

Then he unlinked his hands, slowly brought them forward, and held up the trophy he had just acquired, before setting the blood-drenched organ on fire: the still-beating heart of a female *destiny*, the one who had cried out in concern for her son. He quickly scanned Achilles' memories—*ah yes, the matron, Lily Bratianu*, her heart emblazoned in his hand and dangling before the milieu.

No one had even seen him retrieve it.

Nay, he had moved faster than the speed of light, swifter than the barrier of sound—not one warrior in the piteous courtyard had watched him grasp the female by the neck, encircle her shoulder with a steadying arm, or retrieve her heart through the center of her back. Not one had heard, sensed, or suspected a thing when he had just as swiftly set the organ on fire so that none might bring the wench back to life.

It had all taken place in under a second.

Ciopori and Vanya gasped, even as the males looked around in disarray.

And off in the distance, in that same, far pavilion, a female's body slumped to the ground, hitting the planks of the wooden platform with a thud. A boy, perhaps a teenager—no more than twelve or thirteen summers—cried out in shock and anguish, and another female shouted, "It's Lily! Lily Bratianu!"

Prince Jaegar chuckled. "No," he reiterated, still holding what was left of the incinerated heart, "I'm afraid I cannot do that. And as for your magick, it is no match for my savagery. The only reason you are still standing, dear Vanya..." He locked eyes with his younger sister and peered into her soul, glorying in the shock, fear, and agonized regret he found swirling around in her anima. "The only reason you still live," he repeated, "is because *if* I kill you...*when* I kill you...I will take my time and relish the pleasure."

Three things happened at once.

A male in the affected pavilion roared like a wounded lion in an unmistakable challenge to battle and Blood Vengeance, the black panther pounced, and Saber Alexiares well and truly lost his shit, the latter leaping over two other sentinels in order to get to Jaegar.

Prince Jaegar fell backward, onto the ground, raised his forearm, and tried to block the panther. The panther bit down, snapped Jaegar's radius, and then, frothing, snarling, and whipping its head from side to side, it tugged at the broken limb in a feral attempt to yank the arm out of its socket.

Still, Prince Jaegar kept his wits about him.

He wrestled with the wild cat while deftly dividing his attention: He watched through his peripheral vision as Nuri Bolasek intercepted the female's mate, the wounded lion from the pavilion, the Dark One's albino skin glistening in the moonlight, and he threw up both feet, even as he continued to fight the panther, in a quick, harsh thrust—a desperate, extended leg press— stomping Saber in the chest before the vampire could eviscerate his jugular.

Holy shit; this was wild!

The ensuing tussle on the ground was like a ball of ferocious wild snakes: striking, siphoning, curling around one another, in order to gain greater advantage, and the earth and sky opened up with equal ferocity and fury. Lightning struck the ground three times in rapid, earth-shaking succession. Hail the size of cannon balls began to pelt the courtyard. And the land beneath the vampires began to shake, rumble, and tremble, threatening to

split open in a giant fissure, as a consequence of so much tumul-
tuous energy...too much charged emotion.

Ciopori screamed as Silas and Falcon tried to seize her.

Silas' face exploded as Marquis unleashed his fury,
pommeling the Dark One between the eyes, over and over—*and
over*—wielding his brutish cestus like a jackhammer, brutalizing
bone, stripping flesh, and sending the Dark One's nose ring scat-
tering across the quaking forest into the widening, open fissure.

And the sentinel called Ramsey cut Falcon's head clean off
with one brutal stab and swipe of his trident.

Shiiiit.

Prince Jaegar was as aroused as he was worried, and then
dozens of Dark Ones appeared in the courtyard. The king,
Napolean, flanked by Saxson, Santos, Nathaniel, and Kagen,
prepared to take them on, one by one, all night if necessary, even
as Fabian, Niko, Jankiel, and the princesses began to chant a
powerful spell, heavily laced in Latin.

Then, "Stop!"

Prince Jadon's mighty roar rolled out like thunder, snapping
nearby tree limbs and crackling through the valley. "Not here!
Not now!" He stood atop the center dais and raised both hands in
the air, fingertips pointed toward the heavens, and he did not look
a thing like Braden Bratianu—he must have asked Fabian to
restore the illusion of his former appearance, much like Jaegar
had requested of Salvatore. Jadon whispered a prayer in the
ancient tongue, beseeching the celestial beings who were free this
night to drench the earth with their power, and a multicolored
dome encased the courtyard.

Lightning ceased to strike.

Hail stopped falling.

The broadening gap, the fissure in the earth, knit back
together, and the ground began to settle beneath them.

"Not here," Prince Jadon repeated in a much nobler voice.

"Not now. Brother against brother. Prince against prince. Vampire against vampire, so the legions might live. For all our descendants, for both our houses, for all the Millenia Harvest Moons and battles yet to come—for the fate of one cursed and one honorable species—brother against brother, winner take all." He paused for the space of two heartbeats and added: *"Lasa pe cei puternici sa mosteneasca pamantul."*

Prince Jaegar's ears perked up.

Let the mighty inherit the earth...

Prince Jaegar favored his tattered arm, disentangled himself from the various vampires on the ground, and stood to his full, proud height, even as the warriors and *destinies* around him instinctively dropped to one knee, and the soldiers from the house of Jaegar stood, equally entranced, gawking at the dais.

Nonetheless, the house of Jaegar did not kneel.

They dared not show deference to a traitorous monarch, no matter how ancient, no matter how legendary.

"Brother against brother?" Prince Jaegar tested his voice. He braced his broken arm against his side and stuffed the pain of numerous lacerations, bruised organs, and hanging strips of flesh out of his mind. He buried it somewhere deep—*this was a time to focus.* "Winner take all?" Prince Jaegar repeated. "Be specific; *all what?*"

Prince Jadon frowned, and his dark brown eyes grew murky with tension and disdain. "What is it you most want, my wicked brother? What could possibly assuage your carnal soul, even now, after all these centuries?"

Prince Jaegar smirked and took several cautious steps away from Napolean's warriors. "The redhead, Kristina Silivasi, and my sisters, of course," he said candidly. "All I wish is to finish what I started. I want to defeat you, once and for all, and I want to complete a true, final sacrifice."

"Fuck no!" Saber Alexiares snarled.

"Not gonna happen," Marquis Silivasi barked.

"Have to go through me first," Napolean Mondragon hissed.

"*Warrior*," Ciopori entreated, reaching for Marquis' hand. "Listen...just listen."

Vanya placed her hand on Saber's shoulder and nodded in assent.

"What say you, brother?" Prince Jaegar called out, loud enough for all to hear him.

Prince Jadon's eyes fixed, for the very first time, on the two enchanting ancient females standing in the center of the courtyard, and if Jaegar's own vision had not been clouded by dirt, sweat, and blood, he would've sworn the prince's eyes misted with tears. "Ciopori?" Prince Jadon whispered. "Vanya..." His voice lightly warbled, and then he sucked in a deep, astonished breath.

"Brother..." Ciopori breathed the word, her voice thick with emotion.

Vanya extended her hand toward the stage and began making her way through the crowd as if there was no one else in the courtyard.

"Stop," Jadon cautioned, holding two fingers upright. "Wait." He surveyed the blood, sport, and wreckage strewn about the courtyard; reverently regarded the many vampires kneeling, as well as the body of the lone slain female; and then he turned his full attention back to Prince Jaegar. "I cannot offer you the lives of our sisters. Is there something else you would battle me, and me alone, for?"

"No." Prince Jaegar scowled.

Prince Jadon closed his eyes, cursed beneath his breath, then slowly reopened them. "Then so be it: This mystical, magnetic dome, provided by the gods, will have to hold, and I pray it will shield all the human inhabitants of this valley from the fury of the earth and the outcry of the land, while we, the two sons of

Sakarias, will battle this night, right here and now, unto death. Because I will not cede my sisters or any other female in the house of Jadon."

"No! No, you won't," Ciopori blurted. She immediately turned to regard Marquis. "The children are in the manse—*all of them, including our precious Nikolai*—the *destinies*, here in the courtyard. Brooke, our queen. Napolean, our king. Generations of faithful vampires. No, he cannot. Should Jadon fall, I will go with Jaegar." She turned to face her brother. "No, you will not."

"As will I," Vanya whispered.

Marquis whirled around, fury on his face, and Saber took a scorched step back, away from Vanya. "Are you insane?" the Ancient Master Warrior shouted.

Saber shook his head. "Don't get it twisted, princess. He looks like your brother, but the body he inhabits belongs to Braden Bratianu—that means Braden's age, Braden's knowledge, Braden's skill set in battle."

"And this one"—Marquis gestured toward Prince Jaegar, conspicuously using his third finger to do so—"same thing goes: Achilles' age, Achilles' knowledge...*Achilles'* skill set in battle."

"Nay," Vanya said, even as Ciopori looked on, "the mind and the spirit—the seat of the soul—these powerful entities belong to Prince Jadon and Jaegar. And frankly, I would take Braden's wisdom, psychic talents, and courage over Jaegar's any day of the week and twice on Sunday."

Prince Jaegar snarled, growing restless and annoyed. "Enough!" he barked, repeating the same, simple refrain he had used so long ago in Romania. "What is it going to be?"

Prince Jadon sighed. He closed his eyes and took his time, while massaging the lines in his forehead. Finally, he looked back up. "We move away from the manse, from the women and the children, we reconvene in the Red Canyons at three o'clock in the morning, a half hour before the harvest moon wanes, and we battle to the death, yet again, you and I. Kristina and our sisters for the entire house of Jadon. If I win, Achilles will be no more, your Colony Guard will bring me the head of the snake Oskar Vadovsky, leader of the Dark Ones' Council, as well as the sorcerer, Salvatore Nistor, and you will return to the Valley of Death & Shadows, forever sworn to leave our sisters unharmed. Should you prevail, you will have the three females, but again, you must promise to never return." Before anyone in the audience could object, Prince Jadon held up his hand and scanned the crowd for two vampires. "King Napolean, will you assent? Fabian, High Mage, will you?"

Well, this should be rich, Prince Jaegar mused.

The silver slashes in Napolean Mondragon's dark onyx eyes narrowed as the ancient king considered the weight of Jadon's proposal, and Prince Jaegar could almost see the wheels turning in the silly king's mind as he balanced the far-reaching consequences: To be sure, the king loved the princesses—*perhaps Vanya just a little more than Ciopori, also interesting*—and from the king's perspective, all three females, even the ditsy redhead, were likely irreplaceable: their place in the vale, their duties and friendships, their families, their mates, their existing or future children...

Blah, blah, blah...

To the king's way of thinking, such a loss would be incalculable.

Just the same, he wasn't an idiot.

He had to know that an open battle, waged right here and now in this courtyard, between the house of Jaegar and the house of Jadon, led by their respective patriarchs, would leave untold death, slaughter, and destruction in its wake: Children would die, perhaps his own. Monuments would be destroyed, perhaps the compound. And the economy, all that sustained Dark Moon Vale would be upended—if not ruined—the Academy, the mineral plant, the casino, the lodge, and the resort...all the precious holdings filed away in Achilles' compartmentalized brain. The sons of Jadon might lose their history, their society, and quite possibly, the future of their species.

Nay, any ruler worth his salt must consider the well-being of *all* his subjects.

Beyond that, the king had to know what Prince Jaegar knew: Prince Jadon was only buying time—as long as the fair prince drew breath, whether in this world or the next, Jadon would never truly cede his sisters to Prince Jaegar, nor would he relinquish Kristina.

So be it, two could play this game—all Jaegar needed was the opportunity, the set-up, and the advantage.

"It will be as you pronounced," the king finally said, and Prince Jaegar exhaled with relief.

Jadon inclined his head in deference, noble as ever—*can we just get on with it?* "And you, High Mage? What say you?"

Prince Jaegar turned his attention to Fabian, who appeared to be a million miles away, his silken eyebrows furrowed, his copper skin a few shades too pale. "You must know," the High Mage said, his eyes now linked unerringly with Prince Jadon's, "the time, the hardship, the travails both I and your sisters have come through, the travels, the centuries, the growth we have achieved. The victories we have won and the losses we have grieved." He ran his hand through his long, layered hair—*was he stalling for time or wrestling inner demons?* The fool had to know he was responsible —*nay, guilty*—for setting this entire fiasco in motion. "But I remember you, my beloved monarch, as a prince among princes, one who led with wisdom, compassion, and empathy, a son who revered his father with unyielding fealty, a brother who loved his sisters with unfailing affection, and a leader who served his people, those whose descendants would one day become the house of Jadon, with both honor and duty."

Prince Jaegar puked a little in his mouth.

"Yes, Prince Jadon," Fabian said, "I will defer to your wishes on this fateful night and trust that you will lead us, still, in kind."

Fuuuuck.

Finally, Prince Jaegar groused inwardly.

Prince Jadon released a long, slow breath—*he had probably been holding it this entire time.* "Very well, then my decision is final. Brother"—he turned his attention back to Prince Jaegar, and the dark prince nearly burst with excitement—"take your soldiers and leave us, so that we may reconvene and gather our dead. We shall meet again at three a.m. in the Red Canyons."

Prince Jaegar opened his mouth, then closed it.

What could he say to that?

Gather our dead?

There may have been a lot of injured warriors, but last he had tallied, there was only one dead vampire from the house of a Jadon, a female whom they could not put back together.

Could one be any more melodramatic?

Whatever...

"See you at three." Prince Jaegar smirked, then he spun around to scan the ground, grimacing at all the carnage and mayhem—he was looking for Falcon Zvara's head.

Gruesome?

Yes.

But with enough blood and a little creativity, he could still put it back on Falcon's body and bring the dark soldier back to life. The moment he found it, he dropped into a squat and scooped what was left of it up by the hair—

"No!" Prince Jadon thundered, still perched on the dais like a carnival clown.

Prince Jaegar cocked his brows.

"He stays as he lies until we incinerate him." He gestured

toward the distant pavilion. "A life for a life; you know how this works. Go now, brother, leave us be."

Now this required a strong response.

Who was Prince Jadon to order Jaegar around!?

But it seemed petty, if not immaterial, even by Jaegar's standards.

Very well, he thought. *'Til we meet again.*

He stood to his full height, flicked his wrist over Falcon's body, and sent the corpse up in flames, himself. "Why put off until tomorrow what one can do today?" he called over his shoulder. And then, with a nod and a snarl, he vanished from view, taking his dark servants with him.

CHAPTER EIGHTEEN

MIDNIGHT

Kristina sat in the farthest corner of the lair on the ledge of a sulfuric pool of bubbling water, her five-inch heels strewn haphazardly on top of each other on the floor next to her feet, trying to garner heat from the misty plumes of steam. Her shoulders were curled inward, her arms wrapped tight around her waist, and she was absolutely freezing. As a vampire, she should have been able to regulate her temperature, even raise it a few degrees if necessary, but nothing could stamp out this chill.

Achilles' lair...

She was in Achilles Zahora's lair.

How did she know? It was fairly obvious. From the wicked-looking dagger, carved of bone, sitting atop the heavy chest of drawers, the smooth, antique hilt engraved with the letters *A* and *Z*, to the personal collection of archaic, medieval weapons hanging from the cavern walls, along with a medal or a trophy of some sort, an old piece of brass emblazoned with the word: *Executioner*.

Yeah, two plus two and all that...

And as long as she was doing math, then she might as well solve another equation: Two vials of ancient blood, one fed to Braden, the other to Achilles, plus a rising Millenia Harvest Moon that awakened the same damn blood, equaled a resurrected monster from the eighth century BC. No, she wasn't a guru with history, any more than she could do advanced calculus, but Kristina knew fashion, she knew modern clothes, and the dude who had approached her from behind that ponderosa tree... well, there wasn't a store anywhere in Dark Moon Vale that sold that kind of apparel.

Somehow...someway...Prince Jaegar had been resurrected in Achilles' body, which he had obviously changed back to his own, then dressed in his native garb.

"Shit," she whispered softly, remembering those stark onyx eyes and the overwhelming power that oozed from the vampire's pores. She had sensed that power before—it radiated like the steam from the sulfuric pool all around Napolean and Fabian, an ancient king and a prehistoric mage—that power was unique, primordial, hard to describe but easy to detect.

Yeah, Prince Jaegar was definitely back.

And what made matters worse—all matters worse—was the fact that she could not escape the lair. Hell, trying was not even an option. The way Kristina reasoned, whatever was out there, in the bulk of the Colony, was far, *far* worse than the seclusion she had now in the isolated hideaway. Besides, she wasn't strong enough quite yet to rearrange her molecules and pass through walls. And the door had been bolted from the outside, fortified with some sort of iron- and diamond-embedded beam. Yes, she had examined each and every one of the crude, violent weapons hanging on Achilles' walls—his own private war chest of primeval implements—but she had not survived the streets by being a fool: Taking one of the brutal weapons down, trying to use it against a dark, all-powerful vampire, would probably be the quickest way to lose her head.

How to provoke a predator to kill you in less than three seconds...

Or how to incite a dark vampire to do something...far worse.

Yeah, depending on how bad things got, she might still have to grab one, but for now, Kristina would prefer to try to stay alive, to use her wits to survive instead.

She began to shiver more intensely now as her mind drifted back to elementary math, and she continued to add things up. The calculations automatically led back to Braden, and there was no denying their chilling meaning: If Prince Jaegar had taken over Achilles' body, then it was probably safe to assume Prince Jadon had taken over Braden's. Maybe that was the shift she had felt in the courtyard.

Her eyes began to water, and she swiped them with the back of her hand, scratching her brow with one of the gemstones in her bracelet. *"Braden..."* Was he gone? Dead? Somehow sharing his body with another soul? *"Gods..."* She braced her head in her hands. And then she strained to remember...another time.

A better time.

A time when she and Braden had been especially close.

It had been February 14th, Valentine's Day, and while vampires didn't necessarily celebrate the human holiday, it was still front and center in Kristina's mind as she had climbed the steps to Nachari's brownstone, hoping to convince Braden to take her shopping—she needed a new pair of shoes to go with her blue and gray skirt—and the entire time, from her car to the door, she had been equal parts worried and *titillated* at the thought of seeing Bray again.

On one hand, Braden was always looking for an excuse—any excuse—to plant a kiss on her cheek—or gods forbid, her lips—or to wrap his arms around her, arms that were rapidly growing stronger, more muscular, more...*sexy*. And in her defense, she wasn't having any of that! *How could she?* Braden was still sixteen at the time, almost seventeen, but still...

To Kristina's way of thinking, that made him jailbait, and her a cougar.

Yuck.

No.

She just couldn't get past it.

But on the other hand, they were promised, unofficially engaged of sorts—Napolean had called it *betrothed*—and vampires did mature faster than humans. Way, *way* faster than humans. In fact, Braden's voice was quite a bit deeper, more masculine, kind of...satin, his chest and biceps were practically... titanium, and he was developing a swagger that nearly announced, *Male vampire here*, whenever he walked into a room, a sexy allure that almost dripped from his pores. One sidelong glance from those burnt sienna eyes, and—

Damn, Kristina thought, remembering her inner turmoil.

Why hadn't she just acted on her feelings?

Why hadn't she just risen to her toes and cupped his cheeks the moment he had opened the door?

Why hadn't her heart swelled with both joy and pride—*this gorgeous vampire is mine!*—instead of shrinking with fear and...shame?

Braden had recognized her secret knock and answered the door immediately, flashing a devious smile. "Happy Valentine's Day, Red."

Yep, he had remembered the day.

"Don't," she had warned him. "Just don't." She had rolled her eyes, raised one finger, and placed it between their mouths before he could swoop in for a kiss.

Why had she done that!

Just...why?

True to his good-hearted nature, he had responded with gentle laughter. "So you didn't come by to declare your endless love—what's up then, baby?"

"Kristina," she had corrected. "What's up then, *Kristina*."

"What's up then, Red?"

Despite her current circumstances, she managed a faint smile —*he had always been so funny, so clever...so sweet.* They had talked about the mall, her skirt, and the ankle boots she'd wanted. He had known the difference between her sapphire platforms, her cobalt-blue spikes, and her knee-high, ultramarine leathers. He had asked if he could drive her car. He had also reached out to tuck a lock of her loosely coiled S-curls behind her ear, before brushing her shoulder with the backs of his fingers.

She shivered at the memory, and this time it was not because of the cold.

Soon after, he'd had another one of his horrible headaches, and at least to her credit she had switched her focus, concentrated fully on Braden, helped him breathe...relax...walked him through the painful psychic phenomenon. She had been there for him—

Hadn't she?

She pinched the bridge of her nose and sniffled.

Prince Jaegar, or Achilles—whoever the hell that monster was —could be back any moment, and anything might happen. Kristina didn't know if she would live or die. She only knew that her heart was filled with regret, and honestly, there was nothing The Executioner or the evil prince could do at this point that would wound her more deeply than her own realization—her aching regret—that she had squandered so many precious moments and wasted so much time.

Yes, once they had solved the mystery of Braden's Valentine's Day headache—the vision of the two-toned, black and red rose— his pain had lessened, the *knowing* had gone away, and they had spent the rest of the day at the mall, but not before Braden had reached out with one hand, lifted her jaw, and placed a soft, tender kiss squarely on her lips.

Not before he had whispered, *"Thank you, Red."*

Kristina brought the gemstone bracelet up to her mouth and pressed an equally soft kiss against it. *Too little, too late*, she realized. "I'm sorry, Bray," she said softly, beneath her breath, glancing around the lair. "Shit, what have we gotten ourselves into?" She closed her eyes and murmured a prayer, even though she wasn't usually much for praying: "Monoceros...I mean, Lord Monoceros, please take care of Bray. Just watch over him and protect him—please, for me—and tell him I'm sorry. Tell him... I'm broken. I always have been. Tell him I just couldn't *trust*...any of it. Tell him he's the best thing, the only truly good thing...the one and only true certainty in my entire life."

* * *

"You okay, Bray?" Kristina's soothing voice.

Braden braced both forearms across his knees as he leaned back against the Tree of Light in the Enchanted Forest. The memories were coming faster now—faster and more furious—and this one, Valentine's Day in front of Nachari's brownstone, was particularly insistent.

He had ignored her question, shrugged his shoulders, and held out his palm, hoping to get her car keys. "You gonna let me drive?"

"Hell no!" she'd said. "Never...ever...*ever*. Not unless we're taking your Mustang."

And that's when the headache and dizziness had hit him.

Changing tack, he had walked to the passenger door of Red's pink Corvette, shuttle-stepped sideways, then braced one hand on the panel. "That's cool. You can drive."

She had rounded the car in an instant, leaned against the door, and placed both hands firmly on his chest. "Okay, that's the third time. Braden, what is wrong?"

"Psychic headache," he had teased, trying to sound light-hearted about it.

"Yeah, because our kind really gets headaches. You getting that house of Jadon thing?"

He had nodded.

"In your head, or your gut, or both?"

Braden had felt his eyelids droop, like they were too heavy to hold open. "It's all in my head," he'd replied, still trying to make the best of it.

Kristina had nodded.

Hell, she had intimately understood...

Ever since the king had been attacked by a dark lord in the form of a nasty possession-worm, Braden Bratianu had been linked to the heart of the house of Jadon—he had been linked to the venerable king. While he occasionally had premonitions, he more often had...sensations, bits and pieces of feelings and thoughts, some sort of supernatural knowing, the ability to pick up on random impressions that were floating through the ether. If it affected the house of Jadon, Braden was open game. He could feel it, taste it, smell it, or just sense it, and it often manifested in his body.

Kristina had placed her hands on his knees and softened her voice to just above a whisper. "Okay, so...any dreams? Any visions? Anything concrete?"

"Nope, just a headache, and it's not really even that. Just like a pulse in my temple that makes me a little dizzy."

She had studied him with deep concern. "So, breathe through it then. Let the impression come in fully so it can pass."

His eyes had met hers before he closed them.

"Breathe in through your nose...now out through your

mouth." His chest had risen, then fallen as she'd spoken...as she'd watched. "Good...keep going...now what do you sense?"

"Nothing, really."

"Do you smell anything?"

"No."

"Taste anything?"

"Nope."

"Keep breathing," she'd instructed. "What about physical imprints—can you touch, feel, grab hold of anything?"

He'd shaken his head.

"Okay, what about your hearing? What do you—"

"A two-toned rose."

"Come again?"

"A rose. Two tones. Black and red."

If Kristina had reacted, Braden couldn't tell—her voice had remained soft, calm, and even. "Are you seeing it, or feeling it?"

"Nah," Braden had said, "just...just picking it up...it's just like...it's there."

"Okay. Anything else...about the rose?"

And that's when the vision had grown clearer. "The red, it's more like crimson...for passion. And the black, it's death and foreboding." He'd jolted backward. "The black is swallowing the red."

Kristina hadn't flinched...or overreacted.

She'd simply waited for the *knowing* to pass...until Braden reopened his eyes.

"Feel better?" she'd asked.

"Yeah, that was eerie."

"No shit," she'd agreed, flashing him a cautious smile. "What do you think it was about?"

Braden hadn't known the answer—not quite yet—but Kristina had given him wise advice: She had helped him work through the moral dilemma, what secrets to tell, what secrets to keep, his responsibility to treat his *gift* with discretion versus his duty to the house of Jadon. When to speak—and seek—further counsel. And she had weighed the fact, along with Braden, that the entire incident might just be jitters, concern about his parents' upcoming visit. In other words, she knew him like the back of her hand, the same way he knew her.

Finally, after enough silence had lingered, and Braden had come back to himself, she had switched subjects as seamlessly as Braden switched channels when they were watching TV. "You okay to shop?" she'd asked.

For Braden...

To Braden...

The transition had been...perfect.

She'd known when to push and when to back off—she'd allowed him to be vulnerable but to also save face. Before she could catch it or stop him, he had reached out with one hand, lifted her jaw, and placed a soft, tender kiss directly on her lips. "Yeah. And thank you, Red."

Remember and choose...

Braden allowed the memory to settle.

At this point, he knew each recollection served a purpose, but what was the lesson in this one?

The tree behind him swayed gently to the left, then back to the right, and he rose to his feet, pressed both palms against the trunk, and waited. A soft, perfectly ovoid white leaf detached from a tree limb and fluttered gently to the ground, whispering as it descended: "The gift of *knowing*, the power of *second-sight*, the ability to discern the black-and-red rose..."

A second leaf followed in kind, only this one was a brilliant, shimmering gold: "Only the purest of souls can see the truth... speak the truth...discern the truth. For *truth* must first abide in the heart."

The stems of the leaves came together on the ground as if

linking petal-hands, and just like before, the ground beneath him began to glow with a radiant golden light. Slowly, but surely, one large, oblong disc gradually appeared before him, and a branch from the tree dipped down to scribe something upon it.

Truth.

One word emblazoned in silver.

"Wow," Braden said, as it fully sank in...

Marquis' Blood Moon—*The Blood Canon: Ancient Book of Black Magic*—Braden had fully interpreted the passage Nachari had read aloud, and when Ademordna had possessed Napolean, Braden had felt it, acted it out in his body, relayed the truth to Marquis, Nachari, and Kagen. He had also seen Kyla's deception with Saxson when the black rose had swallowed the red...

Truth.

It was just that simplistic, no more and no less.

The gods had used Braden's life—*no, they had used his honest heart*—to reveal truths to the house of Jadon, illuminated outward, from the light of his being.

As he dropped to one knee to retrieve the badge of *truth* and place it in his pouch, alongside *patience* and *kindness*, he suddenly understood something else, something he had never been able to explain before, the reason he had been willing to one day mate Kristina, long before Napolean had decreed it: "I'm going to be very big and strong one day, like a lion"—he had told her at only fifteen years old—"and I would want you. So, if no one comes along, then, yeah, I'll mate you." He chuckled at the recollection, even as he knew: He had seen the *truth* in Kristina from the very start.

He had seen her pain.

He had seen her scars.

He had seen all the many layers of her defensive walls, but he had also seen what resided beneath them: joy and laughter; playfulness and humor; a fierce, unyielding loyalty; the ability to fight to the death for what she treasured; a heart made ready to love, unconditionally, forged in the fires of tragedy and abandonment; the complete absence of prejudice and judgment—the ability to accept Braden with all his clumsiness, silliness, and slow refinement; the toughness to shore up his sensitivity; and the compassion to match his own.

Kristina was as beautiful as an un-plucked rose.

And beneath the winter ice, there was fire in her bones.

Passion.

Heat.

Eternal fidelity.

She was everything he had longed for, yet never known, growing up with his mortal father, before Dario had come along. Whether she knew it or not, she was one of the best things that had ever happened to Braden...one of the few true certainties in his life.

He only wished—

Well, there was no point in wishing.

Still...

He wished he had not walked away from her so heartlessly the last time he had seen her.

He hoped—he prayed—he might get another chance.

CHAPTER NINETEEN

THE FOREST OF EVIL

Achilles Zahora reclined on the ground, in the thick, moist soil beneath the Tree of Darkness, uncaring that his powerful, strapping body was filthy. He had rolled around in the mud for hours with the siren, sating his every primitive desire like a bestial animal...

Or at least it had felt like hours.

It might have only been minutes.

Time was of little consequence here. It almost did not seem linear—like nothing moved forward and nothing moved back, like everything was circular in nature.

Fine with him.

At first her lips had tasted like honey, and with her fine red ringlets, he had been able to close his eyes and imagine he was bedding Kristina Silivasi. But the more he kissed her, tasted her...*bit her*, the more she tasted like something rotten. The angrier and more dissatisfied Achilles had become, until the sexplay had escalated into something dark, desperate, and violent.

Pulling her hair had not been enough, nor had covering her mouth with his large, rugged hand.

Everything had escalated so quickly.

So savagely.

The siren hadn't stood a chance...

Arching his back and stretching his neck, he glanced off to the left into an outcrop of dead, wiry bushes and stared at the heaping mound, the pile of dirt beneath which he had buried her body. And not out of kindness or some form of ritual—not out of respect or some *last rites* bullshit—he didn't want to look at what was left of her.

He couldn't stand to see her worthless corpse a second longer than he had to.

She had not been Kristina.

Hell, she may not have even been human—

Who knew?

A large, heavy golden goblet had appeared beneath the tree when Achilles had returned from burying the siren's body, a goblet overflowing with the sweetest red elixir, the finest of dark wines, a thick, tantalizing chalice filled with blood and dark gray vapors bubbling from the lid. And much like he had done with the siren's arteries, Achilles drank to his fill.

Two sips of rage, one deep gulp of cruelty, a long, open-throated swallow of vengeance, arrogance, and self-absorption. The more he drank, the drunker he became, and the faster the goblet refilled with decadence.

But now, as he reclined beneath the tree, drunk, sexually sated, and needing to catch some shut-eye, all he felt was envy: Before now, he had been relatively content to serve as the de facto head of the Colony Guard—a punisher, an executioner—to do what he did best, violence for the sake of violence, brutality for the reward of release. But the more he drank from the goblet, the more defiant he became.

He had served the Dark Council for hundreds of years, kept

them alive, protected and defended them, and they should have elevated his position—*why hadn't they?* Achilles should have been one of the most important vampires—if not *the* most important vampire—in the Dark Ones' Colony by now. He had equally tolerated Salvatore Nistor, provided safe space for the sorcerer to practice his magic, unimpeded, and that should have counted for something...more.

Much more...

Yes, Achilles was starting to yearn for more.

He didn't know what *more* actually looked like but more power, more praise, more authority. And if he had to build the damn castle—the Lair of Achilles—one stone at a time, then so be it. If he ever got out of this forest, if he ever returned to the Colony, Kristina Riley Silivasi would help him do it. A new set of offspring every seventy-two hours—he would allow her one full day and night to rest between breeding—a patriarchy of sons, and hopefully daughters, to build Achilles an empire.

He would not have to worry about destroying a body.

He would not have to worry about hunting farther and farther away from the valley.

He would not have to find new prey to inseminate.

He would be the lone male, the only dark soldier, with a vampire-female from the house of Jadon, a *destiny* of sorts to call his own. Superior bloodlines. Superior worth. Only, he would know how to treat her—how to break her, how to command her—unlike his weak, self-righteous vampire cousins.

He would follow the lead of the ultimate patriarch, Prince Jaegar Demir, at the time of The Curse, stopping just short of slitting her throat to drink her blood. His fangs—and her jugular vein—would do just fine.

He folded his hands behind his neck and let his bulging arms fall to the sides.

Sleep was calling...

Time to rejuvenate.

Perhaps he would have sweet dreams of a better siren...a submissive siren...a siren he could claim forever. Perhaps he would have prescient dreams of Kristina.

CHAPTER TWENTY

DARK MOON VALE ~ 1:00 A.M.

Alone in the front parlor of Napolean's manse, Prince Jadon stood in stoic silence. As he awaited his royal sisters, he tried to steady his nerves by admiring the living history all around him: The artistry on the ceiling was positively divine, all the intricate detail in the hand-painted mural of Zeus and Apollo, both exquisite and stunning. The myriad of collected artifacts were as intriguing and they were provocative, so many statues and timeless mementos amassed over so many centuries, from Romania, Greece, Persia...even Egypt...

Napolean had truly seen the whole world.

And every corner of the sitting room—every window, niche, and archway—was encased in hand-carved white moldings, not unlike the castle Prince Jadon had grown up in, and the various windows, the glass itself, were constructed of frosted panes festooned with scenes of ancient battlements and engravings of the gods. Prince Jadon would have liked to spend hours in this rectory, to spend hours with Napolean—to spend hours, going forward, with his sisters—but the much-needed, long-awaited reunion with the latter had been forced to wait until this anxious moment, due to more imminent, pressing matters.

First, there had been the matter of Braden's mother, Lily Bratianu—she had needed to be sutured, bathed, and dressed in a ceremonial robe before she was laid in repose, and Nachari Silivasi as well as his mate, Deanna, were still aiding the bereaved family with the heart-wrenching preparations, supporting Dario Bratianu and his young son, Conrad.

The female's death had been so sudden and overwhelming...

The entire spectacle—the unnecessary slaughter—so gruesome...so heinous...so tragic.

Prince Jadon drew a cleansing breath and forced his ire to cool and his thoughts to pivot. There had also been the matter of Marquis Silivasi and Saber Alexiares, a matter that was still ongoing...

Prince Jadon wrung his hands together in both angst and contemplation. There was no way—*absolutely no way*—the warrior and the "dragon" were going to go along with Prince Jadon's proffered agreement. As far as the two powerful males were concerned, it may as well have been a pact with the devil. And come what may—whether Prince Jadon prevailed in the final battle, or Prince Jaegar won the night—hell would freeze over, thrice times afresh, before the vampires would turn over their mates to be sacrificed.

And should the worst-case scenario occur, there was also the matter of Kristina Silivasi—something drastic had to be done to return her to the house of Jadon, where she belonged. The warriors, along with their sentinel brethren, were readying for war, and alas, that was the reason Prince Jadon had chosen—and offered—3 a.m. for the final conflict: Should something go desperately awry, he did not want his duplicitous brother to have a chance to regroup, to go back to the Colony, devise a new plan, and strike, once again, at the house of Jadon. Come what may, he wanted the outcome to be final...

He wanted Prince Jaegar's time on earth to be finished.

And finally, there had been the matter of the Council of Wizards meeting with Fabian Antonescu, Niko Durciak, and Jankiel Luzanski, as Nachari Silivasi had remained tied up with the bereaved family and the delicate preparations. The wizards had been desperate to divine, once and for all and with absolute finality—or at least as much certainty as possible—whether or not Prince Jadon's soul would wane along with the Millenia Harvest Moon and depart the body at 3 a.m., or not until moonset, at 11:46. They had been frantic to determine whether Braden would return, or whether they would be forced to bury his body next to his mother's. Yet and still, there had been no conclusive answers.

Prince Jadon pinched the bridge of his nose, sucked in a long draw of air through his nostrils, and fingered the outline of a particularly exquisite Grecian statue, wondering at the skill of the artisan. He had not the time to discern the mysteries of the Millenia Harvest Moon, nor could he speak to the will of the gods—what the celestial beings planned to do, if anything, whatever they were doing, with the life and soul of Braden, even as their vampire children labored to fight for their future and to choose wisely, here on earth. He only knew that he had to prevail in the battle yet to come. This time, he had to win the conflict.

He had to slay Prince Jaegar.

The fate of the house of Jadon was resting on its patriarch's shoulders.

His sisters' lives were hanging in the balance, Marquis and Saber not excepted, and the honor of the female who had given her life—nay, lost it in such a violent, unnecessary demonstration of savagery—was his to avenge. To make right.

"Brother." Ciopori's lovely, expressive voice pierced the

207

silence like a cool summer's wind, and Prince Jadon spun around to behold her.

Goddess, she was as breathtaking as he remembered...

She was clad in a stately, flowing garment of ivory silk, with gold and auburn leaves embroidered into the fabric; her long, midnight hair billowed to her waist; and her golden eyes, dotted with amber sparkles, still shone like sun-drenched diamonds. Though her countenance was heavy, her brow was smooth and light, her bearing equal parts regal, composed, and elegant.

"Sister." He crossed the room in an instant, enfolded her in his arms, and held on like she might evaporate if he let go of her, simply breathing in her familiar, springtime scent. "Ciopori," he whispered in her ear.

She clung to his shoulders with equal ardor, and then she began to sob. "There's so much to say, so much to ask...I hardly know where to begin."

He nestled his chin in the thick of her hair and nodded, feeling the same. And then he felt Vanya's sweet, unmistakable presence as she tentatively approached her siblings. Prince Jadon released one arm, extended it outward, and grasped his youngest sister, encircling her shoulders and drawing her into the tight, intimate circle. "Vanya!" He laughed but not in gaiety. He laughed in relief. He laughed in pure joy. He laughed in love and gratitude. "My gods, the two of you made it!"

Vanya's heart-shaped mouth curved upward in a smile, the soft edges of her full lips thinning. "Indeed, my brother; your efforts paid off. We survived the wilderness; we survived the long journey; we survived the long sleep until we were awakened." She pulled free, took a graceful step back, and cupped Jadon's face in her hands. "We survived to look upon your face once more."

Jadon clasped his hands over Vanya's and squeezed. He opened his mouth to speak, then closed it. There were no words

—there simply were...no words—as the children of King Sakarias and Queen Jade remained in a familial circle, drew closer, and pressed their foreheads together. Arms wrapped tightly around each other's waists, the ancient royal family wept.

And time stood still...

Seconds became minutes...

Minutes threatened to become...too many.

An epoch of emotion flowed between them, and their souls embraced in timeless unity.

Finally, Prince Jadon spoke: "We haven't much time—how deeply I regret this—but I must meet your children. I must hold them at least once. I must know how you are faring, and what happened when you arrived in this valley. Not from the perspective I held whilst in the spirit world but from your own mouths, your own stories. I must know that I did right by you both, so that it will fuel my resolve and guide my hand later this night, when I meet our wicked brother."

Princess Vanya sniffled. "And we must know what happened that night in the alps of our homeland, what happened on the desolate mountaintop."

"So that we might aid you as well, dear brother," Ciopori said, "only this time, with our considerable magick."

"Aye," Jadon said, drawing back once again to take their full measure, "you are both so...grown up. So beautiful. So majestic. I haven't the slightest doubt your powers are now considerable."

Vanya's laughter was like a robin's song drifting upon a summer's breeze. "And you, my brother, so strong...so handsome. I had almost forgotten how striking you were." She swiftly corrected, "How striking you *are*."

"I concur," Ciopori said softly. "Your eyes...your smile...oh Jadon, how we've missed you."

Prince Jadon smiled with warmth, appreciation, and he took his sisters' hands. "I will cherish this memory forever, you know.

Hold this singular image in the fore of my memory. And should the celestial gods smile upon us in the canyon—should the gods favor me with victory in battle—then I bid you, always hold the ones you love dear to your hearts. Live fully in every moment. Drink in their sweetness, their spirits, their presence. Remember that each moment is a blessing."

A heavy set of footfalls preceded a silent, stealthy gait as Marquis Silivasi, followed by Saber Alexiares, passed through the archway into the sitting room and strolled toward the three ancient siblings, each vampire with a child in tow.

"Marquis," Prince Jadon called by way of greeting.

"Greetings, my prince, my ancient...brother," Marquis said reverently.

Prince Jadon held the warrior's gaze a moment longer than was customary, in stark acknowledgment of the intimate blood tie. And then he turned his attention to Saber. "Dragon," he said, using the soldier's informal moniker. "How are you holding up? How is your son?"

"Brother...Your Grace," Saber said, making note of each important title, and then he smiled. "Your nephew is doing fine—full of piss and vinegar."

Prince Jadon chuckled.

Overwhelmed with joy, and living in the moment, just as Prince Jadon had bid them, Ciopori released Prince Jadon's hand and pointed toward the raven-haired two-year-old, the bouncy child sitting atop his father's shoulders. "This is Nikolai *Jadon* Silivasi," she said proudly, emphasizing the child's middle name.

Prince Jadon's breath caught in his throat. He met Ciopori's twinkling eyes and inclined his head in acknowledgment. "Thank you," he whispered.

Her eyes glossed over with tears. She bit her bottom lip and nodded.

"And this little boy, the one full of piss and vinegar, is Lucien

Sabino," Vanya said, chuckling. She gestured toward the smaller child wriggling to break free from his father's hold, and Prince Jadon couldn't help but notice—the child's eyes were the color of burnished coal, mixed with hazy, bronzed reflections, as if Vanya's pale rose and Saber's coal black had met in the middle, tussled, and merged.

Lucien Sabino and Nikolai Jadon...

Prince Jadon could barely conceal his emotion—it was truly overwhelming.

He waited for both sires to set their children down, and then he sank to his knees and opened his arms, ushering his nephews forward in a prayerful, heartfelt welcome. "Come," he said, his voice thick with longing. "Come meet your uncle Jadon..." He almost choked on the children's names as he spoke each one with veneration. "Nikolai...Lucien...my two little warriors." He curled his lips around his teeth lest he utter something nonsensical...

Lest joy, gratitude, astonishment...and love...burst from his heart like a fountain.

He did not want to frighten the younglings or get so swept away in the moment that he forgot his perilous duty, his obligation to the house that revered him, the limited time he had left in this parlor to catch up with his sisters...get to know his new brothers, or the critical battle he had yet to prepare for.

Besides, he hadn't any tears left to cry.

CHAPTER TWENTY-ONE

"**H**ear that?" Zeus asked, his spotted black and gray eyes hardening like granite. "The cacophony...the brutal symphony...the screams, the wails, the agony?"

Avoiding his piercing gaze, Kristina stared instead at the Dark One's gnarly, pointed beard, using it as a focal object to obscure his savage features. She leaned back and away from his towering body, closer to the sulfuric pool and the loud, bubbling water, pressed both hands over her ears, and tried to dial down the noise. The rumble of the sulfuric pool and the bluster of the repulsive vampire.

Of course she could hear it...

Even through the thick limestone walls of an underground cavern...

Women screaming...

Sadistic vampires moaning...

The Dark Ones celebrating the Millenia Harvest Moon in the most despicable manner imaginable.

"I asked you a question," Zeus snarled.

Kristina's eyes met his, and she shivered. There was no soul inside this male. His savagery was more blatant than his piercings. This one was wild, barbaric, and way too keyed up. He was needling her, and he was looking for a reason—*any reason*—to attack, to make Kristina just another voice in the brutal, terrifying symphony. "Yes," she murmured, trying to appease his sadism. "I can hear just fine."

He took an intimidating step closer, his tight, rock-hard abs now at eye level, and bent over to run his fingers through her hair.

She drew back, turned her head to the side, and winced. "Don't."

He snarled again, and the tips of his ivory canines flashed beneath thick lips framing the rings in his mouth like a backlight.

Gross.

Kristina shut her eyes.

She needed a second to think, a chance to formulate a plan, but before her brain could come online, Zeus let go of her hair. He let the ringlets fall to her shoulders and squatted down in front of her. "Look at me...bitch."

She grinded her teeth, opened her eyes, and glared right at him.

"You're a hot-tempered little thing, aren't you?" He paused. "Princess Red?" The corner of his mouth turned up in an evil, condescending smirk. "You should guard your thoughts more carefully—your memories are like an open book."

Fuck you. She thought it deliberately. *Can you hear that, asshole?*

Oh, hell, what was she doing?

The backhand came out of nowhere, flipping her off the edge of the pool and into the natural sulfuric hot springs, her head ringing, her teeth rattling, pain overwhelming her senses. And as she flailed her arms, gulped a mouthful of water, her childhood, early years, and entrance into the house of Jadon flashed before her in an instant: her mother and all of Kiki Riley's cruel, predatory boyfriends; life on the streets, the constant threats while being a homeless child; the Dark One who had attacked her in Dark Moon Vale; Dirk and his fist, his boots, his razor-sharp tongue, all the degrading insults and humiliating beatings.

The pain...

The rage and shame...

And the insufferable nature of all of it.

She shot out of the water and gasped for air, her silk black vest molding around her breasts and waist like a corset, her raspberry skirt drenched and clinging to her hips.

No more!

Reaching across the limestone ledge, she quickly scanned the low, angular outcropping for a hanging stalactite, broke it free from the cavern, and spun around in one smooth motion, swinging it like a baseball bat. The jagged edge caught Zeus by the upper jaw, opened a gash in his cheek, and ripped out his lip ring. "I'm no longer human!" Kristina shouted. *Fuck, she was committing suicide!* But she had attended all of Nathaniel and Jocelyn's self-defense classes—hell, she had even worked privately with Mateo Devera.

And she *was* no longer human...

Zeus reached up in shock, grasped the side of his face, dipped his fingers in the blood, and just stared at them. Then he roared like a prehistoric creature, shaking several stalactites loose before diving across the pool at Kristina.

She shot up into the air like a rocket, summersaulted beneath the cavern ceiling, and came back down like a spiraling comet, landing at Zeus' back. She bashed the weight of the heavy stalactite, still in her hands, against the crown of his skull, then swept a nimble leg crosswise, just above his ankles, sending him tumbling headfirst into the pool.

She didn't give him a chance to recover.

She dived onto his back, wrapped her arms around his wiry

but brutally strong shoulders, and sank her fangs into the back of his neck, tearing out a mouthful of flesh and vertebrae.

Zeus sprang to his knees, flipped onto his back, and pinned Kristina beneath him at the bottom of the pool, crushing her slender frame against the limestone, and knocking the air out of her lungs.

She thrashed and squirmed, twisted and kicked, tried desperately to get him off her.

Finally, she reached around, felt for the hard, smooth plane of his lower belly, slid her hand lower, and grasped the family jewels in an iron-clad, vampiric grip; then she yanked for all she was worth—she didn't manage to rip them off, but she stretched them like a bungee.

His back arched, and he snatched both of her wrists and clamped down hard in an effort to crush both arm bones. The bones strained but resisted breaking, and Kristina grew more determined.

She drew back her head, blocked out the pain, then drove it forward, head-butting the vampire from behind, so hard it made her dizzy. He released her arms, and she scrabbled backward, twisting to crawl out of the pool. But he spun around like a nimble tiger, swiveling in one feral motion and grabbing her legs by the ankles. Then he yanked and lifted, whipping her body like a battle rope, slamming her against the floor of the hot springs, then snapping her above the water in one harsh, undulating motion. He spun her over his head like a lasso, tossed her across the lair, and she landed with a hard, unforgiving thud in the middle of Achilles' brass bed.

Oh gods!

Every muscle in her body was burning, every nerve ending was on fire, and surges of pain, like white-hot fire, coursed up and down her limbs in nauseating, pulsing circuits.

Zeus lumbered out of the pool and stalked across the lair like an angry, prowling lion, his dark eyes flashing deep crimson red, his sinewy muscles bunching and contracting with every feline step.

He was going to eviscerate her.

Oh gods, no...

Or much, much worse...

His lightweight sweatpants were drenched with water, sagging to midthigh, and he had obviously recovered from the attack on his privates because his giant staff was fully erect, swaying as he walked and throbbing.

"No," Kristina whimpered, feeling utterly helpless and physically spent.

She didn't have any fight left in her.

He released a dollop of venom into the palm of one hand, crooked it around the base of his neck, and groaned as the torn flesh and bone knitted back together. And then he sank down into a half crouch, half squat, and palmed his junk with the other hand.

"Achilles!" Kristina blurted, her brain finally coming online with a plan. "I belong to Achilles Zahora."

Zeus froze about three paces away from the bed, and Kristina could almost see the wheels turning in his crazed, feral head.

"If you can read my memories then you know damn well that The Executioner wants me *for himself.* He wants me as a rare, individual prize, his own exclusive conquest, his favorite personal...possession. And he sure as hell doesn't want to share me with the likes of you—or any other vampire in this colony!" She paused to catch her breath. "I might not be able to stop you... kill you...defeat you. But Achilles? *He will end you!* And you know it."

Zeus released his package and stood up straight.

He licked his top lip, transferring venom from his upper incisors to the gaping hole the ring had torn out, and healed it instantly. "Achilles isn't here," he hissed, "and Prince Jaegar doesn't give a shit."

"But he'll be back...won't he? The Executioner?"

They could have heard a pin drop in the lair as Kristina held her breath.

Truth was, she was taking a gamble.

Fishing for information—and mostly about Braden...

Would her best friend, her fiancé, ever return to his body?

She honestly didn't know how any of it worked, but Zeus just might.

It was worth the wager.

If looks could kill, Kristina would've been six feet under...the way the Dark One glared at her. His nostrils flared, his features contorted, and the ropes in his neck bulged like hidden serpents, but he didn't take another step forward. "End me?" he echoed. Then he grinned and chuckled. "He is going to *end* you, Kristina. End your freedom. End your future. End every purpose you ever had, except for procreation. You're right, revenge is best served cold. I can wait. Because the cruelest thing I could do to you now is hand you over to Achilles. Think about it. Imagine it. Wait for it."

Kristina sucked in a much-needed breath and almost bit a hole in her tongue. She so wanted to tell him, *Yeah, well, I'm not the one with the bloody, stretched-out balls hanging down my legs,* but she thought better of it. Survival was the name of the game right now, and it was a moment-by-moment process.

Besides, Zeus had confirmed something really, *really* important...

If Prince Jaegar had taken over Achilles' body, but Achilles was going to return, then maybe—just maybe—all wasn't lost.

At least, not yet...

Maybe—just maybe—Braden could return to his body, too.

And even though she had never accepted it...trusted it...

believed in her and Bray's promise, she knew deep down at a cellular level: *Braden was going to fuck Achilles up!*

He would never—ever—leave Kristina in the Dark Ones' Colony.

All she had to do was hope and persevere...

Hope.

And persevere...

All she had to do was stay alive.

Braden drew the back of his hand over his sweat-drenched brow —*since when did vampires sweat like this?*—and lowered the mystical dagger to his side. The Tree of Light had expelled three branches, merged them into a stick-figure combatant, a giant wooden warrior, and Braden had spent what felt like the last several hours sparring...training...being taught by the timber apparition. In truth, he had already been taught many of the basics at the Dark Moon Academy, and Marquis had taught him many more during their regular sparring sessions. Heck, even Julien Lacusta had given Braden a tip or two—maybe three—on the occasions when Braden had swung by to visit the tracker and his son on the northern edge of the vale.

But this...this lesson...was different.

The tree focused on energy and fluid motion—strength, agility, and precognition—how to feel the ebb and flow of the battle, in spirit, how to anticipate the enemy's next movement, how to harness light against a strike of darkness, and how to become one with both your weapon and the forces of nature all around you, energies that could wield it with you if you let them.

Stranger shit...and all that.

At this juncture, Braden didn't question anything—where the magical forest led, he followed.

The stick figure bowed, and Braden responded in kind, watching in rapt fascination as the wooden illusion began to fade and, as if out of the mist, where the figure once stood, a familiar scene appeared: Braden and his mother, Lily, standing on Nachari's rooftop terrace, finally having a much-needed talk...

About the past, what Braden saw as neglect.

About Brad, Braden's biological father.

About Lily's perspective, how much she had always loved him—how broken and defeated...how ashamed she had felt—and about the only thing left that really mattered.

Forgiveness.

Braden had placed his dominant hand on his mother's throat in a vampiric demonstration of bonding, something that had come from an instinct so primordial, it would have been impossible to identify it. And then he had stroked her pulse before allowing his finger to simply rest softly on her jugular. *"Mamica,"* he had whispered, speaking the word *Mommy* in Romanian.

He had allowed the term of endearment to linger.

"Te iert." I forgive you. "I always did."

Lily had melted into a pool of tears, Braden had caught her slumping form, and in an act more healing than any other in his lifetime, he had enfolded his beloved matron in his arms.

The beautiful memory waned and settled, the Tree of Light creaked and groaned behind him, and Braden spun around, only to find another illusion, another far more distant memory, one he had *never* resolved.

Brad Clarke.

Braden's biological, human father...

Drunk as a skunk and hunkered over the hood of an old jalopy car, barking out impossible orders at a four-and-a-half-year-old boy. "Braden, hand me that quarter-inch drive socket. Braden, give me the number fourteen hex key. Braden, what the fuck are you doing? I said number *fourteen!*"

Brad Clarke, spinning around in anger and flinging a wrench at Braden's head.

Braden ducking, but not before the wrench caught his brow, sliced the corner of his eye, and bright red blood spurted out...

All over Brad's tools.

Brad's...

Not Dad's.

Braden hated the man too much to call him father—or maybe he just feared him too much—maybe he just longed for something else.

Someone else.

"Remember and choose," the Tree of Light whispered, and Braden forced himself to look deeper into the scene: His mother had rushed out of the house crying...yelling, his father basically not giving a shit, and later that afternoon—*six stiches later*—Braden had meticulously washed every tool in the toolbox.

Only...there was something else.

Someone else.

A child, even younger, superimposed behind Brad Clarke, and the child was screaming, cowering, covering his head on an oil-stained floor, while an older man with salt-and-pepper sideburns whaled on the child again and again, not just flinging a wrench but beating Brad with a pair of jumper cables...

Beating the child until he passed out.

"You worthless son of a bitch! I'm sorry you were ever born! What the hell did I do to God to deserve such a piece of shit for a son?"

Braden turned away.

He couldn't watch anymore.

"My father's dad," he said absently. "Grandpa Clarke...he beat Dad, too?"

The tree swayed gently in an unseen wind. "Look harder. Remember. And choose."

Braden bit down on his lower lip, dropped into a squat, and stared fixedly at the child inside of the man, and he saw it all in an instant: unrelenting pain, cancerous shame, and a kid who was broken, through and through.

Braden pounded his fist into the dirt. "So what!"

The welts on the child's arms and legs began to swell into nasty raised bruises.

"But fuck you, anyway!"

His left ear was resting in a pool of blood.

"That doesn't make it fair—that doesn't make it right," Braden argued, as the internal battle continued to rage out loud.

The child looked just like Braden, only smaller, weaker, undernourished, and the reality sank in Braden's heart like a stone dropping to the bottom of a murky pond: Every time Brad looked at Braden, he saw his younger self. He saw someone he had been taught to hate long before Braden was born. He saw something he could not hurt enough...damage enough...to stamp out all that hate and self-loathing.

"I hated you, too," Braden whispered, pissed off that he was beginning to cry.

Remember, and choose.

This time, the tree whispered gently in his mind.

"Choose what?" Braden retorted. "I don't *want* to choose." He clutched his head in his hands and fisted his fingers. "Damn you." His shoulders curled inward, and he wept.

Finally, when there were no tears left to cry, he reached into the mirage, placed his hand on the shoulder of the sleeping boy, and breathed the words, "*Te iert.*"

I forgive you.

And something in his chest virtually exploded as all that buried pain broke free.

Braden rocked backward, fell onto the ground, and braced both palms against the dirt to steady his weight. Then he watched as the tree gently swayed, left then right, bent into an arc, and another branch extended its mystical finger. A silver oblong disc appeared, and the edges filled in quickly.

Forgiveness...

Written in sterling letters.

Shimmering. Bright. Luminescent as moonlight.

The scene in the background disappeared, and Braden watched the boy softly vanish, only this time, instead of feeling bottled-up rage, he felt a fresh, new underpinning...a current of compassion.

He reached for the badge, folded it into his palm, and held it against his chest for a prolonged, reverent moment before slipping it into his pouch.

CHAPTER TWENTY-TWO

Prince Jadon moved freely about the numerous underground antechambers and halls of King Napolean Mondragon's compound: the Ceremonial Hall of Justice; the guard room just outside the diamond-embedded holding cell, which now housed many of the Vampyr's children for protection; and even the Chamber of Sacrifice & Atonement, as the extra pews were needed and being utilized to seat the unusually large number of Vampyr gathered at the manse. He had blanched at the anterior door festooned with a skull and crossbones—*Behold the portal to the corridor of the dead* inscribed on the thick, weighty panel—such a dreadful and powerful reminder of how the Curse still played out in recent times. And he had absently wished, more times than he could count, that he still had possession of his own beloved, ancient sword.

Nonetheless, King Napolean had offered Prince Jadon use of The Sword of Andromeda, a Mondragon family heirloom passed down from one generation to the next, taken by Napolean when he was just a lad, after the death of his father, Sebastian. And Nachari Silivasi had equally offered the use of a blade he jokingly referred to as his own Excalibur, also handed down to him by his father, Keitaro, in 1526 or 1527—he wasn't exactly sure of the year.

Prince Jadon intended to try them both.

To try them and test them prior to the battle, and to choose the one best suited to his own strength and skill.

He meandered into the circular Hall of Justice, both mindful and respectful of the body laid so gracefully—and peacefully—on the simple raised pallet at the fore of the gallery, having been bathed and dressed in an elegant ceremonial robe of lavender and ivory: Lily Bratianu, resting in repose, awaiting the final details of her funeral.

He bowed his head in respect, made his way to the back of the room, and approached the seated Council of Wizards, absent those practitioners of magic who still resided at the Romanian University. "Wizards," he said in greeting.

"Your Grace." Niko and Jankiel spoke in unison.

"My sword is in the guard room, on top of the desk," Nachari offered.

"Thank you, Nachari."

"Jadon." Fabian Antonescu stood up. "We do have an answer, but it may not be the clear, concise delineation that you want." He linked his hands behind his back, and Prince Jadon shrugged one shoulder.

"Well, I suppose it is as it is, so what say you?"

Fabian cleared his throat. "Simple. Yet somewhat vague. Much like the moon sets and the sun rises, both bodies still exist in the solar system, yet one gives way to the other's light, to the other's prominence. So it will be when the Millenia Harvest Moon wanes at 3:34 a.m. Your power—*your spirit*—will step back, recede, making way for the true owner of the body to emerge. Assuming Braden is allowed to return, that he has not perished somewhere on a bridge between worlds, his emergence may not be complete or all at once, but like the moon and the sun, one soul will step back, another will come forth, passing one another as if in the night. Both still exist. Both may be still present. At least until full moonset at 11:46."

"I see," Prince Jadon replied, swallowing his grief. There was so much yet to be said and done: the desire to spend more time with his sisters and their mates, the overwhelming yearning to get to know his nephews, the input, the contribution, the mark he would like to leave on the house of Jadon...

The house of Jadon...

His house.

His legacy.

His beloved civilization.

But once again, Jaegar had stolen all of that time, life...love... and so much more from so many innocent beings—it was mind-boggling, unconscionable, truly impossible to comprehend how one evil soul could do so much damage to so many...for so long.

He shook his head to disrupt the train of thought: There was simply no time for regret or recrimination—Jadon's path was clear before him. He had one night. This night. To leave an indelible mark on his kindship...forever. "Well done," he said. "I suppose we shall take it as it comes." He trained his gaze on Nachari Silivasi. "Master Wizard, have you spoken with your eldest brother? On my way to retrieve your sword—and Napolean's—I intend to look in on the sentinels and Master Warriors, to hear the intricate details of their final battle plans, should my twin prevail in the upcoming battle, but a brief summary ahead of time would be helpful. As we all know, time is drawing nigh, and every moment is crucial."

Nachari leaned back in the pew and swept his thick black hair away from his keen, deliberative eyes. He took a moment to collect his thoughts, clearly wanting to speak succinctly and efficiently. "As you know, the wizards are coordinating with the warriors, and the warriors are coordinating with the king. Should you...fall in this battle...Marquis, Saber, Saxson, Keitaro, and a dozen other warriors will encase your sisters in a warded circle, place them inside a protective holding cell, and fight to the death if necessary. Jankiel and Niko will call upon the favor of the gods to drench the Red Canyons with their power and hopefully shield as much of the valley—of our human servants and the surrounding population—with protection, much as you did in the courtyard. Meanwhile, Ramsey will focus solely on taking a high-ranking member of the Dark Ones' Colony alive, and torturing whatever information is necessary out of him to discern where they are holding Kristina. The king, our tracker, Julien, and Santos Olaru will try to make use of the chaos to enter the Colony through the old sacrificial caverns, and use the tunnels to bring Kristina out of the underground fortress. You may as well know, Napolean always risks his well-being when he harnesses the power of the sun, draws upon the energy of the solar system, but his mind is made up—he will incinerate half the house of Jaegar if that is what it takes to return Kristina to our valley."

Nachari paused, carefully considering his next words. "Like you, we will have to take it as it comes, but rest assured that we, as the Council of Wizards, are equally prepared to fight with spells and magick. We have long avoided an all-out war with our cousins of darkness—they outnumber us tremendously, and they are every bit our equals in combat—but if this night is the night when it finally happens, so be it. We are *all* ready and determined."

Prince Jadon closed his eyes, imagining the war...the carnage...the unconscionable loss of life, and the marrow in his bones calcified with both disgust and determination. All of this because Prince Jaegar was spiteful, vengeful, and hell-bent on murdering his own flesh and blood, even though the needless slaughter would ultimately bring him nothing.

Nothing.

No honor.

No power.

No godly reward.

He was simply twisted, self-aggrandizing, and evil.

"Very well." He opened his eyes. "For what it is worth, I do not intend to fail."

Nachari's stunning forest-green eyes softened with both compassion and understanding. "Your Grace?"

Prince Jadon smiled wanly. "What is it, Master Wizard?"

"Before you go, I was hoping..." His voice trailed off as he peered beyond Prince Jadon's right shoulder and extended his hand toward someone or something ostensibly behind him. "My mate, Deanna. Our son, Sebastian Lucas. We weren't here when you offered blessings to the Vampyr—we were retrieving the sword and assisting Dario and Conrad with something personal... meaningful...retrieving a special family heirloom, one they desperately wanted for Lily's burial service."

Prince Jadon nodded solemnly, understanding the vampire's request, and then his heart instantly lightened as he turned around and glimpsed the striking, exotic beauty standing at the end of wooden pew, holding a handsome toddler's hand. Her resplendent blue-gray eyes met his, and she lowered her head in deference, causing a thick, cascading lock of ash-brown hair to fall along the front of her elegant, slender shoulders.

The prince smiled. "You must be Deanna."

The *destiny* beamed from ear to ear. "Yes. And you're..." She was too flustered to get the words out. She tried again. "You're Prince Jadon." She quickly recovered and placed her hand over her heart. "Your Grace."

He waved his hand in dismissal. "Prince Jadon, or just... Jadon will do."

She shook her head, bewildered, and then she gestured

lovingly at the green-eyed toddler who just might, one day, rival his father for otherworldly beauty. His father *and* his mother. "And this is Sebastian," she said.

Prince Jadon bent over, settled down into a squat, and waved the child forward.

"Go." Deanna placed her hand on the child's little back and gently shoved him forward.

Despite the gravity of the night—the loss, the fear, the chaos —the house of Jadon had welcomed their ancient prince with unparalleled awe and reverence, and the prince, in turn, had taken the time to speak the names of each and every member aloud and to bless each one of the children: It was the least he could do in the time he had left. "It is so nice to meet you, Sebastian," he crooned.

"Yer eyes are bwown, like Unka Kagen's," Sebastian said, reaching out to touch Prince Jadon's nose. "But dare's no silva."

Prince Jadon glanced at Deanna and raised his brows in question.

"Silver," she said. "Uncle Kagen's eyes are quite dark brown but filled with beautiful slashes of silver."

"Ah," Prince Jadon said, reaching out to clasp Sebastian's little hands. "Indeed, that's true. And what color are your eyes, little one?"

"Gween."

Deanna chuckled, and Nachari joined her, even as he sidled up beside his mate. "Sebastian, this is Prince Jadon Demir, the... namesake of the house of Jadon."

Sebastian scrunched up his brows. "What's a names...ache?"

"Namesake," Deanna repeated. "It's someone very, *very* important."

He seemed to be pleased with the answer. "Ooooo," he breathed, staring at the prince more intently. "Like King Napol-un."

"Yes," Prince Jadon said. "Just like that." He picked Sebastian up, set him on his knee, and braced one hand against the small of the child's back. The prince raised his other hand to his mouth, released his canines, and pricked his finger with blood before drawing a thin, vertical line along Sebastian's forehead. "Sebastian Lucas Silivasi, I anoint you in the name of the royal house of Demir and by the grace of the celestial deities. May your life be filled with peace, triumph, and purpose. May your path always be blessed."

He ushered Deanna forward and waited for her to kneel.

He drew a similar line along her flawless complexion and repeated the same refrain, taking her full name—Deanna Debois Silivasi—from Nachari's mind. "Keep this little one safe," he whispered in Deanna's ear, referring to the anterior fortress, the diamond-embedded holding cell where the *destinies* and children would wait out the battle, safely locked in together.

"I will," she whispered back.

Sensing the moment, or maybe understanding how much Prince Jadon needed it, Sebastian climbed down from his lap, wriggled between his strong arms and legs, and wrapped his tiny arms around the prince's shoulders, nestling his head in the crook of Jadon's neck.

Prince Jadon accepted the hug with open arms and cradled the child in return, struggling to contain such deep emotion: He had lost his kingdom once before. He had lost his sisters and his loyalists. He had lost everything because of his faithless, wicked twin, and now he was losing a family...a community too precious and dear to fathom.

But all was not lost, he had to remind himself.

Napolean had kept the traditions and customs alive.

The descendants of his loyalists had multiplied and thrived, and Prince Jadon's sisters yet lived.

At least for now—*they lived.*

And Prince Jadon had an opportunity—one harrowing, singular, last opportunity—to finally make things right.

No...

He did not intend to fail.

* * *

On the top tier of the underground colony, Prince Jaegar Demir stood in the Congressional Hall Auditorium staring out at the whole of the house of Jaegar from the center of the dimly lit stage. Though the Millenia Harvest Moon was still in full swing, the vampires in the house of Jaegar had managed to pull themselves away from their various...festivities in order to catch a glimpse of their legendary patriarch. True, the prince and the council had decided earlier that the majority of Dark Ones need not know of his presence, the occurrence of his reanimation—it was best to leave them none the wiser. However, all that had changed in Napolean Mondragon's courtyard, following the female vampire's slaughter, Prince Jadon's challenge to one-to-one combat, and the ensuing battle yet to take place in the Red Canyons.

Now, as Prince Jaegar stood on the strange platform dais, staring out at this odd underground arena with its glistening floors and high, carved-out ceiling, nerves were high, testosterone was flowing, and feral, predatory instincts were at an apex.

Still...

Young and old, soldier and guard, councilmen, fledgling, and ancient held their tongue and restrained their restless energy, hanging on the prince's every utterance. "I wish you could have been there, long ago in Romania," he began, "to witness the power of our movement: the fear we commanded throughout the land, the authority we wielded over the royal court, the noble class and peasants alike. I wish you could have attended the many glorious sacrifices. But alas, I find myself in this peculiar position, reanimated in the body of your infamous executioner whilst reflecting my own glorious persona and asking you—all of you, my faithful servants and distant progeny—to take up my cause yet again, to support me in battle and wage a war of Blood Vengeance."

His speech was met with guttural grunts, feral hisses, and vile expletives as the Dark Ones seethed with rage...and purpose. Yea, they would follow him anywhere. They would fight—and kill—as if their own lives were on the line.

Of this, Prince Jaegar had no doubt.

"Will you join me in the Red Canyons this night?" His voice soared throughout the auditorium. "Will you slay your enemy, male and female alike—will you meet me in the Valley of Death & Shadows if necessary?"

Strong, muscle-bound arms rose high above their heads as the sons of Jaegar pumped their fists in the air and chanted in rhythmic unity, until the combined din of their thunderous voices shook the auditorium in a murderous roar.

Prince Jaegar took a large stride forward and smiled.

Then Zeus approached the stage, head bowed low and shoulders curled forward in a submissive posture. He climbed the stairs to the top of the dais, laid a long, sturdy broadsword at Prince Jaegar's feet, and swiftly backed away: From what Oskar Vadovsky had told him, the blade belonged to Achilles Zahora, and it had been tested in many battles, most notably during the dual beheadings of Damien and Dane Alexiares. Apparently, Saber's adopted father and younger brother had died in the heart of the Red Canyons, eighteen months past—their hearts had been seized from their chests, right in front of the treasonous Dark One, during a perilous meeting with the house of Jadon following Saber's capture.

A good omen to be sure.

Prince Jaegar dipped down lithely, never bowing the length of his back. He lifted the sword and stood up swiftly, his movement as fluid as water, then tested the weight of the sword in his hand. The corner of his mouth curved up in a devious smirk, and he lunged forward, thrust the blade through Zeus' abdomen, withdrew it cleanly, and held it up in fascination...

Rank approval and appreciation.

Yes, this would do.

He searched the first row of the auditorium until his eyes met Salvatore Nistor's, then Oskar Vadovsky's, each vampire in turn. Depending on what happened later that morn, both elder statesmen may—or may not—be dead males walking. "Chairman," he said, addressing Oskar by his esteemed position as head of the Dark Ones' Council, "heal this boy's wounds, would you? Before he bleeds all over my boots." He glared forward, addressing the entire auditorium. "And all of you need to be more wary, remain on your toes. Zeus should not have been so easily skewered."

CHAPTER TWENTY-THREE

THE ENCHANTED FOREST

Following the badge of *forgiveness*, Braden had felt emotionally drained and physically spent. He had sprawled beneath the Tree of Light to sleep a while, and his dreams had carried him back to another place and time...

Dark Moon Vale.

Two years ago...

When he had first met Jocelyn Levi and the Silivasi family...

When he had dressed like a ghastly, embarrassing rendition of Count Dracula—complete with the long, flowing cape, painted white skin, and a high, stiff collar atop a pale silk shirt—and directly gotten into a minor tiff with Marquis Silivasi. Weary of what Marquis had seen as insolence, the elder Ancient Master Warrior had promptly placed Braden in *Time Out*, sealed upside down and hanging in a "bat cave," where he had then been discovered by a lycan named Tristan Hart and ultimately kidnapped and brutalized by both Tristan and his cohort, Willy Jackson. The lycans had nailed Braden to a crude, makeshift cross in a freezing, worn-down outbuilding behind an old, remote wooden cabin. They had tortured him and left him to die.

The dream had seemed so real.

Like he was living it all again for the very first time: being discovered by Jocelyn, watching helplessly as she had struggled to save him—to *feed* him—re-experiencing the effort it had taken to get down from that cross, and the way he had finally fought back, clinging to nothing more than a hope and a prayer, all the while both desperate and determined to prove himself, once and for all, to Nachari and Marquis.

In the end, he had saved Nathaniel's *destiny*.

He had fought off a fearsome lycan.

And he had managed to live to tell about it, thanks to the amazing healing talents of Kagen Silivasi.

Having awakened from the visceral dream, Braden had sat up, stretched his arms, and arched his back, only to find a pair of fresh, perfect discs—two new badges of honor—lying on the ground beside him.

Hope and *Perseverance*.

That had made him smile.

The forest was so strange...

One minute, the branch was curling around his shoulder, leading him through a vision where he had earned the badges of *patience* and *kindness*; the next vision had led him to *truth*. In his mind's eye, he had stood on a rooftop, once again, with his beloved mother and recalled how mercy, compassion, and understanding had healed them both—he had then been catapulted to the most brutal time of his life, where he had struggled and chosen to forgive his biological father in order to earn the badge of *forgiveness*. Still, the next moment, he had simply fallen asleep, entered a dreamscape, and awakened to find *hope* and *perseverance*, at which point, he had figured one never knew where their journey was really taking them, all the lessons and attributes they were learning, discovering...collecting along the way. With gratitude and a newfound humility, he had placed the fresh new discs in his pouch and risen from the ground to explore the forest a little bit more.

Now, as he stood before an odd, gauzy curtain hanging down from the sky and billowing in an unseen wind, he felt both an overwhelming urge to part the gossamer panels and step inside as well as a foreboding sense of dread, warning him to stay put—do not go any further—remain on this side of the veil.

He took a cautious step back and eyed it more carefully.

The ethereal fabric was both silver and gray, like clouds gathering before a storm, peaceful yet turbulent at once, and nestled beside the center of each panel, both on the left and on the right, were two rhombus tiebacks, draped by two shiny braided ropes, each meant to secure its corresponding panel in place.

Braden bent forward to look closer—no, not two rhombus tiebacks—two silver discs.

The one on the left read, *Protect*.

The one on the right read, *Trust*.

He scrunched up his face and considered their meaning. "What is this?" he murmured absently. He tried to peer behind the curtains, between large, windswept billows, but the scenery beyond the veil was too obscured. "Do I just...take the discs?" he said to no one in particular.

The disembodied voice of the Tree of Light floated to his ears on the forest-wind. "You protected Jocelyn in that cabin. You saved her from the lycan. And you protected Kristina when you challenged Ramsey Olaru, believing the Master Warrior was taking advantage of her innocence."

Remember and choose...

Braden stood still and thought back, instantly retrieving the memory, and if he hadn't been so spooked by the gossamer curtains—and whatever lay beyond them—he might have chuckled aloud: Yep, at fifteen years old, before the two had been promised to be mated, Braden had seen a page in Kristina's diary, a page upon which she had waxed all poetic about Ramsey Olaru, wondering if he really cared for her...or just wanted to use her for sex.

Even now, the memory made Braden's blood boil.

Kristina knew darn well that Ramsey would one day have a *destiny* of his own; still, she had still been willing to take a chance. She had been lonely, maybe a little bit desperate, and she had gotten furious with Braden for reading her journal.

Yikes, he thought.

Furious was an understatement, and he cringed at the memory...

'Cause yeah—after that—he had come at her like an angry lion, locked one arm around her waist, pressed his chest against her back, and grasped her chin with his other hand before tilting her head to the side...to expose her jugular.

"Shit," he said out loud. That had been his first real experience with dominant, male-vampire instincts, and his second had been even more reckless. He had confronted Ramsey Olaru, all six feet, five inches, and 240 pounds of the badass, ruthless sentinel, in Napolean's front yard; more or less, directly antagonizing the GQ predator—on purpose—and then hurling a stone at his back in order to protect Kristina's honor. Turns out, Ramsey had never touched her. Saber, who was still a Dark One at the time, had cloaked himself in Ramsey's likeness, the sentinel's persona, in order to do Salvatore and Oskar's dark bidding, but point was: Kristina didn't know that. Braden didn't know that. And he had been willing to get torn apart, possibly limb by limb, in order to defend her.

So yeah, the Tree of Light was right—*go figure*—protection was one of Braden's core attributes. Feeling a bit more confident, he stepped forward, toward the left side of the gossamer screen, and removed the badge, *protect*, from the center of the left-hand panel, tying the curtain back with the braided rope beneath it.

The badge glowed in his hand with golden light, and he placed it inside his satchel.

Then he stared, hard, at the other disc—*trust*—and that deep, wary sense of foreboding rose again in his stomach. "Trust who?" he mumbled. "Trust what?"

And that's when he saw him, the magnificent figure bathed in light, every color of the rainbow radiating out from his aura, the single white cone protruding from his forehead, shimmering like a resplendent, living ray of sunshine.

Braden dropped to one knee and bowed his head. "Lord Monoceros."

* * *

It was time.

Lord Monoceros knew it was time, and Braden was almost ready.

Almost.

Ready.

Monoceros reached out his hand from beyond the veil, the dimension between planes and worlds, and spoke in a gentle but commanding brogue: "Trust me. Trust in the celestial deities. Trust in yourself, son—your wisdom, power, and goodness—and trust in your love for Kristina."

The astonished young vampire raised his head, and the gold pupils within his burnt sienna irises nearly glowed with warmth and curiosity. As Braden rose to his full six-foot-two height, Lord Monoceros could not help but appreciate the impressive adult male he was becoming: proud, broad shoulders; strong, defined musculature; and a powerful, stalwart chest that rose and fell with deep, even breaths. Even his naturally tanned, flawless complexion seemed somehow more mature, to say nothing of such exquisite, sculpted, more seasoned features.

Braden took a graceful step toward the arc between the curtains, and the cotton voile cloth which girded his waist cascaded as he strode forward, revealing lean but powerful thighs beneath the hem of the diaphanous skirt. "I don't understand," he said, reaching out to accept Lord Monoceros' proffered hand, yet stopping just short of crossing the threshold...piercing the veil by stepping beyond the curtains.

Lord Monoceros flashed a compassionate smile. "Not yet, but you will. Until now, I have asked you to remember and choose—we, the celestial bodies, have bid you to remember and choose—we have shown you the past, and you have collected your due, several badges of honor, earned along your journey. But now..." With a gentle tug on Braden's hand, he slowly glided backward in the hopes of ushering the vampire forward. "But now, I must show you more than your past—I must show you the present and once again bid you to make a choice: You may go on from here into the Valley of Spirit & Light, or you may return to Dark Moon Vale."

As curious as Braden seemed—as curious as he was—Lord Monoceros fully understood that the exceptional young male was also highly intuitive—they had fostered him to be so—and he was feeling a familiar pit in his stomach, a terrible sense of foreboding. His arm still extended, his hand still linked with Lord Monoceros', Braden took a deep breath for courage and passed beneath the curtain.

Good lad.

When nothing happened, Braden cocked both brows and waited for the celestial god to instruct him.

"Close your eyes," Monoceros said.

Braden closed them slowly, and the celestial deity sent three haunting visions, one at a time, into the vampire's occipital lobe, allowing each to play out in clear, concise succession: First, Prince Jadon standing on a festive stage in Napolean's lantern-lit courtyard, challenging Prince Jaegar to a lethal battle, "brother against brother, winner take all."

Lord Monoceros allowed the vision to linger, to be fully processed and understood, before introducing the second: Kristina, wearing a wet, raspberry wine-colored skirt, huddled like a fearful child, arms around her knees, on a large brass bed in an underground chamber. Once again, he paused to let Braden sort the information, and then he peered into his thoughts to make sure the vampire understood the vision, clearly.

Dear gods, she's in the Dark Ones' Colony! Braden decried inwardly.

Precisely, Lord Monoceros reflected.

With great regret, yet greater sense of purpose, Lord Monoceros flooded Braden's lobe with the third and final vision: a beautiful female, lying in repose, dressed in an elegant burial robe of lavender and ivory, her hands gently folded across her midriff while resting upon a soft antique pillow embroidered in cross-stitch.

Braden jerked back as if Lord Monoceros had just burned him, snatching his hand away and instantly breaking the connection: *Is this some kind of a joke?* he thought. He blinked several times, and then his knees began to buckle.

Lily!

My mother...

Mamica!

As Braden hit the ground and scrabbled backward, Lord Monoceros could not help but notice that he literally kicked up earth with his heels in his hurry to scurry to the other side of the curtains, and worse than that—far worse than his immediate desire to flee—Lord Monoceros could also feel the young vampire's heart breaking. "Yes," Monoceros whispered, moving to block Braden's path of retreat. "Slain by Prince Jaegar." He paused to infuse as much healing empathy into his voice as possible. "I am so very sorry, Braden."

Braden collided with the celestial god's legs and pushed hard against the hallowed barrier. When Lord Monoceros didn't budge, he dug his nails into the ground and snarled. "No!" He whipped around, sprang to his feet, and landed in a crouch. Then he raised his head, his eyes emblazoned with stark, desperate dread and feral anger, even as he squared his shoulders to the celestial god in challenge. "What the fuck is this!" He stood up slowly. "Fix it! Undo it. Send me back, ten minutes earlier, right before it happens."

Lord Monoceros remained as placid as still water—the lad would need his strength. "I cannot."

Braden glared at him, incredulous. "You can! You're a god, aren't you?"

"I am."

"Then please...*please*! You don't understand—my mother doesn't deserve this. She never meant any harm, not to anyone, and it took us all this time, all these years, to finally work things out...to finally understand each other. You know that! You know what it took me to forgive... You know how badly I needed her love, and now, I finally have it. *I finally have it!* Please, Lord Monoceros, send me back, before her...murder. Let me fix it or let me die trying. *Please*." He waited with wide, hopeful eyes and bated breath.

Lord Monoceros placed his hand on Braden's trembling shoulder. "Look at me, son."

Braden's eyes were so stricken...so haunted.

"Trust me when I tell you, I would never have wished this for you, but what has happened cannot be undone."

"But why not?"

"Braden—"

"You saved Tiffany Olaru! I mean, the goddess Andromeda

saved Tiffany for Ramsey, after she was slain in the Tall Pines Village Park by Tawni Duvall. Andromeda turned back the hands of time so that Ramsey could get a do-over."

Lord Monoceros shook his head. "That was different."

"How?"

"Because the dark lord Ademordna challenged the laws of creation when he reanimated Salvatore Nistor: He created a rift in the cosmos, a tear reaching back as far as time immemorial, threatening to unravel the very threads of life as we know it. One cannot undo the design of the universe without also undoing the laws...undoing their own existence...nay, even undoing the gods. Andromeda stepped in to protect *All That Is*. Not to favor Ramsey."

Braden winced in pain, realizing his argument was futile. "Please..." His voice, nothing more than a faint, hushed whisper, he had to say it anyway—he had to try at least one more time. *"Please."*

"Braden, listen to me carefully, son. This night, Prince Jaegar and Prince Jadon will meet in the Red Canyons at three a.m. to engage in a final, determinative battle. Should Prince Jadon prevail, he will save the celestial princesses, Ciopori and Vanya— he will save Kristina Riley Silivasi, your intended—but should he fall, their lives will be forfeit. The warriors and sentinels will try to save them, but I fear they cannot. What I have given you this night—what I have shown you in this forest—is the most powerful weapon of all, but the choice is yours. You may join your mother in the Valley of Spirit & Light, allow events on earth to unfold as they will, and no one will blame you...hold it against you. Or you may return to your body at a pre-appointed time, determined by the waning of the Millenia Harvest Moon, and fight for the house that you love...the female you love...step into your preordained purpose. I am giving you the choice to walk away from this destiny or to collect one final emblem, the badge of *trust*: to trust me, to trust the celestial deities, to trust yourself, and above all else, to trust in your love for Kristina. As always, you retain free will, but what I will not do—what I cannot do—is restore your mother's soul to her body. You must think it over and decide. Remember and choose."

* * *

Lord Monoceros' words may as well have drifted into the ether like smoke from a banking campfire: thin, wispy, and swiftly dispersed.

Braden couldn't comprehend any of it.

He couldn't catch the celestial god's meaning before it floated away, dissolved into air, and scattered as distant particles of... nonsense, lost to the atmosphere.

His mother was gone, and the celestial deity could not bring her back.

What would become of Dario...and *Conrad*?

What would their family's future look like?

And that was assuming Braden could even prevail in a battle against Prince Jaegar—*no, not Prince Jaegar*—an eventual battle against Achilles Zahora.

Oh, gods...

And Kristina?

Why was she in the Dark Ones' Colony, unless...

Unless...

Oh, fuck...

Achilles Zahora.

Still, what had Lord Monoceros given Braden in the forest— what had the Tree of Light really shown him? What could he possibly possess now that he didn't possess before, that would give him any chance in hell of prevailing in that kind of a battle? Other than a satchel full of silver badges and one single sparring session, where he had learned to wield some energy... Braden could never defeat Achilles.

He sank to the earthen floor, drew his knees to his chest, and wept.

He hated for Lord Monoceros to see him like this, to witness his true inherent weakness, but Lily...his mother...*Mamica!*

And Kristina too?

It was just too much...

Way too much.

The celestial gods had chosen the wrong vampire.

CHAPTER TWENTY-FOUR

DARK MOON VALE ~ 3:00 A.M.

The Red Canyons were shaped like a long, narrow ribbon, nearly fifty miles in length, on the westernmost end of Dark Moon Vale. On the far northern end of the expansive gorge, one would find the house of Jadon's illustrious Academy, Mineral Plant, and the distal back acreage of Napolean's compound. On the far southern end, one would discover the tattered ruins of the Dark Ones' Sacrificial Chamber, the series of caves where the descendants of Jaegar once routinely carried out the hideous ritual of ushering new sons into the world, whereby their innocent, tortured mothers would die wretchedly upon giving birth. Auspiciously named by the early settlers the densest forest in the vale—which flanked the ribbon for miles and miles, jutting east of the canyon—was collectively called the Valley of Shadows, and the flatter, more arid land to the west denoted the staggered border of the Vampyr's valley, where the public lands ended and private lands began.

Now, standing on the valley floor—in the center of the canyon and across from his twin brother, Jaegar—Prince Jadon glanced upward at the high, rocky crevasse, the eastern shelf of the towering ribbon, and watched as Princess Vanya and Princess Ciopori perched on the rocks, each one seated before a member of the Colony Guard, their legs left to dangle off the precarious edge of the cliff.

He held his breath for a moment and tried to slow his breathing.

He knew—or at least he believed—no one would touch his sisters until the battle was over.

But they were so far away from their mates...from the Master Warriors...

So far away from Prince Jadon.

And Kristina...

She was seated several yards to Jadon's right, several yards removed from the princesses and further back from the ledge, but also flanked by a member of the Colony Guard, the male called Zeus. As it appeared, it was not Zeus' job to slay her but to retrieve her, should the battle go in Prince Jaegar's favor, and knowing this only added one more element of concern for Prince Jadon—it further heightened his tension.

At least, Prince Jadon thought, should he blessedly prevail, Ramsey would no longer need to hunt a Dark One to ascertain Kristina's whereabouts through torture, and the king, the tracker, and Santos Olaru would no longer have to enter the old sacrificial tunnels in a perilous mission to rescue the captured female. She was right there, out in the open.

"Gods be merciful," Prince Jadon whispered beneath his breath, knowing that both Julien and Ramsey had now been charged with a far more lethal duty, and he turned his head to examine the opposite side of the cliffs, where Oskar Vadovsky and Salvatore Nistor knelt before the two powerful sentinels, each awaiting their fate based upon the outcome of the battle. Much like Kristina, the council chair and the sorcerer were also seated on the edge of the high bluff, only abutting the western ledge, opposite the princesses, and miles away from their dark, supportive brethren. It was as if the battle were taking place on the floor of a grand, organic, earthen opera, and the VIP theater boxes, on both sides of the auditorium, were filled with the eventual spoils of war.

Prince Jadon didn't like this at all.

But the princesses had agreed to the stakes—to *be* the stakes— and Prince Jaegar had insisted upon fighting for the females. It was the one condition the entire battle had been predicated upon: He would only fight for the right to slay his sisters; anything less, and the ante would not have been high enough to seal the devil's bargain.

In truth, the dark prince had been right not to trust the house of Jadon.

Prince Jaegar had probably known all along that the house of Jadon had no intentions of honoring the wager, that the moment Jadon fell—*if he fell*—Napolean's warriors would rush in to save the females. And it had been equally hard to object to the rules of the gambit as the Dark Ones were willing to turn Oskar and Salvatore over, prior to the battle, so that the house of Jaegar could not easily interfere in the dark vampires' swift execution, should the gods grant favor to the nobler prince and allow him to prevail in combat.

"Please let me prevail," Jadon whispered, considering the flip side of the same treacherous coin: Of course, Prince Jadon got it— treachery flowed two ways. The Dark Ones had no sincere intention of keeping their end of the bargain, either. Should Prince Jadon prevail, they would be just as likely to try to rush in and save the chairman and sorcerer.

He rolled his shoulders to release some tension.

His heart was pounding like a medieval tabor, causing his chest to ache.

Calm down, Jadon, he told himself. *Vampires can travel very,*

very *quickly, and your sisters are warded—well protected—shielded in their hidden, enchanted breastplates. If the Dark Ones try to pierce their backs or retrieve their hearts, the effort will be instantly and magically thwarted.*

Despite the piteous, existential attempt at self-reassurance, nothing could mitigate the fact that Ciopori and Vanya's throats were fully exposed to the Dark Ones' blades—

Stop it, Jadon!

So be it...

It is as it is.

It only means there is no room for error...

Prince Jadon could not make any mistakes.

He took a deep, cleansing breath, then watched...and waited...as a host of the house of Jaegar's soldiers pushed forward, crowding behind the guards and the females like an army of devilish black-and-red fire ants swarming atop the eastern cliffs, possessed with bloodlust and equally determined to slay the detested queen ants. Then he watched...and waited...as the much smaller but far more fearsome force of warriors from the house of Jadon gathered along the western cliffside—beside and behind Ramsey and Julien—their eyes fixed forward, alert, and trained decidedly on the canyon floor.

As the Millenia Harvest Moon waned—only a third of the soft, glowing reddish orb could now be seen in the midnight-blue sky, illuminated by distant, fading starlight—the silence in the canyon grew deafening. Indeed, all would be *listening*, even more than watching, to hear one of the princes' hearts stop beating, the sound that would signal the end of the battle and clearly delineate the victor.

The smell of pine and juniper filled the air in the theater.

A cool, noiseless breeze swept through the ominous canyon.

And electricity rose and fell as Niko and Jankiel called upon the powers of the celestial deities to bathe the ribbon in a hazy, dim light, sealing, insulating, and protecting the valley's humans from the destructive forces of nature and the devastating effects of vampiric emotion.

It was done.

The stage was set and ready.

And the stakes could not be higher.

Facing his evil twin for what, perhaps, would be the last time in his existence, Prince Jadon drew Napolean's Sword of Andromeda and watched silently as Prince Jaegar drew a broadsword of his own.

* * *

Her hind end resting on the back of bare heels, Kristina sat forward on her knees, five or six feet from the edge of the cliff, and wrung her hands in her lap.

She couldn't look.

She wouldn't look.

Oh, hell...

Shit!

She had to look.

Zeus' hot, rancid breath was like damp, sticky steam wafting along the back of her neck, and the cold breeze was carrying the scent to her nostrils, almost making her gag. She turned her head to the side and glanced toward the princesses, hoping to both avoid the stench and catch Ciopori or Vanya's eyes, but both horrified females were staring forward and down, transfixed by the battle—or the tragedy—about to unfold on the canyon floor.

Dear gods, this wasn't happening!

Kristina narrowed her gaze and leaned forward.

She squinted her eyes to get a better look at Prince Jadon, only to realize if she could just relax—just enough to manipulate a bit of her energy—she could use her supernatural vision instead. She could dial the battle in...and out...as needed.

She concentrated on her breathing and tried again.

Unbelievable...

Prince Jadon Demir was really, truly...alive.

Or at least reanimated for a time.

And he was standing on the valley floor, opposite Prince Jaegar, in an ivory pair of trousers, high leather boots, and a ruffled, long-sleeved tunic, with sleeves bound at the wrists. Draped around his strong, broad shoulders, he wore a shimmering gold cloak—Fabian or one of the wizards must have fashioned it for him with magic—and Prince Jaegar was dressed the same way, only his trousers and his tunic were as black as his soulless eyes, his uniform matched his thick, wavy hair, and his cloak was deep bloodred.

"As if we needed the reminder," Kristina murmured absently, construing the gold and red cloaks as *good* versus *evil*—the difference between the two twin brothers was already obvious as hell.

They each drew their swords, and she waited, half expecting to hear a trumpet's blast or the call of a bugle. Anything but this excruciating silence. And then she jerked back and gasped, as *just like that*, Prince Jaegar shifted his sword, over and back, in alignment with his shoulder, and charged forward with dizzying speed.

He launched into a sudden, flying lunge, aimed his broadsword at Prince Jadon's chest, and thrust at his heart, his red cloak flapping behind him.

Prince Jadon moved just as swiftly...

Just as supernaturally.

He dropped to the ground beneath Jaegar's weapon, placed one palm in the dirt for stability and balance, and waited for the perfect moment, when Prince Jaegar was flying directly above him. While doing what Kristina could only describe as a one-handed push-up, he stabbed upward with his sword hand and rotated the tip of his blade in an apparent attempt to disembowel Prince Jaegar—who literally shifted position in midair.

Kristina's jaw dropped open in astonishment as Prince Jaegar sucked in his gut, arched his back like a wild tom cat, and vaulted upward in midflight. He summersaulted forward—over and above Prince Jadon's head—and landed lithely behind him.

Prince Jadon spun around and took several strides backward.

Oh gods, she could hardly bear to watch this...

Her entire life was riding on this battle, to say nothing of the princesses, the house of Jadon, and possibly...Braden's survival. She wanted to bury her head in her hands and start praying, but she didn't dare turn away.

Prince Jaegar spat something vile—Kristina couldn't hear it clearly—but Prince Jadon's eyes glowed red in response, and his fangs descended from his gums. He charged forward in a short series of rapid attacks, lunging at Prince Jaegar, again and again, their swords clattering in a deafening clamor, and then he brought his blade-arm up and around, as if drawing a half-circle around Prince Jaegar's head and shoulders, before slicing it down, crosswise, in an attempt to slit Prince Jaegar's throat.

Prince Jaegar's corporeal body faded in and out as he swiftly dissolved his molecules, allowed the sword to pass through his flesh like air, but not before the tip of Prince Jadon's blade caught the cinch of his crimson cloak and sent it fluttering to the ground.

Prince Jaegar answered the insult with a guttural snarl, and while Kristina didn't know that much about sword-fighting, she had learned a few of the basics from Braden when he had talked about his early training at the Academy or his rounds with Marquis and Julien, and the shit was flying fast and furious now, almost too swift and ferocious to track or process...

Lunge after lunge met with a parry and a counterattack.

A remise—then a riposte—followed by a series of feints.

Drop kicks, aerials, windmills, and summersaults...iron striking iron.

The earth beneath the princes shook, and not from the violent energy of emotion—but from their sheer vampiric strength, and all the while, both males grew angrier. Both vampires grew more feral and determined.

More focused.

More aggressive.

More bloodthirsty and brutal.

And then Prince Jadon raised his sword high above his head and held it in front of his glowing red eyes: The blade caught fire, began to sizzle with electricity, then came back down in a blue, purplish haze.

Kristina's eyes grew wide with wonder. She gazed across the canyon, scanned the ledge for the Master Wizards, and gulped as her mind began to process what her eyes were seeing:

Yep, it was subtle, but it was there.

They were lending their power to Prince Jadon.

And holy shit, Napolean Mondragon—all ten of his fingers were glowing with barely leashed, deadly radiation—the king was prepared to nuke half the valley if he had to, but he couldn't...

Right?

Not without incinerating the princesses and Kristina in the process, not without killing both Prince Jaegar and his better half, Prince Jadon. Not without destroying the host for Braden's body...

Kristina's bit her bottom lip to keep her teeth from chattering, even as Prince Jadon slashed his glowing sword downward and finally drew blood, striking Prince Jaegar's dominant wrist and opening his radial artery.

The evil prince responded with a surge of dark energy originating from the western clifftop near Salvatore Nistor, in the form of thick black smoke. He directed the tendrils like a second set of fingers, wrapping them tightly around the hilt of Prince Jadon's sword.

He ignored his pain.

He ignored the rapid blood loss.

He let go of his broadsword, drew both palms back, and lassoed Prince Jadon's weapon out of his hand, catching the grips of both blades in clenched fingers before either sword could hit the ground. And then he flew forward like a savage animal, fangs gnashing, biceps bulging, and drew both blades across one another in an aerial configuration of an X, determined to dislodge Prince Jadon's head in the crossing.

Kristina screamed in terror as Prince Jadon caught both blades with his naked hands, stopping each just short of piercing his neck. His arms began to tremble as he strained to wrest the heavy blades outward, Prince Jaegar strained to urge them inward, and blood began to drip in bright red rivulets from Prince Jadon's lacerated palms.

The clifftops grew silent.

The air around the princes sizzled...

Prince Jaegar began to weaken from blood loss, and Prince Jadon's grip began to slip.

And then...

Prince Jadon vanished.

CHAPTER TWENTY-FIVE

K nees still drawn to his chest, Braden sobbed until his tear ducts were empty.

Trust Lord Monoceros.

Trust the celestial deities.

Trust himself, and above all else, trust in his love for Kristina...

How could he?

He wasn't ready.

Yet Lord Monoceros believed in him...

No sooner had the latter thought crossed his mind than his satchel began to glow, and the weight of the bag intensified.

Trust had been added to his earlier badges...

"But...but—"

His body rocked backward, and he was suddenly enveloped in darkness.

"Wait!"

He clutched the satchel at his hip and clenched his eyes shut. He was falling...falling...tumbling backward at great speed and velocity, merging into an ocean of dark clouds and dense vapor, crossing eons of space and time as the cocoon surrounding him grew lighter and lighter. As bits and pieces, snippets, and impressions streamed into his consciousness, even as they zoomed rapidly past him.

The soldiers in the house of Jaegar perched atop a high, eastern rocky crevasse.

The house of Jadon warriors gathered in the west.

The princesses surrounded by brutal, would-be executioners...

Kristina Riley—*Red!*—kneeling before a savage, dark henchman, just feet from the edge of a cliff, her bare feet tucked beneath her, her eyes wide with terror and dread.

Pain seared the palms of his hands, and he released his grip on the pouch. *Great lords of the celestial sphere*, he felt as if his fists were being sliced in half. Then just like that, he was standing on a canyon floor, still clothed in a simple, crude tie of cotton cloth, his feet still wrapped in leather sandals, his arms, legs, and chest still bare. Only, his hands were wrapped around twin blades—two separate, mighty swords of iron—and he was struggling to wrench them away from his neck.

His satchel began to glow again, only this time with banked, radiant heat, and the badges he had collected in the Enchanted Forest exploded into eight points of brilliant light.

The light infused his hands, healed his wounds, and streamed into the length of one blade, wrapping around the steel like luminous, ghostly fingers, and Braden, with his corporeal eyes still closed, tuned everything out, except the energy around him.

What had the stick-warrior taught him?

The energy before him was dark and ancient. It flowed from a collective, empty void that had been filled with bloodthirsty hatred, but it ebbed when shown the true empty nature of its soul's reflection. The enemy was flexing the strength in his arms, even as he grew weaker and weaker from blood loss. Yet and still, this Dark One's power was gathered, solely, in the Triple Warmer Meridian, the fight, flight, and freeze response anchored behind his eyes.

And his next move...

His next move would be to drop the hilts of both swords, heal his radial artery with venom, then strike at Braden's heart with an agile clawed hand.

Braden slowed his breathing and opened his entire consciousness to the elements around him, synthesizing the information in under a millisecond: The atomic weight of his own sword—*the Sword of Andromeda!*—was 55.845, with 2.1 percent carbon added. It achieved a physical state at twenty-degrees Celsius, and contained twenty-six protons, thirty neutrons, and another twenty-six electrons. He shifted the atomic structure of his right hand and his sword-arm to match the composition, and the blade became an extension of his body, folding into his flesh and bone.

He slowly opened his eyes and took in the visage of the dark, onyx, hate-filled eyes before him—so it was Prince Jaegar.

But wait—

No...

Coal-black orbs gave way to citrine irises, and a six-foot-tall, broad, muscular frame towered upward into a brawny, malevolent, seven-foot giant.

Achilles Zahora.

So be it.

Just as expected, Achilles dropped the remaining sword, leaped backward, and swathed his wrist in venom, and that's when Braden bent his knees, flattened both heels against the ground, and drew a mighty surge of power up through his feet, borrowing the anima from the earth's molten core. The Sword of Andromeda still merged with his flesh, he raised both arms, lunged forward, and struck inward with the heels of both hands, slamming the atomic strength of steel into each of Achilles' temples in a swift, harsh *whack*! The goal was not to crush his skull but to sear two electrical currents into the Triple Warmer Meridian, stunning the brutish colony guard and freezing the giant in place.

If only for an instant, Achilles froze, and that's when Braden lunged forward and downward. He extended his arm, released the blade, and skewered the giant through the foot—for all intents and purposes, he may as well have been driving a tent-stake made of steel through flesh, blood, and bone, then deep into the ground.

Braden opened both palms, directed the tips of his fingers toward the stake, then sent extreme heat and pressure into the soil all around Achilles' foot and the elaborate spike, crystallizing the carbon into diamond and tethering Achilles to the ground.

He filled his lungs with breath and came up swinging.

A brutal uppercut to the throat chakra, turning the associated aura from blue to brown; a rapid-fire series of six jabs to the heart and seven to the solar plexus, striking the Anahat chakra and wounding the Manipura; a left hook to the brow, the Agya chakra, and a right hook to the crown of the head. And then one last sledgehammer punch for good measure, right between the eyes, the back of Braden's fist laced with the mirror image of an empty, carnal soul.

Prince Jaegar's reflection.

Achilles' spiritual composition.

The giant vampire listed to the side and staggered against the iron tether.

Braden drew the sword from the ground, all eight colors of the badges now glowing like a columnar prism of fire, and brought it upward, above his shoulder, while spinning around in a full 360-degree circle. In five swift slashes, moving faster than both light and sound, he sliced the brachial, carotid, and femoral arteries, and then he braced the pommel of the sword in both fists, one hand locked over the other, and impaled the ferocious colony guard straight through the pulmonary artery. *The heart.*

A collective gasp echoed in the canyon as Achilles Zahora listed forward and fell on top of Braden, both lethal vampires prone on the ground.

Citrine eyes gave way to onyx, and a blood-drenched mouth turned up in a smile.

Braden stared into the hate-filled orbs, watching—*praying*—for the pupils to dim like a fallen, fading star, waiting to crawl from beneath the giant, to take his head, extract his wounded heart, and set all the unholy pieces on fire. But what shone back at him was not Prince Jaegar or Achilles' death but someone else's...

Napolean's courtyard, decorated in the full array of autumn colors: chairs interlaced with leafy vines; candlelit lanterns hanging from trees; arched, slatted walkways leading to twelve elegant white pavilions; and his mother, Lily, standing back and to the side, with Conrad, Colette Nastase, Zayda Patrone, and Natalia Olaru, while Kristos, Dario, and Aric Zander spoke with Keitaro Silivasi and Arielle Nightsong.

Then just like that, faster than an eye could blink or a crow could caw, Lily jerked backward, her shoulders bound by a strong, brawny arm. She arched her back in an unnatural contortion, gasped her last breath of air, and fell to the ground, even as Prince Jaegar Demir appeared once again in the center of the courtyard, holding her blood-drenched heart in his hand like a prized garish trophy before setting the organ on fire.

Braden retched in his mouth.

His heart constricted and he lost all awareness of the battle... of the body lying like a heavy stone weight on top of him.

He lost all desire to finish what he had started.

Emboldened by the sudden shift in energy, onyx eyes flashed back to citrine, and Achilles Zahora crawled off Braden like a wounded, half-dead animal—he bent over into an embryonic position and slowly but steadily began to heal his critical, gushing arteries.

* * *

As if it no longer existed, time seemed to stand still.

Seconds passed...

Maybe minutes...

Could've been hours.

Braden had no sense of anything, other than the pain in his heart and a strange, dull impression of being more and more disconnected from his body. It was as if he were living in a dreamscape, hiding in a dark, hazy corner, and waiting to see if the dream would have a good and peaceful ending or quickly devolve into a hideous nightmare.

Achilles Zahora—at least it seemed like Achilles Zahora, *felt* like Achilles Zahora—crawled back over Braden's prone body, grasped him by the shoulders in two powerful, brawny hands, and jerked him upright before slamming him into the hard, unforgiving ground.

Braden's breath whooshed out of his lungs, but he didn't fight back.

He wanted to stay in the corner.

A solid punch to his rib cage, and several bones broke. Then another. And another. He heard a distant, wretched cough... perhaps his own...and then a voice in his head, foreign yet familiar: "Braden, get up."

He didn't know this vampire—

Or did he?

His brain was too fuzzy, but his spirit crackled like an old transistor radio, dialing in the sound and a faint awareness:

Prince Jadon Demir? Inside his head? Or somewhere, far away, out in the ether?

Either way, it didn't matter.

"Braden, get up!" The prince sounded desperate this time. "I can no longer fully inhabit your body! Your soul is too powerful. Your essence is too strong. Vampire, I need you to come back and fight!"

Come back and fight...

Come back and fight?

Ah yes, Prince Jadon was there—of course—and the prince could definitely fight.

In fact, linked as they were, however obscurely, Braden finally understood what needed to happen: The moment he passed away, Marquis, Saber, Saxson, Keitaro, and a dozen other warriors would surround the princesses in a warded circle, place them inside a protective holding cell, and fight to the death if necessary. Jankiel and Niko would continue to call upon the gods for favor—the entire Council of Wizards would wage war with spells and magick—and Ramsey would most certainly rescue Kristina. Julien and Santos would help him. And the king—if it became necessary—would destroy them all with his solar power.

He would...

He could...

He had to.

The brutal beating stopped.

Either that, or Achilles had already turned Braden's body into hamburger—but no more blows to the chest and ribs. Rather, the sound of dust being disturbed, the fearsome colony guard crawling around in the dirt, scooping up handfuls of soil while sweeping his hand from side to side.

"He's got your sword!" Prince Jadon again. "Napolean's Sword of Andromeda."

Braden's head lolled to the side as he tried to listen.

"He's pitching it atop the eastern cliffs! *Shit*—he tossed the sword to the Dark Ones. Braden, get up! *He is going to kill you.*"

Braden blinked several times.

His eyelids were so heavy, and his heart, even heavier.

Fuck, that wasn't good.

The Sword of Andromeda was gone, which meant so were the badges...

Braden's power.

His celestial assistance...

All he had gained in the Enchanted Forest.

He could not defeat Achilles with his bare hands alone, going toe to toe with the vicious executioner. "Take my body," he tried to murmur to Prince Jadon, but he wasn't sure if the words were audible.

It didn't matter.

He was traveling now...

Ascending out of the safe, hidden corner, speeding across the vale, until at once, he descended, his ethereal feet still attired in rudimentary sandals, inside the familiar circular Hall of Justice, with its ancient walls and copious ceremonial history.

Lily...

Mamica...

She was lying in repose on an exquisitely adorned platform, just like Lord Monoceros had shown him—she was bathed and dressed in an elegant robe of lavender and ivory, her hands folded peacefully across her midriff, resting atop a fine antique pillow—awaiting final rest, to be delivered back to earth...and buried within the same.

He hadn't looked that closely before, while in the Enchanted Forest with Lord Monoceros. Rather, he had snatched his hand away, jerked back, and swiftly broken the connection before any of the details could set in...*cement*...become permanent in his heart or his memory. But this time was different. He approached the platform slowly, studied his mother's tranquil, soft features, then zeroed in on the antique pillow.

He smiled faintly, though there was nothing joyful or light-hearted about this—he just recognized the family heirloom, the embroidered cross-stitch sewn by his great-grandmother and passed along from daughter to daughter over three generations. He remembered how much his mother had loved it, how she had always kept it on the bed, beside her...how she had clutched it in her hands when she prayed, almost like a religious relic: a symbolic crucifix or a beloved rosary.

Funny that after so many years, he had never taken the time to read it.

He bent over the pillow and studied the stitching, and for the first time in his life, he read the aged, cursive words aloud...

"Love is *patient*, love is *kind*. It does not envy, it does not boast, it is not proud." He gasped, and his bottom lip began to tremble. "It does not dishonor others, it is not self-seeking, it is not easily angered, it keeps no record of wrongs."

It forgives...

His eyes swelled with tears.

"Love does not delight in evil but rejoices with the...*truth*. It always *protects*"—he stammered over the words—"always *trusts*, always *hopes*, always *perseveres*." He staggered backward as he recited the last three words: "Love never fails."

Dear gods, the badges...

The Enchanted Forest.

And Lord Monoceros—*trust me, trust the celestial deities, trust yourself, and above all else, trust in your* love *for Kristina.*

"Love never fails."

He felt a strong, loving hand settle on his shoulder, and he heard Lord Monoceros' celestial voice: "That's right, Braden. Love is stronger than hate. You are stronger than Achilles. Prince Jadon was always stronger than his brother. The badges—all that you collected in the forest whilst visiting the bridge between worlds—were never outside of you but within. The sword was never a blade made of steel—*you* are the living Sword of Jadon, my son. You are the embodiment of love."

In that instant, Braden also recalled Lord Monoceros' cryptic words, spoken behind the veil in the Enchanted Forest: *What I have given you this night—what I have shown you in this forest—is the most powerful weapon of all...*"

Love.

Love was the weapon.

Love was the sword.

Braden was the embodiment of love...and love never fails.

Braden spun around to regard his lord—to apologize, to thank him, to seek his blessing—but Lord Monoceros wasn't there. He spun around again, bent over his mother, and kissed her gently on the forehead. Then he leaped from the floor, passed through the ancient ceiling, and shifted into a magnificent giant eagle, rocketing into the cool night air beneath the waning Millenia Harvest Moon, on his way back to his body...

To Achilles...

To the Red Canyons.

To the princesses and Kristina.

CHAPTER TWENTY-SIX

Kristina's heart was breaking for more than one reason...

The secret Zeus had just whispered in her ear to taunt her—the fact that Prince Jaegar had slain Lily Bratianu—*Braden's beloved Mamica!*—and all that was happening to Braden below, on the canyon floor.

Both were beyond imagining...

Kristina's worst nightmares come to life.

But she was solely focused, anchored in the here and now, on one thing—and one thing only—Braden, lying nearly lifeless on the cold canyon ground.

The Millenia Harvest Moon was but a shadow of its former self, dampening in the opaque night sky, sunrise was a little less than three hours away, and based upon Braden's sudden loss of vitality—his complete inability to get up and fight—it didn't look like Prince Jadon was coming back.

It had been so strange...

The transition.

One moment, Prince Jadon had been straining...trembling...

blood-soaked hands prying two blades of steel away from his neck. The next moment, the hands had been Braden's—*the body had been Braden's!*—clad in completely different attire. It had been impossible to tell fantasy from fiction, reality from illusion, and for lack of a saner description, Braden had been rooted to the spot like a tree.

Eyes closed.

Processing information?

And then the pouch at his side had glowed with radiant heat, exploded with light, and wrapped around the Sword of Andromeda—the weapon had disappeared inside his arm!

Prince Jaegar had morphed into Achilles Zahora, and that's when Braden had opened his eyes.

Achilles had dropped his sword, jumped back, and worked feverishly to heal his wrist with venom. Braden had lunged forward, stunned The Executioner with a brutal whack to both temples, then staked the Dark One's foot to the ground, using the sword—*no, using his arm?*—with what appeared to Kristina to be one-half iron and one-half wood, like the strong, studded branch of the same rooted tree.

And Achilles had frozen in place!

Braden had him.

He had beaten the unholy shit out of the vampire, slashed every one of his arteries, and staked him through the heart with his sword.

All that was left was to finish him.

But then Achilles had toppled over, landed on top of Braden, and nothing—*absolutely nothing*—made sense after that. Achilles took all the time he needed to heal his lethal wounds, he had, in turn, beaten Braden like a ragdoll, tossed Braden's sword to the Dark Ones, and all the while, Braden had just laid there...

Like he had simply...entirely...given up.

Horrific did not describe the gruesome beating...

Kristina had felt every vicious blow, every savage kick, every bone, as it bent, broke...snapped in Braden's rib cage. She had absorbed each strike as a hammer to her heart, bludgeoning all four chambers, and the agony had been profound... unbearable...spiritual.

Beyond what she could ever cover up with a Band-Aid.

And in those horrific moments, she had sworn to herself that even if it took a lifetime, she would kill Achilles Zahora. She would wait forever if she had to. She would go on living with one singular purpose: to avenge what Achilles had done to Braden—to avenge the wrong that had been done to Lily—even if it cost her...everything.

Now, as she kneeled atop the eastern cliffs, acutely aware of Zeus Dragavei lurching behind her, she tried to bank her emotions, brace her body, and bolt all four chambers of her ruined heart tightly shut...locked...sealed. Never again to open.

She absently glanced to the right, catching sight of the two royal princesses: Vanya's face was ashen, Ciopori seemed to be holding her breath, and they were both staring fixedly at the canyon floor, painfully aware of what was happening to Braden... what could also happen to them. Only, there was something else in both sisters' eyes, in the slant of their regal shoulders and the cast of their noble jaws: anger, defiance...stark determination.

They were not giving up for an instant.

Kristina gulped, swallowing her surrender and dread.

Maybe Napolean would still come through. Maybe the sentinels could fly across the canyon in the space of a heartbeat. Maybe Saber and Marquis had something up their sleeve—*of course they did; they had to*—in the event, in that moment, when Braden's heart stopped beating.

Bray's heart stopped beating...

No...

No!

This wasn't happening!

And fuck her defenses—why weren't they working?

Her life before Braden—her time *with* Braden—passed by in the space of one tragic heartbeat: unable to love...unable to trust...unable to let herself be vulnerable.

It was all bullshit!

She had wasted every precious, irreplaceable moment, filling up a deep, dark void and nursing wounds from the past with...*bullshit!*

She'd had a choice.

Souls always have a choice.

And now it was too late to make it—or was it?

She took a deep, steadying breath and glanced over her shoulder. Yep, Zeus was still there—with his nasty breath—and he was holding the Sword of Andromeda like his own personal spoil of war.

Nothing from nothing...leaves nothing.

She couldn't live without Braden.

Rising like a suddenly launched space shuttle, all rockets blazing, she sprang to her feet, spun around like a tigress, and snatched the sword from Zeus' hands before he had a chance to see her coming. Without looking back or giving him the opportunity to react, she hefted the sword above her head, cradled it in the palms of both hands, and raced to the edge of the cliff like a cheetah.

She had to time the jump just right.

She had to measure space, calculate time, and cover the exact, perfect distance.

She had to leap with every ounce of vampiric strength she possessed in order to reach her target, to descend behind Achilles Zahora, and pierce his heart as she landed.

She didn't know if the fall would kill her—if the fall *could* kill her—she wasn't even sure what she was doing, but she *did* love Bray. She did trust Bray. And she knew it was now or never.

As she hurtled off the edge of the cliff, springing forward and willing her body downward, a primal scream escaped her throat, and she released a lifetime of pent-up anguish.

* * *

The massive, majestic eagle swooped down from the sky, caught the screaming female in its talons, and dropped her—and the sword—as gently as possible, about ten feet away, before diving at Achilles—claws extended, then curled—ripping several chunks of flesh from the Dark One's shoulders and crushing several of Achilles' bones.

He circled around the stunned executioner three times before shifting effortlessly in the air and landing on mammalian feet. He raised both palms in the air in a provocative gesture. "Yo, dirtbag—I'm right here!"

Achilles staggered to the side, caught his balance, then dropped into a crouch, flexing both hulking biceps. Pain would not deter him.

"Eyes forward," Braden taunted, turning two fingers inward and pointing at his own burnt sienna peepers. It wasn't so much an act of bravado as a tactical calculation—he did not want Achilles Zahora to get any ideas about Kristina, who was as far away as possible, hunkered low to the ground and watching, but still right out in the open. Braden did not want The Executioner to use the wild redhead as bait...or leverage.

Achilles reached for his broadsword, which was lying in the dirt, and tried to scrape it off the hard, reddish soil, but Braden flicked his left wrist at the blade, sent a scorching hot fissure of violet and white flames along the length of the sabre, the fire radiating at 1,540 degrees, and instantly melted the carbon-infused steel.

Achilles dropped the wasting metal, drew back his hand, and snarled, gnashing his fangs.

Braden rooted his lifeforce deep into the ground, like an ageless oak expanding its roots, even as he relaxed the chi in his shoulders and arms, making the limbs more limber. He stared into Achilles' rage-filled citrine eyes, ignoring the rising bloodred glow, deeper...deeper...deeper still, until he glimpsed the naked, elemental seat of his soul: a raw thirst for power, arrogance and pride, dishonor, infinite selfishness, vengeance, and hate. Achilles suckled on malevolence, feasted on evil, and lived for the kill...to beget devastation.

But there was something more...

Something greater than the rest.

He was bathed from his root chakra to his tainted third eye in envy.

Envy...

Achilles envied everyone and everything—he envied the exalted leaders of the Dark Ones' Colony, he envied the house of Jadon, and most of all, he envied Braden Bratianu and any other vampire who was given *one* female to *breed with* for a lifetime. Not out of a desire to love or know companionship but out of a desire to spawn a limitless, superior bloodline. And all forms of envy had been heightened this night by the dark lords of the underworld, beneath the awesome, unrestrained powers of the Millenia Harvest Moon.

So be it.

Wielding his clenched fist like a sledgehammer, Braden exploded from his stance, leaped forward, and struck Achilles in the Adam's apple. He rotated his fist, leaned into the blow, and infused a golden-white light into the vampire's throat. "Sucks to be Salvatore's patsy, doesn't it?" he growled in the Dark One's ear.

Achilles dropped down, then came up swinging, throwing a brutal uppercut, but Braden was already back where he'd started, shaking the errant energy out of his fingertips.

"You protect Oskar, you kiss his ancient ass—but who kisses yours, Achilles?"

Achilles lunged at the ground, scooped a fistful of dirt, heated it to lava, and tossed it into Braden's eyes.

Braden closed them.

He didn't need them.

Five...

Ten...

Fifteen savage blows came at Braden—Achilles was toe to toe, snarling and snorting, yet one by one, Braden blocked them: *left forearm up, slash down like a blade, cross over the midriff...brace the right hand upward.* Like a supersonic windmill whirling so fast its movements were obscured, Braden blocked, guarded, defended...and then he attacked.

A swift snap to the groin, a brutal kick to the gonads...

He used his limber lower leg like a lash.

Two fistfuls of chin-length, black-and-red hair...

He snatched Achille's wild mane, yanked downward, then slammed the Dark One's face into his own rising kneecap.

A mouthful of blood, sweat-drenched flesh, and grisly sinew...

Braden tore chunk...after chunk...out of the Dark One's neck.

"You will never have a *destiny*. You will never procreate. You will die here in this canyon, humiliated, forgotten, and bested by a fucking fledgling!"

Braden leaped back, but not before Achilles caught him by the throat and raised him above his head, broken bones and lacerated shoulders be damned. Braden swung both knees upward, slammed them against Achilles' chest, and summersaulted back-ward, breaking The Executioner's hold. As he landed, he plunged his fist—all five claws, extended and serrated—into Achilles' gut and withdrew a fistful of intestines.

Achilles lunged at Braden's jugular, ivory fangs gleaming in the waning moonlight, yet once again, Braden blocked him with a forearm and stuffed the innards he had just retrieved in the Dark One's mouth.

A vicious strike to Braden's breastbone...

The air left Braden's body, his head snapped back, and he staggered side to side.

A second blow...a third...a fourth...

Then Achilles dug the claws of his thumbs deep into Braden's exposed esophagus and drilled into his jawbone. He shook him like a feral cat taunting a helpless mouse.

"Bray!" Kristina's voice, calling in the background.

Oh shit, she was coming closer...

And lugging the Sword of Andromeda!

Damnit.

Braden could feel Red's energy...the energy of the weapon... all of it, moving, coalescing...drawing nearer and nearer.

Achilles twisted Braden's head to the side, thumbs still lodged in his jawbone, and began to tear through his neck with his canines like a rabid, bestial savage—he was going to decapitate Braden with his fangs.

"No!" Kristina screamed again, and then the entire canyon fell silent.

If he kills me here, he will claim Kristina. Lord Monoceros, how do I beat him?

Help me!

The Tree of Life, with its living limbs festooned in green, white, and golden foliage, appeared before Braden in his mystic mind's eye and swayed back and forth, glowing. Braden released his fear, relinquished his corporeal body, and sank deep into the tree's fluid motion.

Strength.

Agility.

Precognition...

How to feel the ebb and flow of a battle in spirit...

How to harness light against an act of darkness...

How to become one with the forces all around you.

Love is stronger than hate.

You are stronger than Achilles.

You are the living Sword of Jadon—you are the embodiment of love.

Braden reached for the light—the light of The Tree and the light within—he reached for the soft, downy feathers of the mighty eagle, reminding his conscious mind how to shape-shift.

And then he did.

Only, not into the body of an eagle but into the bark, trunk, and branches of a majestic tree.

Limbs, like a hundred hands bearing a thousand fingers, coiled around Achilles' arms, legs, and torso, dissected his back like leeches, worms made of bramble, and burrowed deep. The spiny twigs surrounded The Executioner's heart like thorny sprouts covered in jagged, prickly bristles, and then Braden drew them back, slowly...steadily...retrieving both the branches and the heart of Achilles Zahora as he withdrew them.

He shifted back into a vampire, extended his hand in Kristina's direction, and she tossed him the Sword of Andromeda. Raising the sword high above his head, he spun around in a perfect, full orbit and sliced cleanly through Achilles' gullet, lopping off his head. And then straddling the headless body with both legs, a shoulder's width apart, he murmured softly, "This is for you, *Mamica*." He exhaled slowly through his nose, streaming white-hot flames from his nostrils, as he swiftly...thoroughly...incinerated the body beneath him.

He immediately trained his vision on the upper, eastern side of the canyon—on the Dark Ones gathered atop the cliff—and watched warily as they recoiled in shock and bloodthirsty rage, instantly wanting revenge.

"What happened to brother against brother?" one Dark One snarled.

"The redhead breached the battle!" still another groused. "Cheaters, one and all!"

"She tossed him the sword," yet another insisted as they inched closer to the edge of the cliff like one wild throng, their bodies trembling with vehemence.

Braden took the house of Jaegar's full measure, immediately wondering, *would they retreat...or attack?* Although he had been traveling in the Enchanted Forest when the place and time for the battle had been set, and although Lord Monoceros had shown him a small snippet of Prince Jadon's challenge to Prince Jaegar in Napolean's courtyard, Braden was now back in his body, which meant he still shared one frame, one mind, one seat of the soul with Prince Jadon, and he could now access the entire memory.

He swiftly scanned his corporeal mind until he found the odious pact:

Brother against brother.

Prince against prince.

Vampire against vampire, so the legions might live.

For all our descendants, for both our houses, for all the Millenia Harvest Moons and battles yet to come—for the fate of one cursed and one honorable species—brother against brother, winner take all.

Jaegar would fight for the right to slay his sisters...for the right to keep Kristina.

Jadon would fight for the right to save both Red and the princesses...and for the right to execute both Oskar and Salvatore—Let the mighty inherit the earth.

And now, the Dark Ones believed Braden had cheated because Kristina had tossed him the sword...

Braden swept his gaze over the vulnerable royal females still kneeling at the canyon's edge, and his heartbeat slowed, his spirit lifted, as he eyed the soft, glowing, nearly incandescent light of a holding cell wrapped tightly around them both. He glanced over his shoulder, to the western clifftops, and noted the smug, yet determined look stamped on Marquis and Saber's features—the princesses' mates, the warriors' arms, were linked like a chain with the Master Wizards: Jankiel and Niko on the outside, Nachari Silivasi standing between them. Meanwhile, Fabian Antonescu was seated in front of them, both palms still facing out and turned upward, as he wielded—and held—a shrouded spell.

They had protected the princesses...instantly.

And then Braden felt him before he saw him, Napolean Mondragon hovering in the air, his feet no longer touching the rocky ledge, his entire body pulsing and radiating heat, brimming with barely leashed radiation...all ten fingers splayed and deftly pointed across the canyon at the entire dark horde of vampires.

Yeah, Braden thought, *they had this all along.*

Still, he understood intuitively that the Dark Ones, those who remained in the Colony—the fledglings, the children, those maintaining basic operations—would never stop coming. They would stalk and hunt every soul in the house of Jadon...in perpetuity, to say nothing of all the soulless monsters that would be hatched in the next forty-eight hours.

To say nothing of the fact that the effort might kill Napolean Mondragon—that was *so much* cosmic energy to control and release without lethal consequences.

"It's over!" Braden shouted, and his voice crackled like thunder. "You may have your chairman and your wicked sorcerer. Go back into your hellhole or die like Achilles!" He stormed across the canyon floor, snatched Achilles' head, and held it up in an erect, vertical arm, glaring at the three Dark Ones, all Colony Guard, standing in a loose vertical row with tattoos of jewel-eyed black mambas circling their right biceps. Inadvertently, and led by precognition, his eyes swept from the left to the right and landed on the third and final guardsman: a fiendish vampire with a murderous glare in his granite-gray eyes, spiked red-and-black hair, and a nasty, pointed beard. The vampire's thick upper lip, dissected with multiple piercings, turned up in a contemptuous, mocking scowl—a promise of vengeance—and he stared right back, the black mamba on his bicep twitching and uncoiling, its eyes also boring into Braden's...then Kristina's.

"Son of a bitch," Braden snarled.

And he knew...

He just knew.

He hurled the head like a shot out of a cannon traveling along a bolt of lightning, and watched in primal, possessive, raw satisfaction as it struck its target, unerringly: Achilles' skull exploded in the Dark One's face, crushed his cranium, and bowled him over. They might yet heal the savage bastard, but at least he had gotten the message.

The Dark Ones backed away from the ledge, and their vengeful energy began to dissipate—they did not desire all-out war, any more than the house of Jadon...

As Braden turned around to go to Kristina, he felt a swift, sharp tug between his eyes, as if someone had just unplugged a cord, and a sweep of energy, like a cool winter's wind, whooshed out of his body.

He gasped, jerked back, and spun around.

"Well done, son of Jadon." A disembodied voice. "I have always been with you. Now it is time that I leave you."

"Wait!" Braden spoke into the air, immediately recognizing the soul of Prince Jadon, the spirit who had begged him to get up and fight when he had been prone on the ground...when his eyelids had been so heavy, his heart, even heavier...when he had thought he'd lost his badges, along with Napolean's sword. "I never got to meet you."

"Nay." The ancient prince chuckled. "You know me better than anyone else, save my beloved sisters. Protect our house, Sword of Jadon. My power is always at your disposal."

Realizing the full breadth and meaning of those words, Braden sank to one knee in reverence.

Dear Gods...

Prince Jadon had been with him...leading him...teaching him, protecting his lost, cherished house, all along...through Braden. And it was Jadon's strength, his assistance, his cunning and prowess that had aided Braden through the battle with Achilles.

"Your Grace, I'm not worthy," Braden murmured.

And that's when the Sword of Andromeda appeared before him, dangling in the air like a specter—the blade shimmering with pure, ethereal essence—and began to glow with the radiance of all eight badges. That's when Prince Jadon appeared in the canyon like a spirit of light, in all his nobility, splendid beauty, and timeless glory. The prince grasped the hilt of the sword and held it out in his hand. Then, like a prince of old in a knighthood ceremony, he laid the flat side of the blade on Braden's right shoulder, raised it above Braden's head, then flipped it counter-clockwise, so the same side of the blade would be used to tap the left shoulder. "Arise, son, as my anointed Amadis...the living Sword of Jadon."

Braden stood up, and Prince Jadon vanished.

CHAPTER TWENTY-SEVEN

A sleight of hand.

A delightful artifice.

A low-down dirty trick beneath a waning harvest moon—it did not matter what the Vampyr would call it—they would likely never know it had happened.

Aye, but the lords of the underworld would be fully aware of it.

Free will and all that bullshit...

They had allowed the battle to play out, winner take all, and Prince Jadon...Braden Bratianu...had slayed the dark Prince Jaegar.

Well, Achilles Zahora—

Whatever.

Braden had arisen victorious, and Prince Jaegar's time on earth, living or reanimated, was done with, once and for all. Yea, but the wild redhead had thrown a monkey wrench into the ending when she had entered the battlegrounds and later tossed the Sword of Andromeda to the conquering hero—and thus, she had opened up the tiniest crack, a teensy-weensy sliver, to the dark lord Soreconom.

If the girl could intervene, so could he!

The proud, defiant dark lord had nurtured, indulged, and guided one of his favorite sons of Jaegar, Achilles, for no less than five hours inside The Forest of Evil—he had strengthened The Executioner's vices and planted enough fresh cruelty and envy to last many lifetimes. Far too much work and concentrated effort to be so easily undone. Besides, Achilles' dark soul was over 1,000 years old; whereas, Zeus had only lived for four centuries.

And so it was...

And so it shall be, a sleight of hand to be sure.

An ace for a king.

A jackal for a knight.

A spade for a heart—and an executioner for a Colony Guard.

The soul of Achilles Zahora for the soul of Zeus Dragavei: an even swap, an advantageous trade, a simple malignant replacement.

The sons of Jaegar would most certainly heal Zeus' humiliating injuries—Achilles' head used as a winged bowling ball, now that was kind of funny—and it was still the Millenia Harvest Moon, after all. The rare solar body would not fully set until 11:46 a.m., which still left the dark lords some time to play with.

And so they must...

Indeed, they would...

Interfere with Zeus' healing by swapping his soul with the soul of The Executioner, Achilles Zahora, and planting it firmly in Zeus' body. From this night forward, Zeus would live on but only in appearance, not substance—since Achilles' superior, magnificent form was nay but ash and dust, there was nothing to be done with his glorious body.

But his soul...

Yes, alas, his wicked, carnal, hate-drenched soul—it would

live on in the Dark Ones' Colony, and *Achilles* would never forget.

Though his brethren would be none the wiser, The Executioner would know...

The injury Braden Bratianu had dealt him.

The vampire female he had come *this close* to claiming.

The arrogance, the dishonor, the *envy*...

And he would never rest until he attained Blood Vengeance.

CHAPTER TWENTY-EIGHT

The Red Canyons erupted in feverish activity and frenetic energy. The Master Warriors Ramsey Olaru and Julien Lacusta released Oskar and Salvatore; Marquis Silivasi and Saber Alexiares flashed across the canyon to untangle their mates from the magical protective holding cells; and the Dark Ones reluctantly retreated from the eastern clifftops.

Kagen Silivasi, the Master Healer, rushed to Braden's side, even as his mate, Arielle, hurried to check on Kristina. Meanwhile, in the chaotic background, the remaining sentinels and wizards attended to Napolean Mondragon as he settled to the ground, listed sideways, and fought against the dizziness and disorientation involved in banking all that solar energy.

Well, all except Nachari.

The Master Wizard stood, along with Dario, just a few yards from Braden, his arm wrapped lovingly around Conrad's adolescent shoulders...

Braden sighed, knowing it would be a difficult reunion.

But there was something else—*someone else*—that had to come first.

"Raise your chin," Kagen instructed, feeling along Braden's lower jawbone, turning his head from side to side, then pressing gently against his esophagus. "Amazing." He felt every one of Braden's ribs, examined his stomach and his internal organs, and then he stepped back, switched to infrared vision, and more or less x-rayed Braden's entire anterior torso. "Turn around, son," he said, repeating the examination from the back. "Extraordinary. I can't find a single injury."

Braden shrugged, then rolled his shoulders. "I think the energy from The Tree of Light must've healed me...when I shifted in and out of the branches."

Kagen cocked both eyebrows. "Come again?"

Braden smiled wanly. "Long story. *Really* long story."

Kagen tilted his head to the side, paused, then slowly nodded. He glanced several feet away at his *destiny* and called out, "Arielle, sweeting; how is Kristina?"

Braden's vision followed Kagen's like a trained homing pigeon locking in on home base.

How is Kristina...

She was a hot mess.

Her delicate, dainty feet were bare and covered in dirt and grime. Her hair was tangled, matted in several places, and just like Lord Monoceros had shown him in the vision, she was wearing a raspberry wine-colored skirt, no longer wet but wrinkled, and it was stained with droplets of blood. Braden's throat constricted and his heart skipped a beat...

What had that Dark One done to her?

The broad, U-shaped neckline on her silk black vest was stretched to the sides, the lacy raspberry camisole beneath it was torn, her arms and thighs were bruised, to say nothing of the large, garish fingerprints around her wrists and ankles, and there were more holes in her thin sheer stockings than found in a block of swiss cheese.

"She's doing okay," Arielle said. "Considering she spent four hours in the Dark Ones' Colony and just jumped over the side of a cliff, I would say she's in pretty good shape."

But was she...violated? Braden wanted to ask, but that would have to wait until later, until the two of them were alone, assuming she would feel comfortable enough to answer something so personal.

Besides, he considered, did he really want to know?

What could he do now to change it?

Other than go batshit crazy, he was helpless to go back in time and defend her. He was powerless to undo...anything.

He shoved the wretched thoughts aside, grasped Kagen by the wrist and thanked him. Then he strode toward Kristina with a confident gait, trying to figure out how to break the ice...

Such heavy, bone-chilling, frosty ice...

How to make *her* comfortable, especially considering their last encounter.

The moment he closed the distance between them, he glanced up at the eastern cliffside, used his pointer finger to trace her aerial leap from the ledge and her ensuing path through the air, and grimaced when he came to the spot where the eagle had caught her. "Red," he said lovingly, "*what the actual fuck!?*"

Kristina pressed the palm of her hand to her forehead and chuckled, insincerely. It was funny—*it was Braden*—but at the same time, it wasn't.

She had so very much to tell him.

"Let's just say it was an insane leap of faith," she muttered.

He took her measure from head to toe, then studied her eyes in earnest. "Yeah, maybe...or maybe a desperate leap of...love."

She absently caressed the precious gemstone bracelet around her wrist, and her vision misted with tears. "Bray." The word came out weaker than she intended. "There's so much I need to say to you."

"Kristina, give me your wrists."

She drew back in surprise. "What?"

"Your wrists—let me see your wrists."

She held out both arms, palms facing up, even as she began to shiver. Braden released his fangs, coated his fingertips with venom, and began to slowly massage her bruises until the markings disappeared. He paused—just for a moment—to trace the outline of the familiar bracelet. Then he dropped to one knee and repeated the process on her ankles, his touch as light as a feather, as intense as a blizzard. Without pause or warning, his hands slid up the back of her calves, turned over her knees, and grasped her thighs, his thumbs kneading inward in tender, healing circles.

She gasped. Her breath caught in her throat, and her eyes darted around the immediate canyon—Arielle had already backed away, returning to Kagen and the others.

Braden stood back up. "Better?"

She nodded, growing even more nervous. "*Bray,*" she repeated, "I need to talk to you, to get some things out while I have the courage."

He nodded. "I know."

She shook her head. "No, you don't. There's so much..." Her voice trailed off. "That night, in my apartment, before you left to meet with the king, the sentinels, and the other vampires—"

"I know," he interjected. "Me, too."

She stared at him in earnest. "But I should've said...I should've explained..."

He grasped her jaw and cradled it in his hands. "Red, look at me. *I know.*" He held her gaze, without blinking. "I've always known."

She sighed in exasperation, still determined to explain it. "That day in front of Nachari and Deanna's brownstone, Valentine's Day, before we went to the mall...and that day, a little over four months later, when I acted so selfish and jealous...after you'd rescued Gwen from The Fortress...when she was staying at the brownstone with the three of you."

He pressed two fingers over her lips to silence her. "When I promised you I was not keeping Gwen at the brownstone because I thought she was attractive? When I told you my veins and pulse are attuned to a very different...frequency?" He leaned forward and whispered, "When I bit your bottom lip, healed it with my tongue, and you just stood there for a minute with your mouth hanging open?" His lips curved up in a cheeky grin. "Yes, Kristina, I knew."

She gulped. "But you didn't know *everything*. I mean, about my past."

He cocked one shoulder. "I knew enough."

She shook her head in frustration. "My dad was an alcoholic," she blurted, cringing at the random nature of the words.

"So was mine."

"Yeah, but I never even knew him—he died before I was born."

"I'm aware of this."

"My mother's boyfriends...hell, Kiki, herself...and Dirk—"

"You aren't broken, Kristina," he interrupted. "You're perfectly imperfect, just like the rest of us."

She lowered her gaze in shame. "But you deserved more." A tear escaped her eye, and she didn't try to brush it away. "I couldn't...love. I couldn't...be loved. I've never known how to do...vulnerable."

At this, he tunneled his fingers in her hair, until the tips met her

chin, and then he tilted her jaw upward, forcing her to look at him—
she barely came to his shoulders now, but she strained to meet his
eyes. "Kristina Riley Silivasi, you just snatched a heavy-ass sword
out of the hands of a Dark One, leaped over the edge of a cliff, and
tried to skewer Achilles Zahora—*Achilles Zahora, The Executioner!*
—in the back. For me. For us. To love...to be loved. That was the most
courageous...crazy...and *vulnerable* thing I've ever seen anyone do."

She tucked her elbows into her stomach, clasped both hands
together, and lowered her head until her forehead rested against
her thumbs, and then she leaned into the warmth of his chest and
trembled against him. "And you caught me," she whispered as he
wrapped his arms around her.

"Of course I did," he said. "You and I...we have forever, Red.
You need to tell me every one of your stories—and I need to tell
you mine. Believe me when I say, every road we've traveled,
everywhere we've been, everyone we have ever known has made
us who we are. So it's worth knowing. It's worth sharing. But all
in all, *fuck the past.* You could've been more...affectionate. I
shouldn't have walked away that night...left you on the couch.
But we're standing here now—where we were always meant to be
—and Kristina, you're wearing my bracelet."

She unlocked her arms, wrapped them around his waist, and
sobbed against his chest.

After several poignant moments had passed, she found her
voice again: "I thought I had lost you."

"Shh," he said, then stroked her hair. "Kristina, if I could, I
would stay here, just like this...forever...with you. But Nachari...
my stepdad...*Conrad.*"

She nodded, understanding. And then, "Wait!" She pulled
away, grasped both of his hands, and steadied herself for what
was coming. "Bray, there's something I have to tell you."

He grew quiet, turned inward for a moment...and then his

eyes clouded with deep, haunted shadows. "About my mother? I know."

Her mouth dropped open. "You know about Lily?"

He nodded stoically.

Oh gods.

"I'm so, *so* sorry," she said, allowing the words to linger. She knew there was nothing she could say, nothing she could do, other than to stand there...be there...in the moment, sharing his pain and sorrow. Finally, after another pregnant moment had passed, she whispered his familiar pet name, "Bray..."

He grasped both of her wrists and shook his head. "Not here. Not now. I need to keep it together."

She nodded, rose to the tips of her toes, and cradled his perfect, angular jaw. Then she leaned in slowly, waited for Braden to dip down to meet her, and kissed him softly—sweetly—on the mouth. "Do you want me to come with?"

He shook his head. "No, just wait here for me. Better yet, you might catch a ride with Arielle and Kagen, see if they'll give you a lift home. I'd like to go back to the brownstone, get cleaned up... put on some real clothes. And you need to go back to the penthouse, maybe take a second for yourself"—he swept his hand over her vest, her skirt, then lower, to her dirty, bare feet—"take those off, wash those up." He forced a weak, conciliatory smile. "As much as I'd like to take you...go with you...I'm pretty sure my family, Napolean, maybe even the wizards are gonna want to hash things out. But wait up for me, okay? I'll come to the penthouse as soon as I can."

She brushed a streak of dirt off his chin and nodded.

"And Kristina? You need to keep a warrior nearby—maybe one of the sentinels can stand guard until I get there, or at least until the harvest moon completely sets, whichever comes first. I don't think the Dark Ones are gonna make another play, not this night—not this *morning*—but you never know with those assholes."

"Yeah, okay." She held his gaze a few seconds longer, not wanting to turn away. His beautiful, burnt sienna irises nearly sparkled in the waning moonlight, and for the first time, maybe ever, he saw her...all of her...and she saw him too.

They saw each other.

I love you, Bray...

The words swam in her head, but she didn't want to blurt them out randomly, like she had handled everything else. She wanted to tell him when he could say it back...when he could hold her again, and she could hold him. "Go to your family," she said, instead. "I'll wait for you at the penthouse."

CHAPTER TWENTY-NINE

Nachari Silivasi's heart ached in his chest, even as he tried to remind himself that it was over—Braden had prevailed in the battle, and he was back.

He was back.

The last time he had spoken directly to Braden, not Prince Jadon, had been on the beach at Santos' hidden lake, over eight hours earlier. The battle between the ancient princes—between Braden and Achilles—had stunned Nachari's senses, and now, watching his familiar friend, his cherished acolyte, and the boy he loved like a son both heal and console Kristina moved his soul and constricted his heart.

He exhaled slowly.

No, not a boy—a man.

Yes, his familiar friend—but different.

There was a confidence and a command in Braden that Nachari had never seen before, at least not to this degree. There was a maturity—and a level of self-awareness—that surpassed his usual uncanny insight. His phenomenal abilities. The precognition...

Braden had always been special.

But now, he was...*more.*

His arm still draped around Conrad's shoulders, Nachari felt the young vampire begin to tremble as Braden approached the trio, shoulders back, chin held high, his wise, compassionate eyes filled with deep emotion.

He closed the distance in five fluid strides and stopped short in front of Conrad. "*Conny...*" He searched his younger sibling's eyes. "I know about *Mamica.*"

That was all it took.

The fledgling's shoulders drooped and curled inward, and his entire body shook.

Braden opened his arms and reached for his brother, and Conrad laid his head between the crook of Braden's arm and his strong, unclothed chest. Braden cradled the back of Conrad's head with exquisite gentleness, then nuzzled his chin in Conrad's short, mussed, dirty-blond hair.

He didn't speak, at least not out loud.

He just held the younger vampire until Conrad's tears stopped falling.

Then still holding on, he finally raised his chin and regarded his stepdad. "Dario."

Dario Bratianu nodded sadly.

"I'm so sorry," Braden lamented.

"As am I, son."

A moment of pregnant silence, then Braden asked, "The burial?"

"It's to be held just after sunset on Sunday evening." Despite Dario's stoic resolve, his voice faltered as he pressed forward: "We weren't...sure. We didn't know. The outcome of the battle, the state of affairs in the valley...so Lily"—he cleared his throat and tried again—"so Lily is at Napolean's compound...in the Hall of Justice...she's...*she's...*"

BLOOD HARVEST

"I know," Braden interjected. "I've seen her."

Dario's eyes grew wide. "When? How?"

Braden shook his head. "Later. It's a long story." He removed his hand from Conrad's hair and swept it in an arc, indicating the canyon. "All of this...it's a really long story." Then he turned his attention back to Conrad, angled his body toward him, and braced his little brother by both sagging biceps. "Conny, I want you to know you can stay with me if you want to, as long as you like." He paused to let the words sink in. "We will get through this together." Then he pulled him even closer and whispered in his ear, "I am not the only brother who is strong, or courageous, or...special." He squeezed him tight, with both arms now, his muscular forearms tightening. "I love you, Conrad."

Conrad sniffled. "I love you, too, Braden." He pulled away, nodded faintly, and forced himself to stand taller. "I told you one day you might end up being one of the greatest vampires that ever lived, and now...now you're the living Sword of Jadon."

Braden shook his head in humble dismissal. "No, not to you. As far as I'm concerned, I'm one of Lily's boys, Conrad's brother, and"—he swept his gaze to Dario in both deference and emphasis —"Dario's stepson." He paused. "And whatever I've become, whatever I have accomplished, or survived..." He turned to face Nachari and choked back a sob. "I owe it all to this one." He released Conrad gently, took a faltering step in the Master Wizard's direction, and stole the vampire's gaze. "*Nachari*..." His voice was thick with emotion.

Nachari reached out with a trembling hand and snatched Braden by the arm. He tugged him forward, wrapped his strong arms around him, and the two males embraced like long-lost brothers. "Are you okay?" Nachari murmured.

Braden held him tighter. "I will be."

"What happened? Where'd you go? What the hell was that demonstration in the canyon?" He forced a meek but artful

289

chuckle in an effort to relieve the tension...in an effort to make Braden feel more comfortable.

Braden stepped back and smiled softly. "When the Harvest Moon rose, I sort of...I don't even know how to explain it...but it was like being sucked into a black tunnel, spinning backward, and then I ended up in this unbelievable, astral world...a forest. It was like something out of a fairy tale. And there was this tree, this huge...gold...white...powerful tree, and all these lessons, all these badges. I collected them, one at a time—oh, and Lord Monoceros was there! He told me I had a choice, whether to come back or not. He warned me that I would return to great sorrow, but he also told me to pay attention...to learn and remember. He said nothing that had ever happened to me had been by accident."

Nachari stared at him in stunned, curious silence, momentarily transfixed by the story. "That's unbelievable...extraordinary." And then, "Prince Jadon...he's always been with you, hasn't he? A part of you. Leading you...guiding you...preparing you."

Braden nodded slowly. "I think so...and yeah, through all of it —Marquis' Blood Moon, Napolean's possession, the visions about Kiera and Kyla...even recognizing Gwen's connection to the house of Jadon when I found her in The Fortress...all of it."

Nachari shook his head in wonderment. "And the battle? That thing you did with the extra arms and hands: What the heck kind of magic was that, Braden?"

Braden shrugged both shoulders and raised both brows. "I dunno—the tree. Hard to explain, but I channeled the tree, learned from this lesson it taught me—as a stick man!"

This time Nachari chuckled freely. "*Whoa...*" He eyed Dario and Conrad, who were both listening intently, and reined in his desire to hear the rest of the story, to learn every single detail, right then and there in the canyon...to know everything Braden had gone through in order to assuage his own fears. "I have a feeling this is going to take hours."

"Days," Braden said. "Maybe weeks."

Nachari smiled, and his heart felt...full. "Yeah, and Napolean and Fabian will want to hear every detail, as will Niko and Jankiel. Hell, I think my own brothers, not to mention the sentinels, are going to want to know everything you were shown, told...or taught...by a divine apparition and a celestial deity. *Holy Perseus*...unbelievable." He took a measured step back and regarded him thoughtfully. Then he lowered his eyes and bowed from the neck. "Prince Jadon's Amadis—*model of a chivalric hero*—the living Sword of Jadon."

Braden eyed Nachari warily. "But nothing's changed. I mean, between the two of us—right?"

Nachari laughed out loud. "Oh, everything has changed, Braden. Everything...and nothing." He threw his arms around him and hugged him again. "By all the gods, I love you, *fiule*. Don't you ever forget that—don't ever doubt it."

Braden embraced him with equal affection. "I love you, too, Master Wizard. And thank you." He stepped back.

"For?"

"For everything. *Everything*..."

Nachari nodded, understanding. He felt blessed for having played a role in such an amazing soul's journey—and the journey was only getting started. *What about Kristina?* he asked on a private, telepathic bandwidth, watching as the slender, weary redhead walked away with Arielle and Kagen. *Seems to me, that night you went to see her, before you met with the king, the sentinels, the tracker, myself, and Fabian at the compound, you did not in fact say all you needed to say. Seems to me the two of you have a whole helluva lot more...to say.* He winked, conspiratorially, and Braden actually blushed.

Yeah, well, like I told you that morning in the brownstone: Nunya...

Nunya? Nachari asked.

None ya business, Braden said.

Nachari chuckled softly, then realized they were being really, *really* rude. *Yeah okay,* he said succinctly. *You can fill me in later.* He turned his attention back to Dario and Conrad, more concerned about the latter than the former...

It wasn't that he did not like or respect the Master Warrior—he did—but if the male was feeling a little left out, a bit overshadowed by Nachari's relationship with Braden, then he had only himself to blame. He had wasted so many years...squandered so many opportunities. It hadn't been lost on the Master Wizard that the two males had not even embraced. No judgment implied—Dario was an old-school vampire, stoic by nature, and he had never been all that outwardly affectionate. Just the same, his loss had been Nachari's gain, and Nachari was neither sorry nor ashamed of stepping in to fill that gap. Hopefully, going forward, Dario would mend as many fences as Lily had, make a strong, concerted effort to build that familial foundation, brick by brick, with Braden, ever greater...ever more solid.

As kind, patient, and loving as Braden was, he was already two steps ahead of Nachari.

"Dad," he said lovingly to Dario, his tone far more solemn. "I still have to get cleaned up, put some clothes on. I still have to speak with Napolean, maybe Fabian, and I still...I *need* to spend some time with Kristina." He turned his attention to Conrad. "But I'm here, one hundred percent, for both you and Conny, and I want very much to help with...Mom's final arrangements. I meant what I said about Conrad staying with me if he wants to. Can you give me twenty-four hours?" He eyed Nachari expectantly. "Is that okay with you, Nachari? If Conny comes to the brownstone for a while?"

Nachari nodded enthusiastically. "Of course it is. We would be honored to have him. And you and I, we can catch up more when you're back at the brownstone."

"Conny?" Braden raised his eyebrows.

"Cool by me," Conrad said, even as he smiled faintly, but his voice was still vacant and unmistakably hollow: Grief would continue to weigh on the young vampire's spirit and to rob him of joy for quite some time—there was just no way around it. Having lost both his mother, his father, for centuries, and the twin of his soul, Shelby, how well Nachari understood.

"Take whatever time you need, son," Dario said to Braden. "I'll take Conrad back to the Dark Moon Lodge for tonight, and going forward, when time permits, we can work something out."

Braden declined his head in appreciation. "Thank you."

Nachari opened his mouth to speak, then closed it.

Sometimes words were inadequate, and he didn't want to hijack or disturb the moment.

Braden was here.

Braden was back.

The boy with the painted face, the stiff Count Dracula collar, and a broken wing that he had dragged behind him was now the living Sword of Jadon, and in whatever minuscule way, Nachari had been allowed to play a small role in Braden's evolution. Nachari had been blessed to watch the boy grow into a man. And more than that—so much more—the gods had bestowed the qualities of courage, wisdom, and uncanny insight in Nachari's beloved acolyte, a burgeoning warrior-wizard who hadn't even graduated from The Academy yet.

Or attended the Romanian University...

There were still more precious memories to come.

As the Master Wizard studied Braden's strong, ever-more angular and mature features, his flawless tan skin, and his wise, enchanting eyes, four words came to mind. And if Nachari had been alone, he would have dropped to his knees to breathe them with reverence...

Thank you, Lord Monoceros.

Thank you...Lord Monoceros.

From the bottom of my heart...*thank you for Braden.*

CHAPTER THIRTY

Zeus Dragavei paced around the underground lair like a restless lion, occasionally stopping to eye all the timeless artifacts and ancient weapons hanging on the cavern walls, as Salvatore Nistor stood in the doorway and looked on.

This was Achilles' lair...

And therefore, it was *his* lair, although that last assertion made no sense to anyone but him.

The Colony Guard had patched him up, healed his humiliating injuries with alacrity, and sent him on his way back to his familial cluster. Only, he had approached his brethren—and Oskar Vadovsky—with a rare and unusual request: Would anyone object if he moved his things...relocated...took over Achilles Zahora's living quarters?

To Zeus' way of thinking, it just made sense.

After all, Zeus' father had died over a century earlier, killed by sunlight when he had failed to get his lecherous old ass back to the Colony in time following a night of terrorizing, ravaging, and ultimately dispatching several young girls, and probably boys, in a Scottish orphanage, over four thousand miles away. And Zeus did not have any brothers. He was a guardsman now, formally inducted, which elevated his rank, and there was no disputing the fact—Achilles' living arrangements were superior in luxury, status, and location.

Besides, Zeus Dragavei had hung out with the legend himself, the ancient prince who had given rise to the Dark Ones' society, Prince Jaegar Demir—may he live large in the under-world—before Braden Bratianu had ended the glorious monarch's...brief visit in Dark Moon Vale.

In the end, Oskar had not objected.

In truth, no one among the Colony Guard or on the Dark Ones' Council had balked at the swift, unexplained request by Zeus to change his digs: Salvatore Nistor had been the only one to hang back and watch as Zeus had retrieved a duffle bag of clothes—just one duffle bag—made a right turn instead of a left in the center conical hall, and headed to the now infamous lair.

Salvatore Nistor had been the only one to eye Zeus suspi-ciously and follow him all the way to his new private residence, where he now lurked like a phantom in the doorway. "Like what you see?" the sorcerer drawled, pointing to a particularly grue-some medieval weapon hanging above a heavy chest of drawers.

Zeus bit his bottom lip and ignored him.

He turned his attention to the big brass bed toward the front of the lair and remembered Kristina's angry, defiant features, her wet, disheveled hair, and her slender but perfectly curved body, as she cowered on the mattress.

"Would you like to keep his entire collection?" Salvatore snipped, sarcastically.

Zeus shrugged his shoulders. He was tired...not in the mood.

"You gonna wear his clothes, too? I don't think they'll fit."

Zeus grinded his teeth and tongued the tip of his fangs.

"You're a ballsy little bitch, aren't you?" Salvatore persisted.

Now this pissed Zeus off. He spun on his heel, stalked across the lair, and stopped just short of snatching Salvatore by the throat as the two stood nose to nose in the arched stone doorway. "Had a *really* long night, sorcerer. Why don't you give me some room to breathe?"

Salvatore arched his brows, his dark sapphire eyes narrowed with focus, and his distinctive widow's peak dropped down as his forehead wrinkled. "Why don't you tell me what the hell is really going on? Why you feel the need to desecrate Achilles Zahora's memory? If you'd like, we could piece together what's left of his head, stuff it, and hang it from the ceiling as a centerpiece to a garish candelabra. Then you could stare at it every morning before you go to sleep."

Zeus bristled from head to toe, white-hot energy seared up his spine, and he pumped both fists, straining for control.

"Be careful, vampire," Salvatore warned. "Very, *very* careful. You are sworn to protect me, and don't get it twisted—your strength, even your savagery, is no match for my dark magick." His eyes flashed violet-purple before banking back to sapphire blue.

Zeus tugged on a newly placed nose ring, snorted to dislodge some phlegm—on Salvatore's boots—then grasped the heavy wood-and-iron door and slammed it in Salvatore's face. He bolted it behind the annoying Dark One—of course, Salvatore could likely kick it down if he wanted to—hell, the sorcerer could probably unweave it with his fingers, and the vampire could certainly pass right through. But the bar did contain diamonds embedded in the iron, and Salvatore was old enough, hopefully wise enough, to know what would happen if he ignored the warning and crossed that threshold again.

Two more dead vampires in the house of Jaegar.

Peeling off his tight black muscle shirt and sliding out of his loose gray sweats, Zeus shook his head to dislodge the cotton—unpack the stuffed rage—and made a direct, unswerving path to the natural hot springs. Memories of Kristina Silivasi abounded, once again.

What. The. Fuck. Ever.

Zeus had time...

Achilles had time.

As he crawled into the hot, bubbling water, sank in up to his neck, and sprawled his body like a lazy human tourist sunbathing on a private beach, he let the sulfur, heat, and rippling waves wash over him, carrying the tumult...and angst...away.

He would store it for another day.

But not the envy...

Not the envy.

He would let the envy steep and simmer, rising to a red-hot boil.

He would ponder over his time in the Forest of Evil and mull over Lord Soreconom's life-altering decision to place his soul—*Achilles' soul*—in this weaker, less magnificent body.

He would retrieve the rest of Zeus' things—*his things*—later.

He would give Salvatore Nistor an extremely wide berth as he moved through the Colony and slowly figured out how to make the transition...into a new life...a new body.

A new identity.

And he would determine his next move and redress the wrongs...whenever and however he damn well pleased.

CHAPTER THIRTY-ONE

Freshly showered, his chestnut brown locks still damp, and clad in a pair of soft, stone-washed gray jeans and a short-sleeve, slim fit, casual gray T-shirt with a deep V neck, Braden stood on Napolean's front veranda and hesitated before knocking.

He took a deep, steadying breath—he was tired.

Not only was he eager to get back to Kristina, but his body was beginning to shut down, demanding sleep. It was already 6:00 a.m., the sun would be rising at 6:42, and the Millenia Harvest Moon would be a permanent thing of the past, no more than a memory, in less than six hours.

What a freakin' night...

To his surprise, the queen answered the door, her deep blue eyes brimming with kindness and some unnamable, newfound esteem, laced in wonderment. "Good morning, Braden."

He smiled. "Milady."

"Brooke," she corrected.

"Good morning, Brooke."

Ramsey Olaru cleared his throat in the background, most

likely to let Braden know he was there. He took a healthy step back in the foyer and barked, "C'mon in. The king's in the rectory."

Braden stepped inside quietly. He looked around, made note of the extraordinary silence and the lack of activity—no servants, no other guards or vampires present, besides Ramsey, no children milling around or playing—and he grimaced just a bit as his heavy, cross-laced boots clopped along the hardwood floors. "Where are the other sentinels?" he asked Ramsey.

"Saber's with Vanya, Saxson's at the farmhouse with Marquis and Ciopori, and Santos is posting guard outside Kristina's apartment—the king wanted everyone to remain on their toes, at least until the sun rises. Doubt the Dark Ones will pull any more shit before the harvest moon departs but better safe than sorry."

"Absolutely," Braden agreed. "And Fabian?"

"Last I heard," Ramsey said, "he was meeting up with Niko and Jankiel, some sort of wizardry debriefing—exchanging notes from the earlier ceremonies—then heading back to the guest house to spend the rest of the moon with Gwen and Falcon."

Braden nodded amiably. In truth, he was relieved. The fewer vampires he had to give an account to, the sooner he could get back to Kristina.

"Just one note of caution," Ramsey continued, his deep, gruff voice sounding a bit hoarse, maybe weary, "take it easy with the king—"

"Keep it brief if you can," Brooke interjected, tucking a lock of dark ebony hair behind her ear.

"Lucky for all of us," Ramsey said, "he didn't have to use the full extent of his powers in that canyon, but he banked more of that astral fireball than he's ever stored before. And he was absolutely prepared to unleash every atom if he had to, random consequences and uncontained losses be damned. So, needless to say, he's wasted...spent."

"Got it," Braden said, turning toward the rectory, but just then, Brooke reached out and caught his hand.

"Braden..."

"Yeah?" He cocked both eyebrows.

"I just wanted to tell you...thank you." She stepped closer, wrapped her arms around his shoulders, and placed a gentle kiss on his cheek. "Thank you for your courage, thank you for your bravery, thank you for everything you have always been to the house of Jadon." And then she drew him into a big bear hug and whispered, "I am so very sorry about your mother. My heart is broken, and I am grieving with you. Please...if there is anything I can do, just name it." She paused to let her condolences linger. "We love you, Braden, and we are so very grateful...so incredibly relieved...to have you back in the valley, home where you belong."

Braden returned the hug, feeling touched, honored, and curiously distant. "Thank you," he uttered, "and no problem."

No problem?

He immediately regretted the words.

Of course, losing his mother was more than a problem—it was a living nightmare—and Brooke's words meant everything to Braden, more than she could know. He wished he could've said something more touching...more appropriate...maybe even a little more formal and dignified, but it was what it was. He had to hold it together, and this horror...this loss...was going to take time.

Without missing a beat, Brooke pulled away and stepped back gracefully. She gestured toward the formal living room. "He's waiting for you, Amadis."

Amadis...

She used the accolade like an endearing nickname, more or less referring to Braden as a chivalric knight or hero—wow.

Just wow...

Braden cleared his throat and fixed his gaze on Ramsey. "You coming?"

"Nah," Ramsey said, "not this time. I think the king wants some time alone with you."

Braden drew back his shoulders, nodded in acknowledgment, and entered the rectory more confidently than he felt. He strolled across the floor, took a seat in a red wing-backed chair with mahogany arm supports and legs, cattycorner to Napolean, and drew in warmth from the nearby blazing fire.

The king was sprawled languidly on a royal blue sofa, his feet propped up and crisscrossed at the ankles on a matching ottoman, and while he definitely looked tired, perhaps a bit depleted, there was a faint red flush beneath his chiseled cheekbones and a fresh, radiant sheen in his long, black-and-silver hair—he had clearly fed recently, and fed very well, more than likely from another powerful vampire.

"My lord," Braden said, reverting to more formal protocol.

Napolean snorted, and then he smiled. "Perhaps that is how *I* should address *you* going forward." The deep lines around his eyes creased with mirth. "Your Grace?"

Braden chuckled nervously. "Nah...I mean, no. Definitely not. How are you feeling?"

Napolean flicked his wrist in the air. "I'm fine. No worse for the wear. I think the real question is how are you doing? But before we go any further, I want to express my deepest condolences for the loss of your mother. Son, I know the road the two of you have traveled...how long it took you to get to this juncture... I know how deeply Lily loved you, and I know how deeply you loved her." He shook his head sadly, his dark onyx pupils reflecting the full depths of his sorrow, the silver in his irises reflecting his regret. "So many times throughout the centuries I have questioned the will of the gods: when they intervene, and when they do not. I have wondered at the injustice of the Curse...a child deprived of a parent, a male removed from his *destiny*. And I have even wondered on many occasions why I lost my own father so early, also by the hand of Prince Jaegar."

Braden blinked several times.

Oh, my gods—

That was true...

Napolean's dad had been killed by Prince Jaegar too.

"For what it's worth, and I know it isn't much, every loss to the house of Jadon is a wound to my soul, and this particular loss is especially painful because I've walked the road you're walking now, and I know it isn't easy. But I also take comfort—and hope you will as well—in knowing that when it comes to your life, son, your specific path...your enigmatic journey, nothing has been random, and you have never been alone. The hands of the gods have been on your shoulders since the day you were brought into this world, and we—the house of Jadon—are blessed to have known you. Blessed to have sired you into our ranks. And blessed to have you among our finest warriors—and wizards—going forward. My son, you are beloved by all."

Braden's eyes brimmed with tears, and once again, he blinked, only this time to keep the tears at bay. "Thank you," he whispered softly. "You...all of you...the warriors and the wizards. You've always been my truest family. And maybe now, Conrad too."

Napolean nodded circumspectly. "Yes, Conrad will need you." He paused and narrowed his gaze. "And, of course, there is Kristina..."

Now this made Braden smile.

"Well?" Napolean nudged.

Braden's smile grew wider. "I don't know. Still have to go see her, but I was kind of thinking...hoping...maybe a mating ceremony on my eighteenth birthday? I mean, if you don't mind."

Napolean chuckled softly. "Of course I don't mind. It would be my honor." He clasped his hands, let them rest over his lower belly, and then swiftly changed the subject. "Where were you, son?" he asked softly. "While Prince Jadon resided in your body?" His brows drew inward in a curious, almost mysterious reflection.

"I was safe. I was well. I was in a plane between worlds, some sort of magical forest with this Tree of Light. I was being taught by Lord Monoceros...made ready."

Napolean nodded slowly. "Made ready. Well...that you were." He shook his head in amazement as if replaying a scene in his mind, then shifted his weight on the couch to angle his shoulders more toward Braden. "I will not deny that I'm curious, eager to hear every detail, but I also know that you need your rest—that some of the particulars may be quite private, intimate—and that Fabian should be present when you share...what you will. That said, I do have a couple insistent questions."

"Go ahead," Braden urged.

The king grew quiet for the space of several heartbeats before pressing on: "Were you linked to Prince Jadon the entire time?"

"No," Braden said emphatically. "Not at all. I don't think I ever felt him, saw him, or even knew he was there, using...inhabiting my body, until right before I returned to the canyons. Lord Monoceros showed me...what had happened to my mother. He showed me just a small snippet of Prince Jadon in your courtyard, challenging Prince Jaegar to a battle...*brother against brother, winner take all.* He showed me Kristina in Achilles' lair, and then again, at the very end of the battle in the Red Canyons, I heard Prince Jadon's voice in my head. He kept telling me to get up and fight."

Napolean pondered Braden's words. "I see. Do you hear him now? Feel him now?"

Braden shook his head. "Not that I know of"—he paused to consider the question more methodically, to think it over carefully—"well, I guess in a sense, that isn't true. I guess it depends on how one defines the word *hear*. Because in truth, I think he's always been there, I think I've always heard him...felt him, kind of shared the same heartbeat."

"Indeed."

They sat in silence, allowing the revelation to linger, as Napolean continued to process all he'd heard, and Braden had the strangest feeling, just an inclination, that maybe the king wasn't speaking all he knew—maybe he was keeping much deeper, almost clandestine thoughts to himself.

At least for now.

Finally, the king cleared his throat, and his countenance roused. "It is no small thing what happened in that canyon earlier. And not just the battle, the way you defeated Achilles Zahora, but what happened at the end when Prince Jadon anointed you with the sword. Being sired into our house, as opposed to born, you were never given a naming ceremony like firstborn heirs—you were never formally presented directly after birth. If it is agreeable, I would like to perform a formal naming ceremony for you, Braden, now that you have come of age. Now that you have stepped into your purpose."

Braden drew back in surprise.

"Not this weekend, of course. We all need rest, and there is still the heartbreaking formality of Sunday's burial, but perhaps when some of this bitter dust settles, we might revisit the subject. This season, we shall grieve. We shall honor the cherished life of a beautiful matron, a soul moving on to the afterworld to begin a new journey of Spirit & Light. But, afterward, at some point, we must also celebrate with a ritual honoring new life, a new beginning, a burgeoning journey on earth. 'For every time, there is a season,' and we shall meet each season in time." His voice trailed off, and he waited quietly.

Braden swallowed any immediate questions or concerns. "Can I think it over?"

"Absolutely." There was no hesitation.

"Thank you."

The rectory grew quiet yet again; the orange and yellow flames in the majestic hearth danced and flickered from side to side; and Braden soaked in the warmth, then sat straighter in his chair. "I do have a question for you as well."

"Go ahead," Napolean said, his tone both peaceful and reflective.

"It's about Fabian, something he said...about what he did."

Napolean raised his brows and waited.

"When he traveled in the body of the hawk, then the raven, carrying the vials that night...when he fed them to me and Achilles: 'Drink this blood and welcome life. Drink this blood and welcome death.' Did Fabian know all along? Did he know that I would ultimately survive, and Achilles would ultimately die?"

Napolean appeared to be thinking it over.

He uncrossed his legs at the ankles, switched the dominant foot, then crossed them again, shifting once more on the sofa. "Well, you will have to pose that question directly to him, but I think the reality is more cryptic...the words were more symbolic. Hatred is a death of sorts, a decaying of the soul, a rotting in the spirit, whereas love and light are life-giving, life-affirming...life-enhancing. The ultimate consequence of darkness can never be life, and the ultimate reward of love can never be...true death. I think somewhere deep in Fabian's psyche, despite his confusion and disorientation, he knew the blood in the vials could only be imbibed by a homogenous soul: a soul desirous of embracing light, knowing, and becoming true love, and a soul so lost to depravity that it would welcome ultimate corruption. Perhaps the High Mage was also a tool of the gods, a sword wielded by the hands of the celestial deities."

Becoming true love...

The king's words lingered.

It was uncanny how all these questions—and lessons—dovetailed together.

"Yeah, I think you're right," Braden said, and then he lowered his head in deference, remembering what Ramsey and Brooke had told him. "If you don't mind, I think I'll take you up on that offer to get some rest, and besides, I still need to see Kristina."

The king nodded with understanding.

He studied Braden's features for a moment, looked off into the distance, then brought his gaze back to Braden, and when he did, the silver irises surrounding onyx pupils were glowing with three shades of refracted light: white, gold, and green...

Like the magical Tree of Light.

Napolean? Braden thought, zooming in on the enchanted trio of colors.

Then, *no way!*

Napolean was here...in Dark Moon Vale—he had remained on earth the entire time.

But the lessons, the sparring, the enchanted badges—maybe Napolean and Fabian, together? Or Napolean, with the aid of the princesses and the original, celestial magick...

He pushed the thoughts to the back of his mind.

He really needed some sleep.

Napolean's nose twitched and his eyes twinkled; then he flashed a warm, loving, fatherly smile. "Pay attention. Learn. And remember, my son—always *remember and choose* going forward—knowing you are deeply and eternally loved."

CHAPTER THIRTY-TWO

I t was 6:40 a.m. when Braden arrived at Kristina's penthouse.

A soft, resplendent light, glowing orange, red, and blue, shone below the horizon and caressed the majestic mountain peaks surrounding Dark Moon Vale.

Twilight.

A promise of a new day, a bright, shimmering future—the Millenia Harvest Moon would recede, and a new day would take its place. A new day but an old acquaintance, a time-weathered friendship, a burgeoning love and romance.

Braden parked his King Cobra Mustang, reached for the tightly wrapped bouquet of red roses, pink lilies, and white gypsophila flowers surrounded by gold hypericum and dark green stems, all wrapped in an elegant fold of pink chiffon and tied with a bloodred lace bow, and climbed out of the car.

As he crossed the parking lot, entered the building, and strolled through the lobby to the bank of elevators, he rolled his shoulders to release some tension and sniffed the air a half-dozen times, checking and double-checking the strength of his cologne.

Damn, he hoped he hadn't put too much on.

He didn't want to come across as too eager.

The moment he stepped out of the elevators on the top floor of the casino, he braced himself for what was coming: Santos Olaru's relentless teasing. The sentinel would take one look at the flowers, get one good sniff of Braden's cologne, and probably rib him mercilessly. But as he rounded the corner and caught Santos' eyes, something entirely different happened...

The Master Warrior bowed from the neck, averted his crystal blue eyes, and placed his closed right fist over his heart. "It is with great respect that I greet a fellow descendant of Jadon, the son of Monoceros, and an honored friend: Amadis and living sword of our prince." He stepped forward, gripped both of Braden's shoulders, and locked his eyes with his. "I cannot begin to tell you how good it is to see you this sunrise."

Whoa...

Braden's mouth went dry.

He pulled himself together: "Greetings sentinel, fellow descendant of Jadon, and esteemed Master Warrior. Gotta admit, it feels pretty good to be here. You're a sight for sore eyes, yourself."

Santos chuckled, pulled Braden into a firm warrior's embrace, and then quickly released him, stepping back. "The door's unlocked. She said to tell you to come on in when you get here."

Braden nodded. "Thank you."

Santos declined his head again, then vanished from the luxurious hallway.

Braden stopped to catch his breath. *Gods, this was so overwhelming.* He hoped like hell that once he was inside Kristina's apartment, everything would feel normal...familiar. He just needed a place to be himself and unwind. Just plain Braden. And if he couldn't do that with Kristina, then—

He abruptly cut off the thought.

After all, he was the weirdo carrying a bouquet of flowers and wearing expensive cologne.

He stared at the twin, vertical, long, sleek door pulls mounted on either side of three frosted planes of glass, gripped the one on the right, and opened the mahogany door. The moment he stepped across the threshold, his heart caught in his throat: Kristina was standing in front of the fireplace in a thick cotton bath robe. Her loose red S-curls had dried naturally, framing her face like a radiant halo, and her feet were still bare, toenails freshly painted, but she wasn't wearing a scant of makeup.

Her stunning, bright blue eyes were crystal clear and sparkling in the firelight. Her adorable, pristine features were serene and relaxed. And the coral flush of her cheeks matched the shade of her heart-shaped lips, emphasizing the soft feminine lines of her mouth.

No high heels.

No miniskirt.

No pretenses or...barriers.

Just Kristina Riley Silivasi looking like an angel sent from heaven.

"Bray..." She breathed his name as much as she spoke it, and then she crossed the living room in a quickening stride until she was nearly running. He held out his arms, and she leaped into the invitation, wrapping her legs around him in a full body embrace. He dropped the flowers on the penthouse floor and held her like the gods might take her away if he allowed even a scintilla of space between them.

She sobbed into his shoulder.

And he tunneled his hands in her wild hair. "It's okay, Red. I'm here." He kissed the base of her neck, then the top of her forehead. "I've got you, and I'm not going anywhere."

She clung to him, even tighter.

As if on autopilot, his mind flashed back to the last night he had been there: what she had offered him...and what he had refused her. He could still see her sitting on the couch in that nearly see-through silk blouse, smooth bare legs, the same painted toenails slipped into a designer pair of stiletto heels, trying to pretend she was calm when her pulse was racing, and her heart was pounding.

He set her down on the tips of her toes, and not unlike the time before, he leaned into her, grasped her high, smooth, delicate cheekbones in the palms of his hands, his thumbs yet again anchored beneath her jaw, and bent down to kiss her.

Like before, the kiss was raw, unrestrained, and passionate.

Unlike before, it was also tender, loving...healing, and he didn't pull away.

He gave every ounce of his heart and soul to the slender woman beneath him until both of them were breathless.

He pulled back to search her eyes, and they were both filled with yearning.

She tugged on his hair to draw him back to her mouth and swirled her tongue in a fiery tango, wanting...seeking...needing even more of him.

He groaned into the deepening kiss.

Holy shit...

"Kristina..." His voice was hoarse and foreign.

"I love the way you look in those jeans, that shirt," she teased, nipping his bottom lip, "but I think I liked that loincloth better."

His knees almost buckled.

Oh...fuuuuck.

He swept his hands up the curve of her hips, along the small of her waist, and planted his palms just beneath her breasts, extending his thumbs toward her nipples—no!

Noooo.

No, no, no!

Every primal vampire-instinct in his body warred with his conscience, even as it awakened. He knew *exactly* what to do with her—and just how to do it—how much dominance she needed, how much tenderness she required, what erogenous zones he could tease and titillate...what intimate flesh he could torture.

And his body was ready.

He was ready.

Besides, what he didn't know, she could teach him, and he would have one helluva time learning—but that was not the issue.

"*Kristina...*" He panted her name.

She giggled, seductively. "Braden." Then she sucked his bottom lip into her mouth and bit him, and he almost bit her back, full fangs to jugular, before tossing her across the room onto the sofa—

But nope!

His erection was throbbing.

No!

"Kristina," he tried again, this time sounding both plaintive and desperate. He took a generous step back and locked her wrists in an iron grasp. "I'm not pulling away from *you*. I'm not turning this down—*believe me!* But it's just...it's just...I know you, Red. I know you like the back of my hand. I know your passion, and I know your pain. I know your body is on fire right now, that you need the closeness, the pressure, the intimacy—*so do I*—but I also know you need the touch, the closeness. I know your soul needs more. I've heard your hesitation, your concerns, the dozens of times you've objected, before this harvest moon madness, and I know your mind wrestles with the age difference...with truly believing and giving me all of you. *All of you, Kristina*—mind, body, and soul." He raised her hands to his mouth and kissed the backs of her fingers, one after the other, his lips worshiping every rise and cleft, his tongue savoring each bend with a taste. "And

I'm way too greedy, way too demanding, to accept any less than all of you."

She opened her mouth to speak, but he shushed her, pressing two fingers against her soft, moist lips. "Trust me when I say, I've given this a lot of thought. I want to undress you. I want to explore every inch of your body, and I want you to let me bring you to orgasm." He smiled coyly, but he didn't blink or look away. He wanted full, unabashed vulnerability between them, and Kristina needed to let herself go—fully go—with Braden in order to begin to trust him. "And not just once but over...and over. And then I just want to hold you, *inima mea.*" *My heart* in Romanian. "Hold you and get to know you...all of you...and for you to get to know me."

Her brow creased and her lips tightened, but she didn't object or argue—she just studied Braden's features, watched him intently...and listened.

"Red, I want to tell you everything that's happened to me over the last ten hours, and I *need* you to tell me your stories. All of them. The good, the bad...and the ugly. No censors, no omissions, no shame or regret. I need you to peel back the Band-Aids."

Her face drained of color, and she softly drew back her hands. "What did you just say?"

He cast his eyes up and to the left, trying to remember the exact words he'd used. "I need you to peel back the Band-Aids, sweetheart. And the gods know, I have a few wounds and scars to uncover, myself. I know it's awkward...frustrating...extremely bad timing, and trust me when I tell you, Kristina: I want you so much it hurts. And I mean...*hurts.* But I also know this is right." He shook his head slowly. "I've waited so long...forever...for the two of us to be right here, for you to finally and truly want me." His eyes misted with tears, and he didn't try to conceal them. "And now, I'm just...I'm just too damn selfish, too damn greedy, to accept anything less than all of you. Your heart needs healing—

I've always seen that so clearly. And I want...I need...to be the man who heals you. Not just the man who sleeps with you. Does that make any sense, Red?"

She cupped his cheeks in her hands. "The *male* who heals me," she corrected. "Yes, it makes perfect sense." She bent down to pick up the bouquet of flowers, and froze as she studied them more closely, tracing the bow with a tentative finger. "*Braden*," she breathed, her voice softly breaking. "You brought me lilies...*lilies*." She bit her bottom lip. "Talk about vulnerable. That had to be...so hard."

"Not for you. Or maybe...*only* for you."

She shook her head and sniffled. "I don't know what to say—they're beautiful, Bray. You're beautiful. And by the way, in case I didn't mention it, you smell freakin' fantastic." She forced a stilted smile.

He folded her beneath one arm. "Same."

She giggled. "Same? I smell fantastic too?"

"Well, always," he teased, "but I meant you're beautiful. Really, really beautiful."

Despite the tender moment—or maybe because of it—she nuzzled her head in the crook of his arm and looked up at him sheepishly. "You want to wait until we're mated, don't you?"

"I don't," he said, "but I think we should." He twirled a finger through a loose, silken coil in her hair. "We might be Vampyr—and the gods know I feel like I'm a hundred years old now—but we were both born human, we both spent our formative years in a...different culture. I know it's important to you, Kristina, that I'm at least legal age by human standards."

She sighed, then cringed, probably thinking of her most recent birthday on June 20th—Kristina had turned thirty years old.

And Braden didn't give a shit.

"So, your birthday, then?" she asked.

"Yes. May tenth. I already spoke to Napolean."

She nodded and tightened her arm around his waist. "Okay, but..." She burrowed her head into his chest, as if hiding, and he could feel the heat rise in her skin as she flushed. "But...just me? The...orgasms? All that time?"

He chuckled.

"Braden, that's gonna be...awkward. And selfish on my part. And possibly a little embarrassing."

He laughed more heartily now. "Oh, no, Red. It's gonna be fun. And interesting. And extremely...creative. Believe me, I'm looking forward to every second. Every time. Besides, we're gonna do more than just...get to know each other...thoroughly. Believe me, we're gonna sleep, talk, *play*...sleep, talk, and try some very...creative alternatives."

"Braden!" she scolded. "Stop! You're slaying me here. I'm gonna turn into a red tomato and explode."

He considered going somewhere *indecent* with that comment but thought better of it and chose silence instead. He dipped down, brushed her hair away from her eyes, caught her blushing gaze, and smiled. "Can we go to your bedroom, Kristina?" His voice was deep and throaty.

She shivered.

"I'll take that as a yes."

She nodded, seemingly unable to speak.

"Just one thing," he said, stiffening his spine. "And damn, I might just become the king of ruining intimate moments by the time we get to my birthday, but there's something I have to know. Something I have to ask."

She raised her brows and peeked up at him. "What?"

He sighed. "In the canyon, when I first saw you, before you came home and changed, your clothes were...stained with droplets of blood, and I know the Dark Ones held you in the Colony while I was gone. Kristina, did—"

"No." She spoke firmly. "*No*," she repeated the word. "I promise you, Braden; the answer is no."

He exhaled slowly, then reached for her hand.

Thank the gods, he said to himself.

He wanted to know more—he would need to know more—but that could wait until a later date and time. Feeling blessed, grateful...and more than a little eager, he took her hand, tugged it playfully, and led her down the hall to her bedroom.

CHAPTER THIRTY-THREE

SUNDAY NIGHT

The air was cool.

The night was crisp.

And the sweet smell of pine, sage, and lavender rose like incense from the simple but tasteful organic arrangement placed beside Lily's sweetly embroidered prayer pillow, the family heirloom that had meant so much to the devout female in life...and even more to Braden in the end.

Kristina grasped Braden's hand between both of her palms and squeezed but not too tightly. She was trying to contain her own emotion while simultaneously willing her strength to Bray. After all, it was no longer the Millenia Harvest Moon, the gods were no longer pouring down their power upon the earth, nor were the wizards able to construct an energetic dome of protection over the valley. Such deep, painful emotion could wreak havoc on the humans of Dark Moon Vale if the Vampyr could not control it.

The ancient burial grounds, denoting the final resting place for the fallen descendants of Jadon, were nestled inside a circular clearing, surrounded by towering pines and fir trees, and dotted with simple granite markers.

It was a hallowed clearing.

Sacred earth.

Sheltered by the thick of the surrounding forest and enormous, jutting rocks.

The male vampires—mostly warriors—were typically buried in the interior grounds, while the female *destinies*, the few who had passed, were loosely interred along the outskirts, laid in a sacred circle surrounding their mates, their sons, their beloved defenders, in a crown that symbolized the celestial Blood Moon.

And this night, Lily Bratianu lay peaceful, still, and...perfect, yet adorned in an elegant ceremonial robe of lavender and ivory, upon an ancient stone slab, awaiting final rites and burial. As was typical of the short, solemn ceremonies, there were very few vampires in attendance, only the immediate family and those expressly requested by Braden, Conrad, and Dario. To that end, Braden and Kristina stood on one side of the ancient stone slab, opposite Conrad and Dario, while Napolean Mondragon stood at the head of the slate, just yards in front of Kiera Olaru, who had been requested to attend in order to play her violin one last time for Lily, and Nachari Silivasi stood silently beside his mate, Deanna, at the foot of Lily's final, open sarcophagus. A contention any larger would have been considered superfluous... disrespectful, as the custom was as old as the species itself. The Vampyr were tasked with burying their own, the only exception made for members of the royal family: those who led, protected, and indelibly touched the lives of every member of the community.

Kristina felt the weight of the moment like a boulder resting on top of her heart.

She was truly Braden's family now.

The two of them were in this—were in *everything*—together.

Napolean extended a graceful hand outward, his fingertips pointed toward the ground, and with the exception of Kiera, the funeral party kneeled. As his knees hit the ground, Braden released Kristina's hand and slipped his arm around her waist, his fingers digging desperately into her side, and she leaned into him. *I'm right here*, she whispered, telepathically. *I've got you, Bray.*

A tear escaped the corner of her eyes, and she quickly brushed it away, took a slow, deep, steadying breath, and struggled to bank her emotions. She would've said more—perhaps something poignant or comforting—but she knew Braden too well.

Not now.

Not right here.

Not if she wanted him to get through this.

She rubbed a gentle circle along his lower back instead.

Dario cleared his throat and began to speak softly in the primordial language of the Vampyr's ancestors, offering a prayer for peace and a final benediction, and then he requested *safe journey* to the Valley of Spirit & Light, still vocalizing each word in Romanian.

At last, he switched to English. "May the spirit of Prince Jadon always guide and protect you. May the celestial gods welcome you with open arms." His voice cracked, and he looked at Braden. "Son, if you could..." His voice trailed off.

Braden stared at Lily's face for what felt like an eternity. He seemed to be memorizing every nuance, every feature—every detail—and his shoulders began to shake. *She looks peaceful, doesn't she?* he asked Kristina, still using their private bandwidth.

Yes, she does.

She's okay, right? I mean, she will be.

She is! Kristina insisted, *You, of all people, know this personally. The Enchanted Forest, the Tree of Light, Lord Monoceros...*

the celestial gods and their divine intercession. Lily is not alone, Braden. Far, far from it.

He nodded, almost imperceptibly. And then he drew back his shoulders, raised his chin, and waved his hand from the front of the slab to the posterior. It was then that Kiera began to play her violin, a soft, deeply melodic, soul-stirring rendition of Lily's favorite human song: *Rock of Ages*. As the heavy stone slab began to shift, then sway—ever so slightly, ever so gently—the earth opened to embrace it, and it slowly descended, deep into the ground.

"Travel well, *Mamica*," Braden uttered. "Go in peace."

Kristina nearly lost it, but she clenched both hands into fists and bit down hard on her lower lip, as Dario, then Conrad, repeated the blessed refrain, replacing *Mamica* with *My beloved mate* and then *Mother*...

Napolean Mondragon spoke solemnly: "Travel well, Lilian Bratianu, daughter of our heart...and house. Go in peace."

Nachari—then Deanna—spoke the same refrain as Napolean...

And then the earth closed around Lily, and the service came to an end.

CHAPTER THIRTY-FOUR

TWO WEEKS LATER

Ciopori stood with her hands on her hips, surveying the gorgeous crystal goblets with their long, elegant stems and etched diamond patterns, sitting atop the clean quartz counters in the anteroom behind the Ceremonial Hall of Justice, as she counted each chalice a second time. Braden's naming ceremony would begin in fifteen minutes, and she, Vanya, as well as Kristina and all the Silivasi sisters-in-law had volunteered to show up early, decorate the hall, and prepare the celebratory wine for the casual post-ceremony mingling.

Shelly Winters, a fourth- or fifth-generation human devotee whose family had both been aware of the Vampyr and served them for centuries, had also volunteered to refill glasses and carry trays following the private ceremony, which she would not be a part of. It had seemed like an incredibly generous—and slightly strange—offer, except Shelly used to feed Julien before Rebecca came along and put an end to it, and rumor had it, she still fed Keitaro Silivasi on rare, critical occasions. No one knew the exact nature of Keitaro and Zayda Patrone's relationship, other than the fact that Zayda resided at the Silivasi homestead, but Shelly never passed up an opportunity to brush elbows with the senior Silivasi patriarch. As far as Ciopori was concerned, the poor, lovely lady probably checked the moon and the sky nightly, hoping to see a Sagittarius Blood Moon with her name on it, declaring Shelly Keitaro's...forever.

However, Keitaro had already had a *destiny*, Serena Silivasi, and it didn't work that way, a second Blood Moon...

But no one could fault the poor girl for hoping.

Just then, the *destinies* began to file in from the ceremonial hall, decorations finished.

"I used the very last roll of silk gold ribbon," Jocelyn announced, approaching Ciopori, her stunning hazel-green eyes sparkling with satisfaction. "Good thing we stopped off to get a couple more rolls."

"Same with the black ink refills for the antique brass inkwell, calligraphy pen, and guest book. The first two bottles were completely dried up when I opened them. Sheesh, wonder how old they were," Deanna said.

Kristina walked in behind Deanna, wearing the hell out of a new velvet red dress with a deep V-neck, a high, split-front right thigh, and a modest, sweeping, forward train above a killer pair of strapless red heels, and she smiled brightly at Ciopori. "Everything looks great in the hall."

Ciopori returned the grin and sighed, feeling a deep, newfound appreciation—as well as an even closer sisterly connection—for the pretty redhead. *Holy deities*, Kristina had been through so much the last few weeks and particularly during the Millenia Harvest Moon: First, Achilles had more or less stalked the poor woman, then Kristina had sworn the princesses to secrecy, only to compel them to protect her with an ancient warded spell, a spell their brother Jaegar had unraveled in an instant. If that had not been enough drama for one night, Zeus Dragavei had taken Kristina back to Achilles' lair, where the

Dark Ones had kept her like some primitive, pagan prize, awaiting Achilles' return to his body. All of that to say nothing of the battle in the Red Canyons, where Kristina had been forced to kneel and watch as Braden nearly died—as Ciopori and Vanya awaited potential execution—while knowing nothing of the house of Jadon's plans to rescue the females, no matter the eventuality.

It had to have been harrowing...

Terrifying...

Exhausting.

Having learned about Braden's tragic loss, the passing of his mother, Lily, from Zeus of all vampires, the brave female had sworn to seek vengeance for Braden—somehow, someday—even if she had to do it unilaterally.

And then the wild woman had jumped right off the edge of the cliff, Napolean's sword in hand, trying to impale Achilles.

Ciopori shook her head.

It was over—thank the gods and goddesses.

No point in revisiting the darkest moments.

As it stood, both she and Vanya might be processing all that had happened for a lifetime: the chance to see their brother Jadon again; losing him...twice...without saying goodbye; their sibling Jaegar's never-ending treachery and bloodthirsty vendetta; the *hows*...the *whys*...the utter absurdity.

She blinked to clear her mind, and as if on cue—as if Vanya sensed Ciopori's rising consternation—the beautiful princess sashayed across the room, circled Kristina—twice—then bent to lift the hem of her modest train. "Where are the children?" Vanya asked, her pale rose eyes twinkling with mischief.

"Excuse me?" Kristina slapped Vanya's hand away, took a step back, and smoothed her train.

"The children," Vanya repeated. "The twin girls you are supposed to give to the house of Jadon? It's been two weeks now, well over forty-eight hours. In fact, it's been forty-eight hours, plus forty-eight hours...plus forty-eight hours, times *four*—I thought certainly by now, you and Braden would have...delivered." She smirked, then giggled.

And the other *destinies* joined her.

"Oh, my gosh, Vanya!" Kristina exclaimed. "Maybe give us a minute to get acclimated to all the changes."

"A minute?" Vanya quipped. "Shall I count the *minutes*, too? Hmm, let's see." She touched a finger to her lips. "Three hundred and thirty-six hours divided by fourteen days...twenty-four hours in a day and sixty minutes in an hour—"

"Well, I will say this," Arielle interrupted in an ostensible attempt to save Kristina, her prodding a bit more subdued, "I've never seen any woman smile so much—good heavens, our red-haired sister must have giggled five times while decorating the back pews in the hall. She would place a bundle of gold hypericum on a bench, giggle to herself, then blush and cover her eyes...rinse and repeat with every bunch of hypericum."

Nope, not saving her at all, Ciopori mused.

Kristina turned a bright shade of pink. "Shut up, Arielle."

Oh my, they were onto something, Ciopori mused further, knowing the females would circle like sharks now. But before they could get too revved up, Deanna Silivasi crossed the room in her distinctive, graceful, model's stride and placed an elegant arm around Kristina's shoulders. "No worries, sis; I've got your back."

At this, Vanya leaned in toward Kristina conspiratorially. She spoke in a hushed whisper, knowing full well that all could still hear her: "And I shall always have your back as well, Kristina." She rolled her exquisite eyes. "After all, 'twas I who rode shotgun with you when Saber was being...well, shall we just say, less than faithful. We've been through thick and thin." She held her fist in the air. "Girlfriends forever. Ride or die..."

Now this made Kristina laugh out loud. She squeezed Deanna's hand, then stepped forward and threw both arms around

Vanya, giving her a tight girlfriend hug. "Oh, Vanya," she moaned, "I love you dearly, but sweetheart—a couple corrections." She stepped back and placed a hand on her hip, inadvertently highlighting the red velvet dress. "First, I was the one driving the car, so technically, *you* rode shotgun. And second, Saber was not being unfaithful, not even remotely, and you know this. You had shut him out of your life—remember? He was just going to the bar to feed. And if I recall, you were also the one who slashed his tires. But yes, girlfriend; I will always have your back as well."

Vanya flicked a graceful hand in the air, feigning insult. "Tomato...tomahto...such insignificant details." She smiled like the proverbial cat that ate the canary. "My point simply was: Those were very dark times, and we came through them together."

Deanna leaned toward Kristina and whispered. "Anyone who goes near Saber—"

"*Everyone* who goes near Saber," Jocelyn interjected.

"Well, anyone female," Arielle chimed in.

"All dark times," Deanna insisted.

"*Very* dark times," Jocelyn clarified.

A chorus of laughter filled the anteroom.

Vanya rolled her eyes again. "Whatever." Then she smiled, sheepishly. "Wild dragons need to be tamed from time to time."

"Right," Ciopori said, no longer able to refrain from teasing her blood sister over Vanya's silly grandstanding. She glanced at the hem of Vanya's ruffled, high-waist skirt, a hem that only fell to mid-thigh. "Is that why you have rug burns on your knees, dear sister? Beneath your sheer nylons? You were *taming* Saber last night?"

Vanya blanched.

"Who was taming whom?"

The women's laughter rose.

"Speaking of rug burns, knees, and female children," Ciopori persisted, egged on by the good-natured camaraderie. "So, Kristina, do tell us more: How is the...*sword* of Jadon?" *Oh, dear lords*, she couldn't believe she'd said that.

Deanna laughed so hard she had to press both hands against her stomach, and Jocelyn swiped the back of her eyes—she may have actually shed a tear.

"Oh my gods!" Kristina cried. This time her face flushed pale. "You women are worse than Braden!"

"Worse than Braden?" Deanna probed, sounding coltishly shocked and amused. "C'mon, c'mon; spill the beans!" She fanned her face with her hand. "Because—no disrespect to Nachari's legendary beauty—but that fine young vampire has got to be one of the hottest things on two feet these days. *Holy Monoceros*." She feigned like she was swooning.

"He is...handsome," Arielle said, snickering.

"Ah-hem." Jocelyn cleared her throat. "Can someone say *see-through loincloth*? Had to pull that one out of Nathaniel's memory a couple of times."

"Oh my gosh!" Deanna's eyes grew wide. "You're lucky Nathaniel didn't catch you!"

"Jiminy Christmas!" Kristina huffed.

"Hello?" Shelly Winters chimed in, catching the vampire females off guard. After all, she had no idea what the lewd loincloth reference was about. "He could slide down my chimney any day of the week—and twice on Sunday!" she said, making a rather clever reference to the human holiday.

Vanya spun around on her heel and glared at Shelly, nostrils flaring—Ciopori snatched her by the arm. "Sister, come! We should check the hall, one last time. The guests will be arriving any minute." With that, she tugged the princess so hard, Vanya lost her balance and had to take several stutter-steps sideways to keep from falling over. Then Ciopori dragged her out of the anteroom.

* * *

Braden had only been five years old when he was brought into the house of Jadon...

Not born.

After claiming and mating Lily Clarke, Dario had converted Braden Clarke under the protection of Dario's own celestial lord, Pegasus. He had given the child his surname, and Lord Monoceros had soon revealed to Napolean that he had chosen the child as his own: to lead, protect...and influence. Since the child already had a name, the house of Jadon knew him—or at least knew of him —and since his parents' mating ceremony had already been officiated, Napolean saw no need to replicate the naming of a newborn child for a five-year-old boy, to welcome someone into the house of Jadon who was already a very real and integral part of it.

Rather, Napolean had performed a simple ceremony in Dario and Lily's front parlor, taking Braden's blood so that the king would always be able to track and find him. Napolean had welcomed the awkward, insecure lad to his own broad, extended family—the lighter Vampyr species—explaining the significance of being chosen by Lord Monoceros and assuring Braden's parents that he would be given an appropriate education at the Academy, as well as a formal Induction Ceremony upon graduation, where he would officially receive the Crest Ring of the house of Jadon, just like any other vampire.

He would be free to choose among The Four Disciplines when he enrolled in the Romanian University, and he would be reared in the house of Jadon by all...with love, loyalty, and the customary fealty.

Never in Braden's wildest dreams did he expect to stand on the stage in the hallowed Ceremonial Hall of Justice and look out over a sea of so many vampires: Niko, Jankiel, and Fabian, along with Gwen and Falcon, as well as Napolean's family, were all seated in the front left pew. Keitaro, Zayda, and all Keitaro's sons, plus their *destinies* and children, were seated in the two front, right pews. The sentinels and their mates...their children...were seated behind the Atonescus. A host of Master Warriors, with their families—some clearly Ancients—were seated over several rows behind the Silivasis, and from the way the bodies were crowded in there, Braden could've sworn every vampire in the house of Jadon had crammed into the hall.

Some stood in the outer aisles...

Still others crowded along the walls.

Holy moly...

He took a deep breath to calm his nerves.

And then he bit down on his lower lip with an upper canine to stop his mind from wandering because it kept getting stuck on Kristina and that smoking-hot red velvet dress! Napolean had been gesturing and speaking eloquently for the last two minutes, and Braden hadn't heard a word the king had said. It was just...it was just...now that he knew what was beneath that slender profile, the soft pink areolas beneath the dark, velvet red, on either side of the deep V neckline—

Stop it, Braden!

Just stop.

This is way too important to miss.

Kristina's bright blue eyes lit up, and she flashed him a loving smile—*a loving smile, not a seductive invitation!*—as she stood, relaxed and stately, beside Dario and Conrad, just off to the right from center stage.

Braden returned the smile and straightened his back, fixing his eyes on Napolean.

But those sleek red shoes...

She should've been a foot model.

"It is with great joy that I greet you this day, my brother, a fellow descendant of Jadon, a Master Warrior, mate to the beloved daughter of Pegasus who now makes her home in the Valley of Spirit & Light, sire to the most honored vampire among us, son of Monoceros, the unicorn, who makes his home within the Rosette Nebula in the center of the triangle formed by Betelgeuse, Procyon, and Sirius." Napolean spoke to Dario. "Step forth and declare the name your king and your High Mage have chosen for this newly anointed, adult male vampire."

Dario stepped forward, and he had Braden's full attention.

That, and the painful reminder that his mother was looking down from the celestial heavens, watching from another dimension.

Dario's usual pale gray eyes beamed with uncommon light and pride. "Should it please you, my lord, and find favor with the Celestial Beings, the son of Monoceros is to be forever known as Braden Amadis Bratianu."

Braden inhaled sharply, and his forehead began to sweat.

Lily and Brad had never given him a middle name, but this one moved him to his core: *Amadis*, the title Prince Jadon had given him when the ancient patriarch of the house of Jadon had anointed Braden in the canyon with Napolean's sword.

He gulped, remembering that moment, and Kristina's eyes filled with tears.

They exchanged a knowing glance, and then Braden turned back to Napolean.

"The name pleases me, warrior, and there is no objection from the Celestial Beings."

Like many others in the house of Jadon, Braden supposed, he had always wondered how Napolean knew that—the fact that the gods did not object—but he didn't dare ask. He licked his lips—

they were suddenly dry—and concentrated on keeping his hands at his sides. *No fidgeting!*

Napolean turned to face the crowd. "Let it also be known that this male's formal title is no longer fledgling or acolyte. That even when he attains the title of Master in one—or more—of The Four Disciplines"—he glanced at Braden and winked—"his decorous address shall remain indicative of the rank and title given to him by The Prince himself: Greet and honor the living Sword of Jadon."

Every male in the hall placed a fist over his heart.

Every female placed an open palm over the same...

And all bowed their heads.

Braden's legs turned into spaghetti noodles, and he felt his body sway to the left.

Stand tall, Braden Amadis—Kristina's voice in his head—*you've earned this, you're worthy, and you deserve to take in the moment.*

Braden stiffened his legs, raised his chin, and looked out over the audience.

Nachari Silivasi's deep, forest-green eyes were glazed with proud, gratified tears...full to the brim with devotion...and Braden almost lost it.

Be strong, Braden told himself. *Don't you dare break down and blubber on this stage.*

Julien Lacusta was standing just a bit taller than his usual six-foot-four, towering frame, and his moonstone-gray eyes were as soft as morning raindrops.

Even Marquis Silivasi was beaming with pride.

Holy shit...

"Behold the house of Jadon," Napolean said to Braden, "as you take your rightful place among us: May your life be filled with peace, triumph, and purpose. May your path always be blessed."

As if all that had just taken place wasn't stunning enough, Dario Bratianu stepped forward and extended his hand to Braden, but when Braden reached to take it, his stepdad clasped his wrist instead in a gesture befitting...two warriors. "Behold the house of Jadon," Dario repeated, "as you take your rightful place among us: May your life be filled with peace, triumph, and purpose. May your path always be blessed." Then he released Braden's forearm, clutched his hand, and drew him into a...hug.

A strong, unabashed, openly demonstrative, intimate... father-son hug.

As Dario's strong, muscular arms closed around Braden's broad shoulders, Braden nestled his head in the crook of the vampire's neck. "I love you, son," Dario whispered.

Braden blinked the moisture away. "Love you too, Dad."

They held on a moment longer. Then Conrad stepped forward, and his smile stretched from ear to ear. "Behold the house of Jadon," he said, before going on to repeat the entire refrain. Then, "Told you so, Braden," he added, before wrapping both arms around him.

Braden mussed Conrad's hair—he couldn't help it. "I love you, Conny," he said with a full throat. "And I can't wait until you come to stay at the brownstone for a while. I hope you'll stay until Kristina and I are mated, and even after that, you're welcome at the penthouse."

Conrad squeezed him tighter, as if holding on for dear life, and then he finally released his hold and stepped back, still grinning.

Kristina stepped forward next, although Braden would have called it more of a sashay. Her cute little nose twitched, and her heart-shaped lips curved into a sweet, sly smile. "Behold the house of Jadon," she said softly, "as you take your rightful place among us: May your life be filled with peace, *triumph*, and purpose. May your path always be blessed."

Was it just his imagination, or did she place a strong, sensual emphasis on the word triumph?

He swept his eyes along the curve of her neck, over her dainty collarbone, and slowly down to her wrist, where a sleek platinum band, peppered with flawless, brilliant onyx and ruby gemstones, circled her smooth, pale skin. The bracelet he had made for her, a symbol of their love.

Their love...

He swallowed hard and reached for courage, but she beat him to it. "Braden," she said brightly, loud enough for the entire house of Jadon to hear with their superior, vampiric hearing, "I want you to know that from this day forward, I will always be by your side." She turned toward the congregation and said, "Love is patient, love is kind. It does not envy, it does not brag, it is not arrogant. It does not disrespect others, it is not selfish, it is not quick to anger, and it keeps no record of wrongs." She took a deep breath. "Love does not get off on hurting others or telling lies but celebrates the truth. It always protects, always trusts, always hopes, and always perseveres. And so does Braden—he's all of that and more." She held up both hands and shrugged her dainty shoulders. "And I have no earthly idea why the celestial gods would've chosen someone so good...and so loving...to be with me...forever." She smiled like the sun, the sky, and a host of white fluffy clouds had just been handed to her on a silver platter, and there was a rainbow shining above her. "But I'll take it." She turned, once again, to face Braden. "And I will probably spend the rest of my life trying to learn...trying to be worthy"—he started to object, but she cut him off—"worthy of the living Sword of Jadon."

She took both his hands in hers.

"Bray, I want to say this as clearly as I can, so it leaves no room for doubt. I love you with all my heart, all my soul, and everything that I am: the good, the crazy, and the broken. And I will love you until the day I die. I am so incredibly proud of you, Braden, and it is probably the greatest honor of my life to stand here by your side."

He hung his head and shook it slowly from side to side—she was slaying him, right then and there, and he did not want to cry. Hell, he was Vampyr—he had better not cry. "I love you too, Red." He choked out the words, wishing he had something more poetic to say. "Thank you."

She smiled like a ray of sunshine in the sky he had just described, wrapped her arms around his waist, and held him tightly against her heart. "For ever and ever," she whispered.

"And ever," he replied.

Just then, a fusion of real, true, actual rainbow-colored light refracted off the ornate ceiling above the Hall of Justice, reminiscent of the very first time Braden had laid eyes on Lord Monoceros, right after collecting the badge of *trust*. The light exploded into thousands of golden fragments, falling like snowflakes, dancing in the air. The fragments radiated outward, coalesced, and came back together in the shape of a flaming sword, and then it bathed Braden in a celestial spotlight, from the tip of the pommel to the point of the blade.

"Well done, Sword of Jadon!" Lord Monoceros' voice.

Then, *Carry on in my stead,* Prince Jadon's deep, regal brogue, echoing in Braden's mind.

Braden's heart swelled, then receded, in his chest, and he felt it—*he felt him*—nestled deep inside. Prince Jadon had always been there, and he was not going away. Braden Amadis Bratianu exchanged a breathless glance with King Napolean Mondragon, and then he tightened his arms around Kristina's narrow shoulders, holding her...protecting her...trusting her.

And loving her, right back.

EPILOGUE
THE NEXT MORNING

Nestled on top of a soft, downy sheepskin blanket in front of a roaring fire on the floor of Kristina's apartment, Kristina and Braden watched the sun slowly rise outside the open, floor-to-ceiling balcony doors. As the autumn morning dew settled on the glass panes, Kristina rolled onto her back and rubbed her tired eyes.

"I meant to ask you something," she said, her voice sounding hoarse from first-morning vocal cords.

"Shoot." Braden rolled onto his stomach and propped his weight on his arms.

"Last night, at your ceremony...that hug with Dario. How'd that go? I mean, how did that feel? The two of you seemed pretty...close."

Braden furrowed his brows. "Yeah, we did, didn't we? It was surprising...different. He actually grasped my wrist like a warrior, like an equal, and he even told me he loved me."

Kristina smiled. "Yeah, I heard that. And you said it back."

Braden nodded, then scooted closer to look into Kristina's eyes. "I dunno; things might still be a little awkward going forward, without Mom around to stand in the gap. Rome wasn't built in a day, and it's gonna take a little time for Dario and I to forge a new beginning. But I think we'll get there...in time. Hope so."

Kristina sighed. "I think you will too." A companionable silence settled between them as Kristina ran her fingers through Braden's shoulder-length, chestnut-brown hair, stopping to trace the outline of an unusually stark, blond highlight. "It's a lot to take in, isn't it? All of this. The last few weeks, your new name and title...*Lily*...you and me." She brushed the backs of her fingers along his angular jaw, stopping at the corner of his mouth. "I can still see the grief in your eyes, feel the sorrow in the air, all around us, and I just wish..." She bit her bottom lip. "I just wish there were some way I could carry it for you, but I know that I can't. And saying I'm sorry—so very sorry—about all that happened... doesn't really help, does it?"

Braden forced a paltry smile. "You help more than you know." He shifted his weight onto a single elbow and entwined his fingers in hers. "Just keep doing what you're doing." His smile widened, grew a bit more mischievous, though the merriment didn't quite reach his eyes. "Keep letting me do the things that I do...with you...to you." He swept his gaze from her head to her toes, admiring the silk blue negligee.

Kristina giggled, but she didn't pursue the passion play.

Rather, she rolled on her side to face him, and continued to study his stunning, mysterious eyes. "You do know that you have me now, always and forever, through thick and thin." She paused. "Don't you?"

He cocked his head to the side. "Haven't I always had you, Red?"

She nodded, blushing. "Yeah, I guess you have—but not like this. Just wait, you'll see."

"See what?" he pressed her.

She laughed. "That I may be a lot of crazy, fickle things, but when I love, I love deeply...forever."

He drew back just a bit, feigning sudden insult.

"What!" she demanded.

He frowned.

"*What?*"

"You still love Dirk?" he teased her.

She withdrew her hand from his and slapped his forearm. "Oh, *shut up*..." She rolled her eyes playfully, and then she became more serious: "No, Braden, I don't still love Dirk. In truth, I don't think I ever loved Dirk." She rolled onto her back and stared at the ceiling. "That was different. That was something...sordid. Broken."

"Yeah," he said softly. "I get it, and not just from hearing all your stories." He turned onto his back and lay beside her. "A broken boy, and a broken girl," he mused aloud.

"They come together and make a—"

"Broken couple?" he interjected.

She sat up abruptly. "I was gonna say, a perfect couple!"

He laughed. "Is that what we are, Red? A perfect couple?"

"I don't know," she pondered, "but whatever we are, I wouldn't change it. I think we're just—"

"Forever," he said, completing her sentence.

She was going to say, *meant to be*, but she liked forever better. "Yeah," she said, "exactly. Forever and ever..."

"And ever."

Lying side by side, they both chuckled, and then they instinctively linked fingers.

As Kristina's bracelet sparkled in the golden firelight, she couldn't help but think how far they'd come in such a little time. Well, not really—it had been two years since she had met him and, shortly thereafter, taken him under her wing, so to speak, as her "favorite little brother," wanting to provide support and comfort while Nachari was lost...and away...the Master Wizard's body in a coma. It had been twenty months since Napolean Mondragon had decreed that Braden and Kristina were promised to be mated, and the youngling had harassed her mercilessly, trying to stake a claim Kristina had wanted no part of. She laughed inwardly, remembering that perilous day in the meadow, over a year ago in May, when the Silivasi brothers entered Mhier to find and rescue their father—how Braden had demanded a kiss for good luck, and Nachari had made him apologize...for sexual harassment. Braden had only been sixteen at the time, and Kristina had been utterly horrified.

But these last two and a half weeks?

Time...and the Millenia Harvest Moon...had moved them forward by epochs.

"Braden," she whispered softly. "I really do love you."

He reached out an arm to gather her close, but instead of snuggling against his chest, she rolled on top of him, her feet tangling with his. Their eyes met—and locked—in an enchanted moment, and they lingered, drinking each other in.

And then Kristina lowered her mouth to Braden's and kissed him with the same passionate fervor she had exhibited on the eve of the Millenia Harvest Moon. Only this time, he did not pull away.

She wanted him to know.

She wanted him to feel...everything she felt.

She wanted to seal the promise.

Forever.

Ever...and ever.

* * *

The celestial goddess Cygnus, the Swan, peered down through the cross-shaped cluster of northern stars, this time from her palatial home inside the Veil Nebula, and her golden wings fluttered before folding and receding within her graceful, arched back. She extended an elegant hand to Lord Monoceros, and he took it. "Charming, aren't they?" she commented. "Braden and Kristina."

"Indeed," Lord Monoceros said, leading her away from the portico and into the grand formal living room.

"Pity Lord Pegasus wasn't here to see this."

"Mm," Monoceros murmured, releasing the goddess' hand. "Well, I imagine he is watching from his home within the Globular Cluster. I imagine he is as pleased—and relieved—as we are."

She smiled brightly and bowed her head in the barest hint of a nod. "You did very well, my esteemed, celestial kinsman. I could not have done better myself."

"Thank you," he said, sounding genuinely flattered.

She glided across the see-through crystal floor and took a seat on the edge of a pearly white chaise, folding her hands in her lap. "Perhaps now we shall get some rest." She chuckled softly, and her laughter echoed throughout the grand hall like a set of miniature church bells ringing.

Lord Monoceros took a seat opposite Cygnus, on a matching settee. "But alas, the work of the gods—the sleepless nights and preoccupied days—is never really done."

"No, it isn't," Cygnus said.

"I have a feeling the goddess Lyra and our beloved Lord Aquarius will soon take our place in the worry department."

Cygnus formed her mouth into an "O" and raised her dark, silver eyebrows. "Have you ever heard of such, Monoceros? *A twin Blood Moon!*"

He shook his head. "Nay, I have not. And I imagine Niko Durciak and Jankiel Luzanski have never heard of it either—they won't see it coming."

Cygnus shook her head, revealing both her titillation and her angst. "And what of the girls—sisters, aren't they?"

"Aye," Monoceros replied, "Skye and Sasha Bennet."

This time, Cygnus shuddered. "Two Master Wizards. Two Blood Moons. Two unsuspecting human females—and a whole lot of magick."

"A whole lot of danger."

"Yes." Cygnus bit the tip of her nail. "The Dark Ones' Colony is in a bit of disarray, Salvatore Nistor is miffed, to put it mildly, and that's to say nothing of Oskar Vadovsky."

"Or of Achilles Zahora, parading around as Zeus Dragavei," Monoceros added.

Cygnus released a pair of dainty fangs and snarled. "Now that was a wicked, dirty sleight of hand."

"Indeed," Monoceros agreed. "Yet and still, it was within the boundaries—"

"Barely," Cygnus snarled.

"True, but as we both know, the rules in life are crystal clear; the rules in death are a bit...less so. We collect the souls on their way to the Valley of Spirit & Light—"

"And our dark, despicable counterparts collect—and manipulate—the souls on their way to the Valley of Death & Shadows."

"So it would appear."

Cygnus took a deep, cleansing breath, returning to her previous tranquil nature. "Well, I, for one, shall support dear Lyra in the coming days and nights. It will not be easy to allow her beloved son, Niko, his divine right of free will and self-determination. This game of chance—that blasted Curse—can always go both ways."

Lord Monoceros let out a deep, drawn-out breath. "Indeed. And I shall do my best to support Lord Aquarius—advise him, should he seek counsel on behalf of Jankiel. Heaven knows, he is going to need it."

TESSA DAWN

* * *

Coming Next to the Blood Curse Series:
BLOOD MAGICK

JOIN THE AUTHOR'S MAILING LIST

If you would like to receive a direct email notification each time Tessa releases a new book, please join the author's mailing list at...

www.tessadawn.com

BOOKS IN THE BLOOD CURSE SERIES

ALSO BY TESSA DAWN

DRAGONS REALM SAGA

Dragons Realm

Dragons Reign

PANTHEON OF DRAGONS

Zanaikeyros ∼ Son of Dragons

Axeviathon ∼ Son of Dragons

NIGHTWALKER SERIES

Daywalker ∼ The Beginning

OTHER

Do You Have Any Advice for Aspiring Authors?

(*Free* booklet for readers, who are also aspiring authors)

A SNEAK PEEK FROM ZANAIKEYROS
SON OF DRAGONS

Before time was a recognized paradigm, seven dragon lords created a parallel primordial world for their glory...and their future offspring. They harnessed seven preternatural powers from seven sacred stones and erected the *Temple of Seven* beyond the hidden passage of a mystical portal that would lead back and forth between Earth and the Dragons Domain. And finally, they set about creating a race of beings—the Dragyr—that would exist on blood and fire, and they gifted their progeny with unimaginable powers, unearthly beauty, and immortal life.

For all of this, the dragon lords required only one thing: *absolute and unwavering obedience* to the *Four Principal Laws*...

- Thou shalt pledge thy eternal fealty to the sacred Dragons Pantheon.
- Thou shalt serve as a mercenary for the house of thy birth by seeking out and destroying all *pagan* enemies: whether demons, shadows, or humans.

- Thou shalt *feed* on the blood and heat of human prey in order to reanimate your fire.
- Thou shalt propagate the species by siring *dragyri* sons and providing The Pantheon with future warriors. In so doing, thou shalt capture, claim, and render unto thy lords whatsoever human female the gods have selected to become *dragyra*. And she shall be taken to the sacred *Temple of Seven*—on the tenth day, following discover—to die as a mortal being, to be reborn as a dragon's consort, and to forever serve the sacred pantheon.

And so it came to pass that seven sacred lairs were erected in the archaic domain of the dragons in order to house the powerful race begotten of the ancient gods, each lair in honor of its ruling dragon lord:

Lord Dragos, Keeper of the Diamond
Lord Ethyron, Keeper of the Emerald
Lord Saphyrius, Keeper of the Sapphire
Lord Amarkyus, Keeper of the Amethyst
Lord Onyhanzian, Keeper of the Onyx
Lord Cytarius, Keeper of the Citrine
& Lord Topenzi, Keeper of the Topaz

While a *dragyri* may appear to be human, *he is not.*

While a *dragyra* may appear to belong to her mate, *she does not.*

While the Dragyr may be fierce, invincible, and strong, they are *never* truly free...

* * *

He continued to take the stairs, two at a time, until he had passed her without incident, and then he suddenly stopped in midstride and spun around to face her.

She sensed it more than she saw it.

She could literally *feel* his domineering presence behind her, and despite her immediate impulse to *run*, she turned to face him instead.

The stranger tilted his head to the side and emitted some strange, feral sound. It was almost like a snarl, and Jordan's heart began to race. They locked eyes a second time, and she almost let out a yelp: He was glaring at her now, like she had stolen his first-born child, his dark, sculpted brows creased into a frown.

She unwittingly took a step back, clutched the rail, once again, for stability, and stifled a terrified gasp. Determined to appear calm, she stuffed her free hand into her pocket, hunched her shoulders in some instinctive, submissive gesture, and slowly backed away, feeling carefully for each stair beneath her.

He took a casual step toward her, and she almost bolted.

He halted, almost as if he dared not frighten her any further, and then he did the oddest, most animalistic thing: He inhaled deeply, sniffed the air, and he *groaned*.

Whether it was a groan of annoyance, impatience, or anger, Jordan had no idea, but that was the final straw—she had no intention of sticking around to find out.

Releasing the rail, she spun around in a whirl, leaped the four remaining stairs—almost twisting her ankle—and took off running for her car, all the while digging frantically for her keys as she ran. She could hear the stranger's footsteps behind her, and she cringed at the stupidity of her choice. *Why hadn't she screamed or tried to push past him? Headed back in the direction of the mall, to the safety of other people?*

Rounding the corner of the parking garage, she eyed her forest-green, metallic BMW, only five spaces away, and rotated her key-fob in her hand, pressing the *unlock* button over and over, just to be sure it opened. She glanced over her shoulder to judge the distance between herself and the stranger, and gasped, her feet skidding to a sudden halt.

He wasn't there.

Even though she could have sworn she'd heard his footsteps just moments ago, the man was no longer behind her.

She pressed her hand to her heart and fought to catch her breath, feeling a curious mixture of both relief and embarrassment. She scanned the garage in all four directions, making sure she hadn't overlooked his presence, that he wasn't hiding behind a nearby post or a vehicle, and then she started once again for her car.

Angry tears filled her eyes as she finally reached her BMW, yanked on the door handle, and bent to climb inside.

"*Stop.*" An *invisible* hand snatched her by the arm, slammed her door shut behind her, and pressed her back against the driver's-side panel. And then, just like that, the stranger was standing, once again, in front of her.

What the hell!?

ABOUT THE AUTHOR

Tessa Dawn grew up in Colorado, where she developed a deep affinity for the Rocky Mountains. After graduating with a degree in psychology, she worked for several years in criminal justice and mental health before returning to get her master's degree in nonprofit management.

Tessa began writing as a child and composed her first full-length novel at the age of eleven. By the time she graduated high school, she had a banker's box full of short stories and novels. Since then, she has published works as diverse as poetry, greeting cards, workbooks for kids with autism, and academic curricula. Her Dark Fantasy/Gothic Romance novels represent her long-desired return to her creative-writing roots and her passionate flair for storytelling.

Tessa currently splits her time between the Colorado suburbs and mountains with her husband, two children, and "one very crazy cat." She hopes to one day move to the country, where she can own horses and what she considers "the most beautiful creature ever created"—a German shepherd.

Writing is her bliss.